BLIND SIDE

BLIND SIDE

A novel

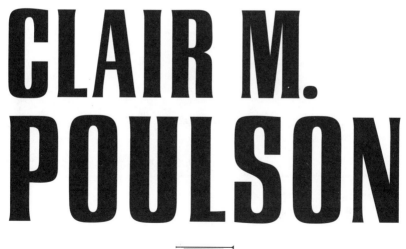

CLAIR M. POULSON

Covenant
Covenant Communications, Inc.

Cover design © 2006 by Covenant Communications, Inc.
Cover image by Gary Cornhouse © Digital Vision/Getty Images, Inc.

Published by Covenant Communications, Inc.
American Fork, Utah

Printed in Canada
First Printing: June 2006

12 11 10 09 08 07 06   10 9 8 7 6 5 4 3 2 1

ISBN 1-59811-097-7

To Brooke and Vicena.
Thanks for all you are to my sons.

CHAPTER 1

It's an October day made for leaf-peepers, Noletta Fahr thought as she pulled off to the side of the road and shut off the engine. A friend of hers from New Hampshire had once used the term to describe tourists who flock to New England to enjoy the incredible fall display. Noletta thought that Utah's splendor today might be just about on par with New England's. The trees in the canyon shimmered with glorious fall colors. She gazed for a moment at the panorama that stretched before her. The sky was a spectacular bright blue, dotted intermittently with white clouds that floated lazily eastward. Their whiteness was a startling contrast to the mountainside beyond—bright red, golden yellow, violet, orange, bronze, yellow-green, and dozens of other shades from the deciduous trees, mixed with dark green from the conifers. Nature had masterminded a scene that made the amateur artist in Noletta quiver with delight.

Noletta's reverie was momentarily interrupted by a gentle nuzzling at the back of her neck. A striking black and tan German shepherd on the backseat reminded her that she wasn't alone. Smiling, Noletta said, "Taffy, should we go for a walk? We couldn't have picked a better day."

The dog's tail beat enthusiastically against the backseat of the Toyota. Taffy whined eagerly, and Noletta said, "Okay girl. I guess we have time to go two or three miles before we need to be heading home. I was just going to look at the leaves today to get an idea for a painting I'd like to do, but it's so beautiful up here in the mountains that I think it might be fun to walk, maybe even jog a little."

Although Noletta had owned Taffy for less than a month, she had already developed the habit of discussing plans with her dog as if she were a roommate. "There's probably a trail-head farther up the road. But first I want to snap a few pictures here. Then when I start painting, I'll have them to help me remember just how this looks."

Noletta snatched her camera from the seat beside her and stepped from the car, instructing Taffy to stay where she was. She took several pictures before getting back in. "There," she said, as she reached back and affectionately patted her dog's head. "That should do for now, unless we see something else up the road that looks even better."

The young woman started her car and pulled back onto State Highway 35. She'd left Salt Lake City earlier that after-noon after completing her last class for the day at the University of Utah School of Law. She'd been tense and irri-table driving home after having been humiliated in front of the class by her professor. She had started to answer his ques-tion, realizing as she spoke that she'd made an error. But when she began to correct herself, he belittled her and silenced her attempts to respond further. Thinking back on the incident, she marveled that she'd been able to maintain her composure. As soon as class was over, she'd left campus and driven directly home.

Noletta lived with her dog in the home she'd grown up in—a large, older house in the Avenues of Salt Lake City that she was watching for her parents while they served an LDS mission in Nigeria. The youngest of four children, she had one brother and two sisters who were all married and lived out of state. She alone had remained in Utah.

It had been lonely in the big house, so just a few weeks ago Noletta had decided to get a dog to keep her company. She'd made a visit to the county animal shelter, where she'd picked Taffy after looking at only a few of the dogs that were available for adoption. At the animal shelter, Noletta had been advised before she took Taffy home that she appeared to have been badly abused. She'd had numerous bruises when she was found wandering the streets. The staff had concluded that she must have been owned by a man; at least she seemed to have an aversion to men.

Despite the warnings, Noletta had felt drawn to Taffy and decided to take her home. She and the young German shepherd had bonded almost instantly. Now more than just a pet, Taffy was a trusted friend.

It had been the look of boredom in Taffy's intelligent eyes, as much as Noletta's own frustration, that had prompted the sudden trek into the mountains that afternoon. With no particular destination in mind, only a desire to get away and perhaps enjoy the fall leaves, Noletta had somehow ended up on the sparsely traveled highway. She knew that if she stayed on it long enough, the road would ultimately bring her over the mountain and into Tabiona. She had no intention of going that far, but after passing through Woodland, she kept driving, enthralled by the beauty of the area.

Spotting a sign announcing a trailhead, she pulled off the highway again and stopped. The only other vehicle there was an older-model, dark green Ford pickup with a rifle hanging on a rack in the back window. Beyond the truck was a small patch of quakies. The artist in her thought, *That's what a money tree would look like if it were covered with Midas's gold.* She opened the door for Taffy, and as the dog bounded out, she reached for her camera. She snapped several pictures, then put the camera in its bag and slung it over her shoulder along with her purse, anticipating other good photo opportunities along the trail.

Noletta shut and locked the car doors and, with water bottle in hand, started up the trail, Taffy running happily ahead.

Less than a hundred feet from the car, she stopped. She shivered and looked back to where she'd left her vehicle. It wasn't exactly cold, but it wasn't warm either. There was a touch of fall chill in the late afternoon air. She shook her head and mentally chided herself, *Hey great law student, have you forgotten all your undergraduate biology? That's what the fall colors are all about—warm, sunny days and colder evenings and nights.* She had a light jacket in the car and decided to go back for it. After slipping the jacket on and once more heading up the trail, Noletta shivered again. This time it was not from the chill in the air. It was something else, something not so easily defined. Suddenly the idea of a walk lost its appeal, and she decided she'd go back to Salt Lake and begin her painting.

"Taffy," she called, but the dog didn't appear. She called again with the same result. Puzzled, she decided to continue up the trail until she had her dog's attention. Then she'd return to the car and leave. Knowing Taffy as she did, Noletta calculated she would be several hundred feet up the trail by now, stopping to sniff at anything that caught her interest and then hurrying on. But she'd soon come back in search of her mistress. She always did.

Noletta turned back to the car, unlocked it, and placed her water bottle and camera inside. With her revised plans, she knew she wouldn't be needing either one now. Then she locked the car again, took a deep breath to settle her nerves, and began walking very quickly up the trail. Every so often she'd call out her dog's name. And when Taffy didn't appear, she'd move on again, wishing that the dog would come back so they could go home.

A single shot rang out somewhere ahead. A squirrel chattered close by at the base of a tall pine tree and then scampered up. A cloud drifted in front of the sun, throwing a chilling shadow over the trail. Noletta thought about the truck parked beside her car at the trailhead. Not a hunter herself, she wondered if there was a big game hunt of some kind going on. That thought caused her more worry, because the tan and brown jacket she was wearing could be mistaken, she supposed, for a deer if someone caught a glimpse of her through the trees. And then there was Taffy. *Surely someone hasn't shot Taffy,* she thought in sudden horror.

Noletta stopped and ran a hand through her long, dark brown hair as her heart hammered in her chest. Instead of calling Taffy's name, she whistled and waited. After a moment, she heard a bark, and with relief she began running ahead, expecting Taffy to appear at any moment. She rounded a sharp curve in the trail and gasped at the sudden, sheer drop-off that appeared at her left. A strangled scream followed the gasp. Twenty-five or thirty feet ahead of her on the trail was a man. Lying on his back, arms flung to either side, his chest soaked with blood, the man gazed sightlessly at the cloud-dotted sky.

Noletta stood immovable for a moment, shocked at the sight. Then she began backing fearfully down the trail, unable to drag her eyes from the body of the dead man. Taffy appeared at that moment, running toward her, and perilously close to the sheer ledge at the edge of the trail. "Taffy," she said in a voice choked with emotion, "we've got to get out of here and call for help."

Taffy stopped and turned just before reaching Noletta. She began to snarl at the unexpected sound of snapping branches on the steep, heavily timbered hillside directly above the body. Shaking now, Noletta continued to back away. Before she had gone far, a man appeared among the trees above the trail. The lowering sun was in Noletta's eyes, preventing her from seeing him well. However, she was sure that he held something in one hand. He thrust the hand and a dark object through the branches. With her heart hammering painfully, Noletta continued to move backward. The man didn't move from the concealment of the trees, nor did he utter a word. Nonetheless, Noletta knew instinctively that she was in great danger. Hardly aware of what she was doing, she offered a fervent prayer.

The last thing Noletta saw was her faithful dog charging into the trees toward the gunman. Then, as she began to turn away, intending to run for her life, there was a sharp crack. She never felt a thing as a bullet entered her head, and her body slumped to the ground.

* * *

Taffy struck the killer only a fraction of a second after the shot. The full weight of her body caught him in the chest, lifting him from his feet and propelling him through the dense branches and onto the trail. He struck the ground with such force that the pistol he'd just fired flew from his hand, bounced once, and then disappeared over the cliff at the trail's edge. Taffy waited and watched as he got to his feet. She bared her fangs as he stepped toward her. With one swift move, he kicked hard at her ribs. Anticipating an attack, Taffy leaped to the side, whirled, and then closed her mouth on the man's right leg.

The killer screamed in agony as Taffy's sharp teeth tore into his flesh. He kicked her with his other foot and pounded on her head with his fists. In pain, Taffy released her hold on his leg and jumped back a step. The killer leaned slowly down, not letting his eyes stray from the dog as he picked up a large stick. Swinging it slowly back and forth with both hands, he threatened, "Stay back, or I'll bash your head in!" As he began to edge his way around her, Taffy lowered her head, fangs bared, and growled a fierce warning but made no move to attack again. The killer heeded the warning, backing slowly down the trail.

He paused only a moment and looked down at the face of the woman he'd shot. He shuddered when he saw that the bullet had entered her head. But he had no time for remorse.

The dog was inching toward him again. He turned and fled down the trail, leaving behind the bloody scene he'd created.

Taffy watched him until he was out of sight, then dropped beside her fallen mistress.

* * *

There was only a single truck in the parking area at the trailhead when, just an hour and a half before sunset, Dylan and Indria Roderick pulled up. Both interns at the University of Utah Hospital, they had a few days off together. Avid hikers and campers, they planned to spend those days doing what they enjoyed most. It took them only a moment to get their backpacks in place, lock their car, and start briskly up the trail, Dylan in the lead.

"I wish we could have gotten away from the hospital sooner," Indria complained. "It'll be dark in a few minutes. We won't be able to go very far tonight."

"That's okay. We have everything we need to make a dry camp along the trail. Then we can get an early start in the morning," Dylan said, throwing a smile over his shoulder at his wife of two years.

They were both tall and sinewy, with long, muscular legs that carried them rapidly up the trail despite the heavy backpacks they carried. For several minutes they hiked without slowing their pace. But when they eventually rounded a sharp curve in the trail, Dylan stopped so suddenly that his wife stomped on the back of his hiking boots.

"Hey, why didn't you give me a sig—" Indria said just before she saw what had stopped her husband in his tracks.

Although it was dusk and getting dark fast, it took Dylan only a few seconds to silently survey the bloodshed before him. Initially dazed, he found his medical training soon taking control. He undid the cord around his waist and, with a couple of quick shrugs, shed his backpack. "You check him," he said urgently to his wife, pointing to the man who lay thirty feet or so beyond the young woman. "I'll see to the girl."

Turning to the German shepherd that stood near the girl's bloody head, he said, "Good dog, we're friends." Despite Dylan's soothing tones, a snarl rumbled from deep within the tan chest and rolled past black lips that were pulled back menacingly.

Dylan quietly extended a hand, the rumbling quieted, and then he touched the dog's head. "Let's see if she's alive," he said calmly to what he was certain was the girl's pet. As Dylan pressed two fingers to the young woman's carotid artery, the dog remained stationary.

Indria called out, "This guy's beyond help. He's dead. It looks like he has been for a while."

"That's what I was afraid of. This girl isn't. But it looks like she might have a bullet in her brain, and her heartbeat is very weak. Give me a hand here," he said. "I need a sleeping bag and my first aid kit. It may not be possible, but we've got to try to save her life."

For several minutes the two young doctors did what little they could for the critically injured woman. They covered her with one of their own sleeping bags in an attempt to reverse the shock they knew she was experiencing. As they cleaned and bandaged the wound on her head, her heartbeat gradually became stronger. Finally Dylan said, "I'm sure we're safe enough, Indria. Whoever did this is undoubtedly long gone. I'll stay with this woman and her dog. I need you to go for help."

Indria leaned down, kissed his head, and then started jogging back down the trail.

Since there was nothing more that Dylan could do for the young woman but monitor her vital signs, he picked up the small black purse that lay beside her on the ground. With the aid of a small flashlight he found inside, he thumbed through her purse until he located some ID. Speaking quietly to the dog, he said, "Your owner's name is Noletta Fahr, I see. And she must be a law student."

He spoke soberly, knowing how gravely injured she was. "I hope we can save her life."

As he spoke he gently stroked the dog's head. "By the way, what's your name?" he said to the dog. Then he felt for the leather collar that was around her neck. "Maybe your name's on here."

With the aid of the beam from the light, Dylan peered closely at the brass plate on the collar in the rapidly gathering darkness. "Taffy," he mumbled. "Well, Taffy, we'll save your pretty Noletta if we possibly can."

* * *

"We'll keep her dog until we can find some of her family to take care of it," Dylan told the sheriff after the helicopter had lifted off from the parking area at the trailhead.

"It's either that or put her in an animal shelter," the sheriff responded. "She seems to have taken a liking to you, Dr. Roderick, so it would probably be best this way. Now, I hate to disturb the camping trip the two of you had planned, but as I said before, the crime scene up the trail has to be preserved. We'll need the daylight to process it properly, so we can't let the two of you continue in that direction tonight."

"I don't think I feel much like camping now anyway," Indria said glumly.

"We'll also need more complete statements from both of you. And it would be best if you could go with one of my detectives back to our office so we can record the interview."

"I'm afraid we don't know much," Dylan said.

"I understand, but right now you know more than anyone else. Detective Jerry Pollard will direct you back to the office where you can give him your statement. I'd certainly appreciate it."

* * *

He watched as the helicopter faded into the distance. Fully aware that his bullet had struck her in the head, he couldn't believe she was still breathing. It was just his luck that someone found her—alive—or else they wouldn't have called for a life flight helicopter. If it had been someone he'd never seen before, he wouldn't feel quite so conscience-stricken, but it was done now. He cursed his rotten luck. He cursed life's capriciousness. And he cursed Lamar.

Lamar was dead. Of that he'd made certain. He told himself that Lamar had asked for what he'd gotten. In fact, Lamar had left him no choice. He hadn't known Lamar long, just long enough that Lamar had discovered his scheme and threatened to turn him into the cops.

But the fact that she had come along when she did had been unfortunate. He'd never dreamed he would have to shoot a woman. He was quite sure she hadn't gotten a good look at him. The sun had been shining directly into her eyes, and he'd stayed back in the shadows of the branches. But he wasn't positive, and that worried him. *I'm sorry I had to shoot her, but I had no choice,* he kept telling himself. *If only she hadn't come along when she did.* Now he could only hope she died from her wound, because if she didn't, he'd have to finish the job at some future date.

He was actually shaking as he recalled the look of terror that had crossed her face as she was turning away and he was squeezing the trigger. It would haunt him for a long time, he was afraid. If he had to confront her in the future, he knew he wouldn't be able to look at her when he killed her.

He wanted to go. His thoughts were becoming more orderly now, and he could finally plan his next move. *There were so many cops, plus an ambulance and a hearse,* he said to himself, *that it will be hours—maybe days—before I can come back and look for the pistol. I doubt the cops will find it right away. I know darn well that it went over the edge of the trail when I dropped it. Anyway, the cops will probably think I took it with me. They might not even look for it,* he thought hopefully.

He ached all over from the fall caused by that wretched dog. And even though it was dark, he was quite sure his leg had bled where the dog had bitten him. He knew that he would need to have it treated. But, for obvious reasons, he couldn't seek medical help anywhere near here.

He wrapped his thigh as well as he could after limping back to his car. He was glad he had parked it farther away from Lamar's pickup truck—one stroke of luck at last. It was with relief that he saw he wasn't bleeding badly. But he knew that he'd need a few stitches to close the wound and something to prevent infection.

With one final look around, he pulled onto the road and headed back toward Kamas to wait a while. Nearly two hours later he entered an emergency room in Murray, about sixty miles away from the scene of the shooting.

The lateness of the hour had left the waiting room empty, except for a woman who was coughing nonstop—deep, wracking coughs that shook both her and her chair. "Well, thank you," he said under his breath when she was finally called back to one of the exam rooms. His turn came a short time later, but not before he had contrived his story.

"That's an ugly wound, young man," the doctor said as he finished removing the wrap from the man's thigh.

"Yeah, and it hurts to high heaven," he said in response, wincing slightly for effect. "I have a pit bull—haven't had him very long—and he bit me."

"Looks like this happened a few hours ago. You should have come in earlier. An injury like this isn't something to take lightly."

"Yes, sir, I realize that," he said meekly. "My dog and I were on our way home from Idaho after visiting a friend when this little accident happened. Actually, the dog originally belonged to my friend. I guess maybe he wasn't too happy to be coming back with me. Anyway, after I wrapped my leg, I felt okay and figured I could make it home."

The doctor spent most of the next twenty minutes telling him what he thought of pit bulls and describing injuries he had treated resulting from similar dog–human encounters. Relieved not to have to keep up his side of the conversation, the man nodded in agreement.

When he was eventually allowed to leave, he turned to the doctor and shook his hand. "Thanks, Doctor," he said, trying to fill his voice with what might be construed as heartfelt gratitude. *Now, just a little more groveling,* he said to himself before he spoke again. "I've been thinking a lot since this incident, and I've decided to have the dog put down."

"Smart move," the doctor said as he took the man's paperwork out to the main desk. "Now, take care of that wound. Here are your instructions. Feel free to call me if you have any problems."

The man left the emergency room, still aching, but feeling less troubled than he had for hours. *You handled that well,* he told himself as he unlocked his car door.

Now he had to find out where they'd taken the woman he shot. He hoped she had died so he wouldn't have to hurt her again. But if she hadn't, she couldn't be allowed to live. *Maybe my luck will change,* he told himself. Maybe she'd be a vegetable, which was very likely, considering where the bullet had lodged. If that happened, he would be in the clear. But he had to know for sure that she didn't pose a threat to him.

He didn't locate her that night, and the next morning he cleaned his old car, wiped it of any prints Lamar may have left in it, and drove it to Provo, where he traded it for a fairly new sedan. He resumed his search for the woman that day, but he gave that up when he read something in the paper that lessened his worry. It appeared that she was no danger to him. Hope surged through him with what he'd learned. He wouldn't be forced to kill her after all. And he could get on with his life now. The cops had no idea who had done the shooting that day in the mountains. And he was confident they never would. It seemed that she also had no idea who it had been. She could never tell. His secret was safe.

CHAPTER 2

Eighteen months later

The bus roared to a stop, the door opened, and a young woman and a dog stepped out. They paused on the sidewalk while she adjusted her dark glasses, shifted her purse to her left hand, squared the full backpack on her back, and gripped the dog's leash. Only then did she speak. "Okay, Taffy, take me to class."

"Hey, Noletta, wait up. I'll walk with you if you promise not to let that dog of yours bite me," a young man called out from behind her.

She smiled as she recognized the voice. Walton Pease, a fellow law student, was a good friend, possibly even her best friend now. When he'd failed to qualify for a mission because of what he explained was a minor health problem that had cropped up the summer after high school graduation, he'd entered the university when she did. Their relationship had been platonic for years. They had dated a few times during high school and occasionally ran into each other on campus during their undergraduate years. Other than that, they hadn't kept up any kind of relationship. After they had both been accepted into law school, they saw more of each other and gradually became better friends, although they hadn't dated until after she'd lost her sight. Apparently, Walton had taken only a few classes during the year Noletta spent in blind school, training to function as a sightless person in a sighted world. Then, when she returned to the university, he seemed to take her under his wing, determined to help her succeed, along with himself, in obtaining a law degree.

Noletta's dog initially didn't seem to care for Walton, but then she didn't care for men in general. To Noletta's relief, however, Taffy gradually came to accept him. Sometimes she even let Walton pet her head, and she growled only sporadically as he approached. Walton and Noletta, with the dog always at her feet, frequently studied together, usually at the library, but occasionally at his apartment. He was a great help to her. She paid another student, a "reader," to help her at times, but whenever Walton was able to do it, he did it for free. And since he too was a law student, Noletta could discuss rather than just listen. More and more she came to enjoy the time they spent together. Very intelligent, Walton was part of the reason she was still in law school despite her disability. She stopped, turned toward him, and listened as his quick, firm steps approached.

"Hi," she said when she sensed his nearness in the darkness that was her world. It had become her world eighteen months earlier when a bullet had severed the optic chiasma where the optic nerves came together, rendering her incurably blind.

"Pretty day," he said easily. "The sky's clear and there's only a touch of smog in the air. And there are some tiny, new green leaves on the trees that line the street here."

"Thanks," she said, referring to his description of the day. Their friendship had become such since she'd lost her sight that he could, without offense, describe things he thought she might appreciate but could never see.

"Feeling okay today?" Walton asked.

"I have a headache, but it's not too bad," she said. Other than her loss of sight, the bullet that had pierced her skull on the lonely mountain trail had done very little lasting damage. The only other thing that still bothered her besides moments of slight dizziness was the almost constant aching in her head. But the headaches were decreasing in intensity, and her doctor repeatedly assured her that they would eventually disappear.

Noletta pictured Walton's curly red hair, dimpled cheeks, and freckled face. It saddened her to think that as he grew older, his boyish looks would change and mature and she wouldn't be able to see those changes. Eventually, she wouldn't know what he looked like.

"Good. Hey, I'm glad I ran into you," Walton said. "I had a question that stumped me last night when I was studying."

"If it stumped you, then you know I won't have a clue," Noletta said with a grin that she directed toward the sound of his voice.

"Actually, I think you can help me," he said. "This is something you know a lot about."

As they talked, Taffy, now a well-trained guide dog, kept gentle pressure on the leash. When Noletta had first suggested that she didn't need a new dog, that her own German shepherd could be trained, she was met with skepticism. "You know nothing about her breeding," she'd been told several times. "It takes a certain level of intelligence and natural instinct to be a successful guide dog," was another criticism. "We have better success when we train a dog from the puppy stage," others told her. "She doesn't like men," seemed to be the most frequent argument she'd heard. But Noletta had brushed them all away.

She knew Taffy better than anyone else, and not for a minute did she doubt the dog's intelligence. She insisted on having her trained, and in doing so, she'd proven the skeptics wrong. Oh, she still growled occasionally at men, but she had never tried to bite. The growling was a failing Noletta was willing to overlook. She and Taffy were inseparable now.

Noletta surprised herself when she was able to answer Walton's question a moment later. If the truth were told, she felt elated to be able to help him for a change after all the help he'd given her. They'd walked a couple of blocks when Noletta sensed a group of people approaching her on the sidewalk. She estimated that there must be four or five of them, all men, and they were walking quite rapidly and talking. More accurately, they were tossing profanity and vulgarity around in much the same manner as she had seen birds discard hulls from the bird-feeder at her parents' home. She felt the leash go slack in her hand, and she stopped as her leg brushed up against Taffy. The dog growled, and Noletta could actually feel the vibration against her leg from the rumbling in Taffy's chest.

The group passed by. Then Walton said, "I wish she'd quit that. People don't know how to take her."

"But you know she's not as fierce as she sounds," Noletta said.

Walton chuckled then. "Well, I'll admit I'm glad for that. I'd hate it if she wouldn't let me near you."

"I think she's actually getting to like you," Noletta said seriously as Taffy started out again, taking the slack from the short leash. "It's funny, though. She hasn't seemed quite that fierce for weeks. Did you recognize any of those guys?"

"Never seen them before in my life," he said easily. "I'm sure they aren't students. They looked and sounded like they weren't smart enough to walk into a classroom."

* * *

That evening, as Noletta was getting ready for bed, she thought about Taffy and her occasional fits of growling. The one time she'd growled that day had been more fierce than she'd heard for quite a while. She was certain that Taffy would never hurt anyone, but she still wished she would overcome the habit. It was embarrassing when she frightened people. *Guide dogs aren't supposed to sound vicious,* she reasoned. But what worried her the most was that it bothered Walton. She wished he wouldn't let Taffy annoy him.

As she slipped into bed, the phone rang. It was her mother. "Are you all right tonight?" she asked Noletta protectively.

"Yes, I am," Noletta responded. "You have to quit worrying so much about me."

"I'd worry less if you lived here with your father and me. You know that there's more than enough room in this big house of ours."

"I know, Mom, but I have to learn to do things for myself. What good will all my months of training do me if I'm constantly taken care of? Besides, I'm not alone. I've got Taffy," she said.

"I know you have her, and I'm grateful for that, but it's still not the same," her mother insisted.

"She's a great companion, she's smart and alert, she hears better than I do, and she is my sight," Noletta said. "How's Dad feeling tonight?"

"I'm worried about him, Noletta," her mother said. "He just doesn't seem to be getting any better."

Having turned the conversation to the health of her father, who'd been quite ill for several weeks, she and her mother visited for the next fifteen or twenty minutes. Later, as she lay in bed thinking about her day, Noletta fought the urge to feel sorry for herself, something she had to combat quite often. Over and over she'd reminded herself that although she had lost her sight, that was all she'd lost. She was alive, she was healthy, and she had a future before her.

Her thoughts turned to Walton. He was a good friend, and without him her life would be much more difficult. But that's all they were—just friends—she thought sadly. She wondered if Walton, or anyone else for that matter, could ever love her as a woman, would ever want to marry her. She used to be attractive.

Her friends and family insisted that she was still pretty, but even their assurance didn't stop her from wondering.

Noletta thought of her great-grandfather, Yousef Fahr, a Palestinian Christian who had immigrated with his wife and children to England from Palestine in 1930 following a political crisis the previous year. Yousef's son Ibrahim, her grandfather, had married a striking young English woman who had helped convert him to the LDS Church. It was this set of grandparents whom she thanked daily for whatever physical attractiveness she possessed.

From Ibrahim, who later became Abraham, she received her abundant, dark, almost black hair, her deep-set brown eyes, and her long, thick eyelashes. During her high school years, she had tried using eye makeup and struggled with it, even as a sighted person. After becoming blind and recovering from her injuries, she had participated in months of various types of training and rehabilitation—independent living, orientation and mobility, braille, and even personal care. In that last class she had received tips on applying makeup and creating a positive image. Once again she struggled and finally confirmed what she had decided years before: her eyes were fine without makeup. From that point on, she had begun reciting a daily mantra each morning as she dressed: "Thank you, Grandfather Abraham, for eyes that need no makeup."

Noletta also thought fondly of Elizabeth, or Grandmother Fahr, with her peaches-and-cream complexion, which she'd passed on to her youngest granddaughter. From the time she was a young girl, Noletta had loved listening to her grandmother speak in her delightful British accent. Grandmother Elizabeth could always make her laugh, but especially when she talked about their shared facial coloring. With a twinkle in her eye and a lilt in her voice, she would say, "I don't know what a peaches-and-cream complexion is, Noletta, but I'll tell you this much. Whatever it is, I'm gratified that they don't call it a steak-and-kidney-pie face." The vision of steak-colored cheeks and mounds of lumpy pie crust over the rest of her face always caused Noletta to giggle. She laughed involuntarily.

Noletta touched the scar where the bullet had entered her head. It was small and far enough behind her right eye that it was often covered by her long hair. She was quite certain that the scar didn't detract from her appearance. As her thoughts gained momentum, she considered other aspects of herself—her physical self. She exercised regularly and ate sensibly. "Pat yourself on the back, Noletta," she said aloud. Appearance wasn't the only reason for her diligence. During her training with Taffy, she had been reminded constantly that she needed the physical ability—strength and stamina—to handle her large dog in daily working situations. Because she had to remain strong and capable, she performed a daily routine with her treadmill and handheld weights.

Although Noletta was slightly on the tall side of average, she remembered her early days at the school for the newly blind before she trained with Taffy. She had hunched over, sometimes almost crouching down, as she learned to use her white cane. Her instructor assured her that this was not too unusual among previously sighted individuals. It was an unintentional attempt to protect herself. Because she had lived in a world where sight had been her strongest sense, she was familiar with the hazards of daily life. Her body was simply defending itself against these now unseen dangers. But Noletta knew it was more than that. It was also a deeply rooted fear of the person who had rendered her sightless.

As she progressed with her training at the school and later with Taffy, she had gradually begun to relax and overcome her stooped posture. One day, her father, with a glimpse of insight, suggested that she always carry with her some pepper spray for her own protection. Noletta actually had two canisters now, one disguised as a fountain pen in her briefcase and the other an unobtrusive cylinder on her key chain in her purse. They gave her an added measure of security.

The final step in her return to an upright stance, a more attractive appearance, and greater competence had occurred one Sunday after a particularly inspiring day at church. With sparkling eyes, the Young Women in her ward had sung: "Walk tall, you're a daughter, a child of God. Be strong—please remember who you are. Try to understand, You're part of His great plan. He's closer than you know—reach up, He'll take your hand." Those were words Noletta needed to hear. They had become her comfort and assurance each day since that wonderful Sabbath.

Noletta was surprised when she realized how long she had been letting her thoughts wander. Finally, her legs began their habitual twitching, and she knew she would soon be asleep.

With no warning Taffy suddenly jumped to her feet, and the familiar, though infrequent, rumble that always began deep in her pet's chest brought Noletta fully awake, her heart pounding with the force of a jackhammer. The rumble became a growl, and Noletta hugged her pillow close, feeling vulnerable. Taffy had never growled at home, not even once. Unbidden, her thoughts turned to the unidentified man who had shot her. Although she tried not to think about him, he was constantly lurking in the back of her mind, a dark force to be reckoned with. Her worst fear was that he might come looking for her someday.

She tried to tell herself she was being silly now. But then, she reasoned, there had to be a logical explanation for Taffy to act as she was tonight. *Could someone—could he—be right outside?* she wondered. *Maybe Mom was right,* she thought as her German shepherd padded softly across the floor toward the window. Perhaps she should move back in with her folks. Their house was certainly large enough, and she knew she was more than welcome. On the other hand, she didn't want to be a burden. She knew her mother kept busy taking care of her father. She didn't need a perfectly healthy daughter to look after as well.

As her growl faded, Taffy returned to Noletta. Then she stood silently but alertly at the head of the bed. The young woman reached out and began to stroke the soft hair. Ten minutes later she hesitantly got out of bed and walked slowly through the house, checking the locks on both outside doors and every window. Then, still feeling apprehensive, she took a sleeping pill, something she hadn't done in several weeks.

Noletta didn't mention what had happened that night in her house to anyone except Walton. When she told him about it the next day, he told her not to worry. "Someone probably walked past your house, a man no doubt, and Taffy took offense," he said. "You shouldn't give it another thought."

He's right. Why should I be afraid anyway? she asked herself. *Who would want to hurt me?*

And then that unwelcome answer entered her mind: *the man who tried to kill me.* But she knew, even if somehow her sight were restored, that she'd never be able to identify him. He'd been too deep in the branches, and the sun had been shining directly into her face. *But he might not realize that,* she thought with a shiver.

And he might not even be anywhere near here. Or he could be. And Taffy might remember him and hold a grudge.

Noletta trembled and tried to shift her thoughts elsewhere. She didn't mention what she'd been thinking to Walton. She told herself that he was more reasonable than she was.

* * *

The next Sunday afternoon, Noletta had a visitor. She always enjoyed the happy chatter and open affection of Harmony Kayser. She lived less than a block up the street but on the opposite side. The nine-year-old loved to visit with Noletta and Taffy. Noletta knew from Harmony's own frank description of herself that her young friend had flaming red hair that hung halfway down her back, and that she had bright green eyes.

Sometimes she would read to Noletta, something she was very accomplished at for one so young. Other times she would sit and stroke Taffy's coat. She would even come over for an evening and help Noletta do her laundry or clean her small house. She helped arrange Noletta's clothes neatly by color and type. That eliminated one worry from Noletta's busy and often stressful life. At least she wouldn't be appearing in public wearing clothes that clashed. Harmony also loved to cook and occasionally helped Noletta prepare a meal and then stayed to eat with her.

Noletta had grown very fond of Harmony, and she looked forward to her visits. On this Sunday afternoon, Harmony surprised Noletta when she asked her for her copy of the Book of Mormon in braille and proceeded to read from it. "Hey, you didn't tell me you could read braille," Noletta said with delight.

"I've been studying it really hard. I wanted to surprise you," Harmony said.

"Well, you did that," Noletta told her. "What other secrets have you been keeping from me?"

She'd intended the question to be in jest, but from her young friend's sudden intake of breath, she wondered if there was something she really should know. For a moment, Harmony said nothing. Then, in a frightened little voice, she asked, "How did you know that I had a secret?"

Noletta didn't know how to respond to that since she hadn't expected a serious answer. So she just smiled and said, "When a person loses their sight, their other senses become sharper." That was a true statement even if it wasn't a direct answer to Harmony's question. But she did want to learn about whatever it was that had suddenly made Harmony so serious.

"You mean like how you can tell what spices I use when we cook just by the smell, but I can't tell which ones you use?" Harmony asked.

"Yeah, like that," Noletta said. Then, hoping to relieve the sudden tension she could feel coming from the young girl, she again complimented her on how surprised she was that Harmony had learned to read braille and how well she read it. Then she said, "Why don't you tell me your other secret."

"Will you tell me one if I tell you mine?" Harmony asked innocently.

"I will," Noletta answered, as she scrambled to think of something.

"I don't know if I should," Harmony countered. "It's kind of scary."

"Lots of times scary secrets don't seem so frightening when we talk about them to someone we trust," Noletta said, wondering what it might be that made Harmony afraid. She wondered if she was being bullied at school. Or maybe her mother, who was a very attractive woman, had a boyfriend. That could be threatening to a child like Harmony who had lost her father. She didn't know what had happened to her dad, because neither Harmony nor her mother had ever discussed it with Noletta. Apparently, that was a secret they didn't want to talk about. She suddenly wondered if that was the very thing Harmony was thinking about now.

"I guess it would be okay if I tell you," Harmony said slowly. Detecting a catch in the girl's voice, Noletta placed her hand over Harmony's.

"Go ahead then," Noletta encouraged her after a moment of silence, during which she could feel a slight trembling in the girl's hand.

"You go first," Harmony finally said. "Then I'll tell you mine."

"Okay," Noletta said slowly, still trying to think of something. She knew it needed to be good. Harmony was an intelligent girl who, she suspected, would be able to see through a phony answer. "You promise you won't ever tell anyone?" Noletta was still trying to buy time.

"I will never tell anyone, Noletta. You're my best friend," Harmony said.

A secret popped into Noletta's mind, and she took a deep breath. Then she told Harmony something she'd never revealed to anyone else. It embarrassed her, but it was the truth. "I sometimes have nightmares about what I would do if I ever lost Taffy. And those nightmares make me very afraid," she said.

Harmony gasped and pulled her hand from Noletta's. Noletta could picture the child placing both hands over her mouth in dismay, and she knew she was right when she heard Harmony's muffled answer. "That would be terrible."

"Hey, it's okay," Noletta said as she put her arm around her little friend and drew her close. "It's just a dream I sometimes have. I didn't mean to frighten you. Maybe I can think of a happy secret to tell you."

"No, that's okay, Noletta," Harmony said. "Your secret reminds me of mine."

That made Noletta's chest constrict. "What is yours?" she asked gently.

"I don't want to scare you," Harmony said. "But it scares me."

"That's okay," Noletta said even as she felt herself begin to perspire. She wondered if it really was going to be about the death of the girl's father.

"The other night my mother and I were coming home really late from my grandma's house in St. George," Harmony began, "and I saw something."

"Did your mother see it too?" Noletta asked when Harmony paused. She was actually relieved, since it didn't appear to be about Harmony's father. She didn't think that Harmony's mother would be happy if her daughter talked about something that she preferred to keep private.

"No, if she had seen what I saw, it wouldn't be a secret," Harmony said sensibly. "Anyway, we passed your house, and there was a man standing beside your door."

It was Noletta's turn to gasp. She tried to appear calm as she asked what night it had occurred. When Noletta told her, she felt a tremor of fear run through her body. It was the same night that she'd been awakened by Taffy's growling. She tried to shake off her fear as much for Harmony's sake as for her own. "He was probably just walking down the street," she said, echoing what Walton had said.

"Oh no, he wasn't out on the sidewalk. He was standing right next to your door. Your light was off, but the streetlight made it bright enough to see that he had his hand on your doorknob. When we passed, he let go and jumped away, like he knew he shouldn't be there."

That night, Noletta had one of her nightmares again, and when she awoke to find Taffy standing beside her bed, she was almost overcome with relief.

CHAPTER 3

Sailboats skimmed across the waves a half mile offshore. The salty ocean air teased the young boy's nose, and the warm sand felt good between his toes. Ritchie turned toward the foaming water as it rushed onto the beach. A gull cried overhead, and in the distance small children laughed and shouted as they played.

"I want to wade in the water," Ritchie told his mother.

"You mustn't go out too far. And when I call for you, you must come back right away."

"Okay," he agreed and began moving slowly toward the water. When it washed over his bare feet, he squealed in delight. "The water feels good," he shouted. "I want to go out until it's up to my knees."

"But no farther," his mother warned.

Slowly, cautiously, Ritchie moved into deeper water. Soon, the water rushing toward him reached his knees. When it receded, it was only to his ankles. He moved a little farther from the shore. Suddenly, a larger wave came in, nearly bowling him over and soaking him up to his chest. For a moment he froze, and his mother started toward him, afraid that he'd be swept away. But then the water began to recede, and he laughed in delight.

His mother called to him anxiously. "Ritchie, that's too far. You come back this way right now."

He backed a few feet toward the shore. "I won't go any farther than this, Mom," he promised as he braced himself for the next wave.

For twenty minutes he played in the water, but finally, at his mother's urging, he moved slowly toward her. He was grinning when she wrapped him in a towel. "You shouldn't have gone that far out, Ritchie. It could be dangerous."

"I was fine, Mom. I had fun. Are the sailboats still out there?"

"Not the same ones, but there are more," Fiona Timmons told her son.

"How many are there?"

"Well, right now I can see six. No, there's another one way off to the west. So that makes seven."

"Do you think I'll ever be able to ride on a sailboat?"

"Maybe someday, Ritchie. But right now we better get home. If your father gets there before we do, he'll be angry," Fiona said. "Come take my hand, and we'll run up the beach while the sun and the breeze dry you out."

Ritchie reached out toward the sound of his mother's voice, and she took his small hand in hers. Then together they ran up the beach, laughing as they ran. Fiona could never understand how he could be so happy so much of the time when he was missing out on so many things because of his blindness.

And when he was deprived of the love of his father.

Her son had been several weeks old before she began to suspect that there was something wrong with his eyes. He didn't look at her when she spoke, and he didn't squint when she turned the light on in his darkened bedroom. She'd mentioned her suspicions to her husband, but Scully had scoffed. "You're making it all up, Fiona," he'd told her.

"No, I'm not," she'd insisted. "Come see him. I'll show you what I mean."

"I'm busy," he'd told her, and before she could insist, Scully was out the door. When he'd finally returned home late that night, the baby was asleep, and Scully reeked of alcohol and tobacco.

Fiona hadn't mentioned her suspicions to Scully again for several days, but she did take Ritchie to a doctor. When she next spoke to Scully of their son's problems, it was no longer suspicion. Now she had facts. She told Scully that Ritchie was blind and that he most likely would always be blind.

Scully had reacted to the news with anger, and he'd told her it was all her fault. From that point on, Scully ignored Ritchie. Only after Ritchie had begun to walk and had spoken his first words did his father show any interest in him. But even then his interest was infrequent and indifferent.

Many times Fiona had been tempted to leave Scully. She never did, though, torn between facing the hardships she knew and those that she didn't. So she put up with Scully's insults, his anger, his beatings, and his sullen indifference toward their son. She did her best to stretch the small income Scully brought home and spent much of her time helping Ritchie. She'd even learned braille so she could teach him, because they couldn't afford to send him to a school for the blind.

Twenty minutes later, when Fiona pulled up to their rundown little house in Whittier, Scully's pickup was in the drive. She knew he'd be angry that she didn't have his dinner ready. He was usually much later than this getting home.

Scully shocked her. He not only wasn't angry, but he seemed to be in a reasonably good mood. Though there was the odor of alcohol on his breath, he wasn't what she considered drunk. That too was uncharacteristic. His good demeanor caused her to worry after a few minutes. It wasn't possible that he'd turned over a new leaf in the few hours since he'd left the house that morning. Scully was lazy, had always been lazy, and never worked at any job for more than six or seven months. Sometimes she didn't even know if he had a job, but he always came home with a few dollars for groceries, rent, and utilities.

So she counted herself lucky. She knew women who were worse off.

Fiona fixed supper while Scully actually spent a few minutes talking to their son. She could overhear him asking about what he'd done that day. Ritchie talked enthusiastically about the beach, the water, the distant sailboats, and the warm sand that felt so good between his toes. "Can you come with us tomorrow?" he asked.

Fiona listened intently for Scully's answer. "Not tomorrow, Ritchie," he said. "I gotta start a new job tomorrow. I'll be making lots of money from now on. Maybe we can even move into a big house on the beach somewhere. Then you can go out every day, and you can play in the sand and the water all you want to."

Fiona's stomach suddenly felt hot and sour; bitter bile rose in her throat. She wasn't stupid. There was no way Scully could get a job that paid enough to buy a house on the beach. They could barely pay the rent on this one. Anger slowly built within her. Scully was not only lying, but he was building up hopes in her son for something that could never be. The boy had enough problems without his own father making impossible promises and then eventually crushing the spirit out of him.

She caught more of the conversation from the living room. "Dad, if we're going to be rich, then you can buy me a dog, one that can help me find my way around so Mom won't always have to do it," Ritchie said, his seven-year-old voice full of hope.

Fiona had heard enough. She raced into the living room and demanded that Scully come clean with her. "You're lying," she accused. "Quit building up Ritchie's hopes when you know you can never afford the things you're promising him."

Scully got to his feet and faced Fiona, his eyes narrowing to dangerous slits. "Don't you ever call me a liar again," he warned. "I'll overlook it this time, but not again."

"Sorry," Fiona said, slightly taken aback. "So tell Ritchie and me about the job you're going to start tomorrow."

Scully's face softened a little. "I'm going to be working for a real important man," he said vaguely.

"Doing what?" Fiona asked, trying her best to show interest while keeping her anger in check so Scully wouldn't explode. She hated what he did when he lost his temper. Drunk or sober, he was almost certain to hurt her, as he had done countless times before.

"Delivering stuff," he said.

She didn't like the sound of this. "What kind of stuff?" she asked suspiciously.

"Lots of stuff," he answered. "Whatever he needs to have delivered. And he'll pay me good money."

Further questions only made him angrier and gave her no additional information. Finally, she gave up, hoping that he would be doing something legal but fearing that would not be the case.

There was a chill over dinner, and Fiona could see that Ritchie had withdrawn into the secret world where he seemed to find solace whenever Scully was in a foul mood. And after Fiona's questioning, he was in a foul one. As she thought about the job he claimed to have found and the promises he'd made to Ritchie, the chill that dominated the dinner table settled into her stomach, making it impossible for her to eat. She pushed her plate away and waited while her son and husband finished their meal.

Ritchie ate slowly and automatically, his mind clearly someplace else, and Scully shoveled in his food, scarcely taking time to chew. It wasn't long before he pushed back from the table and started out of the room.

"Are you going somewhere?" Fiona asked.

"Just to watch TV. Is that okay with you?"

"Sure, just wondered," she said, relieved when she heard the TV come on. It always felt better to be alone with Ritchie.

He was such a good boy. How she wished he wasn't blind. And how she wished that since he was, Scully could accept the blindness and be a real father to him.

* * *

Walton occasionally spoke of his cousin, Creed Esplin. Noletta had met him once just before she'd lost her sight. He'd dropped in at the university when she happened to be walking out of a class with Walton. That was before she and Walton had become such close friends. He was a good-looking man, a little taller than Walton, and he seemed like a nice guy. Walton had mentioned a little more than a year ago that Creed had moved to California because of a great job offer in Los Angeles. He'd told her that Creed worked for a contractor, building houses, and that he made very good money. Other than that, she didn't know much about him.

Walton hadn't mentioned to her that Creed was coming for another visit, so she was surprised when Walton brought him to the library, telling her that Creed was on vacation and had decided to come to Salt Lake for a few days. "Actually, he's been here for several days already. How would it be to be able to get so much time off?" Walton asked.

Taffy was lying against her leg, taking an afternoon nap, so Noletta didn't stand up. But she extended her hand to Creed in a friendly greeting. As they shook, she felt rather than heard the deep rumbling in Taffy's chest.

She withdrew her hand and placed it on Taffy's head, attempting to soothe her. But the rumbling became a growl, and the German shepherd rose to her feet. "Gee, I'm sorry," Creed said. "I didn't mean to upset your dog."

Noletta was embarrassed.

"She doesn't like men," Walton said before she could say anything.

"Looks to me like he's just protective of you," Creed said with a grin as he held his hand out toward the dog. "And I don't blame him."

"Stop it, Taffy," Noletta said.

But Taffy didn't stop. Not only did the growl continue, but the hair stood up on the back of her neck.

"Probably my cologne," Creed said. "A lot of women don't seem to like it."

"Then why do you wear it?" Walton asked as Noletta continued to soothe her dog.

Creed chuckled. "Because I do like it. And when I like something, I get it. And when I get it, I use it."

"That's the truth," Walton said. "You always do like to have your own way."

Taffy's growling ceased, but she remained standing beside Noletta, who visited with the two men for a few minutes. "I won't be able to study with you today, Noletta," Walton said a little later in their conversation. "Creed's truck broke down, and I'm his transportation for a day or two."

"I guess I need a new one, although this one isn't old," Creed said. "It's good to see you again, Noletta. And I must say, you are as pretty as I remembered. Maybe I'll see you again sometime."

"Maybe so," Noletta said. "Sorry about Taffy."

As the two men walked away, she laid her hand on Taffy's neck, and even though there was no growl, she felt the hair rise on her dog. Yes, Taffy just didn't like men in general, she reminded herself. Creed seemed really nice, just like he had the first time they'd met.

She'd known about Taffy's habit from the day she picked her up at the animal shelter. She smiled to herself and sat back down. She had to quit letting Taffy's growling alarm her. It was all so very silly.

A minute later she was engrossed in her studies, her fingers flying over the braille on the pages before her. But she wasn't so engrossed that she didn't feel lonely. This was time she usually had with Walton, and she missed him.

* * *

"Beautiful woman," Creed said as they got in Walton's car. "I know she's blind now, and that she can't look at you, but her face was sure pointed toward you. Is it serious with you and her?"

"Not really," Walton said. "We're just friends. I guess you could say our relationship is more like brother and sister."

"Really," Creed remarked. "I think you're crazy. You should consider her differently. I can see romance as a real possibility for you, my friend."

"Creed, she's blind. I could never marry a blind woman," Walton said with a touch of irritation in his voice.

"Why not?" Creed asked. "She's stunning, and if she's in law school, she must be smart. You ought to rethink things here. After all, not many women are going to fall for that mug of yours."

"I'll have you know, there are plenty of them that think I look okay," Walton retorted with a grin.

"Oh yeah, name one," Creed challenged.

"There's plenty."

"Am I missing something here? Is there a special woman somewhere?"

"No, not really," Walton said.

"Well, I'll tell you what. Blind or not, I could go for that Noletta," Creed said.

"She's really not your type, Creed. And anyway, her dog doesn't like you."

"That can be overcome. He just needs to get to know me."

"He? The dog's a female!"

"Whatever. So is Noletta, and I like what I see. I'd like to get to know her better and let her get to know me. Who knows, if you're not interested in her as a woman, maybe she'll learn to like me."

"Stay away from her, Creed," Walton said suddenly.

"Hey, your face is red," Creed said with a laugh. "Say what you want, my man, but I believe what I see. Brother and sister relationship, my eye."

CHAPTER 4

It happened again the very next day. Taffy growled at someone who passed by her on the sidewalk as she walked toward the bus stop after her classes. Taffy stopped, and so did Noletta. Only one set of footsteps had passed. Whoever was upsetting her dog that afternoon was alone. As she stood waiting for Taffy to start walking again, Noletta listened to the receding footsteps. She could tell that Taffy's attention was directed behind her, and her growl deepened when the footsteps stopped. She scolded herself for imagining things again, but she couldn't shake the feeling that someone's eyes were focused on her back.

Finally, she said, "Let's go, Taffy," and the dog obediently started forward. A moment later she could hear the other person's steps begin again, and she was relieved that they continued away from her.

Despite her resolve after talking with Walton's cousin, Creed, the incident at the bus stop left Noletta unsettled for the rest of the evening. Her first thought was that it might have been Creed, because Walton had mentioned just that afternoon as they left a class together that Creed would be around for a while. But surely Creed would have spoken to her, she reasoned. It could have been anyone. For some reason, Taffy seemed to be reverting back to her old habits. Either that or she was becoming overly protective of her. By evening Noletta had calmed her unreasonable fears.

Sometime after midnight that night, she awoke to the sound of Taffy's deep-throated and troubling growl. She sat up in bed, her heart pounding. It sounded more ominous within the lonely confines of her house. And once again she felt especially vulnerable.

Taffy continued to prowl around the small house for several minutes, clearly agitated. Noletta kept thinking about the man Harmony had seen just a few nights ago with his hand on her doorknob. Thoroughly frightened, she was wide awake when her dog finally came into the bedroom and settled down beside her bed. With an important exam scheduled the next day, Noletta needed sleep. After a prayer in which she asked the Lord to protect her, she again took several sleeping pills her doctor had prescribed and was soon in a deep sleep.

When the alarm awoke her at six, it seemed unusually quiet in the house. It took her only a moment to find her fuzzy slippers. Then she headed for the back of the house where the door opened into the small yard that she let her dog run in. Taffy usually met her before she got to the door, anxious to go out for a few minutes while Noletta showered. It was part of their daily ritual.

But the soft sound of Taffy's feet on the carpet failed to greet her. "Taffy," she called out softly. "Come on, girl. It's time for you to go outside." *Poor Taffy,* she thought, *you didn't have the benefit of a sleeping pill, did you, girl?* She called again.

When the dog failed to respond that time, fear reached out with icy fingers and clutched at Noletta. She called louder, but there was still no response. A cold chill prickling her skin, Noletta walked to the back door and tried the doorknob. It was locked, just as she'd left it. Then she made her way to the front door, where she once again found the door locked. One by one she checked the windows. They were all closed.

She called for Taffy another time, but there was no answer. She wondered if Taffy had taken ill and was lying sick or—

heaven forbid—even dead somewhere in the house. That might explain why she'd been growling at people more frequently lately. It would take her a long time to search the entire house, crawling on hands and knees and feeling around for her dog. The recurring nightmare she'd told Harmony about was actually happening. Noletta felt her knees threaten to give way, and she slumped into the closest chair. Trembling uncontrollably for several minutes, Noletta couldn't decide what to do next. Finally, she picked up the phone and with shaking hands called Harmony's home. Her mother, Terri Kayser, answered. Terri was sympathetic when Noletta told her what she needed, that she couldn't look for the dog alone. And Terri said the early hour didn't matter, that she'd awaken Harmony and come right over.

Harmony was in tears when Noletta opened the door for the Kaysers a little later. She was so upset she couldn't speak when her mother reported a few minutes later to Noletta that Taffy definitely wasn't in the house, nor was she in the little backyard.

Taffy had vanished while Noletta slept. And her world came crashing down. The strength she'd built since learning she was blind evaporated in her sudden grief, and Noletta sank miserably to the floor and sobbed. Even Harmony couldn't console her.

Terri called the police from the phone in Noletta's kitchen while Harmony sat on the floor beside Noletta. With her own eyes full of tears, her head bowed, and her flaming hair scattered on the white carpet beside her friend's shoulder, Harmony clutched Noletta's hand.

After several minutes, Noletta's sobs gradually died away, replaced with paralyzing fear. She felt as if death were overtaking her. She tried to sit up, but she couldn't move. Fear had sapped her energy, and her courage had disappeared. *Perhaps death would be best,* she reasoned. She didn't see how she could go on without Taffy. She had become so dependent on her that without her, living seemed impossible. Slowly the fog of darkness swallowed her, consciousness fled, and Noletta lay still on her white-carpeted living room floor.

* * *

"Is she dead?" Harmony asked, her green eyes full of grief.

"No, Harmony, she must have fainted," her mother said. "This has been a terrible shock to her. You know how she depends on Taffy. The police will be here any minute. I hope they hurry."

"But she's not moving," Harmony persisted. "And her face feels cold."

Harmony's mother knelt beside Noletta on the floor and felt for a pulse. "She's definitely alive, Harmony. Don't worry, sweetheart. I'm sure she'll be fine once the shock of Taffy running away wears off."

Harmony looked up at her mother. "Mom, Taffy didn't run away. The doors were locked. Remember, Noletta had to let us in. Anyway, Taffy wouldn't do that."

"Don't be silly," her mother said. "Of course she ran away. What else could possibly have happened?"

"Someone stole her," Harmony said as her quick young mind recalled the secret she'd shared with Noletta, the secret of the man she'd seen standing at her friend's door late at night.

"For goodness sake, stop it, Harmony. You'll only make yourself scared and give yourself nightmares. You're even scaring me. I'm sure Taffy ran away. The police will be able to tell you that when they get here. Which reminds me, we'd better get you home and fix you some breakfast. You do have school today."

"We can't leave her here like this," Harmony wailed.

"I didn't mean right now," her mother said patiently. "We'll stay until the police get here. Then it's off we go. Hey, I think I hear a car pulling up now."

* * *

When Noletta awoke, she knew she wasn't alone. She also knew she wasn't at home. She'd spent enough time in hospitals that she had no trouble recognizing the hospital bed she lay in. But she didn't recognize the voice that spoke to her. It was a deep voice, a kind voice, but nevertheless a stranger's voice.

"Miss Fahr, are you feeling better?" the voice asked.

"Yes, Doctor, I am," she said.

The deep voice chuckled. "I'm afraid I'm not a doctor, just a cop. But I'll get the doctor for you in a moment if you need him."

"No, that's okay," she said.

"Good. My name's Martin Atkinson, Detective Martin Atkinson. I've been assigned to help you find your dog."

At the mention of Taffy, an almost overwhelming sadness swept across Noletta. But she fought her emotions, ashamed that she'd fallen apart in front of Harmony and her mother, and determined to be positive from that moment on. She'd survived terrible trials before, and she would do it again.

* * *

Detective Atkinson realized that he was staring, but he couldn't help it. He'd come to the hospital to talk to the owner of what had been described to him as a valuable German shepherd. He'd been told that the owner of the missing dog had collapsed when she learned that the dog had disappeared. He'd come expecting to find, well, he didn't know what he'd expected for sure, but it wasn't the young woman who was fighting so hard not to cry now as he stared at her lovely face.

He watched in fascination as a series of emotions crossed that face. He studied her eyes, wondering why she wasn't looking at him, knowing he'd be embarrassed if she did. Her eyes seemed a little dull somehow and didn't seem to focus on anything in particular. When she turned her head away from him, he tore his eyes from her face and spoke to her again without looking at her. "As I was saying, Miss Fahr, I've been assigned, along with my partner, who is back at the office, to look into the matter of your missing dog. He must be valuable, and I can see you must be very attached."

Noletta turned her head back toward him and he looked at her again, but her eyes still didn't meet his. In a soft voice, she said, "*She's* more than valuable, Detective. She's my best friend and my protector. Her name is Taffy."

There was something about those dark brown, rather strange eyes of hers. Slowly, a sense of unease crept over him. "Your protector?" he asked hesitantly.

"Yes, my protector and my eyes," Noletta said.

Understanding struck Martin like a bolt of lightning. Noletta was blind. This wasn't just a nice, expensive dog that was missing. It was a guide dog! No wonder this young woman was devastated. She wasn't some kooky person whose life was wrapped up in that of her pet—walking, grooming, and even clothing it. She was a woman who seriously needed her dog. "I'm sorry," he said, feeling inadequate. "A pair of uniformed officers went to your house. When you'd been taken by an ambulance, they called me, and I came up here. No one explained. No one told me that . . . that . . ." He stumbled on his words.

Noletta was quickly gaining her composure, and she finished for him. "That I'm blind."

"I'm sorry," he said again, feeling terribly awkward. "I had no idea. I'm so sorry."

"So am I," Noletta said, even as her emotions began to change again. "I need Taffy. I don't know what I'll do without her. I can't imagine where she went." Her sightless eyes began to fill with tears. Unable to help himself, Martin grabbed a tissue and gently dabbed at the wet trails running down her cheeks.

"Thank you," Noletta said, and she reached for the tissue that he handed to her. Then she finished the job he'd begun.

Detective Atkinson was reeling. He'd come to LDS Hospital expecting to get a statement and a description of a missing dog. Then he had planned to get back to work on the case he and his partner had been assigned the day before. Now he knew he had other work to do. There was a sense of urgency to this case, and he wanted desperately to find and return this dog.

"Can you get the doctor in here for me?" she asked suddenly. "I want to go home. I'll be okay now."

"I'll need to get some information from you first," the detective began.

"Can't we do it at my house?" she asked. "I need to go home. Taffy might come back, and I need to be there if she does."

Atkinson couldn't argue with that. "Sure, ah, I'll see if I can find the doctor. I'll be right back."

He stepped into the hallway and walked briskly to the nurses' station, where he explained what Noletta wanted. "I don't know if he'll want to release her or not," he was told, "but we'll page him."

Back in Noletta's room a moment later, Martin told her that the doctor would be coming. "My clothes—they must be here somewhere," she said in response. "Would you please find them for me? As soon as I talk to the doctor, I'm getting dressed."

This certainly wasn't the same *basket case* he'd been told to expect. This woman was now in control, and he felt a need to do as she asked. He glanced around the room and spotted a closet. He looked in it, but what he found wasn't what he'd expected. She must have been in her nightgown when she discovered that her dog was missing. The nightgown and a pair of fuzzy blue slippers were the only items in the closet. Gingerly, he touched the nightgown, picked it up, and carried it back to the bed. "This is all I could find," he said as he held it toward her.

"What is it?" she asked.

Oh, yeah, he thought, feeling stupid. *She's blind.* "It's your, ah, a nightgown," he managed to say.

"Oh," she said, "that's right. I wasn't dressed yet when I was looking for Taffy. I'm sorry. Are there slippers in the closet too?"

"Yes, blue ones."

"Okay, but I'll need clothes and shoes. I can't walk out of here in my nightgown."

"But you came in here dressed that way," he said, thinking his logic was reasonable.

"That was different," Noletta responded firmly. "I was in a life flight helicopter, and I wasn't conscious. But I'm conscious now, and there's no way I'm going to leave this room without wearing something proper. I wonder who can get me some clothes. Maybe my mom, if she can leave my dad for a few minutes. He's really sick. We're worried about him."

What a load this young woman must carry, Martin thought. *How can she handle it all?*

"If you'll tell me how to find your house, and how to get into it, and what to bring, I'll go get some clothes for you," he volunteered. Then he wondered if that was something a detective should be doing. He'd been assigned to the division only a few weeks ago. Before that he'd been a uniformed patrol officer. He was still a very green detective.

"Oh, Detective, would you do that for me?" she asked as if in disbelief.

"Whatever it takes to get you to sit down with me and let me ask you a few questions," he responded. Then he thought how lame that must have sounded, and he added, "Of course I'd do it anyway."

Then an amazing thing happened. This woman, this attractive woman wearing a most unbecoming hospital gown and lying in a hospital bed—the woman he'd been told was probably a nutcase grieving over a dog—smiled. And that smile transformed her face into something more entrancing than anything Detective Atkinson had ever seen.

"Your address, Miss Fahr?" he asked.

"Noletta, please," she responded as she recited her address, told him where to find a hidden key if her house was locked, and suggested what he might bring for her. "Really, you don't have to do this. I'm sure that—"

"I'd be glad to," he said.

There was no sign of the missing dog, and the door was unlocked at Noletta's house. Apparently, whoever had been there last had not locked it. That worried him for some reason. He checked to make sure the key was where she said she kept one hidden, since he intended to lock the door when he left and needed to be sure he and Noletta could get back in. It was exactly where she'd told him it would be in her secluded back-yard. It was so well hidden that he was certain anyone who might have gone into her house and stolen the dog had not used that key. He left it in place without touching it and walked back to her front door. This was a crime scene if her dog had been stolen, although that seemed very unlikely. From the brief report the patrol officers had given him, that was certainly the theory of a young neighbor girl. He made a mental note to find and interview the girl after he had a chance to talk with Noletta.

Martin stepped inside the house and looked around. The place was orderly, something that made sense, since a blind person would need things to be where they could be easily found. He moved uncomfortably through the house, feeling as if he were invading sacred space when he entered her bedroom and opened her closet. It took only a moment to locate her cane and the clothes she needed. She'd explained that without her dog, she would need to have her cane.

At the door he stopped again, turned, and looked around her living room. There was a picture of the Savior on one wall, another of the Salt Lake Temple on the opposite wall, and an array of framed photographs—family, he assumed—in another area. A beautiful painting of a small herd of deer beside a forest lake was on the fourth wall. The white carpet was clean, the light blue furniture was attractive, and he couldn't see a thing out of order.

Noletta was blind, and yet she surrounded herself with things others would enjoy. Martin found himself wanting to learn more about the fascinating woman who lived here. His eyes fell again on the painting. It had been done in oils and, even though he was no expert, he thought it looked professional. He crossed the room and examined it more closely. His eye fell on the signature of the painter. It was signed *Noletta Fahr.* So she had not always been blind as he had assumed for no good reason. She'd seen and appreciated the beautiful things of the world and then had tragically lost them. The thought hit him forcefully.

Saddened, but more determined than ever, he again crossed the room to the door. He had work to do, help to give this young woman named Noletta, who, over the past thirty minutes, had affected him so deeply. He shut and locked the door to her house, anxious to get back to the hospital.

A vehicle passed by as he was getting into his patrol car, but his mind was so engrossed in Noletta's plight that he didn't look too closely at the driver.

But the driver inspected him carefully, and there was no regard in that look. In fact, that driver watched him with suspicion and jealousy. Had the driver known the man's profession, a whole different range of feelings would have surfaced, because he hated cops.

CHAPTER 5

"The doctor says I can go home, Detective Atkinson. He said my shock has passed," Noletta said the moment she heard his footsteps come through the door and into her room. She had been positive they were his footsteps. She had listened closely when he'd left earlier, determined to remember the particular sound he made when he walked. He seemed genuine. She hoped he really could find Taffy, that he cared about her loss, and that he wasn't just going through the motions because he was the officer assigned to her case.

"Please," he said, "call me Martin."

"Martin," she said softly. "That was my grandfather's name—my mother's father. I really like that name. I don't suppose Taffy was back when you got there."

"No, I'm sorry. She wasn't."

"Were you able to find my clothes?"

"Yes, it was simple, really. I should get you to organize my house. I'm afraid I'm not a very good housekeeper," he said as he handed her the clothing.

So he was single. She liked that. It would be less awkward working with a single police officer than a married one. Maybe she would actually dare to ask him for a ride home so she wouldn't have to call her mother.

Noletta knew her clothes by touch, and he'd brought the very pants, blouse, and shoes she'd requested. She was impressed. He also handed her the cane she hadn't used much since Taffy had completed her training.

"I'll wait outside your room while you change. Then if you don't mind, I'll give you a ride to your house, and I can get to work on finding Taffy for you."

Of course she didn't mind. And he'd saved her the embarrassment of asking. She was also impressed that he'd called Taffy by name instead of referring to her as *your dog*. That was encouraging. She dressed rapidly and, with the use of her cane, walked to the door and opened it. "Martin," she said. "I'm ready."

"Wow, that was fast."

"I may be blind, but I'm not uncoordinated," she said with a smile. "Would you mind getting my slippers and nightgown for me? The nurse put them in a bag. I think she set them on a chair, but I'm not sure."

He stepped past her. "Sure enough. They're right here."

She started moving in the direction she'd heard him coming from earlier, thinking that the elevator must be that way. But before she'd gone five steps, Martin took her arm. "Do you mind if I help?" he asked.

"Thank you," she responded. "You're very thoughtful."

While waiting for the elevator, he said, "I noticed the painting in your living room. You paint amazingly well."

"I had a lot of room to improve. That's one of the things I miss most about being blind. The day I lost my sight, I was taking pictures of some fall colors in the mountains. I had planned to go home and start a painting that evening. I suppose the film is still in my camera. I never got to finish the roll." In fact, she didn't even know what had become of the camera. She made a mental note to ask her folks if it was at their house.

"I'm sorry," he said. "Would I be rude if I asked what happened to cause you to lose your sight? Were you in a car wreck or something?"

"Something," she said. She didn't consider him rude for asking the question. It was something she had had to face often. But before she could begin to explain, the elevator doors opened.

Walking with the detective, Noletta had an unsettling thought. She loved to be with Walton, but even though he was a good friend, he'd never been quite as thoughtful as this detective whose name was so similar to his. Walton. Martin. *Similar names, both good strong ones,* she thought. And good strong men. Oh, how she'd like to have a good strong man in her life someday, totally and intimately in her life. But she was afraid that would never happen. If only Walton . . . She let the thought drift away to wherever unfinished or unrealistic thoughts sought refuge.

"I'm sorry," Martin said as the cool breeze of a late spring morning greeted them outside.

"For what?" she asked as she held firmly to his arm and used her cane with her other hand to help guide herself down the steps that led toward the street.

"For being rude," he said. "What happened to you is none of my business."

"Oh, Detective," she said, "you weren't rude. I don't mind telling you what happened. For a long time I didn't like to talk about it, but it's okay now. I'm past that point."

"I'd love to hear about it then," he said, and he sounded sincere. "But I do wish you'd call me Martin."

By the time they arrived in front of her house, Noletta had shared all that she remembered or had been told about the day she was shot. And Martin had listened without interrupting. Only after he'd opened the door of his car for her and had helped her onto the walk did he speak. "I remember this case now. And as I also recall, whoever did this has never been caught."

"They have no idea who it might have been," she responded.

"And you didn't recognize him?"

"I didn't really get a good look at him. His face was obscured by branches, and the sun was in my eyes. Before I could get a better look at him, everything went black. I'm afraid I can never help the police find him."

"Oh, you never know. Maybe something more will come back to you," he said.

"I doubt it," she responded glumly.

"You never know," he answered again, and the way he said it actually gave her hope. "Work on your memory of those few moments, Noletta. Since some of what happened has come back to you, maybe more will. You're a painter. You were trained to see details. Think about them. Try to remember more if you can."

"And what if I do?"

"Tell me about it."

"But the crime occurred in Summit County."

"I know, but maybe I can help."

She caught a whiff of new blossoms on the breeze as she approached her door. "I'll get the key," he told her as she breathed deeply, savoring the scent.

When he returned, she said, "I planted some flowers next to the door. I can smell them now. Some of them must be starting to bloom."

"Yeah, there are a few little blossoms," he said.

"What color are they?" she asked.

"Red. And a there are a couple of white ones."

"Are they pretty?"

"Yes, as a matter of fact, they are."

"Thank you," she said.

She listened while Detective Atkinson opened the door. Then she commented, "I guess Taffy still hasn't come back."

"Apparently not," he responded. "But it's time you told me everything you can recall leading up to when you discovered her missing this morning."

They sat at her kitchen table, and again she talked while he listened. Only this time, he inserted occasional questions, which she tried to answer as completely as she could. When she'd finished, she heard him push back from the table and rise to his feet. "Can you describe Taffy for me?" he asked.

She smiled. "I can do better than that. I painted a picture of her just shortly before I was shot. The painting's in the closet in my spare bedroom, along with some of my other paintings. I'll get it for you."

"Do you have other paintings somewhere else?" he asked. "Or do you keep them all here?"

"I have several of them at my parents' home," she said as she pushed her chair back from the table. He took her arm as she stood up, but she said, "You wait here. I'll get it. I know my way around my place very well."

"Yes, I suppose you do," he said. "I'll just take a minute and read over my notes while you're getting it."

When a muted scream came from the direction of Noletta's spare bedroom a few moments later, Martin knocked over his chair in his haste to get up from the table. He didn't take time to upright it as he streaked toward the bedroom that was now silent. He found her on her knees facing the closet, and she seemed to be gasping for air.

"Noletta," he asked in concern, "what's the matter?"

When she turned her face toward him, she was white, and her sightless eyes were wide. "Someone's been in here," she said, her voice betraying the fear that he'd already discovered on her face.

"Is something missing?" he asked as he knelt beside her and gently took her hand.

"Yes," she said in a hoarse whisper.

"A painting?" he pressed.

"Yes."

"The one of Taffy?"

"No, it's right here," she said, and handed him the portrait of the beautiful missing German shepherd.

He glanced at the painting briefly. He could study it later and memorize Taffy's features. He laid it on the floor beside them and asked, "So what *is* missing, Noletta?"

She was already demonstrating her amazing ability to bounce back from upsets. Her eyes weren't quite as large now, the color was returning to her face, and her voice was stronger as she spoke. "I know this sounds stupid, but I painted a self-portrait once. It was here with these other paintings, but it's gone now."

"How long has it been since you've seen it?" he asked. Then, realizing his mistake, he said, "I'm sorry . . . What I meant was—"

She gently interrupted him. "When did I last touch it, or when did I last confirm that it was here?"

"Yeah, that's what I meant."

"It was just last week. I was showing these paintings to a little friend of mine, Harmony Kayser. I mentioned her to you a few minutes ago."

"The red-headed nine-year-old."

"Yes, she wanted to see some of my paintings. But I know I put them back exactly the way I found them, and the one of me was next to the one of Taffy," Noletta said. "I've always numbered my framed paintings by scratching an identification number on the back of the frame. The missing one was number twenty-three. It was definitely here last week."

"Is there any chance that Harmony borrowed it? It sounds like she's very fond of you. Maybe she wanted something in her room to remind herself of you," Martin suggested.

"No, I don't think so. She'd ask. She's very polite and honest."

"Okay, but if it's not there where you left it, then *someone* has taken it," he said, stating the obvious.

"Detective," she began.

"Martin," he interrupted.

"Martin, Taffy couldn't have gotten out of the house if she'd wanted to. It's like I told you a few minutes ago—someone came in and took her. It's possible that the same person also took my painting."

"I suppose it is," he said.

"But why would anyone steal a painting of me?" she asked. "That makes no sense at all."

As they were talking, they'd gotten to their feet, and Martin had picked up the painting of Taffy. An alarming thought occurred to him as he contemplated why someone might take Noletta's picture, but he wasn't about to frighten her with that thought. Instead, he said, "Maybe because you're so pretty."

She flushed and said, "But I'm not."

"Oh, but you are," he countered. And then he added, "And so is Taffy. Would you mind if I borrow this for a little while? I just want to photograph it and get copies made for distribution. I'll do everything I can to find your dog and arrest whoever took her."

"So you do believe she was stolen?" Noletta asked.

"Of course I do. Now all I need to do is figure out why and by whom, and then we'll get her back for you."

"You almost make it sound easy," she said as the doorbell rang. "I wonder who that could be. I'll go answer the door."

Martin stood in Noletta's living room and watched as she walked confidently across the room to the door. She opened it and admitted a pretty, freckle-faced girl with long, flaming red hair and a slender, attractive woman of about thirty-five who had equally red hair. The girl threw her arms around Noletta. "I'm so glad you're okay," she said. "I've worried all day about you. I finally told the teacher why I was having such a bad day, and she called my mom to come and get me so we could check on you."

"And I'm glad she did," Terri said. "We've both been worried sick."

"I'm fine," Noletta said. "I'm so sorry that I upset both of you."

"But Taffy's gone. What will you do?" Harmony cried.

"Harmony and Terri, I want you to meet a new friend of mine. This is Detective Martin Atkinson. He's going to try to find Taffy for me," Noletta told them.

Martin crossed the room, shook hands with Terri, and looked down at Harmony. "I'm going to do everything I can to get Taffy back," he promised. "And I'm glad to meet both of you. Noletta is lucky to have such good friends."

"It's nice to meet you," Harmony said.

"Yes," her mother agreed. Then she said to Harmony, "We'd better not stay, but we can check in with Noletta after you get out of school and I get off work."

"Do I have to go back today?" Harmony pleaded.

"Well, you can't stay home alone. But maybe I could take you to the office with me."

"Terri, if you don't mind, I'd be happy to have her stay here," Noletta said. "I'd enjoy her company. Besides that, without Taffy around, I'll be terribly lonely. I can send her home when you are ready for her if that's okay with Harmony," she said.

"Oh, Mom, please," Harmony begged.

"Well, okay. But I'll come by and pick her up so I can see if there's anything I can do for you," Terri said. Then she turned to Martin. "It's been nice meeting you, Detective. And good luck finding Taffy. I'll be praying for your success."

"Thank you," Martin said as his eyes met hers. They were a light shade of green and very expressive. Their eyes held each other's for just a moment. "I'd appreciate your prayers, and Harmony's too."

After Terri had left, Harmony turned to Noletta. "Noletta, it's after lunchtime. Have you had anything to eat?" Harmony asked with a maturity that Martin knew was far beyond her age.

"I'm fine. I don't have much of an appetite right now."

"You need to eat," the little girl said firmly. "I'll go fix you something while you talk to the policeman."

"Thanks, Harmony. That would be nice. Maybe you could fix enough for yourself and Detective Atkinson, too."

"Sure, I can do that. Do you like tuna fish, Mr. Atkinson?" she asked.

"I'm a bachelor. I eat lots of tuna. Thanks."

Harmony had barely disappeared into the kitchen before the bell rang again. "Pretty popular gal you are," Martin said as Noletta once again stepped to the door.

"Noletta, what are you doing?" a red-haired man in his mid-twenties said the moment he saw her. "Why didn't you come and take the test today?"

"Oh!" Noletta exclaimed as her hand flew to her mouth. "I forgot, Walton. Oh, no! What am I going to do now?"

"How could you forget?" he asked with more than a touch of irritation in his voice. "We studied for two hours yesterday. This was a critical exam. You know that. How do you ever expect to get through law school if you just forget about things, like important tests?" The irritation was approaching anger as he finished his outburst.

Martin watched the exchange, forming a negative impression of Noletta's friend. And at the same time, he was almost overwhelmed to think that she was attending law school. She hadn't mentioned a word of that. *How difficult that must be for her,* he thought, *and how determined she must be.*

"Come on. Grab your coat. I'll take you right now, and we'll go talk to the professor. But you'd better be thinking about a better excuse than *I forgot,*" he snapped.

"How about, *my guide dog was stolen?*" Martin suggested as he stepped forward.

"Who are you?" Walton asked bluntly.

"Oh, I'm sorry," Noletta said. "This is Detective Atkinson. He's here to investigate the disappearance of Taffy."

Walton's face grew darker. "Taffy's been stolen?" he asked as if he couldn't believe his ears. "When?"

"Sometime during the night. She was growling, and I couldn't sleep, so I took a couple of sleeping pills. I guess I slept too soundly," Noletta confessed tearfully. "When I woke up, Taffy was gone. It was terrible."

Martin felt distinctly out of place as Walton comforted Noletta in his arms and, while holding her tightly, said, "She probably just ran off. Dogs do that sometimes."

"She didn't run off," Noletta said. "I'm sure of that."

"I'm so sorry. Why didn't you call me? You know I'd have come right over. This is awful, Noletta."

What made Martin feel even worse was the way Noletta clung to Walton. He was obviously a very special friend, perhaps even more than that. Martin felt very much like an intruder and wanted nothing more than to leave at that moment. Noletta made it easy for him. "Walton, I've got to go up to campus. Will you take me? I'll talk to Professor Simmons and explain."

"Noletta, I'll get my notebook and be on my way," Martin said awkwardly. "You're sure it's okay if I take this painting of Taffy? I'll bring it back later. And I'll keep you posted on what I'm doing to find Taffy."

"Thanks, Detective," she said, and this time he didn't remind her to call him Martin. He was a detective. He was here to investigate a crime. And he reminded himself not to forget what his role was. He had let an attraction to a victim cloud his judgment. He knew better. He was a professional, and he told himself he had better act like one.

"Detective, could I speak with you for a moment?" Walton asked.

He stopped in the doorway and turned back. "Sure," he said.

Noletta slipped by. "I'll hurry and grab a sandwich. I'll bet Harmony has them almost finished. Oh, Harmony! I forgot. I promised her mother she could stay here until after she gets off work. I can't leave her here alone."

"Then bring her with us," Walton suggested. "I'm sure she'll be okay, and it shouldn't take too long."

Martin was watching Walton during the short exchange, trying to rid himself of the distaste he'd so quickly formed. He said, "You needed to talk to me, Walton?"

"Yes, I just want to remind you that Noletta needs that dog back. I hope you aren't planning to make just a cursory search and then drop the whole thing," Walton said.

So much for getting rid of the negative impression, Martin thought. He simply said, "I intend to do everything I can to—"

He was interrupted by a crash in the kitchen. Both men ran in to find Noletta on the floor. Harmony was already beside her. "What happened?" Walton demanded sharply.

"I . . . I'm just clumsy," Noletta said as she began to get to her feet.

"No you're not," Harmony said. "You stumbled over a chair that wasn't where it was supposed to be. It's my fault. I noticed it was tipped over, and I was going to stand it up and push it back under the table, but I hadn't done it yet."

"How did it get tipped over?" Walton asked.

"I did it. I'm sorry, Noletta," Martin said. "It was when you scr—"

Walton interrupted with fury in his voice. "She's blind, Detective. That was pretty thoughtless of you. I hope you give more thought to finding her dog than you do to her safety."

Martin grabbed his notebook and said, "I'm sorry, Noletta. I'll be in touch." Before she could say a word, he hurried from the kitchen and left the house.

CHAPTER 6

Noletta was disturbed about Detective Atkinson's hasty departure, and she couldn't believe the way Walton was acting. As she brushed herself off, she turned in his direction. "Weren't you a little rough on him, Walton?"

"I don't think so," Walton answered defensively. "People need to learn to be more sensitive. You could have been hurt stumbling over that chair. He should have picked it up when he knocked it down and slid it back under the table just like you keep it."

"He didn't have a chance," Noletta said. "He knocked it over when I screamed, and he came running into the spare bedroom to see what had happened."

"You screamed?" Walton said. "What did you scream about? What aren't you telling me?" His voice was urgent now, and he took Noletta's hand as he spoke.

"I was getting the picture I painted of Taffy before I lost my sight. Detective Atkinson wanted to know what Taffy looked like. But when I pulled it out, I noticed that one of my other paintings was missing. And I screamed."

Walton took her other hand in his and said, "Noletta, I don't understand. How could you know if a painting was missing, and why would that make you scream?"

"I've always numbered my framed paintings by scratching a number on the back of the frame with a knife. The one missing was number twenty-three. And I keep things organized now so I can find them. I know where things are in my house. I have to be organized, or I'd forever be feeling around to find what I need," she explained.

"Okay, that makes sense," Walton said. "But again, why did you scream?"

"It was because of the one that was taken, number twenty-three. And also, I guess, because it proves that someone has been in my house. Walton, it makes me feel so vulnerable."

Walton took Noletta gently in his arms and pulled her close to him. Noletta rested her head against his chest, feeling comforted and safe for the moment. She felt bad for speaking harshly to him. "Walton, I shouldn't have spoken to you the way I did. I know you're just concerned about me, and I'm grateful."

"You'd better believe I'm concerned," he said softly. "I've never been so worried in my life."

For several minutes, Walton continued to hold her, and Noletta wished she could remain in his arms. The cares of the world that weighed so heavily on her seemed to be less burdensome when he held her. She finally admitted to herself that this was the type of affection she had been hungering for.

"I have an idea, Noletta," he said suddenly. "Maybe when this is all over, if the cops don't find your portrait, I could do one for you. I know I'm not as good as you, but I think I could do a fair job. And I'd enjoy having you sit for me while I did it."

"Would you really do that for me?" she asked.

"Of course I would," he said. And he continued to hold her, neither of them saying another word.

It was Harmony who broke up the peaceful interlude. "Your lunch is ready, Noletta," she said. "But what should I do with the sandwich I made for Detective Atkinson?"

"I'm sure Walton is missing his lunch to be here, so I guess he can eat it. You are hungry, aren't you, Walton?" Noletta asked as the two stepped apart.

"Starved," he said.

"Then let's hurry and eat, and after that, the three of us can go up to campus. We'll see if I can repair the damage I did by not showing up this morning," Noletta said.

"But I made this sandwich for Detective Atkinson," Harmony protested.

Noletta was surprised at her. "But he had to leave," she said. "And we shouldn't waste it. Walton could eat it."

"He didn't have to leave," Harmony said stubbornly. "He left because Walton made him feel bad."

"That's right," Walton said as he knelt in front of her and looked her in the eye. "And I was wrong. I was so worried about Noletta that I sort of lost my head. Will you forgive me?"

Harmony said nothing, and Noletta wondered what expression her young friend might have on her face.

"Please," Walton begged. "We redheads sometimes have bad tempers, but we don't mean anything by it, do we?"

"No," Harmony agreed softly.

"And there aren't many of us, so we need to stick together, don't you think?"

"I guess so," Harmony said, sounding rather doubtful.

"You do understand why I got upset, don't you? I care a lot about Noletta, just like I know you do. And I'm worried about her."

Noletta felt a comforting warmth pass over her at his words. He'd never spoken so affectionately before, and she loved hearing him speak like that.

Apparently Harmony felt the same. "We love Noletta, don't we?"

"We do," Walton said.

Does he realize what he's saying? Noletta thought, finding herself wondering if it could actually be true. Maybe this terrible thing with Taffy would bring about something in her life that she had hoped for ever since she and Walton had become such good friends. However, even the thought of progress in her relationship with Walton failed to dull the pain of losing Taffy, and she silently prayed that Detective Atkinson would be able to find her.

Things went more smoothly for Noletta at the law school that afternoon than she'd dared hope. And it was all thanks to Walton. He pled her case with eloquence to Professor Simmons. *He'll make a great attorney,* she thought. *Much better than I will.*

* * *

Detective Ted Zobel was fifteen years Martin's senior and had been a detective for more than ten years. There was a bitterness about him after having been passed over several times when he had applied for promotion to sergeant. But he had not given up on his goal. Quite the contrary, in fact. He now wanted it more than ever. As a result, Martin found him hard to work with, as he seemed more focused on impressing Lieutenant Boyd Merrill and others of the brass than on doing his best work on cases he felt were beneath his experience and expertise.

When Martin returned to the office and began to fill Ted in on the current case, he soon learned that it would be difficult to spend the kind of time necessary to find and recover Taffy. After Martin had given him an overview, Ted looked him squarely in the eye. "You might as well forget about this dog case right now. We have a lot more important things to do than look for lost dogs."

"She's a stolen guide dog, and Noletta is blind," Martin said emphatically. "I view this as a serious case, an important one. And it's about more than the dog. Someone, probably the dog thief, also stole a painting of the victim, and that's scary."

"Oh, it's scary, is it? And why is it so scary?" Ted asked in a mocking tone.

"Because Noletta is an extraordinarily attractive woman, and she could be in danger from whoever took the painting. Why else would he take it?"

"*If* he even took it. She's blind, this victim of yours. She can't possibly be sure the painting was stolen," Ted argued.

"She seems to be very sure. But there's still more," Martin said.

"Wonderful, why don't you fill me in?" Ted's voice dripped with sarcasm.

Martin noted the mockery but simply said, "Noletta lost her sight when she was shot. She came upon a murder scene in the mountains, and the killer shot her in the head, clearly intending to kill her. But she lived, and she's very lucky to be alive."

"I see, but the murder and her being shot aren't our problems. They have nothing to do with the loss of her dog," Ted protested angrily.

"I wasn't suggesting that they did, but Taffy—that's her German shepherd—was with her when she was shot. And she's been with her ever since. She's important to her."

"Everybody that has a dog thinks it's important. What you have is a missing dog case, and missing dog cases are as common as the flu. Don't try to make anything more of it than that."

"When you meet Noletta and talk to her, perhaps you'll understand why I think we need to put more effort into this case than we would if it were just any old dog. She's overwhelmed."

"I'm sure she is," Ted broke in, "but that isn't our problem. And I'm not going to meet her. Okay, so she's also gorgeous. So what? All that means is that you've let your bachelor status begin thinking for you."

"Come off it, Ted. She's a victim, and a devastated one at that. The least we can do is give it our best effort," Martin pleaded.

"She can get a new dog," Ted said stubbornly. "They're a dime a dozen. Besides, we haven't the time to run around trying to find a dog thief, if the dog was even stolen, and you haven't convinced me that it was. We have important work to do. So you go check the dog pounds, make a few inquiries, then write an impressive report, and we'll be done with it."

"But we're supposed to be working together," Martin protested.

"When possible. But right now we've got another case, and it actually *is* important. I'll keep working on that while you chase dogs. But wrap it up soon, or Lieutenant Merrill will be breathing down your neck."

Disgusted, Martin stood up to leave, but Ted grabbed his arm. "I mean it, Martin. Hurry up on this one. You can't waste a lot of valuable time on a stupid dog. We have real work to do."

The afternoon had grown blustery, but the wind and cold felt good to Martin after his disheartening talk with his partner. Ted had displayed a bad attitude many times in the weeks they'd worked together. This was the worst yet, and Martin didn't like it. But as the junior partner, he wasn't quite sure how much authority he could exercise. After several hours visiting animal shelters around the valley, he was beginning to lose hope. He wondered if Ted might be right. Then he reminded himself that the answer very likely wouldn't be found at a shelter. This was a more complicated case. Someone had broken into an innocent blind woman's house, and he'd done so very skillfully. It wouldn't have been an easy thing to subdue such a protective dog, as Noletta had described her. And it didn't make sense that the same someone would go to the trouble of stealing a dog just to let it loose or put it in a shelter. No, this dog was stolen and taken somewhere discretely. Also, he figured there had to be a reason this partic- ular dog was taken. What he needed to do now was find a motive in the case.

Martin kept thinking about Noletta Fahr. And although it was clear that she had a serious boyfriend, he couldn't help the attraction he felt toward her. He also admitted that he must not let that affect how he handled the case. Not sure where to go from there, and without an interested partner to discuss it with, he decided to go to the Kayser house and talk with Terri and Harmony.

It was late afternoon when he pulled up in front of the house where the Kaysers lived. He knocked on the door, and Terri answered. Martin explained why he wanted to talk to her and to her daughter. "I can't imagine how we can be of any help to you," she said. "We both feel bad about Taffy. Harmony's especially upset."

"Please, Mrs. Kayser," he said, "I'll be as brief as I can. If I could just get a little more information from the two of you about what happened when you got the call from Miss Fahr this morning."

"There's just not much to tell. We went there when she phoned and said her dog wasn't answering her call. I searched her house. It was clear that Taffy wasn't there. When I told Noletta, she got upset, passed out, and had to be taken to the hospital in an ambulance. I'm sorry I can't be of more help, but that's all I know. And I'm afraid it's all Harmony knows."

"Who's here, Mom?" Harmony called from inside the house somewhere.

"It's Detective Atkinson. I was explaining what little we know about Noletta's dog disappearing," she called back. "Would you come in here for just a moment?"

As Harmony entered, Terri said softly, "Remember, she's very sensitive. I hope you can make this brief."

"Of course," Martin said as Harmony appeared at the door beside her mother. "Hi, Detective Atkinson," she said brightly. "Mom, aren't you going to invite him in?"

"I've told him everything that we—" Terri began.

Harmony interrupted her. "Please, Mom. He's only trying to help Noletta. Maybe we can help."

Terri's face softened, and she stepped back. "Of course, do come in, Detective. I'm sorry if I seem a little stressed. I just got home from work, and I have a lot to do here. It isn't easy being a single parent, you know."

"I'm sure it isn't. But you certainly have a sweet daughter, and I can tell she's used to helping. That says a lot about how you are doing as a parent," Martin said.

Terri smiled at the compliment, and Martin was struck with how pretty she was. And he wondered why she was single. Not that it was any of his business, and he certainly didn't intend to ask her.

The three of them were no sooner seated than the phone rang. Terri stood up. "Excuse me," she said. "I'll get that in the kitchen."

"So how is Noletta doing?" Martin asked Harmony.

"She's okay, but she's awfully sad," Harmony responded.

Just then Terri poked her head back in the room. "I'm sorry, this is an important phone call. It has to do with my work. Would you excuse me? You can just ask Harmony whatever else you need to know. I don't know that there's anything more I can add."

"Of course. Thank you, Mrs. Kayser," Martin said.

She left the room again, and Martin turned to Harmony. Before he was able to ask his first question, Harmony said, "Mom isn't very happy anymore. She really misses my father. I wish he could come back. I miss him too. But I know that he can't."

"What happened to your father?" Martin asked.

"He was murdered," Harmony said, startling Martin with her forthright answer. He controlled his reaction, and she went on. "One morning he left for work, but he never got there. About a week later some officers came to the house and told Mom he'd been killed."

"Oh, Harmony, I'm sorry to hear that," Martin said. There was too much sadness and misery in the world. He encountered it every day and everywhere he went in his business. "What a horrible thing. I'll bet your dad was a really nice man," he added awkwardly.

"He was. We used to have a lot of fun, me and him and Mom," she said sadly.

"How long ago did it happen?" he asked.

"It was before Noletta moved here. I can't remember exactly when. I know that it was in the fall, because I remember that it snowed a few weeks later," she said.

"How old were you then?" Martin asked, trying to get a better feel for when the tragedy had occurred.

"I was seven."

"And now you're how old?"

"I'm nine. My birthday is February tenth."

"Well, you sure are a smart nine-year-old," he said as he thought about the time frame of the killing. About a year and a half ago, he concluded. Martin hadn't come here to talk about the murder of Harmony's father, but he felt compelled to go on. "Where did they find him?"

"It was in the mountains," she said. "I don't know exactly where. My mother won't talk about it. But I do know it was in the mountains."

"What's your father's name?" he asked, determined to find out where it had occurred. He was not sure why it mattered, but for some reason he felt that it did.

"Lamar Kayser," she said.

"I'm sorry about your father," he said. "Did they catch who did it?"

"Nope," she said. "They have no idea."

"Maybe someday they'll find out and arrest him," he said.

"Mom says they won't. She says they don't care and aren't even trying anymore."

"I hope that's not true," Martin said.

"Maybe you could help," Harmony said unexpectedly. "Maybe after you find out who took Taffy, you could look for him."

"Maybe. But right now I guess we'd better be talking about Taffy. I want very much to help Noletta get her dog back," Martin said, smoothly making the transition from Harmony's father to Taffy.

"I feel so sad for Noletta," Harmony said. "She's my best friend."

"I can see why. Noletta is a very special woman," Martin told her.

"You didn't get to eat your sandwich," Harmony said suddenly. "I made it just for you, but Walton ate it."

"That's okay. Walton is Noletta's friend, too, and I'm sure that any friend of Noletta's is a friend of yours."

"He was rude to you. Noletta thinks I've forgiven him, but I haven't. I don't like Walton as much as Noletta does, even if we are both redheads."

"But Noletta likes him a lot, so you need to be good to him," Martin said. "And you should forgive him. I have. He was under a lot of strain today, and he was very worried about Noletta. Maybe you can learn to like him eventually."

"Maybe, but I don't think so," Harmony said stubbornly.

"So, tell me what happened this morning. I know that Noletta called your mother. But what happened after you got to her house?" he asked as he opened his notebook and prepared to take notes.

Although Harmony gave a much more detailed account than her mother had, Martin still learned nothing new. When he had almost finished, he asked, "Is there anything else you can think of that I should know?"

The little girl slowly shook her head, but there was a look in her eyes that puzzled him. So he asked, "There is something, isn't there?"

"But it's a secret."

"Whose secret?"

"It was mine, but now it's mine and Noletta's, and I made her promise she wouldn't tell anyone. And she told me a secret too, and I can't tell anyone hers, not even you," Harmony said very seriously.

Martin watched her thoughtfully for a moment before he asked, "Why can't you tell me your secret?"

"Because I told Noletta."

"But it's still your secret. You can tell more than one person your secret, and it's still a secret," he said.

"Are you sure?" she asked.

"Of course I'm sure," he said with a grin.

"Well, maybe I should. But I hope it's okay with Noletta."

"I'm sure it will be. I'm guessing that it's an important secret," he said.

"It is," Harmony affirmed. "And it's scary."

"Then you'd better tell me."

"You won't write it in your notebook, will you?" Harmony asked with a worried expression on her face.

"Not if you don't want me to," he promised.

"Okay, then I'll tell you." She looked around the room as if to make sure no one else could hear her. Then she went on. "One night, really late, Mom and I were coming home from my grandma's house in St. George. We drove past Noletta's house, and there was a man standing at her door." Martin scarcely breathed. He didn't want to do anything to stop this little girl from continuing her story. This could be critical. "He had his hand on her doorknob."

He waited, but when she said nothing more, he asked, "Is that all you saw?"

"Yes. Wait. I mean, no. When we passed, he jumped away from the door. That's scary, isn't it?"

"Very," he said. "Did your mother see him?"

"No, I don't think so. She was busy driving, and she was really tired."

"Can you remember what night that was?"

She told him, and he hoped he could remember it. He had promised not to write her secret in his notebook, and he felt it was important to keep that promise. "Can you describe him for me?" he asked.

"I couldn't see him very well, but he was really big—I know that. And his head was bald."

"What was he wearing?" he asked.

"He had a coat on. I remember that. It was cold."

"What color was his coat?"

"It was kind of dark that night, but it might have been red. I'm not sure."

"Was he wearing gloves?"

Harmony squinted as she thought about that. Finally she said, "I think so."

"What about his pants?"

"Just jeans, I think."

"And his shoes?"

"I didn't notice his shoes. I'm sorry."

"That's okay, Harmony. I'm glad you remembered what you did. You are a very observant girl," Martin said. "Can you remember about what time of night you saw this big man? I know you said it was late, but how late?"

"I'm not sure, but I know Noletta's lights were out. If it wasn't for the streetlight just up from Noletta's house, I wouldn't have seen him at all."

"Can you guess about what time it was?"

"It was probably after midnight," she said. "I didn't look at a clock."

"That's fine—you've been very helpful," he said.

"Detective Atkinson, this secret of mine and yours and Noletta's . . . is it important?" Harmony asked.

"It's very important."

"Could it have anything to do with what happened to Taffy?" she asked.

"It might."

"Is it something you should write down?"

"Only if you tell me I can."

"Then you can write it down," she said decisively.

"Thank you," he said, opening his notebook and beginning to jot down a few notes. When he'd finished, he asked, "Harmony, is it okay with you if I talk to Noletta about this?"

She nodded her head, and suddenly big tears filled her eyes. As Martin put an arm around her, she said in a heartbroken, nine-year-old voice, "You will protect Noletta, won't you? You won't let someone do to her what they did to my dad, will you?"

"I'll do my very best," he promised. "I'll do whatever I can for her."

As he left a moment later, he pondered the sad coincidence that both Noletta's and Harmony's lives had been tragically altered by such atrocities.

CHAPTER 7

The temperature had dropped, and the wind was blowing harder when Martin stepped out of Harmony's house. He hunched his shoulders into the wind and walked quickly to where he'd parked his car against the curb. After getting in, he glanced down the street toward Noletta's house. He very much wanted to talk to her again. Thinking she might be home by now, he drove to her small house, rang the bell, and waited. There was no response. He tried again with the same result. The wind picked up a notch, and he pulled his coat tighter around his collar. Impulsively, he walked around back and glanced into her tightly fenced yard—just in case. But as he'd expected, the dog wasn't there.

He decided to get something to eat and then return to Noletta's. He wanted to talk to her tonight. And he hoped that when he found her at home, Walton wouldn't be with her. As he ate, he pictured Noletta with Walton, eating somewhere. Not that it was any of his business, and not that he should care, but he did.

It was after seven when he drove back to Noletta's comfortable little home. But he was disappointed again. Maybe she'd decided to stay with her parents, he thought, wishing he had their address. He didn't even know her father's first name, but Fahr wasn't a common name, so perhaps he could try the phone book. Maybe he'd get lucky and locate her parents' place and find her there.

He stopped at a convenience store with a pay phone out front and copied down all the numbers that were listed for people named Fahr in the directory. There weren't many. When he returned to the warmth of his car, he pulled out his cell phone. One by one he dialed the numbers. All but three of the calls were answered, and each time he was told he had the wrong number or that no one by the name of Noletta lived there.

After the last one, he again tried the three who hadn't answered. There was still no response at those numbers. Martin returned to the phone book, wrote down the addresses for the three unanswered numbers, and then started driving toward the first one on his list, knowing that no answer on the phone would most likely mean no answer at the door. But it was worth a try.

As he pulled in front of a large old house in the Avenues, he looked again at his list. He'd written *Elliot and Francine Fahr.* There was a car in the driveway and lights on in the house. Maybe he'd gotten lucky, he decided. Bracing himself against the unseasonable cold, he hurried to the door. When an elderly woman with gray hair answered the door, Martin knew he'd come to the right place. She was a striking woman, and the resemblance to Noletta was unmistakable.

"Hi, my name is Martin Atkinson," he said cheerfully. "And you must be Noletta's mother."

"I am," she answered. "How can I help you?"

"I was wondering if Noletta is here," he said. "She's not at home, and I thought she might be coming to see you folks."

"I'm sorry," Mrs. Fahr said, "but I don't think she's up to visiting with anyone right now. She is here, but she's had a very bad day."

"So I understand," Martin said. "That's why I'm here. Please, mention to her that Martin's here and that I need to talk to her. If she says she'd rather I come another time, that'll be fine, but it really would be helpful if she'd see me now."

"All right, I'll tell her, but she's resting, and I'm quite certain she doesn't want to be disturbed," Mrs. Fahr said with a shake of her head. "We just got home, and she's very tired. But why don't you come inside while I go check with her."

Martin looked around the entryway as he waited. On one wall was a painting, and he knew the moment he saw it that it was one of Noletta's. When Noletta's mother reappeared, he said, "Your daughter's painting is beautiful."

"Why, thank you. She was very talented," Mrs. Fahr said with a distinct sadness in her voice. "Come this way, please. Noletta insists that she wants to talk to you. I take it you're a friend. Although I don't think she's mentioned you before."

"Actually, I'm a police detective. We just met today."

"Oh, she didn't tell me that when I mentioned your name. I don't know if it's wise for her to talk to you right now. She's had just about more than she can handle already," Mrs. Fahr said.

"I realize that, but all I want to do is help," he said.

A moment later he was shown into a comfortable family room. Noletta was sitting in a recliner at the far end of the room.

"Noletta," her mother said, "Detective Atkinson is here."

Noletta began to get up, but Martin said, "Stay where you are, Noletta. I'm sorry to disturb you, but I have just a few questions I need to ask if that's okay."

"Of course it's all right," she said as she settled back into the recliner. "Thanks for coming. How did you find me? We took Dad out to dinner and just got home five minutes ago."

"I'm a detective," he said cheerfully. "I do things like this for a living. I disturbed quite a number of people by the last name of Fahr before I found you."

Noletta chuckled, and he was glad she could. "Of course," she said, "you'd know how to find someone."

"Please sit down, Detective," Mrs. Fahr said graciously. "Can I get you a drink of water or anything?"

"No thanks. I'll try not to be too long."

"How about you, dear?" she asked Noletta.

"I'm fine, Mother. I ate too much at the restaurant. I know Dad needs you, and I'd like to have a few minutes alone with Detective Atkinson."

"Of course, dear," she said and left the room.

"I'm so sorry that Walton treated you the way he did today. He's not normally like that. In fact, he's really a great guy," Noletta said.

"No need to be sorry. He was upset, and I don't blame him. If my girlfriend had just gone through what you went through this morning, I'd be grumpy too."

"I hope your girlfriend never has to go through this," Noletta said. Then she asked, "What's her name?"

Martin cleared his throat, embarrassed. "I was just talking theoretically," he said. "I don't actually have a girlfriend right now. But I do understand what Walton must have been feeling. He's lucky to have you. Did you get things straightened out at school?"

"Yes. Walton was a dear, and everything's okay now. I have to take the exam tomorrow, and I hope I'm up to it. That's why I came here tonight. As much as I hate to upset my folks, especially my dad, when he's so sick, I knew I could never sleep at my place. Without sleep, I'll never be able to pass the test."

"Actually, I'm glad you're here," he said. "I'll worry a lot less about you."

"Oh, you don't have to worry about me."

"But I do. You're an exceptional person, and I don't want anything else to happen to you."

"You are so kind. Thank you. Now, what do you need to know?"

After he told her that he'd spoken with Harmony, he said, "She told me about the secret she shared with you."

Noletta's face became very serious. "Oh my gosh. I guess in all the excitement I had forgotten about that. Plus, I had promised Harmony."

"I understand. But now I know, and I need to talk to you about it. And I have her permission. Odds are good that the person who took Taffy is the same one who was at your door that night. Their driving by might have frightened him off that first time. Did Harmony describe him to you?"

"Not really. Did she to you?"

"Yes. Harmony says he is a big man with a bald head, which could just mean it was shaved. And he was wearing a coat, possibly red. Does that mean anything to you?"

"No, but then anyone could have shaved his head to change his appearance. I'm afraid I'm not much help, am I?"

"Actually, you are," he said. "Now, I hate to pry, but Harmony said that you also told her a secret. If it has anything to do with the disappearance of Taffy, I'd sure like to hear it. If not, then I won't pry further."

Noletta's face lit up again as she smiled in Martin's general direction. "I had to scramble to come up with something when she told me she had a secret but wouldn't tell me unless I told her one. But in a way, I guess what I told her does have a little to do with what happened today."

"Would you like to tell me?" he asked.

"Yes, of course. I told her that I'd been having dreams—nightmares—about Taffy disappearing," Noletta said. "Now I'm afraid it was a warning to me, and I didn't listen to it."

"I'm sorry about that. But I don't know what you could have done. Whoever got into your house knew what he was doing. I hope you're planning to stay here for a while."

"That's what everyone says, but I can't impose on Mom and Dad for very long. They have enough to worry about. I just wish more of my family lived closer," she said wistfully.

"You have brothers and sisters?" he asked.

"I'm the youngest," she said. "One brother, Dirk, and his wife hope to move back here, but they haven't yet. Someday I'm sure they will."

"That would be great," Martin said. "I mean, if more of your family gets to be closer. Well, I'd better get going. That was all I needed to talk to you about—unless, of course, you've thought of something."

Noletta shook her head. "I'm afraid I can't imagine who might have wanted to take Taffy. And as for a big guy, I've only ever met one big man in my life that I didn't like, but that was years ago."

"What was his name?" Martin asked.

"It couldn't possibly have anything to do with Taffy, and anyway, I don't even know if he or any of his friends are even around here now."

"Do you remember his name?" Martin pressed.

"Oh yes, he and his friends, they were real jerks. The big guy was Virgil Weaver. He and his friends crashed our private high school graduation party. They were drunk and barged in on our alcohol-free party."

"Why don't you tell me about it," Martin urged.

"Okay, but as I think back, there's not much to tell. Virgil and another guy, whose name was Evan Guinn, and then still one more who got away before the police came—they called him Skip—came in and started a fight."

"Was anyone hurt?"

"Not too seriously, as it turned out. Jimmy Norse got knocked out, and some of the other guys got a few bruises when they jumped on the big guy after I tripped him. But that was about all."

"You tripped the big guy?" Martin asked skeptically. "Was it intentional?" He laughed. "I'll have to remember not to make you mad," he said. "Could any of those three have a grudge against you?" he asked.

"They did then, but surely they don't still hold one now. That was years ago."

"I see. Well, I'll do a little checking anyway. You never know. The big guy wasn't bald, was he?"

"No, he had kind of short hair. It was greasy. I remember that. But there was plenty of it," she said.

"Hey," Martin said as he remembered the murder of Harmony's father, "has Harmony ever told you what happened to her dad?"

"No, it's never come up. I know her mother's single, but that's all," she said. "Why? Did she tell you?"

"Yes, and it's very tragic."

"What happened to him?" she asked. "Was it bad?"

"You could say that. He was murdered."

Noletta gasped. "Oh, that's horrible. I had no idea. That poor little thing. And that would explain why Terri is so unhappy."

"Yes, according to Harmony, that's why," Martin said.

"How old was Harmony? Was she old enough to remember it?" Noletta asked.

"Oh yes. She was seven at the time. But her mother has sheltered her from most of the details. All she knows is that it happened in the mountains and that they never found who did it."

Noletta got a strange look on her face. "Harmony was seven?"

"That's what she said."

"Did she say what time of year it was?" Noletta asked.

"Probably the fall, because she says it snowed a few weeks after he was killed," Martin explained.

"Martin," she said very softly, "what was her father's first name? Neither she nor Terri ever mentioned him to me."

"Lamar."

Noletta groaned. For a moment Martin thought she might pass out. Her face grew pasty white, and she began to choke. He jumped from his chair and knelt in front of her. "Noletta," he said, grasping her hands. "What is it?"

For a moment she couldn't speak, but she gradually regained control. Finally she whispered, "Lamar Kayser. That's the name of the man who was killed by the man who shot me. He must have been Harmony's dad."

* * *

Scully Timmons brought home his first paycheck, or at least he referred to it as a paycheck, although all Fiona saw was a fistful of hundred-dollar bills. And she accepted the ten he handed her without a word, knowing that if she said anything her voice would betray her doubts to him. No legitimate employer would pay in cash, she reasoned as she shoved the bills into a pocket of her jeans. But this was not the time to argue about that, especially with Scully reeking of alcohol. Anyway, the rent was due in the morning, they needed groceries, and her car was almost out of gas.

Never in their entire life together had Scully given her a thousand dollars. He'd never even brought home a thousand dollars at one time before. And the wad he had left over that he shoved into his own pocket after giving her the ten hundreds was pretty big. She didn't dare even guess how much money he had, nor did she dare think about how he could possibly have gotten such a large amount of cash. It frightened her.

Ritchie came into the room, but he didn't speak to his father. He never spoke to his father unless Scully spoke to him first, and that was the way Scully wanted it. Whenever Ritchie sensed that his father had been drinking heavily, he avoided him. So Ritchie turned to leave again, but Scully grabbed his arm and jerked him back. "Hey, Ritchie, pretty soon we'll have that house on the beach. I'm making big money now."

Ritchie nodded. "That's good," he said so quietly that Fiona barely heard him. She wondered if Scully had heard in his inebriated state. She prayed that he wouldn't hurt their son.

But Scully let go of his arm, and Ritchie, without another word, scurried from the room, narrowly missing the edge of the table in his haste to get away from his father. Scully turned to Fiona. "Ungrateful kid," he muttered. "Just like you. Ain't you even going to say thanks? You shoved that thousand in your pocket like you earned it yourself. I worked hard for that money."

Fiona knew that couldn't be true. Scully didn't know how to work hard. "Thanks, Scully," she said, afraid to offend her husband when his eyes were as glazed as they were now.

But he was already offended. "That wasn't very enthusiastic," he said. "Maybe I gave you too much. Here, give me some of it back."

Fiona backed away. Scully was very drunk. He obviously hadn't come straight home after getting paid. She could always tell when he'd been to a bar. He leaped toward her, but she was ready for him and jumped to the side, letting him crash into the table their blind son had so narrowly missed only moments before. Then Scully was angry, and Fiona knew that unless she fled from the house at that moment, leaving Ritchie behind, she would be severely beaten. But there was no way she would leave Ritchie to suffer the wrath of his drunken father.

She suffered the beating, he took all the money back, and within an hour he had passed out on their bed. Fiona finally managed to clean herself up. Ignoring the pain, she peeked into Ritchie's room. If only she had the confidence to take him and leave, she thought sadly, knowing that she didn't. She did manage to find the courage to dig her thousand dollars out of Scully's pocket and hide it where she knew he wouldn't find it. She doubted he'd even remember taking it back from her when he woke up the next morning. In fact, he might not even remember having given it to her.

She almost took the other wad of bills he'd shoved into a different pocket, but she decided she didn't really want to know how much money he had in there. It would only make her worry more about how he could possibly have gotten it. She had worries enough for now.

CHAPTER 8

When Noletta awoke the next morning, she was momentarily disoriented. She lay in bed, analyzing the sounds and smells surrounding her before she remembered that she was at her parents' house. She lay there a little longer, thinking about the previous day. Four things stood out in her mind as she analyzed all that had happened. First, of course, was the devastating loss of Taffy. The thought of her missing dog brought an unpleasant knot to her stomach.

Next, she thought about Walton. The knot eased, and she felt a little better. He'd been almost affectionate with her yesterday afternoon, something she'd dreamed about for months and had almost given up hope on. Maybe, just maybe, this was the beginning of something that would finally dispel the loneliness from her life.

Then her thoughts turned to her young friend Harmony and what she now knew about the common tie the two of them shared. She thought about the sorrows Harmony had experienced in her short life and felt compassion for her. She also felt a deep sadness for Terri Kayser. Her life had been touched by barbarism at its worst, and it had resulted in the tragic loss of her husband.

Finally, her thoughts turned to Detective Martin Atkinson, whom she kept thinking of only as Martin, a really decent guy who shared her beloved grandfather's name. As she replayed some of the conversations they had shared, Noletta was flustered. She felt drawn to him in a way that she'd tried to reserve only for Walton. She reminded herself that Martin was just a police officer who was doing his job, but strange feelings formed another knot in her stomach. It was not an unpleasant knot this time, just an unexpected one. In fact, the feelings she found herself experiencing as she thought about the sound of his deep voice, the smell of his cologne, the sincerity of his words, and even the sound he made when he chuckled, were some of the more pleasant ones she'd experienced in recent months. To her dismay, she found that they rivaled the feeling she'd felt yesterday when, for the first time ever, Walton had taken her in his arms and held her.

She sat up and swung her feet out of bed. There was a difficult exam awaiting her today that she needed to concentrate on. She felt the hands on her wristwatch and realized that Walton would be there to pick her up in just more than ninety minutes. She needed to get moving. As she put on her slippers and robe, she could hear a phone ringing somewhere deep in the big house. A minute later her mother came into her room and said, "Walton would like to speak to you."

Noletta accepted the cordless receiver. "Hi, Walton," she said. "How are you this morning?"

"Pretty good," he said, "but the important question is how are you?"

"I'm coping. It's not easy, but I'm getting along," she said, comforted by the simple fact that he cared.

"You're strong. You'll be okay," he said. "I'm sorry to bother you so early, but something's come up, and I can't get there to pick you up. Can you make other arrangements?"

"Of course," she said, even as a stab of disappointment pierced her. "I'm sure Mother can drive me over."

"Good, then I'll see you later in the day. I've got to go now. Keep smiling," he said. "And be brave."

Noletta stood holding the phone and clutching her stomach. The knot had returned, and she now felt more confused than before. She wondered what had come up and why Walton hadn't told her what it was. With the new level their relationship seemed to have reached yesterday, she thought he would at least explain himself. She was keenly disappointed, almost sorry for herself. As she squared her shoulders and returned to the bedroom, she said aloud, "You can do this, Noletta. No brooding, and no feeling sorry for yourself."

* * *

Detective Ted Zobel made sure Martin knew he was disgusted with him after Martin had filled him in on his progress on the case. He'd mentioned to Ted that Harmony had seen a large bald man at Noletta's door just a few nights earlier, and that the man who'd been killed by the same person that shot Noletta was Harmony's father, Lamar Kayser.

Ted said, "I can see where you're going with this. My advice to you is simply not to go there. Even though it's a coincidence that the little girl's father and Noletta have a connection they never knew about, that doesn't mean that it has anything to do with the missing dog. It's just a coincidence. Can't you understand that? And the fact that some guy was at Noletta's door one night means nothing. The guy undoubtedly had a wrong address."

"Maybe, but again, I think it bears checking out. Remember, not only is Taffy missing," Martin reminded his partner, "but so is a painting of Noletta. We have more than just a stolen dog here. We have a full-blown burglary."

"If you're thinking that tying a murder case into your runaway dog fiasco is going to give you a big name in the department, you can forget it. And I would advise you to do the same thing with this case—forget it. All you need to do is write your report—without a single reference to murder, since that has nothing to do with the dog—and then get it turned in this morning. And I mean now!" The senior detective pounded his desk for emphasis.

"I can't do that," Martin said stubbornly. "There are still some things I need to follow up on."

"Like chase after a pretty blind woman who can't resist your charms," Ted said with a nasty sneer.

"I'll have you know she has a very serious boyfriend, a fellow law student," Martin said. "So you can knock off the snide remarks. I view this as a serious matter, and it needs more work, that's all."

"Then get out of here and get it done, but if you don't have that report finished by noon tomorrow, we'll be visiting with Lieutenant Merrill. He won't approve of the time you're wasting," Ted threatened.

Annoyed, Martin turned away as he said, "I guess I'll be working alone again today. So I'd better get started."

* * *

With all the pressure her mother was under, Noletta hated having to ask her to drive her to school, and she put it off until it was almost time to leave. Then the phone rang again, and when her mother handed it to her, she felt pleasantly lighthearted. The voice that spoke to her was Martin's deep baritone.

"Could I see you sometime this morning?" he asked. "There are some more things I need to discuss with you."

"Oh, I'm sorry, Detective," she said, wanting to call him Martin but feeling that it wasn't a good idea. "I have to take the exam this morning that I missed yesterday. I was just going to see if Mom could give me a lift. Walton was going to, but he called and said something had come up."

"I can be there in ten minutes," Martin said brightly. "We can talk while I drive you up to campus."

"That would be great," she said. "Are you sure you don't mind?"

"Of course I don't," he said. "I'll see you shortly."

A few minutes later, Martin took Noletta's arm and accompanied her down the long walk from her parents' house to his waiting car. As much as she tried to resist the feelings that his close proximity stirred inside her, she found it impossible. Once inside the car, though, he was all business, and she scolded herself for her schoolgirl thoughts.

His questions had nothing to do with her missing guide dog or the stolen painting. They were all about the guys who had crashed her graduation party several years ago. She answered his questions as fully as she could, but her knowledge about them was minimal. Then he asked, "What about your boyfriend? Do you think Walton could tell me more about those guys?"

"He might," she said even as she thought about Walton and how much like a *boyfriend* he'd seemed the day before. Detective Atkinson had certainly believed their relationship to be something more than just a couple of school chums. *Maybe he's right,* she thought hopefully.

"Will he be at school today?" Martin asked. "I know he had something come up this morning. But I really need to talk to him today if at all possible."

"He said he'd see me later, so I'm sure he'll be there."

"Can you give me his address, just in case I miss him at school?" Martin asked.

"Sure." She recited it from memory.

* * *

Martin decided to try Walton's apartment, on the off chance he might be there, although he doubted he would be. The door was answered by a fellow he assumed was Walton's roommate. When he asked for Walton, the young man said that he'd left earlier that morning and that he didn't expect him back until evening. "He's in law school and he works part-time. He's pretty busy."

"Okay, I'll try him later. Ah, I didn't catch your name," Martin said.

"Creed Esplin. I'm Walton's cousin. Just here for a visit."

"Good to meet you, Creed," Martin said, offering his hand. Creed shook it. "What did you need to see Walton about?"

"I can't say. It's police business."

"Is he in trouble? I can't imagine Walton getting into trouble."

"No, he's not in trouble. I was just hoping he could give me some information I need."

"Well, try the law school. He wasn't feeling well when he left this morning, but I'd bet he's at school anyway," Creed said. "Good to meet you." He shut the door and Martin turned away.

* * *

Walton showed up at school for the one o'clock class both he and Noletta had, but when he approached Noletta, he kept his distance. "You don't want to get too close to me today, Noletta," he said. "When I called this morning, I wasn't feeling well. In fact, I was downright sick. I didn't want to worry you, because I figured it was just something I'd eaten, and I hoped that by now I'd feel better. But I don't, and I don't want you to catch anything."

Another stab of disappointment passed through Noletta. "I hope you're better soon," she said.

"Oh, I'm sure I will be. I hope it wasn't too much trouble for your mother this morning. I know she doesn't like your dad to be alone," Walton said.

"She didn't have to bring me after all. Detective Atkinson called and wanted to talk to me. I rode up with him," she said.

"What did he want?" Walton asked in a tone that Noletta didn't care for. "I'm sure he hasn't found out anything about your dog."

"I'm afraid not, although he's been all over the area looking. He's just trying to determine who might want to cause me trouble. He asked me last night if I had any enemies," she began.

"You don't have enemies," Walton said, sounding disgusted. "Can't he do better than that?"

"He's only trying to do his job," Noletta said with a little more sharpness than she'd intended. "Anyway, I told him about the guys who crashed our high school graduation party. He wanted to know more about them. I'm afraid I wasn't much help."

"Not that it matters," Walton snapped. "Those guys couldn't possibly have anything to do with your dog's disappearance. They don't even know you."

"That's what I told him," Noletta said, wishing Walton wouldn't keep referring to Taffy as *her dog*.

"Well, I suppose that's the end of that line of inquiry for Detective Atkinson," he said, the uncharacteristic rudeness still in his voice.

"Actually, he wants to talk to you about those guys. I hope you'll tell him whatever you can," she said.

"Noletta, I'm afraid that the department has written off your dog. If they hadn't, they'd have assigned someone who knows what he's doing to look for her. Detective Atkinson clearly doesn't know beans," he said. "There's nothing I can tell him, and it wouldn't help if I could. Well, we'd better get to class. It's almost one."

It was a couple of hours later when Walton mentioned to Noletta that since he still wasn't feeling better, it wouldn't be wise for her to ride in his car with him. "I called Creed. He's not busy this afternoon, and his truck is fixed. He said he'd be glad to pick you up and take you home."

"Thanks, but I could have arranged something," Noletta said.

"You don't need to be riding with that detective again," he said sharply. "Creed will meet you at the library at five."

"Thanks," she said, wishing more than ever that she hadn't lost her dog. She hated being dependent on other people, even Walton.

* * *

Although Martin had tried to reach Walton several times that morning, he'd failed. He drove up to the law school that afternoon for another attempt. He spotted Noletta first. She was talking to Walton, who suddenly walked away, leaving her standing alone and looking vulnerable. He almost went straight to her, but he didn't since Walton was walking quickly toward the parking lot. After all the time he'd spent trying to make contact, he didn't want to miss him. "Walton Pease," he called out from behind him.

Walton stopped and turned toward him. "Oh, it's you," Walton said. "Noletta mentioned that you'd been wasting her time and that you also wanted to waste mine. I can save us both a lot of trouble. I don't know any more about the guys who crashed our graduation party than she does. So if there's nothing else, I really don't feel well and want to get home and lie down."

"You're sure you can't—" Martin began.

"I'm sure. So why don't you go do something constructive and look for the lost dog," Walton snapped.

Martin didn't feel like replying and turned back, hoping to catch Noletta before she disappeared. He couldn't imagine why she cared so much for Walton. Yesterday, he could make excuses for his rude behavior, but today he couldn't. He hoped that she hadn't really said what Walton indicated. He hoped she didn't think he was wasting her time. He made up his mind to ask her without being too offensive.

Noletta must have had another class, because she had already disappeared. Martin had really hoped to talk to her for a minute. After he'd first met Walton, he'd made up his mind that he wouldn't think of her as a woman, just as a victim. But after talking with—no, make that listening to—Walton again, he wondered if he wouldn't be doing her a favor by rescuing her from the guy. But she was gone, so it was a moot question. He returned to his car and drove back to the office, thinking about Noletta and what he'd learned that day from the Summit County sheriff and one of his detectives.

They had absolutely no leads, but, unlike his own partner, Detective Zobel, when the sheriff and his deputy learned that Noletta lived just a few houses down the street from his murder victim's wife and daughter and that she was friends with the daughter, the sheriff expressed concerns that Noletta could be in some danger. "Let me know if either my detective or I can help in any way," he'd volunteered.

Martin had promised to do that. The rest of his day, in between attempts to make connections with Walton, had been spent searching for more information about the men he now thought of as the *party crashers*. So far, he'd drawn a blank. He'd also made posters from the painting of Taffy and personally distributed them to every animal shelter in the area, hoping to get lucky and find Taffy at one of them. But, as he had expected, that hadn't happened. Back at the office, he finally did as Ted suggested and wrote a report. However, he didn't close it out. He was a long way from being finished. He was more determined than ever to find Taffy and to learn who'd taken the painting of Noletta from her apartment. He would never admit it to his partner, but he also wanted to help find the man who murdered Harmony's father and who'd destroyed Noletta's sight.

* * *

"Walton said to tell you he was sorry he couldn't give you a ride home, but he really couldn't. He's a lot sicker than he let on this morning," Creed said after walking up behind Noletta and surprising her.

She turned toward him, smiling after gaining her composure. "You startled me," she said. "I heard your footsteps, but I didn't know who it was and didn't expect to be spoken to."

"Sorry. Didn't mean to do that. If you still had your dog, she'd have warned you who it was. She didn't exactly take a liking to me. Anyway, I told my cousin I'd be more than happy to help. If you'll come with me, we'll be on our way."

Once she was in his pickup with him, Creed said, "How about if I buy you some dinner? I have to eat, and I don't feel like fixing something for myself at Walton's pad. In fact, I don't think I'll even stay there again tonight. I don't want to catch whatever he has."

"Thanks, but my mother will—" Noletta began.

"You don't need to burden your mother," Creed broke in firmly. "Walton told me that she's really stressed over your father's health. Please, I insist. You pick the place, and I'll buy."

Not wanting to offend Walton's cousin, she said, "If you're sure it's not a bother."

"A bother?" he said with a hearty chuckle. "It could hardly be considered a bother to spend an hour with a good-looking, intelligent woman like yourself. So, where will it be?"

"Someplace simple would be fine. A hamburger would taste wonderful."

"Okay, a hamburger it is. How would Wendy's be?"

"That would be great."

The meal was somewhat awkward, although Creed seemed like such a nice guy. He complimented her two or three times, but mostly talked about himself. He explained that he built houses in Los Angeles and that he had to get back home to Utah occasionally, since the hustle and bustle of the big city sometimes overwhelmed him. He told her that he'd always liked Walton but still had a hard time believing he wanted to be an attorney. When she asked him why, he couldn't say, only that it just didn't seem like what Walton would have wanted to do.

"He and I used to spend a lot of time in the mountains," Creed said. "We both love to hunt and fish and camp. I just can't see him being confined inside an office and behind a desk for the rest of his life."

"Lots of attorneys like the outdoors," she said. "I've always loved nature. I used to hike, and I'm going to be an attorney. I even have a flower garden, and I plan to plant a small vegetable garden in my backyard this year."

"That's great," he said. "You sound like my kind of girl."

So the conversation went, and Noletta gradually felt less awkward. After eating, they returned to Creed's truck. "Well, I'll take you home now," Creed said.

He did, but as they drove, she began to worry a little. "Are you sure you're going the right direction?"

He chuckled. "Yes. I know exactly which way to go. But tell me something, Noletta, being blind and all, can you tell directions?"

"Not very well, but it just didn't seem like we were headed right. My folks live in the Avenues and—" she began.

"Oh, I see. You're staying with your folks. I thought you'd just planned to eat there. But it makes sense to stay with them. Walton didn't mention that to me, the scoundrel. I was heading for your house. You'll have to tell me your parents' address."

"Actually, Creed, if it wouldn't be too much trouble, and if we aren't too far from it, I would like to stop at my place and get a few things I forgot yesterday," she said.

"I'm taking a few days off work," he reminded her. "I have nothing but time on my hands right now. Whatever you need, I'm at your disposal. I really enjoy your company."

"Thanks, Creed. I really appreciate it. One of the most difficult adjustments I've had to make since I became blind is having to depend on others for things I could always do myself."

"People are glad to help, I'm sure, Noletta. I'd be glad to give you a hand anytime," he said. "In fact, let me give you my cell phone number, and then if you need something, you can give me a call. I'll be around for another week or two. Then I have to get back to L.A., but even then, I'd love to hear from you. Believe it or not, I get lonely."

"Then we have something in common," she said lightly. "I get lonely too."

"Sounds like I need to get after Walton. He doesn't know a good thing when it's staring him right in the face."

"It's not his fault. He's busy. And so am I, for that matter."

"You don't need to make excuses for my cousin. He makes enough for himself. But give him time. I think he's really quite fond of you."

* * *

Taffy growled when Skip entered the abandoned warehouse. Although she was secured in a stout metal cage, Skip didn't trust the dog. She was a hostile animal. But he was being paid well to take care of her for a few days, and he was always in need of money. It seemed like the cost of meth was getting way out of hand. He'd been asked to help out by a friend, a friend he couldn't say no to. This friend was a lot larger than Skip, outweighing him by nearly a hundred pounds, and when he lost his temper, things could get ugly. Skip threw some dog food into the cage as the dog continued to growl. Then he carefully refilled her water pan. Finally, he left. He was only too glad to be out of there. He never had liked dogs, and this one had done nothing to change his mind.

CHAPTER 9

A shrill ringing awoke Martin from a sound sleep. He looked at his digital clock as he reached for the phone. It was almost one o'clock in the morning. He answered with a slight slur, not bothering to check the caller ID. It was a dispatcher. "Detective Atkinson, we just received a 911 call from a young girl who identified herself as Harmony Kayser. She says she needs to talk to you right away. She sounded frightened, so we offered to let her talk to an on-duty officer, but she insisted that you were the only one she'd speak to. Does that name mean anything to you?"

"She's involved in a case I'm working on. What's her number? I'll give her a call," he said, worrying about what could possibly be upsetting Harmony at this time of night.

It was Harmony's mother who answered the phone, and she was clearly angry. "I'm sorry that Harmony bothered you, Detective. I thought I'd taught her better."

"Do you have any idea what she wants to talk to me about?"

"She won't tell me. When I caught her hanging up the phone, she would only say that she saw something that you need to know about."

"If you don't mind, I'd be happy to talk to her."

"Well, I guess, now that she's got us all awake. But I promise, it won't happen again."

Harmony came on the line a moment later. "My mom says I shouldn't have called you. But I didn't know what else to do."

"I don't mind you calling me at any time," Martin said. "But maybe in the future you should tell your mom what's bothering you, and she can make the decision on whether to call or not."

"But it's about our secret, and I can't talk to anyone but you and Noletta about that," she said. "I tried to call Noletta, but she didn't say anything when she answered her phone. I could hear her breathing, but she hung up without saying a word. I'm really scared for her."

"Harmony, listen to me. Noletta isn't staying at home right now. She's safe," he said as a chill settled over him.

"But she answered her phone," Harmony protested.

"Believe me, Harmony. She's with her parents tonight. I know she's okay."

Yet as he spoke, doubts flooded his mind. *Could she have changed her mind and gone home?* he wondered, suddenly almost sick with worry.

But Harmony believed him. "Oh, good, because it's happening again. Our secret, I mean. Maybe . . ." But she didn't go on.

"Harmony, is your mother standing there?" he asked as he shrugged out of his pajamas.

"Yes," the little girl answered.

"Okay, this secret of ours, your mom needs to be part of it now. So here's what I want you to do. First, tell me, with your mother listening, who you saw at Noletta's house tonight. You did see someone, didn't you?"

"Yes."

"Okay, tell me about it, and then later, before you go back to bed, I want you to tell your mother about the last time someone was there. Will you do that?"

"I don't want to, but if you think I should, I guess I will."

"I think you should. Now, what did you see tonight?"

Harmony's voice began to tremble. "I was thirsty, and I got up to get a drink of water. Then I thought about Noletta, so I just went to the window and looked down the street at her house. That man was there again."

"The big man?" he asked as he grabbed for his clothes with his free hand.

"Yes, the same one who was there that other night, the one with the bald head."

"Is he still there?" Martin asked.

"I don't know. Just a minute and let me look."

"Let me talk to your mother while you do that."

A moment later Mrs. Kayser came on the phone. "Is there something I should know?" she asked.

Martin noted that the anger in her voice had been replaced with worry. "Yes, I'm afraid there is. There's something I just learned today, and it might not be relevant, but again, it could be. I'd planned to talk to you later today, but maybe I shouldn't wait. Do you mind if I come to your place as soon as I've had a chance to check at Noletta's house?"

"We're all awake anyway," she said with a sigh. "So I guess you might as well come. Here's Harmony again."

"Detective Atkinson, I can't see him now. Maybe he's inside the house. Could he have answered Noletta's phone?" the girl asked astutely.

"Maybe," Martin said as he pulled on his pants. Had the intruder answered it to make it look like Noletta was home? That could be exactly what happened. He prayed that it was, that Noletta hadn't come home but was safely with her parents. "I'll check out her place, Harmony, and then I'll come to your house. You tell your mom all about it. I'll be there as soon as I can."

When Martin checked with his dispatcher, he thought about having them send a backup unit and, after a moment, decided it might be a good idea. Under normal circumstances he'd have called his partner, but he knew that would only make things worse. So he requested a patrol unit to back him up at Noletta's address. But he made it clear that there were to be no lights or sirens. He had no intention of scaring off the intruder if he was still in Noletta's house.

He raced swiftly through the night, wondering who the bald man was and what he could possibly want at Noletta's house. He suspected that whoever the guy was, he must have been the person that had taken Taffy.

Martin had one of the uniformed officers who met him in front of Noletta's house cover the back door. He asked the other one to watch the front door while he retrieved the spare key. "Then you can go inside with me," he said quietly. "I don't think Noletta's home, and if not, someone else has been in there."

But when he reached for the key in its hiding place behind the house, it wasn't there. He groaned, wondering if the bald man had somehow discovered the key. Perhaps he'd known where it was before and had used it the night he took Taffy. That would explain why the doors and windows were still locked when Noletta discovered that the dog was missing.

"This just got more complicated," he whispered to the two officers a moment later. "The key she kept hidden is gone. That could mean our man—the one who used it—is inside. It could also mean that we can't get in without breaking something, and I don't want to do that. So unless he left the door unlocked behind him, we may have to wait for him to come out, that is, if he's still inside."

"But what if the woman's in there?" one of the officers asked.

"If the door's locked, we'll try the phone. If we need to, we'll break in," he said.

One of the officers took a position in the backyard, the other, his weapon drawn, followed Martin to the front door.

Thinking of fingerprints, he pulled a latex glove on one hand and reached for the doorknob. To his surprise, it turned. A moment later, his heart thundering, he slipped inside. He and his backup moved slowly and carefully through the house, checking each room with their flashlights as they went. When they found no one in any of the rooms, Martin, both glad that Noletta wasn't there but disappointed that they'd missed the bald man, said, "Let's check the closets and under the beds."

They turned on the lights as they entered each room, but the intruder was gone, and so was Noletta's key, it seemed—which was strange since the thief had apparently returned it the time before, the night he took Taffy, if indeed he was the one who had taken the dog.

Knowing that he'd need Noletta to help him determine later if anything further was missing, he conducted a search of her house anyway. As he'd feared, he couldn't tell if anything had been disturbed. He locked the door behind himself, confident that Noletta had another key, but also thinking that he needed to make sure she got new locks on the doors. After thanking the patrol officers for their help, Martin went across the street, passed two houses, and then knocked on the Kaysers' door.

"Was he gone?" Harmony asked the moment her mother invited him in.

"Yes, but I'm sure glad that you noticed he was there and that you called me."

"Did he get inside?" her mother asked. "Was he the one who picked up the phone?"

"It appears that way," Martin said even as another, more terrible thought came to him. *What if Noletta had been home?* he asked himself. *Could the bald man have taken her?* Oh, how he hoped she was with her parents. Maybe he needed to call just to make sure.

"Was anything taken?" Mrs. Kayser asked.

The question startled him. Not wanting to frighten Harmony with the possibility that Noletta had been kidnapped, he said, "I can't tell if anything was taken. I'll have to get Noletta to help me determine that later."

"I see. Now, there was something you wanted to tell me?" Mrs. Kayser pressed.

"That's right. Maybe you and I could talk alone for a few minutes." He turned to Harmony. "Is that okay with you?"

"Sure," she said, although the look of disappointment on her face showed that she felt otherwise.

"But first, did you tell your mother the secret?" he asked.

"I did just like you told me to do, Detective. I even told her that the guy that was over there tonight is probably the same one," she said.

"Thank you, Harmony. You've been a big help. Now there's something else I need to talk to your mom about."

Terri told Harmony to try to get back to sleep. Then she asked, "Okay, what is it that you have to tell me, Detective?" Mrs. Kayser seemed impatient.

"First, I need to make a phone call," he said as he pulled out his cellular phone and began to look up the number of Noletta's parents. As he dialed and listened to it ring, he quickly explained what he was worried about.

"Oh, my!" Harmony's mother said, and the color began to drain from her face.

The phone must have rung ten times before a sleepy voice answered. "Mrs. Fahr, I'm so sorry to disturb you," he began. "This is Detective Atkinson. I need to talk to Noletta."

He prayed that he wouldn't hear her mother say she wasn't there, that she'd gone back to her own house. What he heard was equally as bad. "I'm afraid you can't do that."

Her words struck him like a hammer blow. He raised his voice a little and asked, "Where is she?"

Relief flooded over him when Francine Fahr said, "She's in bed asleep. She took a sleeping pill, and she'd be very hard to wake."

"Oh, I'm so relieved," Martin said.

"Relieved. What do you mean? I thought you wanted to talk to her," a confused Mrs. Fahr said.

"What I really wanted to know was that she was at your house and that she was okay," he said, feeling almost dizzy as the anxiety left him. He'd been more worried than he wanted to admit.

"She's fine, I'm certain, but I'm on my way to her room right now to make sure. Just a moment, Detective."

Martin held his breath for what seemed more like an hour than a moment. But when Mrs. Fahr came back on the phone, she said, "She's asleep, and she's fine. Why did you wonder? Is something wrong?"

Knowing that Noletta was safe, Martin decided not to alarm her mother. "I just wanted to make sure she was okay. I worry about her. I'll talk to her later. Thanks for checking on her."

The earlier fear on Terri Kayser's face had been replaced by tranquility when Martin turned to her again. "She's okay."

"Oh, thank goodness," Mrs. Kayser said. "Now, if you can, I'd appreciate it if you'd tell me what it is that you think I need to know." The impatience was gone. She seemed like a different woman, polite and soft-spoken.

Martin hated to upset her, but she needed to know what he had to tell her. "I'm sorry to stir up old memories, Mrs. Kayser," he began.

"You can call me Terri," she interrupted.

"And I'm Martin," he said. "Anyway, I'm aware of what happened to your husband, and I'm so sorry about that."

"It's been almost two years, but it still hurts," Terri acknowledged. "But what could this problem of Noletta's possibly have to do with Lamar?"

Martin leaned forward and looked straight into Terri's eyes. Thinking that life must be very difficult for her and that what he had to say now would only add to the burden she carried, he nonetheless forged ahead. "You know, I suppose, that Noletta lost her sight due to a gunshot wound?"

"Oh, yes. Noletta has never talked to me about it, but she has to Harmony. And, of course, Harmony mentioned it to me," she said as the worry lines on her forehead deepened. "But I don't know anything other than that. I don't know where or how it happened, or even when," she said. She brushed back a lock of her long red hair, keeping her eyes glued on Martin's.

"Well, in my work on the case of Noletta's missing dog, I learned that she was shot when she stumbled upon a murder scene."

Terri's hand flew to her mouth, and before Martin could finish, she whispered, "In the mountains just past Woodland?"

"Yes, that's where it happened," he agreed. "She caught a glimpse of the man who killed your husband, but not a good look because the sun was in her eyes, and he was behind some branches. Anyway, he shot Noletta, leaving her for dead."

"But she lived," Terri went on, her voice breaking. "But she didn't see him well, you said. And even if she had, she can't see to identify him anyway." Finally breaking eye contact with Martin, she rose to her feet. She approached the window through which Harmony had spotted the bald man, and with her back to Martin, she stood there silently, her shoulders shaking.

Knowing that she was crying, Martin sat quietly, waiting for Terri to come to terms with this new disclosure and hoping he hadn't disrupted the healing process that had already taken place.

Finally, without turning to face him, Terri spoke. "Harmony also told me that Noletta's guide dog was her pet before she was blinded. So now I wonder, and maybe you could tell me, was Taffy there as well?"

"She was, and from what the sheriff up there told me, Taffy attacked the shooter."

"I see. So, whoever killed my husband and then tried to kill Noletta may think that the dog can remember him," she said, her voice steady now.

"That's possible, although it seems rather unlikely."

Slowly, Terri turned and faced him. Once again, her green eyes focused on his. "Lamar went hunting that day with someone he told me he'd met at a job he was on."

"What kind of work did your husband do?"

"He was a plumber."

"Did he tell you this other man's name?"

"No, he just said they both liked to hunt and that the guy had invited him to go with him that day."

"Did he describe him to you?"

Terri was thoughtful. "The sheriff asked me that. And at the time I couldn't remember anything. But I've thought about it a lot since. There is something that it seems like he said at the time."

"And what was that?" Martin asked when she lapsed into silence again.

"I remember Lamar saying that the guy needed to get a new hunting jacket and that he'd offered to let him borrow one. But then he told me that the guy told him not to bother, that Lamar's would be too small for him, that he'd just buy a new one."

"Meaning that he was bigger than Lamar," Martin said.

"I took it to mean that."

"How big was your husband?"

"He was about your height, but very slender."

"He didn't mention the man's age or the color of his hair or anything?" Martin asked.

Terri smiled, although it was only a small one. "You're wondering if he could have been bald?"

Martin was definitely wondering that.

"I suppose he could have been, but, of course, I'd have no way of knowing. I never met him, and Lamar didn't say," she said. "But he must have been bigger than Lamar if Lamar's jacket was too small for him." Terri shivered. "Would you think me silly if I said I'm frightened, Martin?"

"Not at all," he said.

"Well, I am. Of course, I have been a lot of times since Lamar's death."

"That's not surprising, and I'm sorry," Martin said.

"Thanks. Maybe this is all just a coincidence—the dog growling at people, I mean, and then someone stealing her. Harmony told me that Noletta had mentioned Taffy growling. She did say that Taffy growled at men a lot, and that Noletta didn't know why, that it had happened frequently even before she lost her sight. But whoever shot her and Lamar might not have known that, if he's still around here," she said with a shiver.

"I've been thinking the same thing you are."

"So the intruder might have taken Taffy and killed her," Terri said as she wrapped her arms around herself as if she were cold.

"Maybe, or it could be that he plans to sell her somewhere and make a little money while getting rid of the threat he thinks Taffy is to him," Martin suggested.

"Yes," Terri said as she faced the window once more. "I suppose that's possible."

"I have to assume it is and that I can still get Taffy back for Noletta," Martin said.

Again, Harmony's mother was silent for a minute or two. "Does Noletta remember anything about him? I mean, did she see enough to know if he was big and bald?" she suddenly asked. "Or did he say anything to her that might make it possible for her to remember his voice?"

"I haven't talked that much with her about it," he said. "I need to talk to her more. I do know that she remembered that she thought he was wearing a hunting cap of some type. And according to the sheriff, he didn't seem to remember Noletta saying anything to him about that. But I want to talk to her and make sure. I suppose she was quite shocked and probably more than a little frightened. Now, maybe if she thought more about it, she might remember something else. I will ask her some more specific questions about that day when I see her again."

They talked for a little while longer before Martin said, "You and Harmony be really careful, Terri. And if you see any more of this guy that came by Noletta's house tonight, you let me know."

"I've been rather stubborn. I get so wrapped up in the pressures of life that I don't always pay as much attention to Harmony as I should. But you can bet I will after this. And I'll let you know if we see anything suspicious."

"If you don't mind, I might drop by once in a while. You know, just in case . . ." He let his words drift off.

Terri smiled. "Harmony would like that," she said. "And I'll feel a little safer."

Their eyes met again, and Martin wondered what she must have been like before suffering the heartbreak of her husband's death. From what he knew already, he suspected she was well educated and perceptive. The way she reacted to the knowledge about the tragedy she and Noletta shared had given Martin insight into her tender heart. In happier days she must have laughed easily and reached out frequently to help friends and family. Even now he could see compassion in her eyes.

* * *

"Are there any sailboats today?" Ritchie asked his mother as he kicked up sand with his bare feet and giggled.

"There are always sailboats," Fiona told him as she fondly ruffled his curly blond hair.

"How many are there?" he inquired.

Fiona counted. "I can see eleven today."

"Wow, eleven. That's more than ever before," he said happily, satisfied that his question had been answered. "Now can I go play in the water?"

"For a little while, but don't go out as far as you did last time."

"All right," he promised, laughing with delight as he listened intently to the sound of the waves. Then he stepped forward and into the shallow water.

Fiona's heart was heavy as she watched her son splash about. Ritchie was the only bright spot in her otherwise gray world, and she wanted so much for him to be happy. But it was only at times like this, when he was sure his father wouldn't show up, that he seemed truly happy.

A group of children approached from up the beach. They seemed so carefree and full of life. If only Ritchie could be like them, she thought longingly as a dog raced by, barking loudly. The kids laughed, called the dog, and watched it run back to them, its tail wagging. She glanced at Ritchie. He was facing the group of children, his expression turning from joy to sadness.

She called to him, and he came toward her. When he left the water, she could see tears in his eyes. "What is it, honey?" she asked as she put a protective arm around his thin shoulders.

"Those kids have a dog," he said, blinking rapidly. "And they don't even need one. But I do."

"Maybe someday," she said, hoping she wasn't building up false hope in her son. She had absolutely no confidence in Scully's ability to provide a dog. But she did still have another type of faith, and she hoped and prayed constantly.

CHAPTER 10

"Your ride's here," Noletta's mother called from the family room.

"I didn't know I had a ride. I was planning on taking the bus. But I'm almost ready," Noletta called back as she finished brushing her hair. She wondered whether she would ever feel completely confident doing it without the aid of a mirror, not knowing if she looked all right. For good measure she took a few extra strokes. She was certain that Walton was waiting for her, and she wanted to look her best for him this morning.

It wasn't Walton's voice that greeted her a minute later. "Hi, Noletta," Creed said. "Wow, you look great this morning."

"Thank you," she said, hoping that she was not letting her disappointment show. She'd so hoped it was Walton.

"I mean it," Creed said, and there seemed to be both admiration and sincerity in his voice.

She stretched out her hand, expecting that he'd shake it, but instead, she sensed that he had stepped to one side. Then she felt his lips as they brushed her cheek. "You're much too pretty to shake hands with," he said as she felt herself flush.

Feeling awkward, she said, "Is Walton still ill?"

"I don't know. I haven't talked to him this morning," Creed said. "I stayed in a hotel room last night."

"Oh, that's right. You told me you'd be doing that so you wouldn't catch his bug." Realizing that he was looking at her, she smiled. "Creed, you didn't need to do this. I could have taken the bus."

"What a waste that would have been," he said cheerfully. "I have nothing better to do, and anyway, I like being around you."

"Thanks," she said as she felt for her backpack that she had left on the table.

"I'll carry that," he said before she had laid her hands on it.

"Thanks," she said again, and she picked up her cane. Creed put a long arm around her shoulder and gently guided her toward the front door. Of course, she had no need of his help in the house, but she nevertheless appreciated the gentlemanly gesture.

Creed had just opened the door for her when Noletta's mother called out, "Noletta, Detective Atkinson called during the night."

She felt Creed's arm stiffen even as she felt herself become very tense. "What did he want?" she asked.

"He asked to talk to you, but I told him that you'd taken a pill to help you sleep and that you'd be hard to awaken," Mrs. Fahr said. "He said he just wanted to make sure that you were okay, that he was concerned about you."

Creed asked the very question that Noletta was thinking, although in a much harsher manner than she would have. "Why would he call in the middle of the night? That seems rather rude and unprofessional. I wonder how good he is at his job. I would guess maybe mediocre."

Noletta also wondered why he'd called so late, but she didn't consider it rude. Instead, she wondered what had caused him to be awake during the night worrying about her. "Maybe he had something really important to tell me—some good news perhaps," she said hopefully.

"I doubt that," Creed said. "I suspect that whoever took your dog has taken her far from here by now. I know you don't want to hear that, Noletta, but it's probably true."

Noletta couldn't disagree with him. "I'm afraid you're right, but I sure miss her."

"Of course you do," Creed said. "She's been a tremendously important part of your life."

"And she was a friend," Noletta added.

"Yes, that too, I suppose. Have you thought about getting another one?"

"The thought's crossed my mind, but I think I need some time."

"I'd be glad to help you find one. In fact, when I get back to L.A., I'll check into it if you don't mind."

"You don't have to do that."

"But I want to if you'll let me, Noletta."

"Yes, I'll let you. I know I will need a dog. It's just that I wonder how I could ever develop the kind of trust with another dog that I had with Taffy."

Mrs. Fahr spoke up then. "Creed, I think it would be wonderful if you would do that for Noletta. Her father and I have money, and we'll spend whatever it takes to get her another really good dog, but we don't know where to start looking."

"Then I'll definitely check into it," he said, and he guided Noletta with the arm that was around her shoulder.

As Creed drove her to the campus in what he described as his GMC pickup, they talked a little, but she also had time to think. And the more she thought, the more her stomach churned. Detective Atkinson, contrary to what Walton and Creed both seemed to think, was a good officer. He wouldn't have called her in the middle of the night without a good reason. She hoped it was good news, but the more she thought about the call, the more she worried. And soon her worry turned to fear.

When Creed stopped and opened the door for her, he said, "Listen, Noletta. I hope you'll let me pick you up again and take you home."

She began to get out of his truck. "Really, that's so nice of you, but it's not necessary."

"But I want to," he said. "Here, let me help you with your backpack." He assisted her as she slipped her arms through the straps. "What time should I be here?"

"Well, if you're sure it's not too much of a bother," she said.

"It's no bother at all," he replied emphatically. "You name the time. Or if it would be better, you have my cell phone number and can call when you're ready. Then I'll come right up."

"If you're sure, that might be best," she said. "Walton and I might want to study some."

"Don't let him make you ill," he said. "What he has could be contagious."

"I'll be fine," she replied even as she thought about the tone of Creed's voice. *Is that jealousy I can hear?* she wondered. But that didn't make any sense at all. She barely knew Creed.

He surprised her with another kiss on the cheek. Several minutes later she heard footsteps approaching, and Walton called out, "Hey, Noletta, how are you this morning?"

"I'm fine," she said, cheered by the sound of his voice, although still troubled about Martin's phone call. "The question is, how are you? Are you feeling better?"

"Much," he said. "It must have been a short-term bug. But it really laid me out flat. You're here early. How was your bus ride this morning? You must have done okay without your dog."

It isn't my dog. *It's Taffy,* she thought irritably. "Actually, I didn't ride the bus," she said.

"Oh, who brought you then? Your mother?"

"No, Creed gave me a ride."

"Creed?" Walton asked, sounding surprised. "Did you ask him to?"

"No, he just showed up at the house this morning," she said, wondering why Walton hadn't and wishing that he'd done so instead of Creed.

"I see. Well, I guess he has nothing better to do. He moved to a hotel. He's afraid of the bug I had. But then, that's Creed, always thinking of himself."

Noletta, for the second time that morning, thought she detected some envy. She had to admit, though, that it felt good coming from Walton. She reached out her hand, and he took it, squeezing softly. As they walked along together, she felt a measure of contentment and tried not to brood about how Walton hadn't offered to give her a ride that morning. For now, she simply enjoyed his company.

* * *

Skip had just finished feeding and cursing the German shepherd when two other men walked in. He nodded to Virgil Weaver and Evan Guinn. The first to speak to him was Virgil Weaver, whose shaved head glistened. "You taking good care of that dog?" he asked.

"I'm giving her food and water just like you said. That's all you asked me to do. Anyway, she's a mean brute."

Virgil threw back his head and laughed. "Ah, so you're afraid of her?" he asked as they all walked over to the caged animal.

Taffy growled, and Skip said, "See what I mean? She'd take my hand off if I put it in there."

"Well, you're going to have to put it in there. This ain't just any dog off the street. She's worth some money in the right places," Virgil said. "And we'll each get our cut when she's sold."

"She looks terrible now," Evan said as he examined the dog.

"She needs a bath and some exercise," Virgil added. "There's a hose right over there." He pointed across the large empty room. "Make her look good."

Skip shook his head. "I ain't touching her."

Virgil scowled. "You saying you won't do what needs doin'?"

"I just don't want to get bit, that's all."

"Then muzzle her," Virgil suggested.

"I ain't got a muzzle."

"Then get one, you idiot."

"Who's gonna put it on her?" Skip asked.

"You and Evan," Virgil replied. "Now get her looking good. The boss says we can get several grand for her, but she won't bring anywhere near that kind of money if she looks like she's been dragged through a swamp and then locked up."

When Virgil left, Evan stayed behind. "Guess we're dog sitters," he grumbled.

"Where's Virgil headed? Why don't he help us?" Skip asked.

"I don't know for sure. Could be he's going to see the boss," Evan replied.

"Why don't the boss come take care of her?" Skip asked.

"Because he has an image to protect. You know that. Hey, when this dog's gone, Virgil says they've got something going that could make us all a lot of money. So let's don't tick them off."

"I could use a big payday. But Evan, I ain't kidding when I say this dog's mean," Skip warned his buddy.

"We'll handle her," Evan said confidently. "I have a way with dogs, you know."

"No, I didn't know."

"Well, I do. You'll see."

* * *

Noletta had just left class when her cell phone vibrated. "Noletta, it's Martin. I need to talk to you. When would be a good time?"

"I have another class at two," she said. "But I can skip lunch if you want to meet me now." The way her stomach had knotted up that morning, missing lunch didn't seem like a bad idea.

"I'm hungry, and I'll bet you are too," he said. "I'll buy you lunch. We can talk while we eat. I'll pick you up in five minutes if you'll tell me where to meet you."

"Actually, I don't feel too good," she began.

"Did your mother mention that I called during the night?" he asked.

"Yes, but she said you didn't tell her what it was about, only that you wanted to know if I was okay."

"And I was relieved when she told me that you were," he said. "I'm sorry if I've made you worry. Relax and then you can eat a little."

"Well, okay, I'll try," she said. Then she told him where she'd be waiting and put the phone back in her purse.

"Noletta, how about some lunch?" Walton said just seconds after she recognized his footsteps behind her. "I'll buy."

"Oh, Walton," she said, "I can't. I'm meeting Detective Atkinson in a couple of minutes."

"I don't know what you see in him," Walton said with obvious disgust.

"See in him?" she asked in surprise. "He's trying to help get Taffy back. He's a police officer. He's just doing his job."

"I wish I believed that," Walton said. "The way I see it, you're just another pretty face to him, and I think he's milking your case so he can see you and avoid doing real police work. I can't wait till I'm out of law school and can work over guys like him on the witness stand."

Noletta didn't want to talk about Martin. And it upset her when Walton acted disgusted or angry like he was now. It was the gentle, understanding Walton whom she liked. She fought back tears and said, "Could we have lunch tomorrow?"

"I don't know if I'll have time then," Walton said, bitterness evident in his words. "But if I do, then sure, that would be okay."

"Okay . . . well . . . will you be at the library later?" she asked, disgruntled by Walton's temper.

"Probably," he growled.

"Good. I *might* tell you what I learn from Detective Atkinson then."

"Oh, I'm sure it'll be something earth-shattering." He turned away from her, and his last words were muffled. "See you later."

She could hear his footsteps moving away. But then he stopped and faced her again. "Hey, how about after we finish studying? I mean, I could take you home, and maybe we could go to dinner or something on the way."

She knew that the answer was on her face. She was so disappointed. "I can't," she said. "But tomorrow—"

Walton cut her off. "Tomorrow. Always tomorrow," he said angrily. "So who's picking you up and taking you home? Detective Atkinson?"

"No," she said as the combined hurt from his stinging tone and the fact that she had to turn him down made her voice break. "Creed's picking me up here."

"Creed?" he asked incredulously. "My own cousin?"

"Yeah, he's been really thoughtful," she said curtly. As soon as the words were out, she wished she could take them back. It almost sounded as if she were saying Walton wasn't thoughtful. She didn't mean that at all.

Walton laughed then, but Noletta could tell it was forced. "I'll just have to have a little chat with my big lug of a cousin."

"Walton," she called as he started to walk away again, "I'll meet you at the library, and then tomorrow, I promise, I won't let anyone else take me anywhere."

"Great, then it's lunch tomorrow, and dinner," he said firmly.

"I'd love that," she responded, and she was partly sure she meant it.

* * *

Noletta was right where she promised she'd be, and Martin was exactly on time. He helped her into his car. "Any place special you'd like to go?" he asked as he pulled away from the curb.

"I leave it entirely up to you," she said.

"Okay," he replied. "I know of a great place that has tasty food. I haven't had breakfast yet, and they have a good breakfast menu."

"Sounds good to me," she agreed.

"Not that I mean to imply that you have to eat breakfast again."

Noletta chuckled. "Honestly, it sounds good to me."

They rode in silence for a minute or two. Finally, she could stand the suspense no longer. "What happened last night? I'm sure you weren't up in the middle of the night without a reason or that you called just to check up on me sometime after midnight."

She liked the sound of his soft chuckle and his deep voice. "I was actually sleeping quite soundly when the phone rang."

"Who called you?" she asked.

"How about if we wait and I tell you all about it over lunch?"

Noletta had concluded that Detective Atkinson was a very understanding man, so she decided to be honest with him. "I've been a nervous wreck ever since Mom told me you called. Please, can't you tell me now?"

"I'd rather wait, but if you insist, I will," he said.

"I'm sorry, Detective—" she began.

"Please, call me Martin," he interrupted.

He'd asked her to address him that way before, but it seemed too casual, too intimate even. "I like the sound of *Detective Atkinson*," she said.

"I guess that's fine, then. I'm just not much for titles. But whatever you want to call me is okay."

She didn't want to pursue this any further. "Please, tell me what happened last night that was so important that you tried to call me in the middle of the night."

"My dispatcher called," he said. "She told me that Harmony had called 911 and insisted that she talk to me."

"Harmony?" Noletta said with a sudden catch in her voice. "Why did she want to talk to you in the middle of the night?"

"Noletta, please don't be upset," he said.

"What could upset me worse than what's happened to me already?" she asked, hoping that she wouldn't react to whatever it was he had to say in a way that would make her seem like a fool.

"Harmony got up to get a drink at about one o'clock. She said she looked down the street at your house and saw a man standing in front of your door," Detective Atkinson said.

Despite her best efforts, Noletta couldn't stop herself from gasping. Almost instantly, she felt the detective's hand on her arm. "Are you okay?" he asked gently.

His deep voice and the obvious concern it carried helped calm her. "I'll be fine. So what else happened? Did he go inside, or do you know?"

"I know all right."

"Did you have to get up and go check yourself, or did someone else do it?" she asked.

"Of course I went," he said. "But a couple of other officers met me there."

"I'm sorry that you had to get up in the night like that. I'm such a lot of trouble to you," she said, regretting that she was so helpless and dependent on others.

"Noletta, it's fine," he said soothingly. "But when I learned that he'd been inside, I started worrying about you."

"But you knew I was with my folks," she said. "Were you afraid that someone would come there too?" she asked.

"Not really, but I began wondering if you'd changed your mind and decided to stay at your own house after all. You are a pretty plucky girl, you know," he said with a chuckle.

"I don't feel very plucky right now," she countered. "But thanks for worrying about me. I feel safer just knowing that you care enough to check on me. But how do you know he went inside? Did Harmony watch him go in?"

"No, she apparently didn't watch for very long. She must have hurried right to the phone. I knew he'd been inside because the door was unlocked, and your key, the one you had hidden out back, was missing," Martin said.

Noletta could feel the blood drain from her face. "My key was missing? But it was there when Creed and I went by on the way home from school. We used it to get in, because I'd left mine with my mother," she explained in a weak and trembling voice.

"And you put it back?" he asked.

"Yes," she said. She distinctly remembered doing it. "The guy that Harmony saw—was he the same man she saw before?"

"Bald and big," Martin agreed. "She's sure it was the same guy."

"What was he after?" she asked as Martin pulled into the restaurant parking lot.

"I was hoping you could tell me that," he responded. "I'll need to have you check to see if anything's missing. Oh, and with your permission, I'll call a locksmith and have the locks on your house changed this afternoon."

"Oh, you would do that for me?" she asked.

"Sure. So when do you think you could check things out inside your house?"

"Well, let's see. Creed's picking me up to take me back to my folks' place later today. Then maybe Mom could take me over. Dad needs to get out anyway. He'd probably enjoy the ride. But if the locks have been changed by then, I wouldn't have a key, so I'm not sure—" Noletta knew she was babbling, but her mind was having trouble grasping so many details and implications at once.

"I'll see that the new keys are delivered to your mother as soon as the locks are changed. Would that work?" the detective interrupted. "And I'd be glad to meet you and take you over there myself."

"You don't need to do that. I know you're busy, but I appreciate it anyway."

"The offer stands should you happen to change your mind. Let's go inside now. I'm hungry, and I hope I haven't upset you so much that you can't eat."

"Honestly," she said, "I really don't think I want to eat right now. I'm terribly sorry. But I'll go in with you. Maybe I could drink a Sprite. That might settle my stomach."

"Tell you what," Martin said, taking her by the hand and gently turning her around. "I can eat later. Let's go get the key at your mother's, and we can check on your house right now."

"But you didn't have breakfast and—"

His hand tightened its grip on hers ever so slightly, sending pleasant chills up her spine. He said playfully, "If you could see me, Noletta, you'd know that I could miss a few meals without harming myself. So an hour won't hurt me at all."

"You read my mind just now," she said. "And you've done it before."

"No, I finally realized that I was being selfish, so I put myself in your place. If it were my house, I'd want to know right now if anything had been disturbed."

Without really thinking what she was doing, she leaned slightly into him and said, "Thank you, Martin. I appreciate it."

Then she was embarrassed because she'd called him Martin. And it had felt intimate, as she knew it would. But she had liked his name as it rolled off her tongue. She told herself to be careful. There was Walton to think about.

* * *

The bald man was busy cutting letters from a magazine, surgical gloves pulled over his large hands. He had a message to deliver, and he wasn't taking any chances that anyone would ever find out who the sender was.

CHAPTER 11

Harmony was looking out the window when Martin and Noletta drove by. Martin had barely parked the patrol car before she came running down the street. She hugged Noletta fiercely and then spoke politely to Martin. "Is it okay if I come in with you guys, Detective Atkinson?" she asked.

He smiled and mussed her long red hair. He stooped down until his eyes were level with hers. "You may on two conditions."

"What are they?" she asked with delight. "I'll do whatever you say."

"That's a good girl. First, once we get inside, you mustn't touch a thing unless I ask you to."

"Okay, I'll be really careful," she promised. "And what is the other thing I have to do?"

"You have to call me Martin. I've been trying to convince Noletta to call me that, and I want you to do so as well."

The sparkle left her green eyes. "I can't unless Mom says it's okay. She says I should call older people Mister or Missus or Miss, all except Noletta."

Just then her mother arrived. "Are you bugging Detective Atkinson again?" Terri asked.

"He says I can come in with them," she began.

"And I also said I would prefer that she call me Martin. I finally convinced Noletta, and I'd feel more comfortable if both of you would do the same," he said.

Martin liked what he saw when Terri smiled at him. "If you insist, then Harmony has my permission. But it only applies to Martin," she said, turning to Harmony.

"And Noletta," Harmony reminded her.

"Of course. That's been the rule for a long time." Terri then turned to Noletta, and after only a brief hesitation she reached out and pulled her into a warm embrace. "Noletta, I'm so sorry about what happened to you. I had no idea that the same monster who killed my husband also shot you." Her voice quavered as she spoke.

"And I'm sorry about your husband. I wish I'd known him before. He must have been a good man," Noletta said.

"He was, but why do you say that?" Terri inquired as the two women stepped apart.

"Because you would only marry a good man, and because only a good man could be your daughter's daddy," Noletta said.

Martin watched Harmony's face as the two women spoke. She didn't seemed shocked at what her mother had just said. "Terri, I take it that you explained things to Harmony," he said.

Terri turned to Martin. "That's right. I decided that she and I didn't need to keep secrets from each other anymore. She's a very mature girl for her age."

"She is that," Noletta agreed.

"We've done a lot of talking today, haven't we, Harmony?" Terri said.

Harmony smiled, but it was a rather serious smile. Martin suspected that she was sharing a lot of her mother's burden now.

"I took the day off work just so Harmony and I could spend it together," Terri added.

"That's great," Martin said. "Now, if you two would both like to come with us, Noletta and I are going to check things in her house, and we don't have much time. She has a class in a little while."

"And we can't touch anything," Harmony said.

"That's right, unless Noletta or I ask you to," Martin agreed. "Is that okay with you, Noletta?"

"Of course it is," she said with a smile. "In fact, with Harmony's help this will go much quicker."

That turned out to be true. Harmony had helped Noletta enough that she knew where most things were kept. So, while the two of them made a quick search of the house, Martin and Terri waited together in the living room. "That sure is a sweet girl you have," Martin said, making conversation.

"She really is," Terri agreed. "I just wish she had a father to raise her."

"I don't see why she couldn't have," Martin observed. "Her mother is certainly a capable, attractive woman."

Terri blushed. "Thank you. No one has said that to me for a long time."

"Well, it's true," Martin said as he looked into the same green eyes he'd looked into so early that morning. He smiled at her. "I suspect that you might be shutting men out. Perhaps it's time to open up and let someone else into your life."

Terri's eyes glistened, and Martin hoped he hadn't been too direct. "Harmony said something similar to me this morning," she said softly. "And I'm afraid you're both right. But it's not easy. Lamar and I had a really solid marriage."

"I'm sure that's true, but you can have another one. You deserve it," he said.

Just then, Harmony and Noletta came into the room. "Missing anything so far?" he asked.

"Nothing," Noletta said. "We won't be much longer."

Again they left the room. For a moment, there was a companionable silence. Then Terri and Martin began to talk softly, not wanting to disturb Noletta and Harmony in their search. They talked of things they had in common, like the Church, Lamar's mission and Martin's, and even the types of books they enjoyed reading.

After a few minutes, Terri suddenly said, "Martin, this isn't entirely my idea, but Harmony and I would love to have you over to dinner sometime."

Surprised, he said, "I think I would like that. Thank you."

"Would tonight be too soon?"

"That would be great, as long as you understand that there's always the chance that I could get called out. It goes with the job," he said.

"We'll take that chance," she said. "Is seven okay?"

"Seven okay for what?" Harmony had slipped back into the room unobserved.

"Martin's coming to dinner tonight," her mother said.

As Harmony expressed her delight, Noletta also came back in, and Martin wasn't sure what to read into the brief cloud that crossed her face. But it vanished so quickly that he wondered if he'd been imagining that she looked a little hurt. She smiled, and her sightless eyes turned in Martin's direction. "I can't imagine what he was looking for in here. I can't find anything missing, and neither can Harmony."

"That's a relief," he said, even as he had thoughts to the contrary. *If nothing was gone, could it have been the bald man's intention to hurt Noletta in some way?* he wondered. "I'll make a call or two and see that your locks are changed right away."

"Thanks," she said. "I guess I need to get back to school."

"I'll run you up there right now," he said as his cell phone suddenly began to ring.

It was his partner. "Martin, Lieutenant Merrill wants to see both of us in his office in fifteen minutes. I trust that you can drop whatever critically important thing you're doing and be here."

"Fifteen minutes?" he asked. "That will be pushing it. I need to take Noletta back to the university."

"Martin," Terri interrupted, "if there's something you have to do, Harmony and I'd be glad to take Noletta back to campus, wouldn't we, Harmony?"

"Sure," Harmony agreed with a grin.

"Well, if you don't mind," Martin said. Ted had continued talking, but Martin had only half listened to something about important work to do and not flirting with victims. "I'll be there, Ted," he said, unable to mask the irritation he was feeling.

"Good. The lieutenant is not happy with you."

Martin closed his phone. "Sorry about that. I guess I'm needed back at the office."

"My books are in your car," Noletta said.

"That's right. I'll hurry and get them for you," he offered.

"Are they in your backpack?" Harmony asked.

"Yes," Noletta said.

"Harmony, why don't you help Noletta with them while I run and get the car." Terri turned to Martin. "Seven, then?"

"That'll be great," he agreed. And once again, he thought a shadow crossed Noletta's face, but he wasn't sure.

What he *was* sure of was the sparkle in Terri Kayser's light green eyes and the delight on the face of her daughter. Martin wondered what the future held.

He was about to learn.

* * *

Noletta and Terri had a good visit as they rode to the campus. Noletta felt a much deeper friendship developing. Terri had changed, literally overnight. She didn't seem as depressed as she had been before. From a few of the things she said, Noletta suspected that much of the change was brought about by the influence of Martin Atkinson. He was a person who seemed to affect people's lives in a positive way. He'd certainly made these past few days easier for her.

Just before Noletta got out of the car a few minutes later, Terri said, "We'd love to have you join us for dinner tonight. I could pick you up about six, and you and Harmony could help me fix it. She says you're a really good cook."

"That's so sweet of you," Noletta said, "but Walton's cousin is taking me to dinner tonight. Maybe another time."

"Sure, that would be great," Terri said.

As she walked to her next class, Noletta thought about how complicated her life had become the past few days. And more than ever, she missed Taffy.

* * *

Lieutenant Merrill came right to the point as soon as Martin and Ted walked into his office. "We've got work to do, and too much time is being spent on a go-nowhere case. So, as of right now, I'm pulling you two off the case involving the guide dog. There is absolutely no point in pursuing it further. We have a lot of more important cases that need your full attention."

"But, Lieutenant," Martin began as he felt his body heat rise. This was all Ted Zobel's doing, and he knew it.

"No buts, Detective," Lieutenant Merrill broke in. "Detective Zobel tells me you've left him to do all the work on your other cases while you do whatever it is you've been doing. Now I know you're single, and the victim in this case is rather attractive, but that's not—"

Martin surged to his feet and thundered, "This has nothing to do with her looks. That's all Ted's imagination. But she is in danger. Her house was broken into again during the night. A witness saw the perpetrator. He's the same man who was there shortly before the dog was taken. I just need a little more time, and—"

"Sit down, Detective," Lieutenant Merrill said. Out of the corner of his eye, Martin caught Ted smirking.

Martin did as he was told, but he was seething. It appeared to Martin that Ted Zobel would stop at nothing in his desire for a promotion. Looking out for the best interests of the public apparently was no longer one of his priorities. To Martin, that was not only unethical, but it bordered on being criminal. He wasn't sure how he could continue working with him.

"Okay, now, if you're calm, tell me about what happened last night," the lieutenant said, much to Martin's surprise. "Who called you?"

"Dispatch did," he answered. "The witness saw the man at Noletta's door, and she was trying to get hold of me."

"So you went there and checked it out?"

"Of course I did."

"Without your partner?"

"That's right. Ted's refused to help with this case at all, and I knew it would do no good to call him. So I didn't."

"That's garbage, and you know it," Ted growled. "You wouldn't let me help you. All you want to do is be alone with the pretty victim."

Martin's temper again began to flare, but the lieutenant shook a warning finger at him. "We'll settle that matter later. Right now, I want to hear what happened last night. So, you went there alone and then what?"

"I didn't go there alone. I called for uniformed backup. Three of us checked it out, but the suspect was gone. When Ted called me to come in and see you, the victim and a couple of her neighbors were just finishing up a check of the house in an attempt to see what was missing," Martin reported.

"You should have called me," Ted growled. "I'd have come in a heartbeat."

Martin ignored him, as did the lieutenant. "But as far as they could tell, nothing was missing?" Lieutenant Merrill asked.

"That's right."

"Wasn't the victim at home?"

"No, she's been frightened. She's staying with her parents right now, which I think is wise, because I have a feeling that it might have been her he was after this time. And without the dog, she's pretty defenseless."

"How did the intruder get in?" Lieutenant Merrill asked.

"Miss Fahr keeps a key hidden behind the house. It's gone. I assume he somehow found it and used it to enter. I'm guessing that's the same way he got in the night the dog and the painting of Miss Fahr were taken."

"Wait a minute, what painting?"

"It's in my report. It was a self-portrait of the victim, painted before she was shot and lost her sight," Martin said.

"I see. That's a little strange."

"It means nothing," Ted broke in. "Are we about through here? Martin and I have a lot to do. We're way behind because of his playing around with *Miss Fahr*."

Before Martin could respond to that, Lieutenant Merrill said, "This sounds a lot more serious than you indicated, Detective Zobel. I want to hear more. Detective Atkinson," he went on, turning to Martin, "I'd like to hear more details. I also want to know what you plan to do next."

"Well, the first thing I need to do is call a locksmith. I promised to have the locks on the doors changed today."

"Miss Fahr is blind, not helpless," Ted growled. "She can do that herself. Anyway, we're off the case." He turned to the lieutenant again. "Can't you see? He's infatuated with the woman. He hasn't had a date in so long that—"

"I have a date tonight," Martin broke in angrily.

"With Miss Fahr?" the lieutenant asked.

"No, not with her," Martin answered, silently thanking Terri for her timely invitation.

"That's good. Hope you have fun," Lieutenant Merrill said, and for the first time in their interview, he smiled. Then he turned to Ted. "Why don't you go finish some of that work you say has piled up while Martin and I visit."

Ted's face was purple. "This is all a waste of time," he hissed. "I could sure use some competent help." He slammed the door as he left the lieutenant's office.

"I'm sorry, Detective. Now, without your partner's interruptions, why don't you give me a complete rundown on the case."

An hour later Lieutenant Merrill stood up. "It looks to me like we need to do some reshuffling. I don't see how you can continue to work with Ted much longer. He's bucking for promotion, and I think he's lost all sight of what's really important, like this case you're working on."

"Well, I hope he gets his promotion, as long as I don't have to work under him," Martin said.

"That's not going to happen. Ted Zobel is not sergeant material. Do the best you can for a few days. I'll make some changes and give you someone you can work with. It might actually be best for both of you. In the meantime, even if you have to work alone some of the time, I want you to follow every lead you can on this case," Lieutenant Merrill said. "And you'd better get looking for a locksmith right now."

"Thanks. I'll get on it," Martin promised.

"And enjoy your date tonight," the lieutenant added with a grin.

"I'm sure I will," Martin said.

Ted was glaring at him when he approached his desk a moment later. "Ready to go to work now?" he demanded.

"I am," he said, and he sat down and grabbed a phone book. A short time later he had a locksmith on the line and arranged for the locks to be changed. After setting a time to pick up the keys when the job was finished, he hung up.

"That was part of the case we've been taken off," Ted snarled. "You don't care much about your career, do you?"

"We've been given the case back, and I could use your help. But I guess it's up to you."

"You lying, backstabbing—" Ted began.

But he was interrupted when Lieutenant Merrill called, "Ted, I need to speak to you for a minute."

Ted glowered at Martin before heading for the lieutenant's office. Martin hoped he would have a new partner—and the sooner, the better. This partnership wasn't working, and he could tell it never would. He rubbed his forehead, thinking about the perpetual conflict between Ted and him. Although sometimes he tended to place all the blame on Ted, he told himself that in reality there was probably enough for them to share.

When Martin took his lunch break at about one o'clock, he picked up a hamburger at a nearby fast-food place. He was still seething about his partner, he was disturbed with some of the loose ends he kept finding in Taffy's and Noletta's case, and his life had reached a deadlock. Almost on autopilot, he finished his burger and headed toward the cemetery. Martin's mother had died three years earlier of cancer. Whenever he needed to think clearly or resolve inner conflicts, he spent time sitting on the bench across from her grave site.

Martin's father had died two years before his mother. So, when his mother, Sheila, was diagnosed with rapidly spreading breast cancer—the doctor had compared it to a wildfire—he and his older brother, Noel, had taken turns caring for her. Noel, fourteen years older, had chosen a safe, secure profession— public accounting. Martin, on the other hand, had followed in his father's footsteps when he chose law enforcement.

Martin remembered the last month before his mother's death. She had pleaded with him almost daily not to let himself become hard like his father. Certainly, his father had been a good man. But his constant exposure to corruption and the baser things of life had affected him, hardened him. He seemed incapable of appreciating refinement and goodness. He became a "glass half empty" person whose conversation was generally critical, complaining, and even coarse.

Martin had promised his mother that he would never lose the gentler part of his nature, which he knew he had inherited from her. In describing Sheila, many people used the trite expression "salt of the earth." Yes, she was kind, generous, humble, obedient, loving. But Martin preferred to think of her as "the Lord's handmaiden." Whenever he thought of this phrase, he pictured her surrounded by a special radiance that he felt was reserved for the righteous. That was generally all it took to release him from his slump and clear his mind.

As he began walking through the cemetery back to his car, Martin straightened his shoulders and looked upward, reaffirming what he had promised his mother: *I will not allow anyone to callous my soul, and that includes Detective Ted Zobel.*

* * *

Taffy did not cooperate. Both Evan and Skip suffered several minor bites before the muzzle was in place. And despite the warning that this dog was worth a lot of money, Skip kicked her hard half a dozen times after the muzzle was on. They gave her the bath they'd been ordered to, but Taffy fought them through every minute of the ordeal. When she was finally back in her cage, Skip said, "I thought you said you have a way with dogs, Evan."

"I do, but this creature is not a normal dog. I pity the person who buys her."

"So do I, but I hope it's soon. I'm sick of this beast," Skip complained.

"Me too, but you had better hope you didn't injure her when you kicked her. Virgil will beat you to a pulp if you did," Evan told him.

"He'll never know unless you tell him."

"I'm not saying anything. You know Virgil. He'll blame me, too. He'll say I should have stopped you."

The two men left a little later, after cautiously pushing some food and water into Taffy's cage.

* * *

Scully had been drinking, but he wasn't drunk when he arrived home from work late that afternoon. "I've got news," he announced to Fiona. "Where's Ritchie?"

"In his room," Fiona answered.

"Well, tell him to come in here right now."

Fiona did as she was ordered. When she and Ritchie had joined Scully, he said, "My boss says he can get us a guide dog for you, Ritchie."

The little boy's eyes widened, but he didn't smile. His father had disappointed him too many times before. Fiona wanted to warn Scully to quit building up Ritchie's hopes, then dashing them. But she kept still. She was reasonably certain Ritchie had learned that his father was a liar, and so there was no need for her to make things worse.

"Aren't you happy that you're getting a dog?" Scully asked when his announcement elicited no reaction from his son.

"Sure. I want a dog," Ritchie agreed. "When can you get one?"

"Soon. You're gonna have one soon. I'll have to do a little extra work to earn it, 'cause dogs like this aren't cheap, but I'll get one soon. And that's a promise," Scully said.

Fiona made sure Scully didn't see her when she rolled her eyes.

CHAPTER 12

Since Noletta wasn't at her parents' home when Martin took the new keys by, he left them with Mrs. Fahr. While he was there, he inquired about her father. "He's not well," Noletta's mother said sadly. "I keep hoping that a miracle will occur and that he'll get better, but we haven't had a lot of miracles the last few years."

"You have Noletta," Martin said solemnly.

"She's blind," Mrs. Fahr said with a touch of bitterness in her voice. "I don't know that I'd exactly call that a miracle."

"But she's alive," Martin said. "She's intelligent, she's beautiful, she's determined—in fact, everything about her is praiseworthy. All things considered, I'd call her life a miracle."

Noletta's mother studied Martin's face for a moment before she sank to the sofa, her head in her hands. For a minute or two she sat silently while Martin stood near her, quite uncomfortable. Finally, she looked up at Martin. "Thank you for reminding me," she said. "Sometimes I get so tired and discouraged that I forget to count my blessings. Noletta's a wonderful, vibrant girl, isn't she?"

"She is that," Martin said with sincerity.

"And Walton's a good man," Mrs. Fahr added.

Martin wasn't quite so quick to answer that time, but when he did, he said, "I don't really know him." He hoped she didn't notice his hesitation.

"They've been friends for quite some time," Mrs. Fahr said. "I'm not sure, but I suspect that Noletta cares quite deeply for Walton."

"Then he'd better be good to her," Martin said a little more firmly than he'd intended. In an attempt to move Noletta's mother's mind away from Walton, he asked, "Would you mind if I met and visited with your husband?"

"Not at all. In fact, I think it would be nice for him to have a visitor. This business with Taffy has upset him quite a bit, and maybe you could reassure him a little."

"I'd be glad to try," Martin said.

Elliot Fahr, Martin could see, had once been strong and active. It was clear that Noletta's dark brown hair and brown eyes had been inherited from her father. Even now, although he was clearly weak from the mysterious illness that had bothered him for several months, his eyes shone with intelligence. He was in his mid-sixties, Martin surmised. It was sad to see him so weak now, as Martin suspected that with better health, there was still a lot he could do.

It was easy for the two of them to begin an amiable conversation. Before Martin knew it, half an hour had passed. He needed to be at Terri's for dinner in a few minutes. "I'm probably tiring you," he said. "I didn't mean to stay so long."

"Oh, no, Martin, it's been an enjoyable visit. And I want to thank you for all you're doing for our daughter."

"I only hope I can do more," Martin said as he rose to his feet. "But I'd better be going now."

"Martin, thank you for spending time with me," Elliot said. "I've felt isolated, not to mention useless, lately. Your visit has revitalized me. Please come again."

"Of course. I'd be glad to," Martin said.

He left shortly thereafter, hurrying to make it to the Kaysers' on time. He didn't want to make a bad impression by being late.

* * *

"Thanks for sharing dinner with me," Creed said as he laid a big, calloused hand across the table on Noletta's small, soft one. "I really enjoy being with you."

"And I with you," Noletta said. When he'd invited her to dinner, she'd accepted reluctantly. But now she was glad she'd gone with him. It had been a pleasant evening. Walton had studied with her for a while at the library, but he suddenly said he had to leave, that he had an appointment. He didn't say what the appointment was. But he had reminded her that they were having lunch the next day and dinner the next evening.

Noletta had then dialed Creed's cell phone, and he'd picked her up at the library ten minutes later. She thought about Terri's dinner invitation, but she had a feeling she'd have been intruding there. From her viewpoint, it appeared that a blossom could be budding between Terri and Detective Atkinson.

Creed had been a lot of fun. Once again he'd promised that he'd look for a suitable replacement for Taffy, something which, although she hated to think about, she realized was wise.

"I'd love to do this again tomorrow night," Creed said softly as his fingers gently caressed her hand.

"Oh, Creed," she said, "I have a date with Walton tomorrow. I'm sorry."

Creed chuckled. "Maybe he's not as dumb as I credit him. But I'm going to make him earn every hour he spends with you. I don't think he recognizes a good thing when he sees it. And I don't like the idea of a day going by without seeing you myself. I'll give you a ride again in the morning."

"You really don't have to do that, Creed," she said. "I'm becoming much too dependent."

"There's nothing I'd like better than to have you dependent on me," he said quite seriously. "I'll be there at nine in the morning. Is that early enough?"

"Thanks, Creed," she said. "You're much too generous."

She liked his voice, and his arm felt strong and steady around her.

* * *

Harmony met Martin on the sidewalk. She was wearing an ear-to-ear grin, and her long red hair glistened in the rays of the lowering sun. She looked remarkably like her mother. *She'll be turning the boys' heads in not many years,* he thought to himself. "Come in, Martin," she said. He could see that she was proud of the fact that she was allowed to call him by his first name.

"Thank you, Harmony," he said. "You look pretty tonight."

"Thank you, Martin. So does Mom," she said. "I hope you'll tell her so."

A little matchmaker, Martin thought.

When he met Terri in her living room a minute later, he realized that Harmony had understated her mother's appearance. Terri's green eyes sparkled, her long red hair glistened as brightly as her daughter's, and the dress she wore, though modest, flattered her beautiful figure. He hadn't needed Harmony's prompting. The words tumbled from his mouth. "You look stunning, Terri."

She blushed and turned away. "Thank you, Martin."

Martin couldn't remember having spent a more delightful evening or enjoying a better meal in years. He complimented Terri more times than was polite, knowing from his first bite that she was no newcomer to the kitchen. Roast, mashed potatoes, country gravy, petite peas, rolls, tossed green salad, fruit salad, and lemon meringue pie. Had his stomach been larger, he could have eaten for hours just for the sheer pleasure of it.

Later, they all retired to the living room. Terri sat on the sofa on one side of Martin and Harmony on the other. He accepted their invitation to watch a movie with them. It almost felt like they were a family, and he had to admit to himself that it was a good feeling.

Halfway through the movie, reality rang. Martin answered his cell phone. "Detective Atkinson, we've just had a call that we think you might be interested in. A man who was out running tonight says a dog is barking in an empty warehouse on the west side of the city. He says it sounds distressed."

"Give me the address, and I'll head right over there," he said.

"Would you like us to call your partner?" the dispatcher asked him.

"Please do," he said, pretty sure that Ted, despite his earlier statements to the contrary, would find an excuse not to come. "Have him meet me there."

"What is it?" Terri asked with wide, frightened eyes as Martin shut his cell phone and put it back in the carrier on his belt.

"Probably nothing, but it needs to be checked out. Someone reported a dog barking in an old warehouse," he said.

"Taffy!" Harmony cried. "I'll bet it's Taffy."

"We can hope," Martin said, moving toward the door.

"And pray," Terri said softly as she caught his arm. "Thanks for coming over tonight."

"Thank you," he said. "This has been the nicest evening I can remember in a long time. I'm sorry I have to leave so early."

"So are we," Terri said. "Be careful."

"I will," he said.

"And if you're not too long, you could come back and finish the movie with us," Terri said shyly.

"I'd love that. I'll let you know what happens."

"Please come back, Martin," Harmony pleaded.

"Of course I will," he answered. "If not tonight, then another time."

His eyes met Terri's for a moment. Then he stepped toward her, kissed her lightly on the cheek, and hurried out the door, his stomach fluttering with strange emotions.

As Martin approached the address he was looking for, his emotions changed. The strange new feelings were gradually replaced by old familiar ones, feelings that always came when he was responding to a call—a little adrenaline mixed with a touch of fear of the unknown and the unexpected, topped off with the natural elation he felt in anticipation of solving a case.

The dispatcher called just before he arrived at the warehouse. "Detective Zobel says to tell you to get stuffed," she said into the phone. "I couldn't believe he'd say something like that, especially on the phone. Doesn't he know the phone calls are recorded?"

"He's having a bad day," Martin said generously. "And he's probably really tired."

"Would you like us to send a backup unit?" the dispatcher asked.

"If there's one in the area that could respond, I'd appreciate it very much."

Martin stopped across the street from the warehouse. No sound could be heard from inside. Attaching a radio to his belt and checking his concealed pistol, he crossed the street and approached what looked like the main door. He touched the door handle and turned it, expecting to find it locked. It wasn't. He looked up and down the street, but his backup unit wasn't in sight yet.

He keyed the radio and said to the dispatcher, "I'm going in, but I don't hear any dog barking. How far away is my backup?"

"They're almost there," he was told.

"When they get here, have them cover the front and back of the building."

He placed the radio back on his belt, pulled out his service weapon, and gently pushed on the door. It creaked as it swung open. Martin moved rapidly inside and away from the doorway, pressing himself against a wall. For a moment he listened. It was as still as a morgue for several seconds before he heard a creaking sound, like another door opening. His gut tightened, and he wished his backup was there. He decided he'd step back outside and wait. But before moving toward the door, he stood and continued to listen. When he heard nothing more, he assumed that what he'd heard was just the normal sounds—creaking, groaning, and settling—in an old building such as this. He started walking back the way he'd come in.

Suddenly a dog barked, stopping Martin in his tracks. He listened. The dog barked once more, and then it whined. Then silence again. Martin reversed his course, slowly working his way deeper into the warehouse, his gun in one hand and a flashlight in the other. He turned the flashlight on for only brief moments to keep from stumbling.

Another bark caused Martin to readjust his direction. The dog barked more vigorously as he moved closer, and he knew that the dog, whether Taffy or another one, was aware of his presence. He prayed that it was Taffy. How he'd love to see Noletta's face wreathed in smiles when he presented her with her companion and protector. Then he had another thought, one that brought a brief smile to his own face. Perhaps Terri and Harmony could go with him to deliver Taffy to her. They'd all enjoy that.

But first it had to be Taffy. Reality told him that was unlikely. *It's probably just a stray that found its way into the building and became trapped,* he reasoned.

The dog was barking vigorously now, and it was close, perhaps in an adjoining room, one just beyond the large area he'd been making his way through. Martin reasoned that the dog must have smelled and heard him. He turned the flashlight on briefly, located the door, and then immediately turned it off again. A moment later he was opening the door.

The dog seemed almost deranged, its barking incessant. Martin slipped through the doorway and paused again. Then he turned on the flashlight. It took only a moment to locate the dog. It wasn't trapped.

It was caged!

And it was a German shepherd!

"Taffy?" he said.

The barking stopped.

"I'm coming, Taffy. I'll get you out of here, girl." As he spoke, he moved toward her.

She was silent now, and Martin was sure he'd found Noletta's missing guide dog. But that thought had no more than triggered excitement in him than she began to growl. It was a fierce and menacing sound. Suddenly, the room was flooded with light, and Martin looked for cover as he heard a male voice. "Let's get Taffy in the van."

It was definitely Noletta's dog, he concluded, as he realized there was no place to hide. He decided to make a dash for the door he'd just come through. He couldn't see anyone, but he knew they were there, just beyond the light.

Someone shouted, "Shoot him, Skip!"

Martin turned, ducked, and made a zigzag run for the door, his heart beating a drumroll.

He had made it almost to the door when he heard gunfire. He dropped his pistol as his right arm went numb. A second shot reverberated in the almost-empty building, and he felt himself being propelled forward by the bullet that struck him in the back. As he fell, his head hit something solid. Martin was immediately engulfed in blackness.

* * *

Her watch read 9:55. A disappointed Harmony had finally gone to bed. Terri had been sure she'd hear from Martin by now. She was beginning to worry. *Maybe he just forgot,* she told herself. After all, she and Martin barely knew each other.

She waited a few more minutes before trying his cell phone. Because he'd given her the number, she was reasonably sure he wouldn't mind. It rang several times before it was answered. She didn't recognize the voice that said hello. It definitely wasn't Martin's deep voice. She wondered if she'd misdialed and was about to hang up when the voice said, "Are you trying to reach Detective Atkinson?"

"Yes," she said. "I've been expecting him to call. Who is this?"

"My name's Sergeant Witherton with the Salt Lake City Police Department," he responded. "And who are you?"

"I'm Terri Kayser, a friend of Martin's. Why didn't Martin answer his own phone?" she asked as a sickening, terrifyingly familiar feeling began to crush her. The image of two officers standing in her living room, telling her that her husband had been murdered, filled her mind, and she sank to the floor. She didn't want to hear the answer to her question, fearing what it might be. But still she clutched the phone and held it tight against her ear.

"I'm sorry, ma'am, but Detective Atkinson's been shot."

Whatever else the officer might have said was lost when Terri dropped her phone and began screaming. Seconds later she felt Harmony's arms around her neck. "Mommy, Mommy," she sobbed. "What happened, Mommy?"

But Terri couldn't speak. She felt helpless, terrified, and suddenly very lost. She and her little girl clung to each other as if they were alone in the world.

* * *

"You fools," Virgil shouted. "Now you've done it."

"We had no choice, man. He recognized the dog. He called her Taffy," Skip said.

"Yeah, and besides stealing a blind woman's dog, now the cops are after us for killing one of their own."

"Maybe he's not dead," Evan said.

"You mean you didn't make sure? If he lives, that's even worse," Virgil raged. "What if he saw you? He could identify both of you, and that could lead the cops to me."

"Nah, he didn't see us," Skip said confidently.

"Are you sure?"

"He definitely didn't," Evan agreed.

"That's the only good thing you've told me so far," Virgil said. "Do you know who the cop was?"

"No. I'm not even sure he was a cop. He didn't have a uniform on, but he was carrying a gun," Skip said. "And he had a radio on his belt. It started squawking just after I gunned him down."

"Then he was a cop," Virgil snarled. "I hope he dies. You'd better pray he dies."

"He was probably dead. I'm a good shot," Skip said.

"Let's hope you are," Virgil hissed. "Did any cops see you leave in the van?"

"Nope. We passed a marked patrol car, but we were a block from the warehouse by then. They didn't pay any attention to us," Evan answered.

"You'd better hope they didn't."

"We got clean plates now," Skip said proudly. "And we changed the signs on the sides of the van."

Virgil glared at Skip and Evan. "What I'd like to know is why you didn't have that dog out of there sooner, like you were told. You knew she'd been making a fuss, and I told you to sedate her, just like I did when I stole her. And I told you to head out of state with her in the van. What were you halfwits doing?" The anger in his voice was punctuated dangerously by the fire shooting from his narrowed eyes.

"We blew a tire on the van, and the spare was flat," Evan said. "We hurried as fast as we could, but it took us an extra hour. Wasn't our fault."

"Well, you'd better step on it now," Virgil said angrily. "You guys head out of state right now—pronto—and keep that dog sedated."

"Which way should we go?" Skip asked.

"Do you think I care? It doesn't matter," Virgil said. "Just make tracks, and call us when you're several hundred miles from here."

"We'll go east," Evan suggested.

"Why east?" Skip asked.

"I don't know. Colorado's that way. I've been in Denver before. We could go there and hide out for a few days."

"Then go already!" Virgil ordered. He was losing his temper, his voice reaching shrill tones. "But don't you lose that dog, and don't you hurt her. The boss—he's got a guy who says he can get us top dollar for her. So don't you let anything happen to her. One of us will call when it's time for you to head somewhere to meet the buyer."

They jumped in the van and drove. Neither one wanted to see Virgil any angrier than he already was. They knew what he was capable of when he was in a rage.

* * *

An hour had passed, and Terri finally had herself under control. She desperately wanted to call the police department and find out more about what had happened to Martin. But she couldn't; she lacked the courage. She wished she'd listened to the rest of what the officer had been saying, but it was too late for that now. And in a way, she wasn't sure she wanted to know. As long as she didn't know the very worst, she could always hope. It was after midnight when she finally decided that she and Harmony might as well try to get some sleep. "Let's check the doors and make sure they're locked and see that all the windows are closed. You can sleep with me tonight, Harmony, if you'd like."

Harmony paused at the living room window, which had a clear view of Noletta's house. Terri heard her muted scream and raced to her. "What is it?" she asked urgently.

"That man—he's at Noletta's house again," she said, pointing a shaking finger.

There was no mistaking him. He was big and bald and was moving his hands across Noletta's front door. A moment later he looked briefly in their direction before walking down the street a couple of houses. He got into a car Terri couldn't see well and drove away in the opposite direction from their house. She said, "We should call 911, Harmony."

After they finished checking the doors, they went into the kitchen, where Terri reached for the phone. Just as her hand touched it, it rang. Terri jumped. *Who could that be?* she wondered as she looked at the caller ID.

It told her nothing. It appeared that it was blocked. "Don't you even think about calling the cops," a menacing voice said after she'd uttered a shaky greeting.

"Who is this?" she asked.

"Don't you tell nobody that you saw somebody at the blind woman's house if you value your life." There was a pause. Then he added ominously, "Or if you value your daughter's life."

Chills ran up and down Terri's spine, and a splitting pain shot through her head. She couldn't speak. She couldn't move. She held the phone, frozen with fear.

The man on the phone hadn't finished. "Don't test me on this, lady, or you and your kid will end up just like Lamar." The line went dead.

"What did he say, Mom?" Harmony asked.

Terry hesitated. She didn't want Harmony to feel the terror she was experiencing at that moment. She also remembered the pact she and Harmony had made about not keeping secrets from one another. *But does this situation apply to that promise?* she asked herself.

"Mom," Harmony said, sounding very grown up now, compared with the whimpering little girl who'd hugged her around the neck and called her Mommy only a few hours ago. "No secrets, remember?"

"Yes, I remember. But this is a frightening thing," Terri warned her.

"I'm already frightened," Harmony said. "I don't think I can be any more scared than I am right now. The bald man scares me. I think he saw us at the window watching him."

"I'm afraid you're right. I think it was the bald man on the phone," Terry said, and Harmony barely flinched when she said it.

"Did he tell you that we shouldn't tell anyone we saw him?" Harmony asked.

"That's what he said," Terri confirmed.

"What will he do if we tell someone?"

"He'll hurt us really bad."

"Like somebody did to Daddy?"

"Yes, like that," Terri said. Her voice was breaking, and tears were flowing freely.

"Martin can help us," Harmony said.

"He's been shot, remember? I just told you about that a little while ago."

"The man didn't say he was dead, did he?"

"Not that I remember, but I only partly heard what he said."

"Maybe he's still alive, and if he is, he'll know what to do," Harmony insisted. "Let's go find him. He's probably at a hospital."

"I don't think we should leave the house right now," Terri said. "The bald man could be waiting for us to do that. We can't take that risk."

"Then call Martin's phone again."

Terri was amazed at how logical, even in the midst of all this terror, her daughter was. She picked up the phone and hit the talk button. Nothing happened. She put it to her ear. It was silent. She looked at the display. It was blank. Her heart nearly seized up. Their phone lines had been severed, she reasoned.

"Aren't you going to call, Mom?" Harmony asked.

"The phone's dead. He's cut the lines," Terri responded.

"What about your cell phone?" Harmony asked. "You can use it."

"I left it at work, remember? I told you that earlier. It had gone dead, and I plugged it in the charger and then forgot it. I haven't been to work since."

Harmony's face looked stricken with that news. Her strong facade was beginning to crumble. Terri took her in her arms. "I swore I'd never touch Daddy's guns after he was killed by one, Harmony, but I think we need to get one of them now."

Harmony nodded in agreement, and the two of them entered the room that had been Lamar's den. Neither one had spent much time in there since his death. His guns still stood in the gun cabinet. The only one missing was the rifle he'd taken hunting with him the day he died. The police still had it. She'd told them to keep it, that she didn't want it. Because Terri had avoided looking at the gun cabinet, even when she cleaned the den, she wasn't sure what else Lamar had.

Terri wasn't ignorant about guns. Her father had been a hunter, and she and Lamar had also hunted together. She unlocked the cabinet and looked the guns over carefully. A sharp rapping on the window immobilized them. Through the closed blinds they saw the silhouette of a large, bulky body, an arm outstretched, and something held in the extended hand. A sound like metal hitting against glass sent mother and daughter into each other's arms. As suddenly as it had appeared, the image was gone.

With hands that wouldn't stop shaking, Terri reached into the cabinet and pulled out Lamar's twelve-gauge shotgun. She found some shells in the drawer beneath the guns, loaded the shotgun, and hurried with Harmony to the living room. They sat together on the sofa, the gun across Terri's knees, and Harmony snuggled tightly against her mother. All thoughts of sleep had vanished.

For several minutes they sat that way, each in her own private world of fear. Cars passed occasionally on the street, but that wasn't unusual. The only time Terri flinched was when a knock at the door sliced through the silence of the room. The thudding of her heart was so intense that she felt she might pass out from lack of oxygen. The knocking was loud and insistent. Harmony clung fiercely to her mother. Terri jacked a round into the chamber of the shotgun and pointed it at the door. The knock continued. Terri waited, the shotgun amazingly steady in her hands.

CHAPTER 13

After regaining consciousness in a hospital bed, Martin had been told that someone had called his cell phone asking about him. He'd tried to call Terri, but her phone was dead. There could be several reasons that her phone didn't work. Two of them frightened Martin. Although it seemed unlikely that anyone would do that intentionally, both possibilities that kept worrying him involved foul play. One was that her line had been cut outside the house. The other, and more frightening of the two, was that someone had entered her house and had jerked the phones from the wall.

He prayed that neither was the case as he knocked again on the door. If Terri and Harmony were gone, if someone had taken them . . . He tried not to think about that and knocked once more. Then he called out, "Terri, it's me, Martin Atkinson. Please, if you're in there, come to the door."

"Martin?" a frightened voice called from inside.

"Yes, it's me," he said.

"But an officer said you'd been shot,"

"Just a nick. It wasn't serious," he said. "My arm's bandaged, but I can use it."

Just then the door opened, and Terri threw an arm around him, the one that wasn't holding a very menacing shotgun. Harmony's arms reached around his waist. "Let's get inside," Martin said.

They moved back quickly, and he swung the door shut behind him with his bandaged right arm as Terri flipped on a light. "That's better. Now, tell me—why were you sitting in the dark with what I suspect is a loaded shotgun with the safety off?"

"Oh," Terri exclaimed. "Here, you take it."

Martin did so, and in a moment he'd rendered it safe. "Now, let's hear what happened."

The words gushed from Harmony's mouth, describing the man who for at least the third time had been at Noletta's house. Terri finished the story, and Martin was very worried about what he'd heard. "You can't stay here," he said. "It isn't safe. Not until we catch that guy."

"But we have no place else to go. My mother lives in St. George, Lamar's parents in Vermont," Terri said.

"We'll think of something. Right now, I think I should have a look at Noletta's," he said.

"But the bald guy didn't get inside. It looked like he was trying, but I saw someone there this afternoon changing the locks."

"I want to look anyway."

"But Martin, you're hurt. You've been shot," Terri said with a catch in her voice.

"My arm will be sore for a while, but it barely creased me. My back hurts too, but—"

"You were shot in the back too?" Terri cried.

"Yes, but I'd been smart for once in my life and put my vest on before I went into the warehouse."

"Vest? Warehouse?" she asked.

"Bulletproof vest," he explained. "It saved my life."

"Your head's hurt too," Harmony broke in.

"That's from when I fell. The bullet that hit my back knocked me down, but it didn't go through the vest. I must have struck the doorframe when I fell. I'll tell you all about it later," he explained.

"Oh, Martin, does it hurt?" Terri asked.

"Yes, it hurts, and I have a bump, but it's not bad. Believe me, I'm fine."

"And I'm relieved, Martin. You can't imagine how worried we've been." Terri looked at him with anxiety, and Martin put an arm around her shoulders and pulled her close. "We had such a wonderful evening, then this . . ." she said a minute later.

Martin called for another set of officers to back him up before he checked on Noletta's house. What he found there was a surprise. The burglar had left a note: *Noletta, your dog's dead now. So call off the cops, or you'll wish you had.* It had been composed using letters cut from a magazine or magazines. Almost impossible to trace.

Martin spent the rest of the night on Terri's sofa. He couldn't bring himself to leave Terri and Harmony there alone, and he didn't know what else to do. Terri had worried about his injured arm and bruised back and told him he needed to go home to get some rest. She insisted that they'd be fine alone now. But her face and eyes told a different story. She was terrified, and Martin knew it. He also knew that telling her about the shooting would only add to her fears, but he realized that she needed to know everything. She was now involved.

The first order of business that morning was to contact Noletta about the latest trespass on her property. Terri needed to go to work that day, although she admitted to Martin that she'd probably be worthless. Martin offered to drop Harmony off at school. But since it was still early, he took her with him to Noletta's parents' home first.

Noletta, who was almost ready for school, seemed excited to see both of them until Harmony broke the news of the previous night's activities at both Noletta's house and the Kayser home. Not a word was said about Martin's having been shot. Martin had told Harmony before coming over that he didn't want Noletta to worry about that, too.

Noletta's dark, sightless eyes filled with tears. Then she did as she always did: she pulled herself together—both physically and emotionally—and faced the new problems head-on. "What are you and your mother going to do now?" she asked Harmony.

"I don't know. Martin says we can't stay at home, that it's too dangerous. Mom and I are both scared to anyway. We don't know where to go," she said with a catch in her little voice.

Noletta took Harmony in her arms and held her close for a moment. "I have an idea," she said. "Give me just a minute, and then I'll get back to you."

Harmony stood beside Martin as Noletta moved quickly through the room and into the kitchen, which bordered it. There were muffed voices there for a minute or two, and then Noletta returned. "My mother says you may stay here," she announced. "This is a huge house, and you and your mother could have plenty of privacy and come and go as you needed."

Mrs. Fahr came into the room as Noletta was speaking. "And I'd like for you to stay here with me when you aren't at school, Harmony. Noletta has told me a lot about you, and I think you'd be a big help to me in caring for Mr. Fahr while he's ill."

"Oh, I'd love to do that," Harmony said as she squared her shoulders. "Thank you very much."

"Let's call your mother and explain to her. She needs to agree to all of this before we make any firm plans," Martin cautioned.

He placed the call to Terri himself and explained the offer.

"Oh, Martin, I hate to impose on anyone," she protested.

"Please, Terri," he said. "You'll be much safer here than anywhere else I can think of. And both Noletta and her mother very much want you to come. It won't be for long. I'm going to do everything I can to catch this guy soon."

"I don't know," she said again. "Noletta's father is sick, and Harmony might annoy him."

"Not a chance. Harmony's already agreed to help Noletta's mother take care of him."

"But still, we'd be such a burden, Martin."

"Please, Terri. I would sure worry less," he pleaded.

That seemed to convince her. "Well, I guess we can. But we won't stay for long," she said.

"Great. Let me meet you when you get home from work. Harmony can stay here while you pack a few things," Martin suggested.

When he shut his cell phone a moment later, he turned to Noletta. She was smiling. "Terri's a nice person, isn't she?"

"Yes," he said, "she is at that."

"Thanks for talking her into staying here," Noletta said sincerely. "I'd hate to have anything happen to Terri or Harmony because of me."

Harmony had gone to the back of the house with Mrs. Fahr to meet Noletta's father. So Martin spoke freely. "The man who shot you killed their father and husband," he reminded her. "You have a connection with Terri, and it certainly isn't your fault."

"But surely all of that has nothing to do with what's going on now," Noletta said.

"I'm afraid it may have a lot to do with it, but I'm just not sure how or why. However, I intend to get some answers," he promised.

"Well, anyway, I'm glad they've agreed to stay. I appreciate it," Noletta said.

"You and your parents are the ones to be thanked, Noletta. Harmony puts on a brave face, but she's a very frightened little girl. She'll be fine here."

Noletta's face dropped. "Unless that guy, whoever he is, finds out where we're all staying."

"Don't worry. I'll arrange for officers to keep an eye on things here. And whenever I can, I'll check by myself. It'll be a lot easier having all three of you in the same place at night," he said.

Harmony and Mrs. Fahr came back in. "We should get you to school, kid," Martin said with a grin. "Don't want you to be late and get me in trouble."

"Oh, you won't get in trouble," Harmony said. "You're a cop. And cops don't get in trouble."

Martin smiled to himself. Getting himself shot had been trouble, but he didn't mention that to Harmony. As they left the house, Martin placed a call to his lieutenant to see what it would take to arrange surveillance at the Fahr home.

* * *

Noletta listened as Martin and Harmony left the house. Her mother was still back with her father, and it was suddenly very quiet. She stood thinking about all that had happened in the past few hours. The stillness was broken by the ringing of the phone. "Is this Noletta Fahr?" a voice she hadn't heard before asked when she answered.

"Yes, who is this?" she asked as her body tensed.

"I'm Detective Ted Zobel. I've been trying to call my partner, Detective Atkinson. His cell phone seems to be tied up. The dispatcher told me he'd checked out there. Could I speak to him?"

"I'm sorry. He just left," Noletta said as relief swept over her. "He was talking on his cell phone when he went out the door. But I suppose he'll be through soon."

"Okay, I'll just keep trying his cell phone. I'd think with his getting shot during the night, he'd maybe let things go, but I guess he'll never learn," Detective Zobel said.

"Shot?" she asked as once again she felt an attack of anxiety come on.

"Yeah, he ran off without waiting for proper backup in the middle of the night to check out some barking dog in a warehouse. He got a bullet in the arm and one in the back for his troubles," Ted said coldly. "He was wearing—"

Noletta cut him off. "Are you sure?" she asked. "He seemed fine and—"

Ted broke in this time. "Didn't you see his bandaged arm?"

"I'm blind," Noletta said.

"Oh, sorry, of course," he said. "Well, I'll get hold of him. He should be in bed, not running around playing the macho cop. Seems all Martin wants to do is make a name for himself. And he's doing a fine job of that, the young fool."

Noletta was worried, but she was also getting angry. And the anger was overpowering the worry. "He's only trying to help me," she said. "For one, I'm grateful for what he's doing."

"Well, be careful," Ted said. "Don't let Martin fool you. He's not what he'd have you believe."

"Really?" she asked dubiously. "In what way?"

"He's easily swayed by a pretty face. That's what I mean. He loves to impress attractive young women like yourself, but then he leaves them with a broken heart," Detective Zobel said. "So whatever you do, don't let him make you believe he cares about you in any way, because he's as phony as a three-dollar bill."

It was clear to Noletta that Martin's partner disliked him. What she didn't know was whether it was because what he'd just told her was true or because Martin worked harder than Zobel did and he was jealous. She hoped it was the latter. But seeds of doubt had already been planted. "Thanks for your advice," she said coldly, and before he could say anything else about Martin, she ended the call.

A moment later the doorbell rang. She answered it herself since her mother was somewhere else in the house. She recognized the scent of Creed's cologne. "Thanks for coming, Creed.

Come in. I'm not quite ready. We've had some interruptions here this morning. But I won't be long."

He stepped past her, and she shut the door. When she turned, he was blocking her way. He put both his arms around her and said, "It's good to see you, Noletta. You look beautiful this morning. Of course, you always do."

"Why, thank you," she responded as she felt the blood rush to her face.

She felt his face move toward hers, and she felt a tingle when he kissed her lightly on the cheek. "I should let you finish getting ready, I guess," he said as he removed his arms from around her. "I don't want you to be late for your class this morning."

Noletta tried to think about Walton as she finished preparing for school, but Creed crowded him out. She wondered at that. She really cared for Walton, but Creed was the one who seemed to care whether she was okay or not. She was impressed. Rubbing lightly at her cheek where he'd kissed her, she smiled. He'd already made her day brighter.

On their way to campus, Creed asked, "What was Detective Atkinson doing over here this morning? I'd swear that was his car that I saw a few blocks from here. Looked like he had a little girl with him."

"That was my neighbor's daughter, Harmony. He was taking her to school. Detective Atkinson came to tell me what had happened during the night," she said.

"Oh? What happened?" Creed asked.

"Lots, actually. But he didn't tell me everything," she said, thinking of the disturbing call from his partner and wondering how badly Martin had been hurt. It couldn't have been too bad, she thought, or he wouldn't have been able to come by at all. She wondered, at that moment, why Harmony hadn't mentioned anything about Martin's being shot.

"Really? That doesn't sound right. You have a right to know everything about your case that goes on," Creed said quite sternly. "But tell me, what happened that your cop friend *did* tell you about?"

Noletta completed her thought about Harmony before she answered Creed's question. She knew Harmony well enough to know that if Detective Atkinson told her his getting shot was their secret, that she'd say nothing. With that issue settled in her mind, she turned her attention to Creed's question. "Like I said, Creed, a lot happened—it was a horrible night." And she recounted what she knew about Martin's injuries. "But I don't know where it happened or anything about it," she said. "I only learned about that from his partner, who called me just after Detective Atkinson and Harmony left."

Creed had remained silent as she spoke, and only when she'd finished did he speak. "We'd better do something, Noletta. I gather your detective friend must not have been hurt too badly, but it only adds to my concerns that he isn't the best officer in the world. However, that's the least of our worries right now. We've gotta keep you safe."

The way he said *our* and *we've* was so sincere that she felt grateful to him just for caring and for making it his problem. But she didn't see what he could do. "I don't know what else can be done. Detective Atkinson said he'd try to put a patrol of some kind on my parents' house so that Terri and Harmony and I will be safer. And he promised to check by himself from time to time."

"I worry if that's enough protection," Creed said. "Really, Noletta, you can't imagine how sick I'd be if anything happened to you. You're one of the best women I've ever met."

That both calmed and worried Noletta. It was nice to have someone like Creed say such sweet things, but it worried her about Walton, Creed's own cousin. *Am I coming between their friendship?* she wondered. She hoped not.

Creed went on. "I have an idea, Noletta," he said thoughtfully. "I'm not a poor man, so don't protest when I tell you what I'm thinking," he said. "I'd like to hire someone to watch your parents' house. I want to be sure that bald man—or anyone else, for that matter—doesn't bother you."

"I can't let you do that, Creed," she said. "The police will take care of us."

"But what if they don't? I'm sure Detective Atkinson didn't mean to get shot, but he did. He wasn't careful enough. I don't want his or anyone else's carelessness getting you hurt," he said firmly. "I'll make some calls. I want to know you're safe."

"I'll be fine," she said.

"That's right," Creed responded, "because I'll make sure you are." He reached over and took hold of one of her hands, squeezing it gently. Then he said something that made her wonder what his intentions really were. "Whether for me or my cousin, I want to get you through this thing. And I will. And if it's for Walton, all I can say is that he had better be grateful."

When he let her off on campus, he helped her from the truck. Once again he kissed her on the cheek, but this time his kiss lingered a little. "What time should I pick you up?" he asked.

"You don't need to do that," she said feebly.

"Don't you get it, Noletta?" he asked with a chuckle. "It's a pleasure I've not had in a long time."

"In that case," she said as her heart did cartwheels, "I'll call you. I'm just not sure what time."

Noletta accepted one more kiss on the cheek and let Creed help her put her backpack on before taking her cane firmly in hand and starting up the walk. A couple of minutes later, Walton met her. "You made it okay again?" he asked.

"I did," she said.

"Did you ride the bus?" he asked.

"No, Creed brought me."

There was stony silence for a moment. Then Walton took her firmly by the hand. "You remember we have a lunch date and a dinner date, don't you?"

She did now, but in all the excitement of the morning, and

especially the last few minutes with Creed, she hadn't thought about it. "Of course. I'm looking forward to both," she said, hoping he didn't notice the hesitation.

He seemed not to. "Great," he said enthusiastically. "And I intend to give you a ride home from school, too."

"But, ah . . ." she mumbled.

"Creed again?" he asked.

"Well, yes. I told him I'd call when I was finished," she said. "He insisted."

"Don't worry," Walton said firmly. "I'll call him and explain that you have other plans," he said. "Now tell me, how did your night go?"

She told him, and he too sounded genuinely worried about her. But unlike Creed, he didn't offer to provide protection. Not that he had the means, she told herself, because he almost certainly didn't. If he did, he'd help. She felt fairly confident of that. But she was troubled. A dangerous triangle was developing. She didn't want to hurt Creed or Walton, and the way things were going, one of them was likely to get burned.

And she thought about Detective Atkinson. She prayed that he would be okay, and she wondered at the call she'd received from his partner. At least, she reassured herself, she didn't have to worry about Martin trying to become romantically involved with her. It was pretty clear that he'd developed an interest in Terri. And for their sakes, she hoped things would work out.

* * *

Skip and Evan called. They'd made it safely to Denver, but the dog was getting more agitated by the hour. "Should we sedate her again?" they asked Virgil.

"Better not. Too much could make her sick, and we don't

want her to be sick."

"But she keeps barking," Skip protested.

"Then put the muzzle back on," Virgil said sharply. "Don't you mess up that dog."

"We won't, but we don't want to get bit."

"Just be careful, you fool," Virgil responded. "And one more thing. We want one of you to come back. Come on a bus."

"I'll be coming, then," Skip said almost gratefully.

"No. I'll choose Evan," Virgil said.

Skip began to protest, but Virgil cut him short. "Just do as you're told. And by the way, I hear the cop's out of the hospital and back on the job. You two are blundering idiots. Now tell Evan to catch a bus. We want him here by morning. He has a job to finish."

"Doing what?"

"Making sure that fool cop doesn't mess things up any more," Virgil said.

"I can do that," Skip suggested.

"No, I think it'd better be Evan. You've already proven you're a lousy shot. We don't want Detective Atkinson to keep snooping around."

"Then what do *I* do?" Skip whined.

"You take that dog and head for Albuquerque, New Mexico. There'll be a potential buyer meeting you tomorrow sometime. So call me when you get there, and I'll give you the details. Now get Evan on the phone."

CHAPTER 14

After dropping off Harmony at her elementary school, Martin drove to the office. He was in pain, he was tired, and he was angry at himself for coming so close to getting Taffy back only to lose her, not to mention allowing himself to get shot in the process. He expected the lieutenant to be furious with him, and he supposed he deserved it. He'd really botched it. He hadn't yet gathered the courage to tell Noletta how close he'd come to recovering Taffy—and then how he had lost her again. If the dog was dead, as the note indicated, then it was his fault.

Lieutenant Merrill was furious, all right. Martin had barely managed to sit down at his desk before the lieutenant yelled, "Detective Atkinson, I need to see you in my office." His eyes were flashing, and his face was dark with anger.

The officers nearest to Martin's desk all seemed to be totally absorbed in their own paperwork when he got to his feet and looked around. Not one of them looked up or mentioned his injured arm, head, or back. Yet, there were subtle indications that word of his close call during the night had been thoroughly discussed by now. He guessed none of them would want to change places with him as he made his way to the lieutenant's office.

Lieutenant Merrill had already sat down behind his desk by the time Martin walked in. "Shut the door. Then have a seat."

Martin did as he was instructed. For a moment the room was quiet. The lieutenant glared at him before he said, "I gave you a break yesterday. I thought you'd appreciate it."

"I did, and I'm sorry that I messed up," Martin said contritely.

"Care to fill me in on the lurid details?" the lieutenant asked. "Start with why you didn't bother to call Ted and at least give him a chance to back you up before you went into the warehouse. I told you I'd make some changes, but until I get it done, Ted is still your partner."

Martin thought about his response for a moment. "Who told you I didn't ask for Ted's help?"

"Ted did, of course. As soon as he came in this morning, I had him in here. He had no idea that you'd been shot until he came in and the office was buzzing with it." Then before Martin could respond, he asked, "How are you feeling?"

"I'm fine, just a little sore."

"You got lucky this time," Lieutenant Merrill said.

"Yes, I guess that's true. I did call for Ted's help, though," he added.

"That's not what Ted claims. So I guess it's your word against his."

"Not exactly," Martin said. "I didn't call him personally. I asked the dispatcher to."

Lieutenant Merrill leaned across the desk toward Martin. "Are you sure of that?"

"Yes, I'm sure," Martin said defensively.

"So did the dispatcher forget to do it or what?"

"No, she made the call. Ted told her to tell me to get stuffed."

"He did what? That seems a little much, even for Ted," Lieutenant Merrill said in disbelief.

"Check the recordings. The dispatcher told me that she couldn't believe he'd say that on the phone, knowing it was recorded."

The lieutenant sat back, frowning. "He refused to help you?" the lieutenant asked after a moment of tense silence.

"Sounded like a refusal to me," Martin said. "So I asked for a patrol unit to back me."

"And did they come?"

"I guess so, but it took forever. I thought they were right behind me when I went in, but they apparently got delayed. I should have waited."

"That would have been a good idea," the lieutenant said. "So, give me the details."

Martin recited the facts, up to the point where he'd felt the bullet hit his arm. The next thing he was able to tell the lieutenant was that he awoke in the hospital.

"I tried to call your apartment when I got word that you'd been released from the hospital. You didn't answer your phone," Lieutenant Merrill said.

"I wasn't home," Martin confessed, as he wondered whether he was prepared for the suspension that just might be coming. "Would you like to know what else happened?"

"I think it would be a good time to tell me, Martin."

So Martin told him about the note left at Noletta's door, and he handed it, enclosed in a plastic bag, to his superior officer. The lieutenant read the note. "Do you think they killed the dog?"

Martin shook his head. "I don't know. I hope they didn't." Then he went on to explain about the threatening phone call and the man at the window at Terri Kayser's.

"Mrs. Kayser and her daughter will need protection," Lieutenant Merrill said.

"They'll be staying with Noletta Fahr and her parents. I thought that would be best since you'd already arranged for their house to be kept under surveillance. Whoever is behind all this is dangerous," Martin said.

"That's an understatement, Detective," the lieutenant said. "And I think you should be careful yourself. Now, while I get you some help, you had better get some rest."

"I'd like to follow up on a couple of things first," Martin protested. He felt guilty that he hadn't told Noletta about finding Taffy and intended on going up to the law school to find her.

"Think again, Martin. You're not doing anything or going anywhere until after you get more rest. And you need a partner that *will* back you up. Give me until three this afternoon, and I'll have someone assigned to take Ted's place. I'll also check the dispatch records before I talk to Ted again. Not that I don't believe you, but I want to have proof when he comes in so that he can't continue to play his word against yours. Can you be back here by three?"

"If you want me to be," Martin agreed.

"Good. I'll see you then. In the meantime, get some rest. And that's an order."

* * *

"I called Creed," Walton said over lunch.

Noletta merely nodded since she didn't know what to say. It was embarrassing to her that Walton would tell him not to give her a ride home.

"He sounded a bit put out," he went on. "Noletta, I think he's smitten by you. I'd be concerned, but he has to go back to work in California in a few days, and he shouldn't be bothering you much more."

She remained silent. She still didn't know how to respond. Even though she'd longed for a deeper relationship with Walton, theirs had never gone beyond that of a very good friendship. It made her uncomfortable now as he acted like the jealous boyfriend. It was true that Creed had to go back to Los Angeles soon, but she found that she liked him better than Walton at times. And he was, as much as she hated to admit it, more of a gentleman than Walton had been lately.

"Noletta," Walton said, "are you listening to me?"

"Sure," she said, attempting to smile.

"Good, because I'm worried about how much time you're spending with Creed. I know he's my cousin and all, but you're too good for him," he said very seriously.

That surprised Noletta, and she asked, "In what way?" She remembered asking the same questions about another man during the past twenty-four hours.

Walton hesitated. "He uses people and then discards them when they aren't useful to him anymore."

"Really?" she asked skeptically. "How?"

"Take me for example. He comes here from California, bums a room in my apartment, then suddenly leaves with nothing but a short note of explanation and gets himself a hotel room," he said. "I put myself out for him, and then he did that."

"But you were sick, and he didn't want to catch whatever you had," Noletta explained.

"At least that's what he wants us to believe," Walton said, as anger seeped into his voice.

"Is there some other reason that he's not telling me about?" Noletta asked.

"You'd better believe it," Walton said. "There's always another reason with that guy."

"So why did he move out on you?"

"That's easy. He moved out because of you."

"Me? What do you mean? Why would he move out because of me?" she asked, honestly puzzled.

"Because it made it easier for him to see you, to interfere with the friendship you and I have," he explained. "Believe me, Noletta. He'll only end up hurting you. He may be good-looking and act like the knight in shining armor, but there's a dark side beneath that facade."

Later that afternoon, as she thought about what Walton had said, Noletta was torn. She cared a great deal for Walton, and she hoped he was beginning to care for her in the same way. Yet Creed had been such a gentleman and was downright sweet to her. It was hard to believe he was the kind of person Walton described. She couldn't help but think that the unkind picture Walton painted of Creed was out of jealousy. If it was, she supposed that should make her feel good, but it didn't. It only made her suspicious of both men.

She hoped that having dinner that evening with Walton would be more pleasant than their lunch date had been. Then thoughts of a third man interrupted, and she wondered why Martin hadn't mentioned that he'd been injured. She wondered if what his partner had said about him was true. Maybe the safest thing would be to distance herself from men in general. Perhaps her handicap made her too vulnerable. And once again she missed Taffy. Her heart ached with loneliness.

* * *

Terri was worried about Martin. She feared that his injuries were worse than he'd let on. Because he was strong-willed, she could imagine him checking himself out of the hospital before the doctor felt it was safe for him to go. Finally, around two, she called his cell phone. She was surprised when it went to voice mail. When she tried his home number, it rang several times before she heard his deep and very groggy voice say, "Hello."

"Martin, it's Terri. Did I wake you?" she asked, feeling suddenly both foolish and worried. She felt bad for waking him, but she needed to know he was okay.

"Yes, but that's okay. My alarm was about to go off," Martin said. "I'm supposed to be back at the office to meet my new partner at three."

"I'm sorry I disturbed you," she said.

"Please, don't be. My alarm is about to—"

She heard his alarm as it cut him off with its loud blast. She could hear him fumbling with it. "Like I was saying, it's time I get moving."

"Martin," she said hesitantly, "are you really okay?"

She enjoyed his deep chuckle, and her heart lifted when he finally spoke. "Really, I'm fine, Terri. But I appreciate your asking. I wasn't planning to rest, but the lieutenant ordered me to. And I guess I needed it, because I slept soundly. How about you—are you doing all right?"

"As well as can be expected," she said, even as she considered the turmoil she'd been experiencing all day. She was frightened—for herself, for Harmony, and for Noletta. And even though she hated to admit it, she was also frightened for Martin. There was just something about him that lay over her like a warm mist, and it felt good. She trembled to think that he could so easily have been killed last night. It brought back horrible and haunting memories.

"Hang in there, Terri. I'll drop by tonight if that's okay," he said.

It was more than okay, she realized. In fact, she looked forward to seeing him. "I'd like that a lot," she said.

"Good. Then I'll see you later. I should get going now."

Terri looked at the phone in her hand for a long moment. Then she shook her head and mentally scolded herself. *You hardly know the man*, she thought. *Be careful. You don't need this in your life right now.*

But a little voice in her head disagreed, and she shivered. Although she knew she hadn't been truly happy since Lamar was killed, life had been going quite smoothly for her and Harmony, especially the last few months. Now it was in turmoil again. And yet she couldn't deny the fact that she liked being around Martin Atkinson more than any man she'd known—with the exception of Lamar, of course.

* * *

Ted was nowhere in sight when Martin entered the office that afternoon. He'd worried about meeting him there. He didn't like the friction that had developed between the two of them, and he was sure that the next time he saw Ted, his partner would have plenty to say. He took a deep breath, glad to have the inevitable confrontation delayed.

He tapped on Lieutenant Merrill's door at three o'clock sharp. "Come in," the lieutenant called.

"Oh, I'm sorry. I didn't mean to interrupt," he said when he saw that someone was already with the lieutenant. A short-haired woman wearing a police uniform was sitting with her back to Martin.

"No, you're fine. We were expecting you. I'd like you to meet your new partner, Madison Reed, more generally known as Maddie," Lieutenant Merrill said, as the woman rose to her feet and turned toward Martin. "You may have seen each other before, but I don't suppose you've ever worked together. Madison, this is the officer I've been telling you about, Detective Martin Atkinson."

As they shook hands, Martin tried to remember when he'd seen her before. He supposed their paths might have crossed sometime in the past. One thing was for sure: she had one of those faces a man didn't easily forget. He decided it was her eyes. "Hi, Detective," she said. "It's a real pleasure to meet you."

"Same here," Martin said awkwardly.

"Maddie may not be as big as Ted," Lieutenant Merrill said with a grin as Martin both looked at her and tried not to, "but she comes to this division highly recommended. She'll be ready to work with you in the morning. She's covering a shift today, and her supervisor is trying to reshuffle so she can be freed up by tomorrow."

"That's great," Martin said with more enthusiasm than he was feeling. The last thing he'd expected was to be partnered with a female officer. That could be a distraction he didn't need.

"Sorry about your injuries," Maddie said. "I hope you're going to be okay."

"I'll be fine, thanks," he said.

"Did you get some rest this afternoon?" Lieutenant Merrill asked.

"I did, and you were right. I needed it. But I'm feeling pretty good right now," he said.

"Excellent. Maddie, who by morning will officially be Detective Madison Reed, is excited to be working with you," Lieutenant Merrill said.

"That's right," she beamed up at him.

"So train her well," the lieutenant said.

"I'll do my best, but I'm just learning myself."

"Lieutenant Merrill says you have all the right instincts," Maddie said. "He also says you're working a very difficult and dangerous case." She smiled, and her whole face lit up. "But then I guess that's pretty evident," she said as her dark blue eyes moved upward to the lump high on his forehead.

"Yeah, and I sure welcome the help," he said.

"Well, Martin, if you can keep yourself in one piece until morning, you'll have dependable help." The lieutenant grinned as he spoke, but Martin knew he was being told to be careful. "Maddie may not look the part, but she has a black belt in karate and is a crack shot with her sidearm."

"That's great," Martin said, beginning to feel overwhelmed. He'd studied karate but had barely made it to brown belt. "I'll know to behave myself. I'm only brown," he added with a smile. He had almost said something about her being his body-guard, but he stopped himself.

"Ted will have his gear moved later today, and Maddie, you can take over his desk in the morning. If you could meet Martin here at eight, he can fill you in on the case. Then you two can get right to work after that."

"So is Ted going to be okay?" Martin asked.

"Yes. He's got a couple of days' suspension, and then he'll be returning to the division. I'm not sure who we'll pair him with yet," the lieutenant explained.

"I'm sorry this happened," Martin said sincerely.

"So am I," Lieutenant Merrill said. "By the way, I did get a chance to listen to the dispatch recording. And it was just like you said. When I confronted Ted with it, he said he didn't remember exactly what he told the dispatcher but that he felt bad about it. He said he'd eaten something that made him really ill that night. He'd been throwing up and was in no condition to go out. He said that when the call came in, he didn't understand exactly what was happening because his head was throbbing so bad. I hope that makes you feel better about him."

"Yeah, it's fine. I'm just glad I don't have to work directly with him anymore. Detective Reed will, I'm sure, be a great partner," Martin said as he thought about the lies Ted tossed about so smoothly. There was no way he'd been so sick. He was just covering his tail. *But it doesn't matter now,* Martin reminded himself, thinking of his mother. It was history. He would move on and abandon his hard feelings toward his former partner. He just hoped Ted would do the same.

Maddie walked out with Martin after they'd received a few more instructions from the lieutenant. To Martin's dismay, Ted was at his desk, and he rose the moment he spotted them, glaring at both of them.

"So, you have a new senior partner, Martin. Maybe she can do what I couldn't. You have your work cut out for you, ah . . ." Ted hesitated. He clearly didn't know Maddie.

"I'm Madison Reed," she volunteered as she held out her hand to him, "and I'm the *junior* partner. I'm excited to be working with Martin."

"It'll be more exciting than you know," Ted said snidely, rebuffing her outstretched hand. "But if you work at it, you might be able to ace out the beautiful blind girl he's fallen head over heels for."

Madison looked genuinely puzzled.

"He's referring to the victim in the case I've been working," Martin said icily. "Ted has his own warped view of the world."

Then, although Ted began to say something else, Martin ignored him and spoke to Maddie. "So eight o'clock in the morning?"

"I'll be here," she said with a grin as she turned her back on Ted.

Martin headed for the door, and Maddie fell in step beside him. After leaving the large room, she said, "Ugh. You had to work with *that*?"

"It wasn't pleasant," Martin agreed.

"Well, I promise I won't be half as bad," Maddie said with another big smile.

"Thanks. It'll be refreshing," Martin said, and despite his earlier misgivings, he was beginning to think that they might make a good team.

CHAPTER 15

Noletta answered her phone just after five, wondering if Creed was trying to call. She was unsure of herself with him after what Walton had said, but on the other hand, she was also not so sure how she felt about Walton at this point. She wished she could find an excuse to skip the dinner date with him that evening.

"Hello," she said and was surprised to hear Detective Atkinson's deep voice on the other end.

"Noletta, I need to talk to you for a few minutes. Would now be a good time?" he asked.

"You're right, Detective, we do need to talk. I've been worrying about you all day. Why didn't you tell me you'd been shot?" she blurted.

"That's one of the things I wanted to talk about. Would now be okay?" he asked again.

"Now would be fine. I have a date at seven, but until then I'm free," she said.

"Okay, I'll be right in," he said.

She was surprised when the doorbell rang less than a minute later. She realized he must have been parked on the street when he called. As he shook her hand, Noletta kept thinking about the derogatory remarks Martin's partner had made about him. She had debated whether to tell him about

Detective Zobel's call. As she felt the warmth of his hand, she decided to tell him. If he was to help her out of the trouble she was in, they both needed to trust each other. Of course, if she felt like he was stringing her along and not doing his job, she'd ask for someone else to take the case.

"Would it be okay if we sat down?" he asked.

"Oh, sure. I guess I'm a little distracted," she said.

She led the way into a large family room and then sat, inviting him to sit near her on a large sofa. "What are you distracted about?" he asked. "Is it over the note that was left at your house during the night?"

"Well, that too, I suppose," she said. "But it's actually more than that. It's about the call I got from your partner, Detective Zobel."

"Oh, so that's how you learned that I had a little trouble last night," he said.

"Yes, he told me about it and quite a bit else."

"Well, I guess we should clear something up right now, Noletta. Ted Zobel is no longer my partner. He was suspended today for a short time."

"Suspended?" she asked with surprise.

"Yes, and I have a partner now who will begin helping me tomorrow. I think this time I'll actually have someone who's willing to work. All Ted could think of was getting promoted, and he didn't care who he hurt to get there. Unfortunately for him, it backfired," Martin said. "But enough of that. I don't know what he said to you this morning, but please, Noletta, don't hold it against me."

She was relieved and decided to give Detective Atkinson the trust he needed, at least for now. "So, tell me what happened, how you got shot," she said. "And I hope you're okay."

"I'm fine. I just got a little impatient last night," he admitted. "And by being impatient, I got careless. It's my fault that I was shot. I shouldn't have let it happen."

"Where did the bullet hit you?" she asked, even as she subconsciously fingered the tiny scar where the bullet that blinded her had entered her head.

"I was wearing a bulletproof vest," he said. "One of the bullets hit me in the back, and even though I'm bruised there, the vest saved me."

"Oh, so you weren't really shot?" she asked.

"Well, actually, another bullet hit my arm, but it was only superficial. What hurt the worst was when I fell and struck my head. That knocked me out."

"Oh, Detective," she said. "What happened after that?"

"I don't know for sure, except that the guys who did it got away, and I lost what I'd gone into the building for. Would you mind if I told you the entire story?" he asked. "And if you're angry with me, it's okay. You have a right to be."

"How can I be angry?" she asked. "I know what it's like to be shot. You could have been killed." Putting into words what she'd been thinking made her subdued.

The hand that held hers squeezed gently. "I'm fine. Now, let me tell you what happened. I was responding to a call that a dog was barking in an abandoned warehouse. My partner refused to help me, and the backup patrol unit that I called got delayed. So I went in alone. I shouldn't have done that."

Noletta took a deep breath, slowly letting it out. "Was it Taffy?"

"I'm so sorry, Noletta. I let you down. I'm almost positive it was Taffy, but by going in alone, I got myself shot, and whoever shot me got away with Taffy."

"And they killed her, according to the note that you found on my door," she said.

"That's what the note says, but I'm having a hard time believing that, Noletta. Taffy must be worth some money to them—quite a lot of money—and with me out of the way, they had no reason to hurt her. No, I think they just moved her somewhere else. I feel bad that I was so close and then muddled the case," he said, his voice filled with emotion.

Noletta turned toward him on the sofa, freed her hand from his, then gently took his face in both hands. "You risked your life for me," she said with great feeling and gratitude. "Thank you for trying so hard. And I'm sorry for letting Detective Zobel create doubts about you in my mind."

"He's good at that," Martin said as she released his face. "But I don't blame you at all. And Noletta, I promise I'll keep trying to find Taffy for you. With a little luck, we just might get her back yet."

"Martin," she said urgently, surprised at herself for using his first name. She'd tried to avoid that. But she went on. "Don't risk your life again. These men, whoever they are, are dangerous. It's okay if you let it go now. I'll get another dog. Creed said he'd help me find one."

"It's too late to back off," Martin said very seriously. "These men, and I now know there are at least three involved, must be caught. They're dangerous, Noletta. And I may be wrong, but I wouldn't be surprised if one of them killed Terri's husband and stole your sight from you. I can't stop now until I find that man."

They talked about the case for a few more minutes. Then Noletta said, "Terri and Harmony should be getting here pretty soon. I wish I didn't have to leave this evening. But I have my doubts that Walton will release me from our dinner date."

"It's nice of you and your folks to take them in," Martin said.

"We wouldn't consider anything else," Noletta said. "Harmony is such a sweet girl. I just love her. And Terri is a great person, too, and a big help."

"She is a good woman," Martin said awkwardly.

"Is she pretty?" Noletta suddenly asked.

"Oh, yes," he responded. "She's a very attractive woman. She and Harmony look a lot alike."

"And her hair's red like Harmony's? I mean, I know they both have red hair, but is it the same shade?" Noletta asked.

"Almost identical," Martin told her. "And they both wear it very long."

"What color are Terri's eyes?"

"Green. A vibrant green," Martin said.

Noletta smiled. "I think she likes you, Martin."

"Oh, no, I doubt that," he said awkwardly.

"No, I mean it. And so does Harmony. I hope they get here before you have to go so that you can see them."

The doorbell rang. "I'll get it, Noletta," her mother called as she hurried past the family room.

"That's probably them now. I'll let you visit with them while I go study for a little while. Walton will be here at seven," she said.

Just then Creed entered the room. "Hi, Noletta," he said. "Sorry I missed you earlier. Looks like my young cousin's getting a little possessive." She could feel the warmth in his voice, and she felt her doubts about him melting away.

"Hello, Creed," Martin said as he rose to his feet.

"Detective," he answered. "I hear you had a rough night. Are you feeling okay?"

"Yes, I'm fine," Martin said. Then he turned to Noletta. "I'll be in touch," he said. "Oh, and there will be officers keeping an eye on the place."

"I appreciate that, and I know Terri and Harmony will too. Thanks for all you're doing," Noletta said.

The doorbell rang again. "That had better not be Walton," Creed said, but there was a lightness to his voice. Noletta suspected that he was smiling.

"It's probably Terri and Harmony," she said. "Martin's been sort of waiting for them." She was teasing now, and she hoped that Martin could tell that from the tone of her voice.

"I'll get it," Mrs. Fahr called out again.

* * *

It felt awkward, ringing the bell at the very place they were going to be living for a while, but Terri couldn't just barge in. She and Harmony had spent a few minutes after work doing some shopping, but they hadn't bought a thing. What she was really doing was stalling. It felt strange having to live with people she barely knew, but she was grateful that she could.

Her heart felt light as she waited. She'd recognized Martin's car parked on the street. Harmony voiced her own feelings. "I hope Martin's here, Mom. I really like him."

The door opened, saving Terri from having to respond to her daughter's awkward statement. She liked Martin too. To her delight, standing right behind Terri's mother was Martin. Despite the lump on his head and the small bandage on his left arm, he looked so handsome. Mrs. Fahr invited her in, then stepped back, leaving her facing Martin. Her heart skipped a beat when he smiled at her.

"Hi, Terri. It's good to see you."

"And it's good to see you, too."

Then he bent over and put an arm around Harmony and pulled her against him. "How's my girl?"

"I'm really good, Martin," she said with a huge grin.

"Your rooms are all ready," Mrs. Fahr said. "And I'll get busy and fix us some dinner. Noletta won't be eating with us. She has a dinner date."

"You don't need to fix dinner for us, Mrs. Fahr. We'll go out and get something," Terri said.

"I have an even better idea," Martin chimed in, and Terri looked at him hopefully. "Why don't the three of us go to dinner? It's either that, or I have to eat alone, and why should I do that when I could be in the company of two beautiful women?"

"You would be welcome to eat with us, Detective," Mrs. Fahr offered.

"Maybe another time," Martin said. "I appreciate the thoughtfulness, but you have more than your share to do. Anyway, if they're willing, I'd love to spend the evening with Terri and Harmony."

"Mrs. Fahr, you are so generous. But if you don't mind, I think I'll take Martin up on his offer," Terri said as her heart raced with anticipation.

"That would be fine. In fact, maybe Harmony would like to keep me company and help me fix something for Mr. Fahr. Then you two could have the evening to yourselves," Mrs. Fahr volunteered.

"I think that's a good idea. Anyway, I have some homework to do. I'd love to stay here with you. Thank you, Mrs. Fahr," Harmony said. Terri smiled proudly at her daughter.

"And thank you, Harmony," Noletta's mother said. "You are such a sweetheart."

"Mom and Martin would like to spend some time together," Harmony said in a very mature voice.

Martin's eyes caught Terri's. "It's true for my part."

"And for mine too," Terri said as she realized how much she would enjoy spending some time alone with Martin. She'd been too lonely for far too long.

"I'll give you time to settle in a bit," Martin said. "What time should I be back?"

Right now would be great, she was thinking. But she said, "Can you give me thirty minutes?"

"I'll see you then," Martin said. As he stepped past Terri, his hand brushed lightly against hers, sending pleasant chills through her. Then he was out the door and gone.

* * *

Creed left just a few minutes before it was time for Walton to pick Noletta up. She barely had time to get ready. But her visit with Creed had been pleasant. And just before he left, he'd said, "If you hear of a strange car hanging around, don't be alarmed. I told you I'd make sure you were safe here, and I meant it."

Over dinner, Noletta filled Walton in on all the details of the last twenty-four hours, which she couldn't do at lunch with all their discussion about Creed. Their evening went quite well until he asked her if she'd heard from Creed. That was just as they were eating their dessert. When she told him that he'd been by, Walton's mood soured. "I'm telling you, Noletta, he's not what he wants you to think he is. He's nothing but a ladies' man. He'll lead you on and then drop you like a hot coal."

"I guess I'll be the judge of what he's like," she said angrily. "Why don't you get off Creed's case? Like you said, he'll be leaving soon anyway. It won't hurt to be good to him while he's here. And I think maybe you and I shouldn't talk about him anymore."

The subject was dropped, but the rest of the evening was ruined. When he left her at her parents' house, it was nearly eight-thirty. Martin was just pulling away from the curb. "There goes your cop friend," Walton said. "Wonder what he's doing back here. Why doesn't he go get your dog back instead of trying to hang around you all the time?"

More jealousy, and this time entirely unfounded, Noletta thought with more disgust than she liked to feel. But she tried to be sweet. "He took my friend Terri to dinner tonight. You know, Harmony's mother."

"I know who Terri is," Walton grumbled.

"Of course you do. I think she and Detective Atkinson have a thing going," she observed, hoping to defray some of the ugly jealousy she sensed in Walton. "I think it would be nice for Terri if something developed there."

"Do you really think she'd want to be married to a cop after what happened to her husband?" Walton asked. "I'd think that after what you just described to me that she went through, she'd want to steer clear of someone who could get killed just about any day."

"You don't like Detective Atkinson, do you?"

"Not particularly," Walton agreed. "If he'd done his job right, he'd have recovered your dog by now—last night for sure. I just don't think he's much of a cop, that's all. He's the kind I'll eat up on the witness stand someday."

"What do you mean?" Noletta asked.

"The more I think about it, the more I want to do criminal defense work. There's good money in it, and it would give me a chance to put guys like Atkinson in their place when they do shoddy work."

She couldn't help herself. She felt compelled to defend Detective Atkinson. "I think he's done a good job on this case, Walton. It's not his fault his partner let him down. It's Detective Zobel's fault Martin got shot and Taffy wasn't recovered, not Martin's."

"So it's *Martin* now, is it?" Walton sneered.

"Detective Atkinson then!" she said angrily as she opened her door and got out.

Walton also got out and caught up with Noletta before she reached the door. "I'm sorry. I shouldn't be so hard on Detective Atkinson. I'm just so frustrated that you are without your dog, and I want so badly for you to have her back."

"That will probably never happen," Noletta said. But she felt bad that she was angry with Walton. She didn't want it to be that way. She felt for his face, reached up, and kissed him lightly on the cheek. "I'll talk to you tomorrow?" she queried.

"I'll be here to pick you up for school at eight," he said, "if you'll still let me."

"Of course I'll let you, Walton," she said, and then she let herself into the house.

Noletta tried not to think about Creed or Walton the rest of the night. The emotional roller coaster she was on with them was just too much to deal with right now in addition to all the strain and stress and danger in her life. She wished they'd both back off and give her some space.

Terri and Harmony were both in a good mood, making it easy for Noletta to concentrate on something else. All they could do was talk about Martin, and she listened attentively. There was no question that Terri was falling for Martin. In a way she envied her, because she knew that Martin was a good man.

* * *

Martin's phone rang at midnight. It was one of the officers on shift keeping an eye on Noletta's parents' house. "There's a strange man hanging around here in a car," he was told. "Would you like us to stop him and check it out?"

Martin was already rolling out of bed. "No, just keep an eye on him. I'm on my way. We'll stop him when I get there. And he had better have a good explanation for what he's doing there."

CHAPTER 16

Determined not to make the same mistake again—walking into another dangerous situation alone—Martin debated whether he should call his new partner, Madison, or rely on the patrol unit that had contacted him. It hadn't been clear whether she was his partner now or not officially until eight in the morning.

He'd almost decided to rely on the patrol unit, but at the last minute, as he left his house, he changed his mind and dialed the number Maddie had given him. She answered on the second ring. "Hello?" she said, sounding drowsy.

"Hi, Madison, this is Martin Atkinson. I'm sorry to bother you, but I've got another one of those middle-of-the-night calls," he began.

"I'm glad you called," she said. He was surprised at how quickly she shook the sleep from her voice.

"I wasn't sure if I should, and there are patrol units available, but—" he began.

"No, I'd have felt bad if you hadn't," she responded. "What's the call about?"

He told her as he started his car. "Let me give you my address," she said. "It's not far out of the way, and by the time you get here, I'll be ready." She read off the address and then added, "Thanks for trusting me to help."

"No, thank you for being so willing," he said. "I'll see you shortly."

* * *

It was a new feeling, but a good one, for Maddie—being needed and appreciated. Police work had not been her first vocation. Following graduation from the university, she had been a high school physical education teacher and gymnastics coach. Although she enjoyed working with her students, after six years of blowing whistles, spotting for jumps and flips, and dealing with incessant demands and complaints from parents and their children, she had experienced burnout.

Of course, it wasn't just six years. It was a lifetime. Her father had insisted that his children not be stereotypical. There were no dancing lessons, cheerleading, or piano lessons for her. Instead, she had participated in equestrian training, gymnastics, and karate. And she had excelled.

Maddie wasn't sure when and why it was that she had decided that law enforcement appealed to her. She knew it had something to do with a desire for an intellectual challenge as well as a desire for good to triumph over evil—the latter sounded hackneyed, she knew, but it was true nonetheless.

Her training at the police academy had felt comfortable and natural. And now, as she began her first real work as a detective, she silently thanked her father for his influence. Her early training had indeed prepared her for today.

Madison looked unbelievably fresh, considering the hour when Martin picked her up in front of the apartment complex where she lived. She hopped in his car and smiled at him. "Let's go, partner."

When they approached the immediate vicinity of the Fahrs' home, Martin called the unit that was watching the house. "Is that other car still hanging around?" he asked.

"It just drove by," the officer said.

"Can you still see it?"

"Yes. It's less than a block away."

"Good. Why don't you pull it over. My partner and I will be right there. Just do the usual driver's license check and so on. Leave the interrogating to us."

"Will do."

When he and Madison pulled in behind the patrol unit, which was now directly in front of the Fahr home, the patrol officers were standing beside the suspect's car talking to the driver. Martin and Madison joined them, and one of the officers handed a driver's license to Martin. The name on the license was Frank Jones. *Very generic,* he thought as he slipped over to the driver's window and leaned down. "I'm Detective Atkinson," he said, presenting his shield for a quick inspection. "Would you care to explain what you're doing driving around in this neighborhood at this time of night?"

"Just making sure nobody tries anything at the Fahrs' house," he said.

"That's our job," Martin said coldly. "Who are you working for, or are you doing this on your own?"

"Actually, I was hired by Noletta Fahr's boyfriend," he said. "My instructions were to call the cops if I saw anything suspicious."

"Well, so far, you're the only suspicious thing the cops who are watching this place have seen," Martin said.

"I'm legal," the suspect said. "Just helping out an old acquaintance."

"So you were hired by Walton Pease?"

"No. I wouldn't work for him if someone paid me to," Frank said.

"He's Noletta's boyfriend," Martin said. "Why don't you step out of the car, and we'll visit some more."

Frank did as he was asked. And then he moved to the back of his car when Martin directed him. Once there, Martin handed the driver's license to Maddie. "Would you run him through dispatch for me. And while you're doing it, would you jot down his name, date of birth, etc.?"

"Sure thing," she said.

Then he turned again to Frank. "So if you're not working for Mr. Pease, who are you working for?"

"Noletta's boyfriend, Creed Esplin. He works for a building contractor in California," Frank said.

"I know Creed. But I wasn't aware that he was Noletta Fahr's boyfriend," Martin said with ice in his voice.

"That's what Creed says. And he's paying me decent money to keep an eye out on this house, so that's what I'm doing."

"Not anymore, you aren't," Martin replied sternly. "This is police business. You must stay out of the area. And you can tell Creed Esplin that he can rely on the police to protect Noletta Fahr."

"Whatever you say," Frank said.

"He's clear," Maddie said a moment later.

"Then am I free to go?" Frank asked.

"Yes, you may go. But remember, this is police business. Stay out of it," Martin warned him.

"No problem," Frank said jauntily, then got in his car and pulled away.

After he was gone, Martin told the officers running the surveillance to keep a close watch on the house. If Frank Jones came into the neighborhood again, they were to detain him and call Martin. "I'm not sure what I'll charge him with, but I'll think of something."

* * *

"Are they gone?" Noletta asked in a trembling voice.

"Martin just pulled away," Terri said.

"I wonder what was going on," Noletta said. "Aren't we going to have a single night of peace?"

"I suppose he was a suspicious person," Terri said as she let the drapes fall back into place. She'd been lying awake when she saw the reflection of flashing blue lights in the window of the bedroom she was using. She got up, went downstairs and into the living room, where she could get a better look outside, and then began to watch as the patrol officers talked to the driver of the older silver car they'd stopped. She'd been especially interested when Martin had arrived. She'd been watching for two or three minutes when Noletta had approached her almost silently and asked what was going on.

"I hope that's all," Noletta said, referring to Terri's answer about a suspicious person. "I guess we should be glad the police are on the job."

"Yes, but I wish Martin didn't have to come out in the night like this," Terri said. "It worries me. After what happened last night, you'd think that he could be allowed a full night without having to be interrupted."

"You like him, don't you?" Noletta asked shrewdly.

"Truthfully, yes. He's one of the nicest guys I've ever met," Terri said. "But I hate having to worry about him."

"Don't let him get away," Noletta counseled. "Because I get the feeling he likes you, too. And I know Harmony thinks he's just about the greatest."

"You're right about that," Terri agreed.

"You may have times of worry with his job, but I think he would take good care of you," Noletta added.

Terri chuckled. "We're not that serious," she said. "I barely know him. Anyway, there's that girl that was with him just now."

"There was a woman with him?" Noletta asked in surprise.

"Oh, yeah," Terri said. "I suppose she's an officer too, but she's one who could turn a guy's head."

"That's funny. He said he got a new partner, but he never mentioned a female officer working with him."

"Maybe she's a girlfriend," Terri said morosely.

"I don't think so," Noletta countered. "But no matter what, you go after him, Terri. Like I said before, he'll take good care of you and Harmony. I think he's a great guy."

* * *

Martin was at his desk by seven-thirty. He hoped it wasn't too early to check on Terri, Harmony, and Noletta. He dialed Terri's cell phone, and she answered. "Hi, it's Martin," he said. "I hope I'm not calling too early."

"Not at all. Harmony's already getting ready for school, and I'm getting ready for work," she said. "Thanks for calling."

"Did you sleep well last night?" Martin asked.

"Not really. I was awake when those two officers stopped that car in front of the house during the night."

"I'm sorry. So I take it you got up to see what was going on?"

"I did. And my moving around woke up Noletta. So what did that guy do? It must not have been too serious, or you would have arrested him."

"He was hanging around the area, and the officers on duty watching the Fahrs' house called me. But he checked out okay. Nothing to worry about," Martin said.

"Who was the woman with you?" Terri suddenly asked, and Martin was almost certain he detected a hint of jealousy in her voice.

Martin answered even as he spotted Madison approaching their desks. "She's my new partner. And she's already taken an interest in this case. I think she's going to make a good detective."

"Who's going to make a good detective?" Maddie asked, raising her eyebrows as she sat down at her newly assigned desk and looked over at Martin.

"You are," he mouthed. Then into the phone he asked, "So are you guys all okay this morning?"

"Other than worrying about you, we're fine," Terri responded. "But we're tired."

"You were worrying about me?" Martin asked. "You don't need to worry about me."

"But I do, and I can't help it," Terri said with a catch in her voice. "Am I going to see you today?"

"Absolutely. I'll give you a call after you get off work. And say hello to Harmony for me. Give her a hug for me, too."

"I will. You be careful now."

"I will, and tell Noletta I called. Explain, if you would, about the little disturbance last night. Make sure she understands that there was nothing to it," Martin emphasized.

After he'd hung up, Maddie said, "Someone special?"

Martin shrugged. "A nice gal, but we barely know each other. I'll tell you more about her later. She's involved in this case. In fact, she and her daughter are staying with Noletta Fahr and her parents since they're in danger too. When I fill you in on the case, you'll see how they fit in."

An hour later, Martin decided he'd told Madison everything she should know about the case. "What do we do next?" she asked. "Remember, I'm brand new at this investigation business, so you'll have to point me in the right direction."

"I'm not exactly an old hand at it myself," Martin confessed, "but I was thinking that we should go back to the warehouse where they were holding Noletta's dog, Taffy."

"And where you were shot," Madison said.

"Yeah, that too," he conceded.

"And what will we do there?"

"Have a thorough look around. Maybe we could try to lift some fingerprints in the area where they were holding the dog."

"Didn't somebody do that after you got hurt?"

"I don't think they did much," Martin said.

"Won't we need a search warrant?"

"Not if we can locate the owner of the building and get permission."

"Okay, what can I do?" she asked, and Martin smiled. "What are you grinning about?" she asked.

"You have no idea how good it feels to have a partner who's willing to work. With your help, we may crack this case yet."

* * *

"Thanks for the ride, Walton," Noletta said after they'd started across the parking lot to a class they were both enrolled in.

"Anytime," he said. "I've just got to make sure Creed doesn't bother you again until his vacation is over. Once he's gone back to California, you'll never hear from him again."

Or hear from you again, Noletta thought. Noletta decided that in this case no response was a good response. However, she did hope she'd see Creed again before he left. Shortly after she and Walton parted, following their class, Noletta's phone rang. "Hello," she said.

"Hi, Noletta. It's Creed."

"Oh, hi, Creed," she said, feeling strangely relieved to hear his voice.

"I came by to pick you up, but your mother said you'd already gone with Walton. Sorry I missed you."

"I'm sorry too," she said. Walton was making her feel uncomfortable with the way he kept demeaning his cousin.

"Do you have a few minutes right now?" he asked.

"Yes, but I'm up on campus. It might take you a while to get here."

He chuckled into the phone and said, "I'm admiring your beautiful face even as we speak," he said.

"Oh, so where are you?"

"I'm walking toward you. Just a minute, and I'll be right there with you."

Creed was true to his word. Noletta heard his footsteps and smelled his aftershave just moments before he put his arms around her and pulled her close. "I'm going to have a hard time going back to L.A.," he said, brushing his lips against her cheek. "Would you like a little snack somewhere so we can talk?"

"I'd like that very much," she said as she realized how good she felt when she was with Creed.

Creed and Noletta chatted for the next fifteen minutes, and she found herself relaxing more the longer she was with him. The slight damper Walton's earlier words had placed on her feelings was beginning to let up. And then, after seating themselves in a small snack bar, Creed altered the mood. "Have you talked with Detective Atkinson this morning?"

She tensed at the change in his tone of voice. "No," she said. "But Terri did. Why would I have talked to him?"

"I just wondered if he'd explained to you why he ran the man off that I'd hired to keep an eye on your parents' house. I don't think he had the right to do that, Noletta," Creed said very firmly. "I'm concerned about you, and I think I should be able to hire someone to protect you without the cops interfering."

"Maybe that was the guy he and the other officers talked to during the night," she said. "I wasn't aware that it was someone you'd hired."

"Well, it was. Frank Jones is an old friend of mine, and believe me, you'd be safe under his watchful eye," Creed said. "I wish you'd talk to Detective Atkinson and see if you can't get him to let Frank continue to help, at least until the danger to you is past."

"Creed, it's so sweet of you to help like this, but you don't need to be spending your money on me. The police will keep a close eye on us. Really, there's no need to worry now," Noletta said.

"But I do worry," he said as he reached across the small table and took hold of her hands with his. "I care about you, Noletta. I know we don't know each other very well, but I've never met anyone that has affected me in quite the way you do. But please, please, talk to the officer for me. Try to convince him to let Frank keep an eye on things at night. Tell the detective that I'll make sure Frank stays out of the officers' way and won't cause any trouble. Please, I'd just feel so much better about your safety if I knew someone I trust is helping out."

He was so sincere that it was hard for her to rebuff his continued request. Finally, she said, "If you promise that you'll do whatever Detective Atkinson says after I talk to him, then I'll try to get him to let your friend help."

"You won't regret it," Creed said as he leaned across the table. She felt his face near hers, and she leaned forward herself. He kissed her forehead. "I wish I didn't have to go back to work next week, but my boss needs me."

"When next week?" she asked.

"Wednesday," he said.

She calculated quickly in her head. "Only five days," she said, and she knew after these past few minutes that she'd miss him. He had, in that short time, made her feel special. She just wished she knew more about him. One thing that had never come up in their conversations was the Church, and that was crucial to her.

"Yes, only five days," he said, "and I intend to spend as much time with you during those five days as I can, whether my dear cousin likes it or not." Then, as if he'd read her mind, Creed said, "My bishop's executive secretary called me last night. He said the bishop wants to see me. He'd hoped it could be Sunday, but when I told him it would be at least the next one, since I wouldn't be home before that, he said that would be fine."

"Do you have any idea what he wants?"

"A new calling, I suppose. You know how that goes."

"What are you doing in the Church now?"

There was a slight hesitation before he answered. "I'm a Sunday school teacher."

"Young people?"

There was another hesitation. "Yes, but I don't think I'm very good with them."

"I'll bet you are," Noletta said warmly. "And I'll bet they all miss you." Then she felt the dial on her watch. "I've got another class, Creed. I'm afraid I have to go, or I'll be late."

"I'll walk you there," he said.

"Thanks. I'd like that."

Had Noletta been able to see, she would have flinched at the look of rage on Walton's face as she and Creed left the snack bar together.

It wasn't until she was in class a few minutes later that she began to feel alarmed. *What if Walton's right about Creed?* she thought. *What if he really is just leading me on? I can't let myself fall for him, not yet anyway.* And she promised herself she'd try to limit her time with him over the next few days. Then, after he'd been back in California a little while, she'd see how things were going with Walton, and maybe, if Creed called, she'd see how she felt.

* * *

It had taken more than two hours to track down the owner of the warehouse. So by the time Martin and Madison began to search, it was almost noon. They worked for an hour before stopping for lunch. They ate together at a nearby barbecue place and had almost finished their meal when Martin's cell phone rang.

He was surprised to hear Noletta's voice. "How are you doing?" he asked her. "I guess you know about the little incident during the night. It was nothing to worry about."

"Yes, Terri told me. That's what I called to talk to you about. Creed asked me to tell you that he really wished you'd let his friend Frank Jones spend a few hours watching my parents' house each night until you get the guys who are doing all this."

"There really is no need for that," Martin said, irritated that Creed would use Noletta to try to persuade him to change his mind.

"I know that, Martin," she said in a plaintive voice, "but I told him I'd ask. He said he'd tell Frank to stay out of the way and that he wouldn't be any trouble."

"I'm sorry, Noletta," Martin said, "but I don't know this Frank guy, and having him around would only be a distraction to our surveillance teams. I just can't let him do that."

"Okay," she said. "I told Creed I'd ask. So how's it going? What are you doing now?"

"My partner and I are just finishing lunch. Then we're going back to the warehouse where I let Taffy slip through my fingers," he said.

"Detective, please don't blame yourself. You did the best you could. And I appreciate it," she said.

"I do blame myself. I should have gotten her back then. But that's all water under the bridge. Detective Reed and I are going to carefully examine the area in the warehouse where they kept Taffy, just to see if we can find any clues that will help us identify the guys who took her."

"When do I get to meet Detective Reed?" Noletta asked. "Terri tells me she's pretty. I think she's a little jealous."

"No need for her to be," Martin said, a little shaken by Noletta's comment.

"Thanks for talking to me," Noletta said. "I'll tell Creed. He said that he'd stand by whatever you decided."

* * *

Scully Timmons had been spending less and less time at home lately. He said it was his job. Whenever Fiona tried to draw information from him about the kind of work it was, he would get angry, and she'd back off. She was almost positive now that whatever he was doing was illegal.

He came home early that Friday afternoon, and though he'd been drinking as usual, he was in an extraordinarily good mood. "Where's Ritchie?" he asked.

"He's in his room," she said.

"Get him. I have a surprise for the two of you."

"What kind of surprise?"

"A good surprise. Get him, and I'll tell both of you at the same time," he promised.

After Ritchie had joined them in their small living room, Scully asked, "Ritchie, do you still want a guide dog?"

Ritchie nodded his head but said nothing.

"You know he does, Scully," Fiona said. "But don't you go promising something you can't deliver."

"I'd never do that," he said, and she chose not to remind him of the countless times he'd done exactly that. "Ritchie, I've found you a dog, and it's all trained and everything."

"Scully!" Fiona said in anger. "You know we can't afford a trained guide dog."

She cringed when he stepped toward her, his fist raised. "You'll see," he told her, lowering his hand before he struck her. "It'll be here in the next couple of days."

"How much is it costing you?" she asked. "And how are you going to pay for it?"

"That's none of your business," he snapped. "I've worked it out with my boss. I'm going to do a big job for him, one I'll be paid a lot for. Then I can pay for the dog."

"You can't let Ritchie down," she said, knowing she shouldn't be provoking Scully, but unable to stop herself.

He ignored her and left the house. A moment later, she heard his pickup leave, and she took Ritchie in her arms. "Will Dad really get me a dog?" he asked.

"Honey, you shouldn't count on it," she said. "Then you won't be disappointed."

"Okay, Mom," he said, "but I really want a dog. Maybe this time Dad will do what he says."

"Maybe," Fiona said, trying not to let her anger at her husband show. Despite what she'd said to Ritchie, she knew that he wanted to believe his father. That could only mean one thing as far as she was concerned—her son was going to be hurt again. And she hated the fact that she was powerless to prevent it.

CHAPTER 17

"The cage they had the dog in was about right there," Martin said as he surveyed the large room from the doorway and pointed to an area about fifty feet away. He set his camera bag and briefcase on the floor as he spoke.

"Is this where you were shot?" Maddie asked as she pointed to a spot of blood on the floor.

"Looks like it," Martin said. "Although I never saw them, I'm quite sure there were two men, and they were over there somewhere." Again he pointed, this time to the far side of the room where there were several large crates and beyond them, two more doors. One of the doors was large enough to drive a truck through.

"What do we do now?" Maddie asked.

"Let's walk through the room without disturbing anything and just see what we find," he answered. "Then we can try to lift some fingerprints if we see a spot it seems likely they might have touched."

"Would you like me to take one part of the room and you another?" she asked. "This is awfully big."

Martin was thoughtful for a moment. "No, I could easily miss something important. Why don't we work together."

"Whatever you think's best," Maddie replied cheerfully.

Martin glanced at her, and as usual she was smiling. He couldn't believe how pleasant she was and how much he was already enjoying working with her.

It was Maddie who spotted an empty Camel packet, crushed and thrown behind a crate. "It may not have anything to do with the guys we're after," she said as she pointed it out to Martin.

"But then again it could," he said. "Clearly, the officers that were here after I got shot missed it." He pulled on a pair of surgical gloves and placed the empty package in a bag. "Good job," he said. "I hope we find something more."

They did, but it was in the room beyond where the dog had been caged. The criminals had apparently been careless. There were some empty candy wrappers, a couple of beer cans, and in an oily area on the floor, what appeared to be fairly fresh shoe tracks. Fingerprints were taken from door handles and light switches. There were no empty .38 caliber pistol casings. Martin had hoped to find some, but he hadn't really expected to because the officers had previously found one. It had contained only very small and badly smudged prints that had proven to be of no help. He hoped what he and Maddie had found would be more useful.

* * *

Virgil answered his cell phone by snapping angrily, "What now, Evan?"

"Detective Atkinson's in the warehouse," Evan told him.

"So why are you telling me? You know what to do. Get rid of him. We're tired of that cop snooping around so much," Virgil growled.

"It won't be easy, because he's not alone," Evan reported.

"Who's with him?"

"A woman."

"Must be a cop," Virgil said. "So there's two of them. You'll just have to deal with it. Get in there and do what you have to do. And don't leave any bodies behind when you're done. Call me when you're finished."

"I may need help," Evan whined. He could handle one, but two, and the second one a woman at that? His palms began to sweat, and he glanced toward the warehouse. Detective Atkinson's car was still parked near the main door.

"Skip's still in Albuquerque getting rid of the dog, and we're not close enough to help you. Anyway, you know the boss doesn't ever get involved personally. So you just get in there and take care of 'em," Virgil ordered, and the call was abruptly terminated.

Sure, I need the money, Evan thought. *But this is more than I bargained for. If only it hadn't been for that layoff.* He felt cornered and wondered fleetingly if Taffy might have felt the same way—caged and no way out.

Evan was the first in his family to attend college. So, maybe he didn't finish, but he had stuck it out for almost three years—and he was going back. He was actually proud of what he had accomplished, especially when he thought about high school. He had barely graduated. Part of that, he knew, was because of his reputation as a hood—he and the other guys he hung out with. Good buddies like Virgil and Skip.

After high school he had drifted from state to state for a few years, a job here, a job there. Nothing permanent. Then he had become hooked on computers. The whole field fascinated him, and he found that he had the innate skills necessary to become a programmer. By working three-quarter time, he earned enough money to stay in school. Till the layoff. Jobs had been scarce after that, and he finally ended up back with Virgil. He knew it was only temporary, just till he had enough money for another year's tuition.

Wiping the sweat from his forehead, Evan thought about running. He wasn't sure he could kill a woman, even if she was a cop. *What am I thinking?* he asked himself. *I don't know if I can kill anyone.* He also didn't know if he could run. He was certain Virgil would come after him, and he dreaded thinking about the consequences if his old buddy ever caught up with him. Virgil didn't like being double-crossed.

Evan cursed the world in general, and his bad luck in particular, and glanced again at the warehouse. He began to shake as he thought about going in there alone.

* * *

Martin pulled out his new digital camera and began photographing the location of everything of interest they'd found. While he did that, his new partner walked to the front of the building and looked outside. When she came back a few minutes later, she looked worried.

"Are you about finished?" she asked.

"Almost. Is something wrong?"

"I don't know for sure, but there's a car out there with a guy sitting in it. I know he wasn't there when we came in. And he keeps looking this way. He's too far away to get a good look at him, but he makes me nervous."

Martin looked at her for a moment, feeling grateful that she was cautious. He'd been lucky once in this place. He wasn't about to take any more chances. "Thanks for noticing, Maddie," he said softly. "Let's use my zoom lens and see if we can get a good look at the guy before we go to the car."

From the darkness of the building's interior, Martin focused his camera on the man who was still sitting in his car. The vehicle appeared to be a gold-colored, rental Toyota. Martin took several good pictures of him, but he didn't recognize the man. "We'll take a look at some mug shots when we get back to the station," Martin suggested as he put his camera away.

"What if he's waiting for us?" Maddie was only putting into words what Martin was already thinking.

"We'll just have to be careful," he responded.

"Could there be others out there with him?"

"I suppose there could. But we can't stay in here all day waiting to see what happens."

"I know, and I'm sorry if I seem paranoid," Maddie said.

"It's not paranoia. It's called caution, and I appreciate the fact that you're so careful."

"Hey, look. He's getting out of the car," Maddie said suddenly. "And he has something in his hand!"

Martin saw the object for just a moment before the man stuffed it in his waistband and pulled his shirt over it. "It's got to be a gun, Maddie. And he's coming in after us," Martin said as his heart began to pump like that of a runner approaching the finish line. The recent shooting was still too fresh in his mind.

Placing the briefcase with their new evidence and the camera bag on the floor, he called quickly for backup using his cell phone. Then he pulled out his pistol and flashlight. Maddie did the same while they moved deeper into the darkness. The man from the Toyota was heading straight for the warehouse, although he was moving slowly. He kept looking nervously around him.

"We'll have to take him by surprise," Martin whispered to Maddie. "As soon as he steps through the door, I'll order him to stop. At that point, we'll both turn on our flashlights. But remember, keep it away from your body so you won't be a target if he decides to resist arrest."

"Okay," she said softly. "I've done that in training before."

"This is real," Martin reminded her. "If he tries to make any moves for his gun, we'll have no choice but to shoot. Can you do that?"

"If I have to," Maddie said, sounding less than confident but nevertheless determined.

"Okay, step over there and take cover behind those crates. I'll be over by that wall."

A minute later the man's form filled the doorway for only a fraction of a second before he was inside, crouching against the wall near the door, his pistol in hand. "Police! Don't move!" Martin shouted.

As both his and Maddie's flashlights lit him up, the man rolled to one side and began firing rapidly in Martin's direction. The report of Martin's and Maddie's pistols sounded like one. Groaning, the gunman fell face down, his pistol sliding across the floor.

"Keep me covered," Martin instructed his partner as he moved cautiously forward. "This could be a hoax."

But the gunman wasn't faking. "Call for an ambulance," Martin said as he felt for a pulse. "He's alive, but it looks like we both hit him."

Sirens began wailing nearby as the officers that had been responding quietly to their call for help now responded with urgency when they heard Maddie's call.

Maddie knelt beside Martin, who was applying pressure to one of the wounds. He could see that she was trembling. "Find some lights if you can," he said. "That doorway and our flashlights aren't enough. But listen for anyone else who might be here to help this guy. He might not be alone."

* * *

It had been a warm afternoon in Albuquerque, and Skip again wiped the perspiration before it dripped into his eyes. A man who had introduced himself only as Joe was looking Taffy over carefully. Taffy had growled at first, but Joe had spoken gently to her, and she'd eventually calmed down. Soon, he had her out of her cage and was petting her and giving her small chunks of jerky.

"She looks pretty good," Joe said after a little while, "although it appears that she's been roughed up a bit not too long ago. She's tender in the ribs and on her flanks."

Skip remained silent. He knew why she was tender, but he wasn't about to admit to the prospective buyer that he'd kicked the dog.

"Someone's abused her," Joe said accusingly after a closer inspection of Taffy.

"Not me," Skip said. "So are you taking her or not?"

"Don't know yet. I've got to see if she's really trained the way your boss says she is."

"She's trained, all right."

"We're talking a fair chunk of change here," Joe said with ice in his voice. "I intend to make sure I get my money's worth."

"How you gonna do that?"

"I'll let her work for me. And while I do that, you'll wait and keep your mouth shut."

"You ain't taking her out of my sight without handing over the eight grand," Skip said. "That's my boss's orders."

"Didn't intend to," he was told.

Thirty minutes later Joe was convinced. "She's a right good one."

"Give me the money, and you can take her," Skip said, anxious to rid himself of the dog he hated.

The exchange was made, and Skip counted the money. "This ain't right," he said. "My boss said eight thousand. You're five hundred short."

"Eight thousand was for a very experienced guide dog in top physical condition. You've roughed this little lady up," Joe said.

"She's fine," Skip argued angrily.

"I know dogs," Joe said. "You've beat her. Now take your money and scram."

Skip was thinking about how angry Virgil and the boss would be when he was unable to deliver the full purchase price. He tried once more. "Sorry, I guess the deal's off," Skip bluffed.

Joe's face grew dark and dangerous. "Deal's not off. Now get out of here before I rough you up like you did this dog," he threatened.

Skip knew he had lost. He began to think of how he'd explain the shortage to Virgil as he backed away from Joe and

Taffy. He wished he'd never seen the dog. It had caused him nothing but trouble.

* * *

"So, are we suspended?" Martin asked. "I know that after a shooting that's usually what has to happen."

"It generally is," Lieutenant Merrill agreed, "but your case is going to have to be different. I've already spoken with the chief about it. There will be the normal full investigation, but we need the two of you to keep working the case. Too much would be lost to put someone else on it right now. Time could be critical here, and we're clearly dealing with something more than just a stolen dog. So you two keep at it."

"Thanks," Martin said. "I just wish the guy hadn't died. He could probably have cleared things up for us."

"Well, look at it this way," the lieutenant said. "At least we know who he is. And we also know he was in the place before because of the prints you found. So you two go ahead and get back to work."

Maddie stood up and looked at Martin. "I hope every day isn't this rough," she said with a somber look. She was still clearly shaken from the ordeal they'd been through. Martin had to admit he didn't feel so great himself.

"It'll get better," Martin said. "Let's go talk to Noletta and see if this is the same Evan Guinn that helped disrupt her high school graduation party."

* * *

Noletta was expecting Creed. He'd called and invited her to dinner that evening. She'd tried to turn him down but hadn't succeeded. She'd spent much of the afternoon with Walton, who had once again cautioned her about getting too friendly with

Creed. Disgusted with his contentious attitude, she'd cut him off short. It was hard not to believe him, but it was harder not to believe Creed. He was so gentle and solicitous with her. It was when Creed had told her that he'd be leaving Monday afternoon instead of Wednesday that she finally accepted the date.

Her mother had taken her father for a ride to get him out of the house for a while. Harmony had gone with them, and Terri had insisted on fixing a dinner for them to eat when they got back. So when the doorbell rang, Noletta answered it.

Noletta fully expected Creed to be there, but it was Martin Atkinson's familiar aftershave that she smelled, along with perfume she didn't recognize. "Detective," she said before Martin had a chance to say anything. "I wasn't expecting you."

"We needed some information and were hoping you could help us," Martin said.

"You sound discouraged or something," she said, noting an unusual drag in his voice.

"It's been a hard day," he said. "Oh, I'd like you to meet my new partner, Detective Madison Reed."

Noletta reached out, and as she shook hands with the detective, she noticed how soft her hand was and yet how firmly she gripped. "Please, come in," she said. Then she called out, "Terri, Martin's here."

Terri joined them before she'd even had a chance to invite the detectives to sit down. Noletta smiled to herself. She was quite certain Terri was smitten. "Hi, Martin," she heard her friend say.

Then she listened as Detective Atkinson stepped toward Terri, and she felt her heart pumping a little strangely. She was fairly sure that Martin had kissed Terri, probably on the cheek, but a kiss, nonetheless. Martin introduced Terri to Detective Reed, and then he and Terri talked briefly about Harmony. Terri excused herself to go back to the kitchen a moment later. "I can't let dinner burn," she said lightly. "And if you're through and can join us, we'll be eating about seven."

"I'd love to," Martin said, "but it looks like Detective Reed and I are going to be busy this evening."

Martin came right to the point after Terri had returned to the kitchen. "Noletta, you mentioned to me before that one of the guys who crashed your graduation party was a fellow named Evan Guinn," he said. "Can you describe him to me?"

Noletta felt the blood drain from her face. Even though several years had passed, she hadn't forgotten the night of her graduation. Evan was the guy who, in his drunken state, had tried to force her to dance. The mention of his name brought back all the unpleasant feelings of that ruined evening. She could still feel the strength of his grip on her arm and smell the stench of alcohol as he pulled her toward him, leering all the while.

"Noletta," she heard Martin say solicitously, "are you all right?"

"I'm fine," she managed to say. "It's just that Evan Guinn was someone I'd sooner forget. But yes, I think I can give you at least a vague description of him."

Noletta then described what she could remember about him, and at Martin's prodding, again recounted what had happened that night. "Why are you asking about Evan?" she asked after finishing. "Did he have something to do with Taffy?"

"It looks like it," Martin said. "We found his fingerprints in the warehouse she was in earlier, his and those of someone we haven't identified yet. We were hoping you could help us with that too. I can't help but wonder if one of them was the big guy you said was Virgil Weaver, or if it might have been the one you called Skip."

"You're wondering if Virgil could be the guy who's been breaking into my apartment, aren't you?" Noletta said. "If Evan's involved, then I'd guess that Virgil Weaver could be too. But I can't imagine why after all these years, they'd begin to bother me now."

"Maybe Detective Reed and I can find out if we can locate Virgil," Martin said. "I've already tried to find him, but we'll give it another try. Is there anything else you can remember about him or Skip? Anything at all?"

"I don't think so. Maybe Walton could help."

"I talked to him before. He says he can't remember anything more than you told me about that night," Martin said.

"What about Evan? You obviously know who he is. Do you also know where he is?" Noletta asked.

"I'm afraid so," Martin said softly; the strained sound that she'd noticed when she first answered the door was back in his voice.

Noletta was aware of Terri's presence again. She had heard her footsteps returning from the kitchen just seconds before. "Where is Evan?" Noletta asked. "Can you talk to him?"

"Well, you see—" Martin began.

Detective Reed broke in. "Let me, Martin," she said. "Noletta, Evan Guinn is dead, so we can't talk to him."

"How did he die?" Terri asked. Noletta detected an unmistakable note of fear in her voice.

"Martin and I tried to arrest him in the warehouse this afternoon," Maddie said. "He'd been watching us from outside, and he'd come in with a gun. But when we challenged him, he began firing at Martin. We shot back," she finished, leaving them to figure out the result.

Terri gasped, and then Noletta heard her say, "Oh, Martin. Not again."

Then she fled from the room. Martin followed, leaving Noletta alone with Detective Reed, who filled her in on the details. "What is going on?" Noletta asked in despair as the young detective put a comforting arm around her shoulders.

"That's what we intend to find out," Maddie assured her.

After the detectives left, Terri came from the kitchen. She was sniffling and was clearly upset. When Noletta asked her what the matter was, she said, "I'm so afraid for Martin."

"And you have a right to be," Noletta said, and she began to tremble.

"I can hardly stand to think about it all," Terri said. "A man finally comes into my life after losing my husband, and now I'm scared that something's going to happen to him. I just don't know what to do."

Nor did Noletta. She feared this whole affair was somehow her fault. And it cut her to the core. The two women hugged each other for support.

The doorbell interrupted them a few moments later. "That will be Creed," Noletta said as she wiped her eyes and put on her dark glasses to hide her swollen eyes.

"I'm sorry to upset you," Terri said.

"You're a good friend," Noletta replied. "We can both pray for Martin's safety."

"Thank you for your understanding," Terri said. "I'd better get back to the kitchen and get myself under control. I don't want to upset Harmony when she comes back. And you should answer the door. Try to have a good time tonight with Creed. I'll be in a better mood when you come home. I promise."

The two hugged again as the doorbell rang once more. This time it was Creed, and he was immediately concerned about her. They were close enough now that she was unable to hide her emotions from him. He took her gently into his arms and said, "I don't know what might have upset you, Noletta, but whatever it is, I'll try to help."

"Oh, Creed, I wish you could. It's all so dreadful, but I don't know what you could ever do."

"I can hold you and tell you I love you," he said softly. "Because I do."

His words rang in her ears. No man had ever said that to her before. She'd often dreamed of Walton saying such a thing, but he never had. She was unsure how to react, and so she simply leaned harder against Creed's firm body and let him hold her tightly. Finally he said, with a smile in his voice, "Let's go get some dinner, love. And you can tell me all that has happened."

Later, during their dinner, Noletta related the new developments to Creed. He listened attentively, interrupting infrequently. When she'd finished the account of the encounter the detectives had with Evan, he sighed deeply. "They only did what they had to do," he said of Evan's death.

"I know that," Noletta said, "but it still upsets me. And I wonder when someone else will try to kill Martin. He hasn't done anything wrong, Creed. All he's trying to do is help me."

"He's a cop, love," Creed said as he reached across the table and ran a finger down her cheek. "Some people hate cops. It's not your fault. Detective Atkinson chose his profession, knowing he was putting his life in jeopardy."

Noletta found little solace in that, but the feel of Creed's hand against her cheek, then covering her own hand, did provide comfort.

After finishing a piece of cheesecake for dessert, they left the restaurant. "Let's take a walk around the block," Creed suggested. "The fresh air would do you good, and I'm not ready to take you home yet."

Noletta readily agreed. They strolled slowly, and she depended entirely on Creed, giving no thought to where they were going. It felt good. She soon realized that it was more than a walk around the block they were taking, but she said nothing. Finally Creed said, "It feels so good being with you, Noletta." A gentle pressure on her arm brought her to a standstill, and instinctively she turned toward him, her face upturned.

His lips met hers, and she responded, hoping no one was watching. It wasn't a long kiss, but it definitely wasn't a brotherly one either. When Creed pulled away, he said, "Noletta, come with me to Los Angeles. You'll be safe there. I'll take care of you, I promise."

Caught off guard, she stammered, "But Creed, I can't. I have law school."

"And you have constant danger threatening your life," he countered. "Please, I can't stand the thought of something happening to you. I realize we've known each other for just a few days, but I love you, Noletta. I want to be with you."

"Whoa," she said. "I need some time to think." His suggestion had clearly confused her, but as the two of them stood there, leaning easily into one another, his idea began to make some sense. She was so afraid for herself and her friends. Maybe moving would ease things for them. Then she thought of Walton and felt herself give a little jump. She needed Walton.

"Noletta, what is it?" Creed asked as he held her even tighter.

"What about Walton?" she asked, feeling stupid and instantly wishing she hadn't mentioned his name. She hadn't thought of him for more than an hour.

"What about him?" Creed asked with a laugh. "He doesn't care about you."

"But he does," Noletta protested as she pulled back from Creed's embrace.

"Not in the way I do. He cares about you only as a friend," Creed said. "Think about it, Noletta. He's like a brother to you, not a boyfriend. He's leading you on. Please, come with me. You'll never regret it."

"Can I think about it?" she asked, even as she continued to think about Walton. She'd come closer to loving him than any other man . . . until now. Not that she loved Creed, but she was beginning to have strong feelings for him. She felt happy with him, and safe.

"I'm leaving Monday. You have until then to decide, my love," Creed said.

CHAPTER 18

Noletta was restless, tossing and turning in bed that night. The more she thought about Creed's offer, the more she tossed. She liked Creed. He was easy to be with. But to move to L.A. to be near him was a huge step. For one thing, it would be almost akin to accepting a marriage proposal from him, and she was a long way from that point. She didn't know him that well. In fact, she barely knew him. He was nice. She'd enjoyed the time she'd been with him. But what he wanted seemed more impossible to her the longer she thought about it.

She had worked hard to be where she was now in law school. She couldn't just walk away from that. And there was Walton. Her friendship with him would be hurt badly, if not totally destroyed, if she accepted Creed's offer.

She sat up as the deep sound of another voice entered her mind. *What would Martin think?* she wondered. *Does that even matter?* For a reason she couldn't quite define, she felt that it did. She honestly cared about what he thought. And despite both Walton's and Creed's misgivings, she believed Martin was doing everything possible to help her. He'd even risked his life for her, or at least he'd risked it while trying to solve the crimes that had been committed against her. Accepting Creed's offer felt like a betrayal of Detective Atkinson. But it shouldn't. It was her life, she kept telling herself. And if long-term happiness for her was with Creed, then that was what she should care about, and only that.

Noletta slipped from her bed and made her way to the kitchen, where she poured herself a glass of milk and sat at the table to drink it. A soft patter of slippered feet a minute later told her she wasn't alone. "Are you having as difficult a time sleeping as I am?" Terri asked.

Noletta smiled in the direction of her friend's voice. "I'm wide awake," she admitted.

"Do you need to talk?" Terri asked.

"Actually, I'd like that," Noletta said.

"I'll make you a deal then. I'll listen to you if you'll listen to me," Terri said as she also stepped to the refrigerator. "Because I need a listening ear, too, and it's not something I can talk about with my daughter."

"Okay, it's a deal. Who goes first?"

"Will you?" Terri asked.

Noletta told Terri of her dilemma, of Creed's offer, which sounded very much like the precursor to a marriage proposal. Terri listened intently. "Sounds like you aren't ready to make the kind of commitment to Creed that he wants from you."

"Please don't get me wrong. I like Creed a lot. And there are things that make it an attractive idea," Noletta admitted. "But I've thought it over for several hours now. I can only think of two good reasons why I should go with him."

"And those reasons are?"

"First, I'd very likely be safer. And second, so would my family and friends, including Detective Atkinson and you and Harmony."

"Okay. That may be true, but what are the reasons you've found why you shouldn't go?"

"My father is ill, for one thing. And there's law school. I've worked so hard . . . I can hardly bear to think of just leaving it all now. Then there's Walton. And those are just the main reasons I think I should stay. There are others."

"Those are good reasons. At least the first two are," Terri said.

"What do you mean?" Noletta asked.

"Let me ask you a question," Terri suggested. "Are you in love with Walton?"

Noletta thought about that question for a long moment. "I've almost been, at times. But right now, I'm really not sure of myself with him."

"If he came to you later today and took you in his arms and told you he loved you, would that make a difference in what you're feeling?"

Noletta answered that very quickly. "Of course it would. I've wanted to hear him say something like that for a long time."

"So you do care for him more than just as a good friend?" Terri asked.

"Yes, I do," Noletta admitted.

"Now, what about Creed?"

"He's been really nice to me. Actually, he's been nicer to me lately than Walton has."

"So, what if Creed took you in his arms and told you he loved you? How would you feel?" Terri asked.

"He did that tonight," Noletta said.

"Really!? And did you feel something special?"

"Sort of, but I don't really know Creed. I think I'd like to get to know him better. But I'm not in love with him."

"Sounds to me like Walton still has the upper hand," Terri said. "Am I right?"

"Yes," Noletta admitted.

"Then what are you going to do?" Terri asked pointedly.

"I guess I'll stay here and pray that things work out in whatever way is best," Noletta said. And she realized as she said it that going with Creed, at least at this point in their relationship, didn't make much sense. She didn't see how she could seriously consider it.

"Okay, then you go after Walton. Find out how he feels. And let him know how you feel," Terri counseled.

Noletta slowly nodded her head. Then she said, "But I don't want to write off Creed completely. I'd like to get to know him better."

"Then write to him after he goes back to California, talk to him on the phone, but don't give up on Walton."

"Thanks, Terri. I hear you. And I appreciate the advice. Now it's your turn to talk and my turn to listen. What's keeping you awake tonight?"

"Martin," she said flatly. "I think I might be falling for him."

"Is there something wrong with that?" Noletta asked even as the sound of his deep voice and the touch of his rough hands came clearly into her mind.

"There could be," Terri responded. "I loved Lamar a lot. I still do. And even though he wasn't living the way he'd been living before we were married, I still loved him. He was good and gentle to me."

"What was he doing that was different than before you were married?" Noletta asked, hoping she wasn't prying where she shouldn't be.

"We were married in the temple. And it was the greatest experience of my life. But less than a year after our wedding, he quit going to church. He didn't start smoking or drinking or anything like that, but he quit going to church, and he quit paying tithing. He'd never tell me why, and I think that maybe in time, he would have changed back. I always hoped and prayed for that. I think Harmony would have helped him change even if I couldn't. But anyway, I loved him deeply. And when he was murdered, I didn't know if I could go on living. It was horrible."

"I'm sure it was," Noletta said sympathetically.

"And that brings me to Martin. I don't know if I could go through something like that again. The close calls he's had this week are almost more than I can bear, and I'm not even sure yet how I feel about him."

"You must feel something pretty deeply."

"Maybe I do, but I keep telling myself I shouldn't let myself fall in love again. That way I can't be hurt like I was before."

"You deserve some happiness, Terri," Noletta said. "You've got to go on with your life, and loving someone could be part of that if you'll let it be. And I think Martin is a great guy."

"So do I, but I'm so afraid," Terri admitted. "I'm terrified."

"Is it partly because the man who murdered your husband has never been caught?" Noletta asked shrewdly.

"Probably. I know he's out there somewhere, and I hate that thought. But it's also because Martin's a cop. He has to deal with guys like that all the time. That's what frightens me the most, Noletta. So many people hate law enforcement officers, especially good ones like Martin. It's awful just to think about."

* * *

It took until noon on Saturday, but Martin and Maddie finally learned who Skip was. His name was Hugh Rushton, and he had a criminal record—auto theft, burglary, shoplifting, scams, and more to boot. By early afternoon they'd traced him through credit card transactions to Denver and on to Albuquerque. The trail ended there.

They were also able to learn a great deal more about Virgil Weaver after many phone calls and personal contacts. "My guess is that Virgil is the driving force behind the threesome's criminal activities," Martin suggested to his partner. "And I also suspect that Hugh Rushton, alias Skip, has Taffy with him, possibly in New Mexico."

"Unless he sold her somewhere along the way," Maddie suggested.

They had enough to convince a deputy district attorney to seek a warrant for Skip for the assault on Martin, but not for taking the dog. They had nothing they could bring against Virgil Weaver.

"That frustrates me," Martin told Maddie. "I just can't help but think that Weaver is not only a dog thief and burglar, but I would guess that he could be the person who shot Noletta and killed Lamar Kayser."

"And if it's not the same man?" Maddie asked.

"Then I'm wrong in my guess. However, if it's not Virgil, I wonder if it could be Skip or Evan. I'm thinking it must be one of those three."

"So what do we do now?" Maddie asked.

"First, as soon as the D.A.'s office has the warrant on Skip, we'll fax it to Albuquerque," Martin replied. "Then I think we should contact the sheriff up in Summit County. It may be a long shot, but I think he might want to look at his case again with the theory that Virgil Weaver or one of his pals is Lamar Kayser's killer."

* * *

Fiona caught her breath in disbelief when she saw Scully pull up outside their home that evening with a dog in the back of the truck. *Surely that isn't really a guide dog,* she thought. She resisted the urge to run out and meet Scully before he brought the dog into the house.

"Ritchie," Scully called out the moment the door opened, "come meet your new dog."

When Ritchie didn't immediately respond, Scully turned to Fiona, who was staring at the big German shepherd. It was a beautiful animal. "Where's Ritchie?" Scully demanded.

"Scully, is that really a trained guide dog?" she asked.

"You have no faith in me, do you?" he said with a laugh. "Of course it is. I told you I'd get Ritchie a dog, and I got him one. Now where is that boy?"

"I'll get him. He may be asleep in his room," she said.

Ritchie, very much awake, was trembling when Fiona entered his bedroom. "Does Dad really have a dog?" he asked.

"Ritchie," Fiona said, taking her little boy into her arms and hugging him fiercely, "don't get your hopes up. He has a dog, but it might not be trained."

"What if it is?" Ritchie asked, the hope in his voice almost breaking her heart.

"We can hope, I guess, but even if it's not, I'll bet you and that dog can become friends. Let's go in the living room and see what happens," she said, anger already building at Scully just in case he was lying about the dog's credentials.

"Hi, buddy," Scully greeted Ritchie. "Come over here and meet Taffy. She's your new dog. And she's a good one."

Ritchie held out his little hands. They were still trembling. Fiona watched as the dog her husband had just called Taffy turned her face toward the boy. Her tail began to wag, and she touched one of his hands with her wet black nose. Fiona hardly dared to breathe. Scully didn't say anything, but he pressed the blue nylon leash into Ritchie's hand. The leash was attached to a matching harness that went around the dog's front shoulders and her chest. "Here, take this," he said. "I don't think she likes me."

Ritchie took the leash, gripping it tightly, but his other hand had gone from the dog's nose to her head, and he was petting her with light, gentle strokes. Taffy stood quietly as the boy continued to explore with his hand, moving it down her neck and to her back. Finally, in a voice filled with emotion, he said, "Taffy."

Taffy wagged her tail again and turned her face until her black eyes were looking directly into Ritchie's face. "Tell her to take you somewhere," Scully suggested.

Fiona could scarcely believe her eyes when Taffy responded to Ritchie's soft voice. "Let's go outside, Taffy."

The dog took the slack from the leash, and then, as soon as Ritchie took a tentative step forward, she began to walk toward the open doorway. Ritchie followed for a moment, but when he stopped and the leash drew tight, Taffy stopped as well. "Go, Taffy," he said as he stepped beside his new dog. She responded instantly. And in a minute, she'd led Ritchie through the door and into the cluttered yard.

For the first time in years, Fiona felt a rush of warmth toward her husband. She put an arm around him and said softly, "Thank you, dear."

But he pulled away from her without a word and followed Ritchie and Taffy as they circled all the way around the house and back into the front yard again. Fiona was fascinated, but she also knew that she had to find someone who could help Ritchie. It was obvious that the dog knew what to do, but Ritchie would need training before he could give her meaningful commands.

After about ten minutes, Scully called Ritchie and Taffy back to the house. "See," he gloated to Fiona, "I told you I'd get him a dog."

"Thanks, Scully," she said, her full heart almost to bursting. "That's the nicest thing you ever did. But I still don't see how we can afford her. Dogs like this must cost thousands of dollars."

"I make good money. I told you, I'll be doing some extra work for my boss. He paid for her, and when I finish what he wants me to do, she'll be all ours," he said.

"Will there be enough money to have someone work with Ritchie and the dog? I can see that she knows what to do, but Ritchie needs some help," she suggested.

Scully's good humor soured, and an ugly expression covered his face. "Don't even think about asking anybody for help. The boy will just have to learn on his own. Is that clear?" he demanded as his fist clenched threateningly.

It was clear, all right. "Maybe we can help Ritchie learn," Fiona dared to suggest.

"If you want somebody to help Ritchie, you'll have to do it. I got the dog. It's your job to make sure he learns how to work with her," Scully said sullenly. "Anyway, I've got to get going now. My boss expects me back at six. And I'll be gone for a few days."

He left without so much as a good-bye to either his wife or his son. Fiona was glad when his vehicle pulled away. It would give her and her son a chance to become acquainted with Taffy.

* * *

Harmony squealed and ran out the door when she saw Martin's car pull up outside. "Hi," he said. "Have you had a good day?"

"I've had a great day. I've been helping Grandpa Fahr, and he says he's feeling better," she said as she threw her arms around Martin and hugged him.

"Grandpa Fahr?" he asked, lifting an eyebrow and grinning.

"Yes. Noletta's dad said I have to call him Grandpa. He's a really nice grandpa too," she said. Then, typical for her age, she instantly changed the subject. "Have you found Taffy yet?"

"Detective Reed and I are working on it."

"When do I get to meet Detective Reed, Martin? My mom says she's really pretty."

"She's gone home for the night. We've worked hard today. One of these days you'll get to meet her," Martin promised. "And yes, she is pretty, but not as pretty as you."

"Or my Mom?" Harmony asked, suddenly very serious.

"You and your mother are beautiful," Martin said seriously. "Is your mother here?"

"She is, and she just brushed her hair. I think she likes you a lot."

Martin laughed and followed Harmony into the house, but it wasn't Terri whom he saw first. It was Noletta, and she was smiling, her face turned in his direction. He was struck once again at what a lovely, poised woman she was.

"Hello, Martin," she said. "How are you coming along on the case?"

She sounded very formal, despite the smile, and he wondered why. "We're making progress, thanks to you," he said.

"What kind of progress?"

"We've identified Skip. He's a petty crook whose real name is Hugh Rushton. And we've traced him from Salt Lake to Denver and on to Albuquerque, New Mexico," he said as Harmony left the room.

"I've never heard that name before," Noletta said.

Martin moved toward her and stopped when he was only a couple of feet away. "He's definitely a player in all of this, but Virgil Weaver is the one behind Taffy's disappearance, if I'm not mistaken. But I suspect Taffy was taken to New Mexico by Skip. We have officers down there looking for him. So, how are you holding up?" he asked.

"I'm fine, I guess. I'm just sorry my problems are causing so many other people so much trouble," she said.

"You are not the cause of anyone's troubles," Terri said as she came into the room, followed by Harmony.

"Terri's right," Martin said, and then he turned toward her. She approached him slowly, gently tossing her long red hair over her shoulder while holding her eyes on his. He held out his arms, and she stepped into his embrace. "And how are you doing, Terri?" he asked.

"I'm okay," she said.

Martin looked deep into her eyes for a moment and then pulled her close and kissed her cheek. "You're looking good," he said awkwardly.

For the next few minutes, they all chatted together. Finally, Noletta mentioned that Creed was coming to pick her up. When she mentioned that, Martin noted how happy she looked, and he supposed the radiance was for Creed. He turned to Terri. "I could use a little company tonight. Are you and Harmony free?"

They were, and he outlined a plan for the three of them.

He left before Creed arrived, wondering if Walton's cousin was squeezing Walton out. Although he wasn't terribly fond of either man, right now Creed was the better of the two in his estimation.

CHAPTER 19

Creed had been in a jovial mood since the moment he'd picked Noletta up, but that mood soured when Noletta told him there was no way she could leave school and go to California with him—that she had invested too much time, money, and effort to give it all up now.

"But you're not safe in Utah," he pleaded. "You know all that's been happening. You need to get away from here. Your life may depend on it. Anyway, I want you to come with me. I need you, Noletta."

"I can't leave law school," she told him again. "I just can't."

"This isn't about law school," Creed said sadly as he laid his fork down on the table in the small restaurant where they were eating. "I think it's about my cousin Walton."

"No, it's not about Walton. But he is a good friend. And he helps me a lot in school. But that's as far as it goes," she said, wondering if it might be as far as it would ever go. "Please, Creed, don't be angry. You and I can talk on the phone every day, and I'll let you know everything that's happening. I honestly don't think my life's in as much danger as you seem to think. But if things do get too bad here, then I might come down there for a while."

His mood lifted at that, and she heard him begin to eat again. "So how is your detective friend coming on the case? I assume he's as stumped as ever," he said a minute later.

"Actually, he and his new partner are making good progress," she said. "They believe that Taffy was taken to New Mexico, and they know that a guy by the name of Hugh Rushton went there from here by way of Denver. They think he has Taffy with him."

"Really!?" Creed said, sounding very much surprised. "But how do they know that this Rushton guy, whoever he is, had anything to do with your dog?"

"Skip, that's the guy's nickname, left his fingerprints in that warehouse where Martin was shot," she said. "So did Evan, the guy that died," she told him.

"I guess that cop friend of yours is smarter than I give him credit for," Creed said grudgingly. "So they think that Skip and Evan took your dog?"

"Yes, along with a guy named Virgil Weaver," she said.

"So there's a third guy too?"

"That's what the detectives think."

"Do they know where he is?" Creed asked. "I mean this Weaver guy?"

Noletta shook her head. "Detective Atkinson's got a warrant out on Skip, and he's faxed it to the authorities in New Mexico. He plans to go down there and question him as soon as they find him."

"If they find him," Creed said. "I'd be surprised if he stays anywhere for very long. I'm sure they don't know what he's driving, so how do they go about looking for him?"

"I don't know," she admitted. She wanted to get off the subject. "You will keep in touch with me after you go back to L.A., won't you, Creed?"

"Of course I will. Remember, I love you, Noletta. I'm not going to let you get away from me. And I'm pretty sure that in time you'll come to love me too. That's what I pray for every day." He touched her cheek lightly as he spoke. They were both silent for a moment, and she was thinking about his recurring statements of love for her. He really meant it. She was almost certain of that now. So why didn't she have those same feelings for him even though she found herself attracted to him? She reasoned that maybe time would bring that about, just as he had suggested.

He took hold of her hand. "Are you sure you can't come with me? Nothing in this world would make me happier. I'd help you find a place to live near me, and I'm sure we can find a law school that will admit you. Please come, Noletta."

"I can't, Creed."

"Well, I guess in that case, as much as I hate to, I've got to do what my boss asked me to do earlier today."

"What's that?"

"He wants me back there Monday morning in time to work. That's a day earlier than his last change, and I told him I might not be able to, but I didn't tell him it was because I was hoping you'd be coming with me. I knew you'd need time to arrange things. But I guess I'd better call him and tell him I can make it after all. I really don't want to jeopardize my job."

"You can come to church with me tomorrow before you leave, can't you?" Noletta asked.

"It will depend on what time your meetings start. I'll need to get back tomorrow night," he said. "What time did you say they were held?"

"I'm on the late schedule," she said. "We start at one o'clock in the afternoon."

"I'm afraid not," he said. "I'll have to be on my way long before that. It's a long drive, and if I get back too late, I'll be exhausted Monday morning. But I'll come up for the weekend in a few weeks—maybe hop a plane—and then we can be together."

"That would be great," Noletta said. "I'll look forward to it. But I wish you didn't have to leave so soon."

"I do too, but—well, you know why," he said. "Are you up for another walk?"

"Sure. I'd like that," she responded as she reached for his hand.

Noletta was more confused and unsure of her feelings when she walked into her bedroom later that evening. She felt a distinct loss, knowing that Creed was going back to Los Angeles so soon. But she also felt hopeful that she might see more of Walton now and thus be able to sort out her feelings. Even though she enjoyed the time she'd spent with Creed, she still felt something for Walton and didn't want to discard it.

When she heard Terri and Harmony come in as she was turning down her bed, she decided to see what kind of night they'd had. Or maybe what she really needed right now was to talk to a good friend.

"Hi, Noletta," Harmony said, and the little girl's feet moved quickly across the floor. In a moment Noletta was being hugged around the waist. "Did you have fun tonight?" she asked as she shook her fiery hair from her eyes.

"Actually," Noletta said as she thought about her evening with Creed, "it could have been better."

"Why's that?" Terri asked. "Didn't he take your decision to stay here very well?"

"He was actually pretty good about that," she said. "But he's leaving for L.A. tomorrow morning. And you know what? I'm going to miss him."

"Why's he doing that?" Terri asked. "I thought he was going back sometime Monday."

"That was his plan, but he says his boss called and wants him back to work Monday morning."

"Okay, so while you're missing him, you can see more of Walton," Terri suggested brightly. "Isn't that what you wanted to do?"

"Yes, that's true. I just wish I knew how I felt about both of them. Right now I'm really confused."

Terri turned to Harmony. "Why don't you go get ready for bed," she said, "while Noletta and I have a *grown-up girl* talk."

The two women were far from being through talking when Harmony returned a few minutes later. "My teeth are brushed, and I have my nightgown on," she announced.

"Then I'll help you with your prayers and tuck you into bed," Terri said firmly. "If you'll excuse us for a little bit, Noletta."

"Of course."

When Terri returned, Noletta explained how torn she was between Walton and Creed.

"Do you think you're falling in love with either one of them?" Terri asked bluntly.

"Like I told you before, I like them both a lot," Noletta hedged. "I've thought at times that I was in love with Walton, but I'm not. It would be more accurate to say I'm fond of him. But I'm also fond of Creed. I just don't know him as well as I do Walton."

The two were silent for a moment. Noletta wished she could see her friend's face to read her expressions. That, she'd found, was one of the truly exasperating things about her blindness. That rather effective method of communication had been taken from her.

Finally, Terri spoke again, and although Noletta couldn't see her expression, she could tell a lot from the tone of her voice. Terri was serious. "Think hard about what I'm going to say, Noletta." Noletta did pay close attention as Terri went on. "I told you before that I thought you should tell Walton how you felt and see if he'd open up to you. But now I don't know if that's such good advice. Maybe neither one of them is right for you, Noletta."

Noletta tried to keep her disappointment from her face as she felt the impact of Terri's words. She knew that Terri might be right. She spoke slowly, trying to keep her voice from showing the sudden sadness she felt. "You're probably right, Terri. There may be no one for me, but that would be better than marrying someone I didn't truly love and who couldn't fully understand me and what I'm going through. I don't want my blindness to be a handicap for someone else." Even as she said that, Noletta wondered if her blindness had already become a handicap for Walton, and if he was privately struggling with it.

"Oh, there'll be someone," Terri consoled. "I'm the one who might never find another husband."

"But I think you already have," Noletta said quickly. "Don't you even *think* about letting Martin get away from you. He's genuine. He's a really good man, and he'd make you a great husband and Harmony a great father."

"I agree that Martin is a tremendous guy. And I like him a lot," Terri said.

"You told me that you thought you were falling for him. Think about it, Terri, and tell me, and yourself, the answer to this question. Do you love him, Terri?"

"I barely know him. But I am attracted to him. He's so easy to be with, he's caring, intelligent, and a very good man, but . . ." she drifted off.

"Terri," Noletta began, "you need to give yourself some time. I think you'll find that you will fall in love with him. And I also think he'll fall in love with you."

"To be totally honest, I'm not at all sure about that," Terri said, and there was a sadness in her voice now. "Tonight, when we were together, it was fun, and he absolutely doted on Harmony."

"Like I said, he would make a great father for her."

"That's true. He would. But to finish my thought," Terri said, "I felt something disconnect between me and him."

Noletta said nothing. She was stunned. She didn't know what to say. She'd convinced herself that Terri and Martin were perfect for each other.

Terri went on. "It's partly my fault, because I'm so afraid of falling for someone who's in a dangerous profession. I know that things can happen to anyone, but I don't think I could be married to a law enforcement officer because of what I went through after Lamar was shot and killed. Even though he had his failings, I loved him. I still miss him. I know I can love again, but I don't think I could marry a policeman. His life would always be on the line."

"Hey, there are lots of dangerous professions," Noletta said. "You would just have to trust his life to the Lord."

"I know that, but even then, I'd worry constantly. I just know I would, and that would make my life miserable—and his too. But that's not the only problem for Martin and me," she said, her voice fading until it was difficult for Noletta to hear her.

"What's that?" Noletta asked.

Terri's voice was marginally louder when she spoke again. "I get the feeling when we're together that his mind is on someone else. I think he cares deeply for someone, and maybe he even denies it to himself," Terri said.

For a moment, Noletta's heart beat a little faster. But she quickly thrust unwanted thoughts from her mind. "Who? You don't mean his new partner, Madison, do you?"

"That would be conceivable, because Maddie is not only pretty, but she's smart and seems like a really nice person. But no, it's not her."

"Do you have any idea who?" Noletta asked, wondering at how badly she wanted to hear the answer to that question and yet not wanting to hear it at the same time.

"I don't know who," Terri said evasively. "But I have a question for you."

"Oh, and what's that?" Noletta asked.

"Why do you still call him Detective Atkinson sometimes?"

"Because that's who he is."

"No, I mean, why don't you call him Martin more often? You did for a while, you know."

Noletta felt her face redden, and she hoped Terri didn't notice. She had to admit to herself that her answer was lame. "We have a professional relationship. He's a detective, and I'm the victim of the crime he's investigating."

"So am I," Terri said, "because he's become very interested in finding out who killed my husband. But I still call him by his first name."

"I guess that's your choice," Noletta said, forcing a smile.

"I guess so," Terri agreed with a laugh. "Hey, it's getting late. We both should go to bed."

Noletta was glad she'd talked with Terri, although their conversation hadn't taken the direction she'd expected. But she was also relieved that Terri didn't want to talk more, because the last few minutes had brought feelings to the surface that had been deep inside her heart. And she needed the quiet of her bedroom to put them firmly back in their place again. *It is true,* she told herself sternly, *that my relationship with Martin is purely a professional one. And that is how it must stay.*

* * *

The bed creaked as Martin rolled from side to side. His bed had made noises for months now, but tonight he was more active than usual. Part of it had to do with worry over what had become a very complicated case. And partly it had to do with his sore shoulder and back. Then there was the threat to his life. For all he knew, someone could be outside right now, preparing to enter his home and take him out of the picture. He felt his gun where it lay beside his pillow and was slightly reassured.

Even with that assurance, he still tossed and turned. He finally admitted that his disquiet was caused by something more. He was attracted to the victim in the case he was working, and he knew that he shouldn't allow that to happen.

For one thing, she had two boyfriends. He didn't particularly care for either one of them, but that didn't mean that Noletta shouldn't be allowed to like them.

Martin had to admit that he was attracted to Terri, but it didn't have the same intensity as his attraction to Noletta. He'd kept those feelings he had for Noletta hidden, even from himself—until tonight, that is. When he was talking to Terri, he kept finding his thoughts drifting to Noletta. He felt guilty about that even as it happened, but he hadn't been able to stop it at the time, and even now, his thoughts kept searching for her.

It might have been easier if it wasn't for some things Terri had said. She hadn't come right out and been clear about her thoughts, and that might have been because Harmony was with them. However, he had gathered from her conversation that she never wanted to go through what she'd experienced after her husband was killed. And it was also fairly clear to him that she thought being a police officer was a very dangerous job. The lingering pain in his shoulder and back made it hard for him to argue that point.

He'd concluded that she was trying to tell him, without hurting his feelings, that they should back off from their budding relationship. As he lay in bed worrying, he decided that he would do that. Right now he needed to concentrate on the case he was working. Noletta needed her dog back, and if in the process he could somehow find out who shot Terri's husband and her, it would be so much the better.

With sleep eluding him, Martin got up and went into his kitchen, where he drank a glass of cold water. Then he looked out each of his windows in turn. He took a double take when he saw a car pass by with what looked like a large, bald man driving it. From the light of the closest streetlight, Martin was almost certain the man had a cell phone to his ear. For a moment he thought about giving chase, but by the time he got dressed, he knew the car would be hard to find. The best thing to do, he decided, was to wait and see if it came by again. If it did, then he would call for backup and see if he could make an arrest, because at that point, he was convinced that he would find the same man who had broken into Noletta's house. Right now, having not seen the man clearly, he couldn't be sure it was his suspect.

Martin pulled on his clothes, and then, for the next hour, he intermittently watched for the car to come by again while he placed pans and pots and other household items at each door and window—his makeshift burglar alarm. If someone came in, he wanted to have enough warning so that he could at least defend himself. When his preparations were finished, he hadn't seen the bald man again. Feeling somewhat reassured, he finally made himself lie on his bed again, fully clothed.

* * *

"Hey man, what do you think you're doing calling at this time of night?" Skip asked angrily. He was not only sleepy, but drunk.

"Shut up and listen," Virgil growled. "Get yourself out of bed, and head back up here."

"Tonight?" Skip asked.

"Yes, tonight. You got a problem with that?"

"Yeah, I'm tired, and I've had quite a bit to drink. I don't know if I can drive without falling asleep."

"Wake yourself up. Lose the van. Lose it fast, but lose it good. Catch a bus, and get on your way. You can sleep on the bus. Call me when you get here," Virgil ordered. "Things have changed."

Skip groaned after closing his cell phone. But he did as he was told. He almost always did as he was told. He was afraid of Virgil, but he was even more afraid of the boss, the man who gave Virgil his orders. He left the motel without paying. He didn't care. He'd registered under a false name anyway. And the van didn't matter. Even if they'd taken his plate number, they would only discover that the plates were stolen. And the van itself was about to get dumped.

* * *

There were no phone calls during the night, although Martin had hoped to receive a call informing him that Hugh Rushton, better known as Skip, was in custody in New Mexico. If that call had come, he'd have headed for New Mexico to question the man. But it hadn't, and no one had broken into his house during the night after he'd finally fallen asleep.

He took a shower, washed the grit from his eyes, and tried to banish the fatigue from his body as he got ready for church. He looked forward to his meetings today. He needed a spiritual break from the pressures of his job.

* * *

Creed called Noletta at six that evening. She hadn't heard from Walton at all, and she felt somewhat slighted, wondering why he was ignoring her. Creed told her that he was just going through Baker, California, and he asked her how she was doing.

"I'm doing okay," she said.

"How was church?" he asked.

"It was good. My bishop spoke, and it seemed at times like he was talking straight to me."

Noletta expected Creed to ask what the bishop talked about, but instead, he said, "I had to miss church today. I feel guilty, but I had to get started back to L.A. But next Sunday I'll be in my own ward, and I'll learn what the bishop wants to see me about."

"Have you had good weather?" Noletta asked, disappointed that the conversation was so humdrum and that Creed apparently didn't want to hear more about her meetings.

"Excellent," he said. "I've made good time. But I sure miss you. I wish you were with me."

"I'm glad you're thinking about me," she said and then wondered why she'd said that. She wasn't sure that she was glad he was thinking about her. She was afraid of where this relationship would go. Maybe it would be better for both of them if he didn't call again.

"I just wanted to see how you were doing. If it's not too late when I get home, I'll call you then," he said.

After hanging up, she had another call. She hoped it was Walton. She needed to talk to him, to be reassured that he was still her friend. But it wasn't his voice she heard. The deep voice that greeted her gave new life to her suppressed feelings. She tried unsuccessfully to shove them back where she didn't have to acknowledge them.

"Hello, Martin," she said, deciding to drop her earlier pretenses. "Has something happened? Have they caught Skip?"

"Not yet. I was just calling to see if you're all right."

"Of course I'm all right."

"Good. I just needed to be sure."

He sounded so sincere, but she worried that there was some other danger out there that she should know about. "Thanks for calling," she said awkwardly as she tried to slow down her heart rate. Despite herself, she wanted very much to be in his presence. Suddenly she found herself saying, "We were all going to eat at six-thirty. Why don't you join us?"

"Sounds good," he said cheerfully. "See you in a little bit."

"Who was that?" Terri asked. She had entered the living room a moment before the call was ended.

"Martin."

"Oh, and you invited him for dinner. That's nice," Terri said with what Noletta could only interpret as a mischief in her voice. She wished again that she could see her face.

"Just before he called, Creed called. He's just passing through Baker," Noletta said.

"I see. What did Martin call about?" Terri asked.

"He was just checking to see if I'm okay. But that worries me. Is there some other threat that I don't know about?" she asked.

The grin was gone from Terri's voice when she spoke again. "I hope not. But if there is, surely he'll say so when he comes. Relax, Noletta. I'm going to see if I can help your mother."

* * *

Scully had his assignment, and it made him break out in a cold sweat. "This could be risky," he said to his boss.

"That dog cost me a bundle, Scully," he was told. "And this is how you're gonna pay me for it. Keep your wits about you, keep your eyes open, and don't let them frighten you. Just complete the deal, and the dog is paid for. Screw it up, and I'll take the dog back from that kid of yours so fast your head will rotate full circle. You got that?"

Scully swallowed hard, nodded, and took a long drink from the glass he was holding. His hands were shaking, and the glass almost slipped when he put it back on the table. To steady himself, he put his hand inside the new jacket he was wearing and felt the cool steel that was concealed there. The boss had told him the gun was his to keep, unless he had to use it. In that case, he was to get rid of it where it would never be found.

He felt the pistol's grip in his hand, and he was slightly reassured about the trip he was about to make into Mexico. He could do it. There was no way he would fail. He didn't want to have to listen to Fiona if the boss took the dog back. She'd never let him live it down, and he couldn't—wouldn't—stand for that.

* * *

When the phone rang again, just a few minutes before dinner was to begin, it was Walton who was calling. Noletta tried to be happy that he was finally calling, but she felt awkward as she spoke with him. Finally, he asked, "Are you okay, Noletta?"

"I'm fine."

"You don't sound fine."

"Well, I'm worried, of course," she admitted. "I just wish this whole nightmare would end. And I wish they'd find the man who shot me."

"A lot of time has passed," Walton reminded her. "It might not be possible now."

"I know that, but it still haunts me that he's out there somewhere. And I know it would help Terri to know that the guy who killed her husband is no longer running loose," she said.

There was silence on the line for a moment before Walton spoke again. "I have an idea, Noletta. I know it's a long shot, but who knows—maybe it'll help. I don't want you to get your hopes up, though, because it may not work."

"What's that?" she asked, hoping he had a good idea, not just some half-baked proposal he thought might make her feel better.

"You and I both paint and draw. I know I'm not as good a painter as you are, but I do a good job with pencil sketches."

"I know you do," she said, wondering what he might be leading up to. "In fact, you're really good."

"Thanks. But anyway, I just wondered if you might be willing to try to help me make a sketch of the guy who shot you? You could describe what you saw, and I could try to sketch it," he said.

"But I didn't see much. The sun was in my eyes, and there were branches covering his face," she protested, disappointed at his idea. She didn't see how it could possibly help.

"Noletta, I think we should try," he said, sounding hopeful. "I spent all day yesterday and all afternoon today reading up on the way that police artists work. And I've also studied how a computer can be used to enhance a drawing. I even bought a program to help with that. Please, let's at least give it a try. It can't hurt, and it just might help."

She thought about it for a minute. "Okay, I guess we can try. I don't doubt your ability; it's me that I doubt. I just don't remember much and couldn't see him well."

"Can I come over tonight and pick you up?" he asked. "I want to get started."

"Sure," she said. "What time? We're having dinner in just a few minutes. In fact, why don't you join us?"

"I can't be there that soon. How about eight?"

"That would be fine," she said.

"Noletta, I want to get this thing over with as much as you do. It's tearing me up seeing you suffer so much," he said, and she was sure she heard his voice break as he spoke.

"Thanks, Walton," she said as a lump formed in her throat. "I'll see you at eight."

"I'll pick you up, and we'll work on this at my place because I don't want anyone else to know what we're doing, just in case it doesn't work. Is that all right?"

She agreed that it was. Then he said, "But honestly, I think this will help. I just feel really strongly about it. In fact, I already have everything set up for us to start."

After Walton hung up, Noletta sat and thought about what had just occurred. She didn't see how his idea could possibly help identify her assailant, but she was deeply touched by his concern for her and for his desire to help. She almost wished she hadn't invited Martin to dinner so as to not further confuse her feelings.

And yet, despite herself, she couldn't help feeling happy that he was coming.

CHAPTER 20

Dinner was enjoyable that Sunday evening. It had been a dazzling spring day, and as they ate, a comfortable breeze drifted through the kitchen window. Martin had found himself seated between Terri and Noletta, and across the table from Harmony, who seemed in an especially good mood. Noletta's father, Elliot, sat at the head of the table, nearest to Harmony, who kept watching him closely, almost possessively. Elliot seemed to be a different man. There was color in his face, he sat straight, and he smiled frequently. He appeared to be on the road to recovery.

Francine Fahr, Noletta's mother, was also cheerful—lifted in spirit, it seemed, by her husband's sudden turn toward improved health. Terri was relaxed and seemed more at ease with Martin than she had the previous evening. Their budding romance may have faded, but they both felt more comfortable with each other. Harmony seemed unaware of the change between her mother and Martin.

As for Martin, though his mind was full of worries, he found himself relaxing as they ate and talked and even joked around the friendly dinner table. Noletta was the only one who seemed tense. She was quieter than normal, and whenever Martin addressed her directly, she seemed to shrink a little. Finally he said to her, "Noletta, you look worried. Is there something we need to know about?"

"No," she said. "It's just that . . ." Her voice faded away.

"Just that what?" her mother asked.

Noletta smiled, although Martin thought it looked forced. Finally, she said, "Walton's coming over to pick me up at eight. He said he wants to see me."

Which he has every right to do, Martin told himself sternly. He forced himself to say, "I don't blame him, Noletta. After all, he's a good friend, and you've been going through a lot lately."

She nodded and responded in a soft voice, "Yes, he is."

"Dinner has been great," he said as he stood and prepared to leave. He didn't want to be there when Walton came.

"Thanks for coming, Detective," she said.

"Please, Noletta. As I've said many times, you can call me Martin," he requested. It just didn't feel right when she called him by his title. It seemed too formal.

Noletta nodded but said nothing.

Martin spoke to Harmony; his tone was serious, but his eyes twinkled and his mouth broke into a grin. "Harmony, don't you think *Miss Fahr* should call me Martin? All my best friends call me Martin, don't they?"

The little girl grinned. "Yes, Martin, we do," she responded.

Noletta's face suddenly blossomed with a large smile, a beautiful smile that seemed to fill the room. "I guess if Harmony can address you that way, then so can I. Martin it is."

* * *

Walton was in an exceptionally good mood when he picked Noletta up. She worried, as she had all through dinner, that she was going to fail him. But he was being so sweet about their project that she was determined to describe everything she could as precisely as possible. Then it would be up to him to sketch as well as he could.

They sat across a small table from each other, the drawing pad between them. "Okay," Walton said, "I'm ready if you are. Describe what you saw through the branches as completely as you can."

"All right," she said, and slowly she began.

For the next hour they worked. Walton said very little except to occasionally ask her to repeat herself on one point or another. He was even particular in asking her to describe the hat the killer had worn and also his jacket.

"Well, I guess that's it for now," he finally said.

"What do you think?" she asked.

"I don't know. I'll run you back to your folks' place. Then I'll come back and scan this into my computer and see what I come up with," he said.

"But have we done any good?" she asked tensely.

"It's too early to tell, Noletta, but I think we have. I just need to clean it up a little and let the computer add a few details. Then we'll see what we have."

Walton seemed taciturn as he drove her home, and even when he walked her to the door, he seemed to be deep in thought. Finally, unable to stand the suspense his reticence was causing, she asked, "Are you mad at me, Walton? I told you I couldn't remember much."

"Actually, you did very well. And no, I'm not mad, not at all. In fact, I'm very pleased."

"You mean it might actually work?" she asked hopefully.

"Yes," he said decisively. "I think it just might. I'll let you know more later." Then, to her surprise, he kissed her lightly before opening the door for her. She stepped into the house, and he said, "I'll see you tomorrow, Noletta. Thanks for helping me with this idea of mine. I wish we'd tried it a long time ago."

Terri came in just moments after the door closed behind her. "Creed would like to speak with you, Noletta," she said.

"He just barely called and asked to have you call back when you came in."

She nodded. "I'll go to my room and call him back," she said, wishing she didn't have to. She didn't feel much like talking to Creed right then.

* * *

Terri was surprised when the doorbell rang just moments after Noletta had disappeared to make her phone call. She opened it to find Martin standing there.

"Martin," she said in surprise, "it's late. Have you learned something more? Have they caught Skip?"

"No, I was just wondering if you have any idea why Noletta was so withdrawn at dinner. I've been worrying about it."

"So have I," Terri said. "Walton just brought her home."

"Is he here?" he asked.

"No, he left right away. Noletta's on the phone with Creed right now. Come in, Martin, and sit down."

He did as Terri asked. Then he said, "You know, Terri, I get the feeling she's really torn between those two guys, and frankly, I don't think either one of them is that good for her."

Terri grinned at him. "I agree with you."

"But it's none of my business. I just wanted to see if you knew what was bothering her, or if her folks did."

"I'm sorry. They've both gone to bed. I don't know for sure what's going on with Noletta. She was so secretive when she left with Walton. It seemed strange that he wanted to pick her up and take her to his place so late. I don't know what's up."

"Maybe he's afraid Creed is getting the upper hand on him," Martin suggested. "And I suspect that he is."

"Martin," Terri said, an unusual intensity in her voice, "there's something you need to know."

"Oh, what's that?" he asked.

"It's not either one of those guys she thinks of the most. It's you," she said bluntly.

"What are you talking about?" Martin asked.

Terri smiled. "You know very well what I'm talking about. I don't think she'll be on the phone long, and when she comes back in here, I'm going to disappear and let you spend some time with Noletta. She needs you."

"But, I . . . we . . ." he stammered.

Terri touched his arm again, looked deep into his eyes, and then spoke with a catch in her voice. "You're a great guy, Martin. But we both know that it would never work for us. Be good to her. She may not recognize it yet, but Noletta cares for you. Don't let Creed or Walton or anyone else come between the two of you."

He shook his head. "You're serious, aren't you?"

"Quite. And here she comes. I'll leave. Spend whatever time you need with her, even if it's already late."

* * *

Noletta couldn't quit thinking about the conversation she'd just had with Creed. He'd again expressed his love for her. But more than that, he'd practically demanded that she come to Los Angeles. "You're not safe up there," he'd insisted. "You've got to get away from Salt Lake. You can't trust the police, not even Martin. He'll let you get hurt. He's not the perfect cop he wants you to think he is. I'm afraid there's a side to him you haven't seen."

He'd gone on like that, repeating himself over and over, becoming more emotional as the minutes passed. She'd protested at first, but then she'd listened. Doubts about Martin's ability to keep her safe had begun to creep into her mind. She'd finally ended the phone call without promising him that she'd come, but with the assurance that she'd think seriously about it for the next day or two.

Now, as she realized Martin was there in the house with her, her mind became clouded with confusion. She wondered if she really did trust Martin too much. He certainly seemed sincere, but was he all that competent? Was he truly capable of keeping her safe and solving the crime, even though his intentions were nothing but good? And was there a side to him she hadn't noticed, that Terri hadn't noticed either? She also wondered if Creed wasn't being totally honest with her. She even suspected that Creed could somehow read her mind and had figured out that tender thoughts of Martin kept slipping in there, quietly crowding out both Creed and Walton. She honestly didn't know what to think at this point.

She smiled as she felt Martin step close to her. She tried to shrug off the mood of discontent that Creed's phone call had put her in. She didn't want Martin to sense how she was feeling.

"Are you all right?" Martin asked. "I was just driving through the area to make sure the officers assigned here were on the job and alert."

"Are they?"

"Yes, and they haven't seen anything suspicious."

"Good, and I'm fine."

"You don't look like you're fine, Noletta. Did something Creed say upset you?"

"Martin," she said more sharply than she'd intended, "let's not talk about Creed."

"Okay, that's fine with me. But you seemed so withdrawn at dinner. Is it something Walton said that—"

She cut him off. "It's nothing. But I appreciate your coming by to check."

She was thinking about what Creed had just said. And despite Creed's warning, she felt a stirring inside that made her heart flutter. Martin's distinctive cologne, his deep voice, and his concern seemed to have caused the stirring to intensify. Being alone with him felt right. Yes, it felt so good.

But then there were Creed's repeated cautions, and as they replayed rapidly in her mind, the stirring eased. Confusion set in again. She didn't know whom to trust. Then she suddenly felt that she needed to be honest with Martin. "Creed says not to trust you," she blurted.

"Oh he does, does he?" he said. "So do you or don't you?"

"Oh, Martin, I don't know what to think. I mostly trust you, but Creed has become a very good friend. I trust him too," she said.

"And do you trust Walton?"

"Of course."

"What does Walton do in the Church?" he asked, surprising her at the sudden turn his question took.

"He teaches in the elders quorum in his ward. Why do you ask that?"

"Just wondered. What about Creed?"

"He teaches Sunday school."

"I see."

Noletta was very puzzled at Martin's questions, and yet she felt comfortable in his presence, and safe. Still, Creed's warnings kept running through her mind. And she couldn't help thinking about how critical Walton had been of Martin. Maybe she should trust their instincts. She was so confused. But by the time Martin left a few minutes later, she was once again feeling that Martin was both competent and trustworthy. She was glad that he'd come and that the distrust was nearly gone now.

* * *

Martin couldn't quit thinking about Noletta as he drove home. He kept telling himself that Terri was wrong. *There is no way Noletta thinks about me in any way other than professionally.*

He pictured her face, and as he did, a feeling of warmth enveloped him. He tried to deny what he was feeling, but he could do it no longer. He'd never been attracted to anyone else the way he was attracted to Noletta Fahr. And it was far more than just her physical attractiveness. There was a depth to her that he hadn't found in others. Her genuine goodness was palpable. And she had a spiritual strength that simply drew him to her.

Martin was deep in thought and nearly back to his house when he was surprised by a call on his cell phone from Walton Pease. "I'm sorry to call you so late," Walton said, "but I have something you need to see."

"What's that?" Martin asked suspiciously. He'd gotten the feeling the first time he met Walton that the man didn't care for him, and with tender thoughts of Noletta still on his mind, he wasn't sure he even wanted to talk to Walton.

"It's about Noletta," Walton said.

As Walton said her name, Martin suddenly tensed. "Have you heard something about Taffy?" Martin asked, thinking that such a thing was hardly likely.

"Of course not, and I'm afraid you're wasting your time looking for that dog," Walton told him. "This is much more important. It's about who shot Noletta. Please, Detective, can I meet you somewhere right now?"

"Of course," Martin said, wondering what Walton could possibly have learned that was important enough to make him call. "Why don't we meet at the police department?"

"We don't need to do that, Detective. This will only take a few minutes. Give me your address, and I'll go there."

"All right," Martin said, and he gave his address to Walton.

"I can be there in ten or fifteen minutes," Walton said.

Martin pulled into his driveway and shut off his engine. For several minutes he sat thinking about Walton and Noletta and even Creed. He was afraid that she cared for one of those two men, if not both of them, and it made him feel, well, miserable.

He recognized his feelings as jealously, and he angrily told himself to knock it off. He slammed the door in frustration when he finally got out of his car. *How can I be effective in this investigation if I let my personal feelings become involved?* he asked himself. *It's time to bury anything other than professional feelings—and do it now.*

After entering his house, Martin moved the crude elements of the makeshift burglar alarms from his living room. He was embarrassed to have Walton see them. He'd scarcely finished when the doorbell rang.

Walton carried a rolled-up paper in his hand when Martin answered the door. "Look at this, Detective," he said sharply as he opened the paper. "Who does this look like to you?"

Martin found himself staring at the face of a man on the paper that Walton now held open on the coffee table in his living room. There was a familiarity about the face, but Martin was more interested in where this picture had come from than who the face might belong to at this point. "Where did you get this?" he asked.

"It's a sketch I made from a description Noletta gave me earlier of the man who shot her!" he said, intense anger seeping into the conversation.

"You drew this?" Martin asked. "But it looks like it was printed on a computer."

"Let me explain," Walton said impatiently. "I'm an artist, as is Noletta. We both have the training and experience to remember details. I had her describe everything she could remember about the person who shot her. I know that she had the sun in her eyes and that the foliage partially blocked her view as well, but I've done a lot of study, had some practice, and drew the face the best I could from her description of what she saw. And as she described it to me, she found that she remembered more than she'd realized. After I took her home, I went back to my place and scanned my sketch into my computer. I have a program that helps to fill in the details. This is what I came up with."

"I see," Martin said as he looked more closely at the sketch before him. "Noletta didn't mention this to me."

"I asked her not to until I finished it, in case it was a total flop. But as you can see for yourself, it's not a total flop," Walton said.

Martin became agitated. The man in the sketch bore a striking resemblance to someone he knew. *But it can't be,* he told himself.

"Who do you think this is?" Walton pressed, urgency in his voice.

Martin straightened up. "May I take this?" he asked.

"Of course. That's why I brought it to you," Walton said. "But you haven't answered my question. I've got to know if you see what I see. I'd like to think I'm wrong, but I've got to know." Walton was practically shouting now.

Martin looked Walton in the eye and told him what he thought.

"Exactly what I thought too!" Walton said. "Find him, Detective, before he does something to Noletta. Go find him!"

Walton was angry. He seemed desperate with concern over Noletta. And for once, Martin had to admit that he felt the same as the angry, red-haired man for whom he still felt unwanted jealousy, despite his best efforts to bury his feelings. If the face looking up at the two of them was whom they both suspected, Noletta was in terrible danger.

"Thank you, Walton," Martin said. "You've been a great help. I'd better call my partner right now."

"You do that," Walton said. "If you need more copies of this, just let me know. I can print as many as you need from my computer."

Martin thanked him again, and Walton left. For another minute, he studied the image on the paper Walton had left, feeling a terror unlike any he'd ever experienced before. He had to protect Noletta. He picked up his phone. "Maddie," he said when she answered, "I'm sorry to call so late. But we may have just gotten a huge break, and if we did, Noletta is in terrible danger."

"What have you learned?" she asked.

He quickly explained.

"So at least we might have a better idea of who we're after," she said. "But it also means Noletta may be in far more danger than we thought."

They planned what to do next and both agreed that, other than making absolutely certain that Noletta was safe during the night, there wasn't much they could do until morning.

Martin thanked Maddie for her input and promised to do what he could to ensure Noletta's safety that night. As he hung up the phone, he was once again grateful to have a partner who had faith in him, who didn't second-guess his every thought and move.

CHAPTER 21

Virgil met Skip about a block from the bus depot as they had arranged earlier. The sun was already up, and Virgil was nervous. "That cop, Detective Atkinson, I'm afraid he knows too much. The boss wants us to do something about him. And he wants it done today."

"He ain't easy to waste," Skip said nervously. "He's got luck on his side. Look at what happened to poor Evan."

"Evan was careless. We won't be. Come on. We've gotta meet with the boss in thirty minutes and decide how to do this," Virgil said as he started his car and eased it from the alley where he'd waited for Skip.

"What about the blind woman?" Skip asked.

"What about her? For now, we leave her alone," Virgil growled. "Boss's orders. He says they've doubled the guard on the house where she's staying with her parents. He also says that the other woman, the redhead, and her little girl could be trouble, and they're in the same house as the blind woman is. He says he'll decide later what to do with them, after the cop is out of the way."

* * *

Martin met his partner at seven that Monday morning. Their first order of business was to make sure all occupants of the big house in the Avenues were protected that day. A short visit with Lieutenant Merrill was all it took to get officers assigned to shadow all of them, including Harmony. Once those assignments had been made and the officers had their subjects covered, Martin called the sheriff in Summit County.

While he was waiting for the sheriff to come on the line, his former partner, Ted Zobel, strolled up. "Still think you're going to find the dog, do you?" he smirked.

"I hope to," Martin said.

Ted shook his head, and his lips curled into a snarl. "You're a fool, Martin Atkinson. You really are a fool." He swaggered across the room.

Martin watched him warily, hoping he wouldn't try to interfere in his case in an attempt to make him look bad. He worried that Ted might be willing to stoop to such a level, no matter whom he endangered. Just then the sheriff came on the line, and Martin got right to the point with him. "There's a chance I can tell you who killed Lamar Kayser," he said. "But I need more evidence."

"Hey, that's great. What do you have right now?" the sheriff asked.

Martin explained, and the sheriff said, "I'd like to see the sketch."

"I thought you might. If you like, we'll bring it up."

"Great. I'll meet you in Park City."

"My partner and I will head that way in a few minutes But first, there's something else I wanted to ask," Martin told him.

"What's that?"

"Is it true that the murder weapon was never found?"

"That's correct."

"Could it still be in the area of the crime?" Martin asked.

"We searched the trail and the vicinity. The couple who discovered the murder scene, two young doctors, said they never saw a gun there at all, except for the victim's hunting rifle, and it hadn't been fired. We assumed the killer took his weapon with him. Or it could be somewhere along the trail or even in a stream. He might have thrown it anywhere."

"What about over the ledge near where Noletta and Lamar were found? Was that searched?"

The sheriff was silent for a moment. "I sent a deputy down there, but he didn't find anything. I suppose he could have missed it though. It's a rugged spot with lots of brush and timber at the bottom. Frankly, we didn't think it was worth spending a lot of time on since the most likely thing is that the gunman took it with him."

"Would you mind if we had another look?" Martin asked.

"Not at all," the sheriff responded, "but I think it'll be a waste of your time. I can't make it today since I have an important matter to take care of in a couple of hours. But I can send Jerry Pollard with you. He was the lead detective on that investigation."

"I've talked with Jerry before. That would work just fine. I know it's a long shot, but I've thought a lot about this lately. And I keep coming up with one question: why did the killer let the dog live after shooting Noletta?"

"I wondered that too," the sheriff agreed. "But we finally assumed the dog ran off the moment Noletta was shot and that it came back later, after the killer had left the scene."

"I thought about that, but then I wondered if the dog might have attacked him. And if that occurred, I wondered if the gun might have somehow gone over the ledge," Martin reasoned.

"Well, that's a thought my deputies and I never had," the sheriff admitted.

"That's why I want to have a look."

"Sounds reasonable to me. So how soon can you get up here and show me the sketch?"

"Give us an hour and a half," Martin said. "Or will that make you late for your other appointment?"

"That'll work if you're no longer than that."

"We won't be late," Martin promised.

* * *

Noletta phoned Walton and asked him if he'd give her a ride to campus that morning. It wasn't so much that she needed the ride, because she could have asked her mother to take her, but she wanted to talk to Walton. She had to clear the air with him. She wanted to hear him say how he felt about their relationship and where it might be going. She knew that it was a bold step she was taking, but she was tired of the confusion and mistrust that surrounded her.

She placed the call to his cell phone. "Hi, Noletta," he answered cheerily. "It's good to hear from you. How was your weekend?"

"It was okay," she said. "How was yours?"

"Better now that Creed's gone home. Maybe you could use a lift to school this morning," Walton offered.

"Thanks, Walton, I'd appreciate that. I need to talk to you."

They arranged a time, talked for a minute about what lay ahead in school that day, and disconnected. *Walton sounds almost like his old cheerful self,* Noletta thought as she put her phone in her purse. *Maybe Creed's leaving really was a good thing if that's why Walton is acting so much more like himself this morning.*

Noletta bid both Terri and Harmony good-bye as they left for work and school. She was relieved when her mother mentioned that a marked police car was following them down the avenue. Terri had already explained that Detective Reed had called a little earlier and informed her of the increased protection. It made Noletta nervous while it also made her more at ease. Nervous because it meant the police were concerned about more violence. More at ease because there were so many officers providing protection. She thought about Creed's request for her to live in Los Angeles, his insistence that she'd be safe there—that she wasn't safe here.

Even as she was thinking of Creed, he called from his cell phone. "I'm on my way to work," he told her. "I'd almost forgotten what a nightmare it is to drive in the rush hour down here. I wish I could be up there with you instead," he said. "And how are you this morning, sweetheart?"

"I'm doing very well," she said.

"Hey, you be careful, my love," he said. "I'm worried about you."

"I'm fine. The police have increased their patrols. They're watching out for me."

"Why have they done that?" he asked sharply. "Has there been another threat of some kind?"

"No, there's no new threat, at least not that anyone's told me about. I don't know why they have."

"Like I keep telling you, don't put too much trust in that detective. If he knows something, he should tell you. It's your right to know. Call him, Noletta, and tell him that you want to be brought up to speed on everything he knows or even suspects."

"Can I do that?"

"Of course you can. Demand that he tell you what's going on. Who knows, he may even have a suspect in mind besides this Skip guy you talked about and might be keeping it from you," Creed said angrily. "Make him come clean."

"If you think I should," she said tentatively.

"I know you should. And then let me know. I'm worried sick down here. I should have stayed up there to take care of you myself."

"But you have your job."

"What's a job? There are other jobs, but there's only one of you. Noletta, I love you, and I don't intend to lose you. Maybe I just need to come back."

"Don't. I'll be fine."

"How about if I come up and get you this weekend? You can make arrangements to move by then, can't you?"

"I could, but I don't think I should. And I want you to quit worrying."

"That's easy for you to say. Be careful. How are you getting to school today?"

She explained that Walton was coming to get her, and he nearly exploded over the phone. "He doesn't care a hoot about you!" he thundered. "Don't you let him lead you on. Oh, how I wish I hadn't had to come back to work."

"It'll be okay," she told him soothingly.

But he didn't seem to think so. However, he gradually calmed down, and the last few minutes of their conversation were amiable. He had barely disconnected when the doorbell rang. Noletta's mother answered it. "It's Martin and his partner," she announced through Noletta's closed door.

At the mention of Martin's name, her heart began to race, and she hurriedly finished getting dressed. She could smell the familiar cologne before she entered the living room. It was mixed with the scent of perfume—his new partner, Maddie, she presumed.

"Good morning, Noletta. You look very much like a spring morning today," Martin said.

"Thank you," she responded cheerfully, "and good morning to both of you."

"Hi, Noletta," Detective Reed greeted her.

"I see you're ready to go to school. Was your mother planning to take you?"

"No, Walton's coming for me."

"I'm sorry to interrupt your plans, but Detective Reed and I wondered if there was any chance you could help us this morning."

"Doing what? I don't have a class till early this afternoon, but I really need to study. I was going to spend the morning at the library."

She stiffened a little as he moved near her, but in spite of herself, she relaxed when he took her hand in his. She knew he was looking into her face, and she imagined she could feel his eyes penetrating hers. She suddenly wanted to reach up, touch his face, feel the shape of his chin, his mouth, his nose, and then run her hand through his hair. *What am I thinking?* she thought. *Come on, girl; get a grip on yourself.*

"Noletta, we really could use your help, but if you can't or if it makes you too uncomfortable, we'll understand. We're meeting the sheriff of Summit County this morning, and then one of his detectives is going to take us to the place where you and Terri's husband were shot."

Noletta stiffened, and she felt herself gasping for air. "Oh, Martin, I don't know if I can go back there," she said, having to force herself to speak.

"I understand, Noletta," Martin said as one of his strong arms encircled her waist and supported her as she sagged. "But we really need your help."

"I don't know what I can do. Why do you need to go there? Surely you don't expect to find anything useful after all this time."

"We're going to look for the weapon the shooter used," he said. "It could be very helpful at this point. We think there's a chance it might have fallen over the ledge you were standing by. I've wondered a lot about why he didn't shoot Taffy. Now I'm thinking that she might have attacked him when he shot you. She may have made him drop his weapon."

"You could be right." Noletta was trembling.

"Maddie and I think it's worth a try. The sheriff up there agrees. We may not find the pistol, but we need to try to hunt for it down below the cliff. If you can help us figure out about where he was standing when he shot you, we might be able to narrow our search and save some time."

His grip around her waist tightened, and he pulled her close to him. She thought about the doubts both Walton and Creed had concerning Martin. But at the moment she felt that she could trust him. But still, going back would be very punishing. "Why do you need the gun? What good will it do even if you find it?" she asked, knowing she should go with them, but seeking any reasonable excuse to avoid returning to that nightmarish place.

"Walton showed me a sketch he did last night, the one you helped him with," he said. "It could prove to be helpful. But we need evidence to go with what we may be seeing in the sketch. Sometimes guns can be traced using serial numbers. Who knows, it might give us a break."

"Walton showed it to you?" she asked fearfully. "He didn't tell me that when he called. Who do you think it is?"

"We're not positive, so we don't want to say for now. But it would certainly help our case if we found the gun," Maddie said.

"I'm frightened," Noletta admitted. "That place terrifies me."

"Please," Martin said.

"Okay, Martin, I'll go with you on one condition," she finally said. For some reason he was hedging about Walton's sketch. She thought she might have found a way to force his hand.

"Great," he said, his face only inches from hers and making her slightly dizzy. But she had no desire to step back. "What's your condition?"

"That you tell me who you think Walton drew."

"But like Maddie just said, we can't be sure," he said, sounding evasive.

She pulled herself away from him, stepped back, and then faced him again, her hands planted firmly on her hips. "I mean it, Martin. Either you tell me who you think Walton drew, or else I won't go with you."

She knew she had him when he began to chuckle. "You drive a hard bargain," he said. "What about it, Maddie? Should we tell her?"

"I don't think we have much choice, Martin. We need her help."

"Okay, so tell me," Noletta insisted.

Once again Martin moved close to her, and a second time he put an arm around her. "This is going to come as a shock," he said. "If you don't mind, I'd like to hold onto you when I tell you who I think I see in your sketch."

"Okay, tell me," she said again, but she leaned comfortably into his body, knowing that what was to come would not be pleasant.

He told her, and if he hadn't been holding her, she would have collapsed. "Oh, Martin," she said as both his arms held her tightly. "You must be wrong. Walton must be wrong. It isn't possible."

"Yes, we could be wrong. That's why I didn't want to tell you. And that's why we need more evidence."

"Okay," she said as she turned her face against his jacket and began to sob. What she'd just heard was a blow, and she hoped they were wrong, but deep down, she began to worry. *What if they are right?* she asked herself. "I know some things you can check. They might prove that the sketch is wrong."

"Or that we're right?" he prodded.

She lowered her head. "That too," she agreed reluctantly.

"We'd better talk in the car. I promised the sheriff that we wouldn't be late. I'll call Walton and tell him that you won't be needing his help this morning. He'll understand."

"Thank you. I could never do it myself."

Madison drove, and Noletta sat between her and Martin, who kept a comforting arm around her shoulders. At that moment she didn't know what she would do without him. She now trusted him—unequivocally. She leaned into him and realized that there was more to her feelings concerning him, but she dared not even consider that subject as they headed up Parley's Canyon.

She told them some things they needed to check out, and even as they drove, Martin began to make phone calls, beginning with Walton. What he learned didn't do what Noletta had hoped. Rather, it seemed to confirm their suspicions. The number of calls increased the closer they came to Park City. Noletta's emotions escalated in direct proportion to the number—disbelief, sadness, betrayal, fear, and fury.

* * *

Virgil and Skip, disguised as employees of the natural gas company, easily picked the lock at Martin's house. It took only a few minutes to complete their assignment from the boss. Then they headed for their car, making sure they left no incriminating evidence behind and bantering about the violent end Martin would meet when he came home. They would watch the news that night and laugh some more. Then, in a few days they would leave Utah, for at least a year or so while things cooled down. The boss wanted them gone, more for his protection, they suspected, than for their own. Things had become complicated, and they were more than glad to comply.

* * *

"He's not familiar to me," the sheriff said as he looked at Walton's sketch. His deputy, Jerry Pollard, agreed.

Martin then produced a photograph he'd copied and enlarged from a high school yearbook. "Does this fellow look familiar?" he asked.

The sheriff shook his head. "I'm afraid not, but I can see a resemblance to this sketch. Yes, there's a strong resemblance." Then he pointed to the photo. "I suppose this could be our man, all right. If I get done in time, I'll come up and meet you and Jerry at the crime scene. But I hope you find the weapon sooner if it's there to be found. With Noletta's help, you have a good shot at it."

Later, as they walked up the same trail that Noletta and Taffy had traversed that tragic fall day more than eighteen months earlier, Noletta clung tightly to Martin. He had no idea what would happen after the authorities arrested the man who had blinded her, and was, he suspected, behind the theft of her dog. But of one thing he was certain: he wanted to get to know Noletta a lot better and hopefully on a new level. He also wanted to return Taffy to her, although hope of that was fading. No sign had turned up of the man who'd taken the dog to New Mexico.

Once they arrived at the spot in the trail that was forever imprinted in Noletta's memory, Martin described it to her.

"It hasn't changed much since then," Detective Jerry Pollard observed.

Noletta listened carefully, and in her mind's eye she tried to recall the scene from a year and a half ago and place it in the picture Martin was painting in her mind now. It was painstaking, and more than half an hour passed before Noletta was confident that she had been able to place herself where she'd stood then, as well as pinpoint where the body had lain and where the killer had been standing when he fired at her. Then Martin and Maddie tried to determine the most likely direction he would have gone as he stepped from the trees after shooting her.

Once that was done, Noletta and Maddie waited while Martin and Jerry headed back down the trail until they found a place where they could work their way off the trail and into the ravine below. When they were finally down there, Martin called back up to his partner. Maddie stepped to the edge of the trail. "This was about where we decided he might have stepped to if he came out of the trees there after he shot Noletta," she said.

Martin and Jerry then began their search. An hour passed, then another. The pistol simply wasn't there. "I wonder," Jerry said thoughtfully, "if he came back and found the gun later, that is if he didn't take it with him in the first place. And I still think that might have been the case. It just seems logical that he would take it and ditch it elsewhere."

Martin's heart sank. The killer returning later to find his weapon was a distinct possibility—not at all beyond reason—he admitted to himself, especially in light of what he now knew about the man he considered the prime suspect. "You're probably right," he finally admitted to Jerry. "I guess we might as well quit hunting. We've covered every square inch of ground where it could possibly be if he had dropped it over the edge."

"Maddie," Martin called up.

She appeared at the edge of the trail a moment later, Noletta at her side. "Did you find it?" she asked.

"No, and we're convinced it isn't here. If he didn't take it with him, then he must have come back later and recovered it himself."

"So you're coming back up now?" Noletta asked.

"I don't think there's much more we can do down here," Martin agreed as he gazed up at her. The sunlight had broken through the trees and lit her face. It created a halo effect around her, and Martin couldn't tear his eyes from her face. He'd never been in love before, but he knew that what he was experiencing at that moment was the beginning of love. There was no denying it any longer.

"Martin, should we go?" Jerry asked.

Embarrassed that he'd been caught staring at Noletta, he slowly and nonchalantly moved his eyes down the face of the cliff. Suddenly he cried out, "Jerry, look."

"At what?" the other detective asked.

"Right below where Noletta's standing there's a small outcropping of rock. It's down about twenty feet. I'm not sure, but I think it might lead into some kind of small depression in the ledge. What if the gun fell right there?" he asked.

"That's possible," the deputy said. "But there's no way to tell from down here."

"What are you looking at?" Maddie called down to them.

"There's an outcropping of rock right below you guys. Could you get on your stomach and look over the edge? It's straight below where Noletta's standing," Martin said. "It's maybe twenty or twenty-five feet down."

Maddie crawled out to the edge and looked over. "I see what you're looking at," she said after studying the area below her for a minute. "It goes down quite steep, right into the cliff. There could be a hole there, I suppose, but I can't tell from here."

"I have some rope in my truck," Jerry said. "I'll get it, and we can lower one of us over the edge and have a look."

While Jerry went for the rope, Martin joined Noletta and Maddie. "Martin, I've been thinking while you guys were searching for that pistol," Noletta said. "If Taffy attacked him, bit him, he'd have a scar of some kind."

"Yes, that's likely," Martin agreed.

"And what if Taffy bit the hand that held the gun?" she asked.

"Then he might have a scar on his right hand. You did say he was holding the gun in his right hand, didn't you?" Martin asked.

"That's right."

"Noletta, does—" Martin began.

She cut him off. "No, I don't think he has a scar on either hand. I surely would have felt it if he did."

"Of course, Taffy could have just struck him, maybe knocked the gun from his hand," Martin said thoughtfully. "I guess the truth is we really don't know."

When the Summit County detective arrived with the rope, they tied it to a tree. "The murder is my case, so I guess I'd better be the one to go down there," Jerry said.

"I'll do it if you'd like me to," Martin volunteered.

"No, I'll do it."

"Do what?" a voice called from behind them.

"Oh, hi, Sheriff," Jerry said. "Glad you made it."

"Any luck?" the sheriff asked.

"Not yet, but we have one more place to check out."

"What's with the rope?"

They explained, and then with the sheriff's help, Martin and Maddie lowered Jerry over the edge. "Far enough," he said. He was silent for a minute or two. Then his excited shout rose up the cliff. "I found it! It's back a few inches in the hole in the face of the cliff."

Later, after Jerry had returned to the trail, the sheriff said, "I'll get this pistol processed right away, and I'll call as soon as I know anything."

"Thanks, Sheriff, and we'll do some more checking on his story. I have a feeling he's told us a lot of lies," Martin said.

"And those lies will help us put him away forever," the sheriff added.

A few minutes later, they all started back down the trail toward the cars. Martin and Noletta brought up the rear. He could tell that she was torn up inside. Suddenly, very softly, she said, "It *was* Creed, wasn't it?"

"It looks that way," he said.

"I don't understand why," she said sadly. "He doesn't seem like that kind of man. He teaches Sunday school."

"Maybe," he said. "And maybe not. Much of his life is probably a fabrication."

She nodded silently, tears spilling from below the dark glasses she was wearing.

Martin looked at her for a long moment. Then he said gently, "You liked Creed quite a lot, didn't you?"

"I was beginning to," she answered. "He seemed so gentle and kind. But it was all a facade. I'll bet he not only doesn't teach Sunday school, but he's probably not even a member of the Church. He probably made it all up. I feel like he used me, betrayed me."

"All but his attraction to you," Martin corrected her. "I think that might have been very real. But I promise, we'll keep you safe from him."

"I'm safe for now," she said, "because he's in California."

"How do we know that?" Martin asked.

"He keeps calling me from there."

"How can you tell? Didn't you say he used his cell phone? He could be anywhere," Martin pointed out.

Noletta leaned heavily into Martin. "Oh, Martin," she said nervously. "What if he comes after me?"

"I'll never let him touch you. You have my promise."

"But if it really was him, he'll try. I know he will. He took Taffy, or had Virgil and his friends take her, and he must have done it so he could get close to me. But Taffy remembered him, didn't she?" Noletta said. "She seemed a little more fierce around him than around other men."

"I'd say that's exactly why he took her, Noletta. I suspect that when he saw you that day, he thought exactly what I thought the first time I saw you, and that is that you are the most beautiful woman in the world. He'd never have shot you except that he had everything to lose if you ever talked. His was a split-second decision. Then later, when he learned that you had survived but could never recognize him, he started coming around you, figuring he could ingratiate himself with you. But he must have decided Taffy would, at the very least, make it more difficult for him. So he got rid of her."

"Do you think Taffy's dead?" Noletta asked tearfully. "I so desperately want her back."

"No, I think she's alive, and as soon as we can catch Creed and his gang, I'll do everything I can to find her."

"I know you will," she said.

They walked in silence for a moment, lagging farther and farther behind the others. Martin glanced occasionally at Noletta, savoring the moment. Then he said, "Thanks for helping us find the gun."

"But I didn't do much," she countered. "You're the one who spotted the outcrop of rock."

"That was an accident. I'd been standing down there looking up at you, thinking that I'd never seen anyone more beautiful. It was only when Jerry broke the spell you had me under, and said that we needed to go, that I began to lower my eyes. They just fell on that spot," he said.

"Do you mean that?" she asked, confident now that she could always trust him. "I mean, that you were under a spell because of me?"

"Yes, Noletta, I mean that. With all my heart I mean that," he said.

She stopped, forcing him to stop too. "I can't hear the others," she said.

"Yeah, we're slow."

"Are they out of sight?" she asked.

"Yes, why?"

"Because I would like you to kiss me," she said, "if you want to, that is."

Martin wanted to, and he did. He thought of Walton and felt somewhat guilty. He was quite sure Walton must feel about her as he did. But the choice would be Noletta's, he told himself. That was her right.

* * *

"Is the bomb set?" the boss asked.

"It is. It's all set to send Detective Martin Atkinson to the promised land. All he has to do is step into his house tonight," Virgil said.

"This had better work," the boss said coldly. "And there had better not ever be any connection to either of you or to me."

"Don't worry, boss. It'll work. He's as good as dead right now."

CHAPTER 22

Fiona watched quietly as Taffy led her son up the beach. This was the first time they'd come here since Scully had brought the German shepherd home. The way the boy and the dog had bonded was unbelievable.

From the moment they'd left the car ten minutes earlier, Fiona hadn't needed to hold Ritchie's hand even once. Taffy had taken him through the parking area, weaving among the parked cars. Taffy had stopped and waited while a small foreign car backed out, then again when a truck came through the lane ahead of them. Fiona had gradually allowed them to take a bigger lead as they crossed the grass and then started up the sandy beach.

The tide had washed large piles of seaweed onto the sand, but it wasn't a problem for Ritchie. Taffy led him around those and other obstacles, including sunbathers, without a single incident. Fiona's eyes welled up as the boy urged the dog to go down to the edge of the water. There they walked slowly, Ritchie kicking up sand and water and laughing with delight. Even though the dog got wet, she never shirked her duty.

Three children about Ritchie's age ran down the beach toward them. They stopped short of Ritchie and Taffy, and one of them, a little girl with dark blonde hair, said, "Your dog is beautiful. Can I pet him?"

"Taffy is a girl," Ritchie said. "But you can pet *her*."

The little girl stretched out a hand, and Taffy touched it with her nose. Then the girl touched the proud head, and before long, all three children were petting Taffy. Finally, the little girl said, "My name is Polly. What's yours?"

"I'm Ritchie," he said.

"Is something wrong with your eyes?" one of the boys asked.

"Yes, I'm blind," he said.

"Then how can you tell where you're going?" the second boy asked.

"Oh, Bobby, don't be so stupid," Polly said. "His dog helps him, doesn't she, Ritchie?"

"Yes, she makes sure I don't bump into things. She stops when there's cars, and she goes when there's not," he said proudly.

"You're lucky," Polly said. "I wish I had a dog."

The three children played with Taffy and Ritchie for ten minutes or so before they decided they had better get back to their mothers. Ritchie shouted as they left, "Will you play with me again sometime?"

Polly turned around and waved. "Sure," she said. "See you later."

Fiona was touched. Never before in his life had other children treated him so well, and she knew it was because of Taffy. Again she felt gratitude toward Scully. She wondered when he'd be home. He'd been gone for several days. Surely he'd be home soon, and when he came, she'd make sure he knew how much she appreciated what he'd done for their son.

The rest of the afternoon was delightful. Ritchie and Fiona ate a picnic lunch on the sand. Fiona smiled as Ritchie shared bites with Taffy. After they started home, Ritchie asked if they could come again soon.

"Yes, we'll come often," she said. "Me and you and Taffy."

When they drove up to the house a few minutes later, they saw a police car parked there. Two officers, who were leaning against it, straightened up when Fiona pulled past them and into the driveway. Her heart was thudding when she got out.

"Are you Mrs. Timmons?" the older of the two officers asked.

"Yes," she said, wondering how they knew her name.

"I'm Sergeant Powell," he said. "And this is my partner, Officer Lopez. Can we go into the house and talk with you?"

"Yes, but what's the matter? Is it about my boy's dog?"

Both men looked at Ritchie, who was just getting out of the car. They watched as Taffy waited for him to take her leash. Then he said, "Let's go in the house, Taffy," and the dog obediently led the way.

The men exchanged glances. Then Sergeant Powell said, "No, it's not about your boy or his dog. Please, can we go inside where you can sit down?"

"Of course," she said. "Come in."

Fiona couldn't imagine what the officers wanted. After sending Ritchie to his room with Taffy, she sat down on a hard-backed chair and offered the sofa to the officers. Sergeant Powell said in a soft, mellow voice, "Are you Scully Timmons's wife?"

"Yes," she said. "Is Scully in some kind of trouble?"

"You might say that, ma'am. I'm sorry to have to tell you this, but your husband is dead. He was found by the border patrol just a few feet this side of Mexico early this morning. I'm so very sorry."

"What—what happened?" she asked in a daze.

"He was shot, murdered," the sergeant said. "And I know this isn't a good time, but we need to ask you a few questions."

"Like what?"

"Like what kind of work he did," Sergeant Powell said. "And who he worked for."

* * *

At Martin's insistence, Noletta stayed with him after they returned to Salt Lake. It didn't take them long to learn that Creed Esplin hadn't been truthful with Noletta. His boss had eventually been located in the Los Angeles area. Creed had not been back to work, nor was he expected until later in the week. When officers located his apartment, they reported that no one was home. Neighbors reported that he'd come in late one night, had left the next morning, and hadn't been back. These lies, when considered with the other evidence, made Creed look guiltier.

Then the real clincher came. Detective Pollard called and said that the gun they'd found was registered to Creed Esplin. Working with the Summit County authorities, Martin and Maddie held a warrant for Creed's arrest in their hands by six o'clock that evening. Noletta sat alone at Martin's desk as Lieutenant Boyd Merrill met with half a dozen officers, including Martin and Maddie, planning their next moves. She perked up when she heard someone behind her. "Poor little blind girl. Maybe sweet Martin will make you feel better."

Noletta spun around, but the speaker's footsteps were receding. She had no idea who it might have been, but the incident made her nervous. *I'm not even safe here at the police department,* she worried, hoping that Martin's meeting would soon be over.

She tried to concentrate on the book she'd been studying, one from a class she'd missed earlier today. She ran her fingers swiftly across the pages, but she soon realized that she was just going through the motions and was comprehending almost nothing from what she read. She went back to the beginning of the chapter and tried again.

The door to the lieutenant's office opened, and Noletta could hear the officers as they came out and headed in different directions. Recognizing Martin's footsteps, she turned toward him. "You okay, Noletta?" he asked. "You seem a little pale."

"I'm fine," she said.

Noletta's phone began to ring, and she pulled it out, popped it open, and answered, expecting to hear from her parents or Terri. But when she heard Creed say, "Hi, love," she had to lower herself into a chair and take a deep breath.

Then she forced herself to talk to him. "Hello, Creed. Are you off work?"

She knew that Martin was looking at her now. Then he touched her arm. "Be careful what you say."

Noletta nodded as she wondered where Creed was calling from. Was he in Los Angeles, or was he right here in Salt Lake, almost within striking distance? She shivered and tried to concentrate on what he was saying, but she couldn't. She knew that if she didn't end this call immediately, she might unintentionally reveal something. She silently prayed for inspiration.

"Creed, my phone's dying," she said right over the top of something he was trying to say. "I can't hear you. I forgot to charge it last night. I'm only getting part of what you're saying."

He sounded angry. "You need to pay more attention to what you're doing, Noletta. A blind girl like you should make sure that things like cell phones are kept charged. Plug it in and call me back."

"What did you say?" she asked even as she both heard and felt Martin move close to her. At that point she clicked her phone shut, disconnecting the call.

"Noletta, what's going on? That was Creed, wasn't it?" Martin asked.

"Yes, but I couldn't concentrate," she said.

"So you pretended that your battery was dying?" he asked.

"I didn't know what else to do," she admitted. "Please don't be angry with me, Martin. I couldn't talk to him right then. I was afraid I'd say something wrong."

He put an arm on her shoulder and sat down next to her. "Noletta, I could never get mad at you. I think your idea was clever. He'll call back, and then maybe we can be ready for him."

"He told me to plug in my phone and call him back," she said. "He must think I'm home."

"Probably," Martin agreed. "All right, let's see how we'll handle this. We need to do it right away, so pull yourself together, Noletta. I know you can do it."

Noletta nodded. "I'll try," she said.

"Good. Okay, first I'll see if Lieutenant Merrill will let us use his office, where there will be less danger of sudden background noise."

"You're right. It will be easier in there. Oh, I hope I don't mess it up," she said. "I'm frightened, Martin."

"Don't worry. I'll keep you safe," he said, and she could feel the sincerity of his words.

"Thank you, Martin," she said.

"Oh, shoot. It looks like the lieutenant still has someone in there with him. We'll just have to make sure people stay quiet here for a while," he said.

Just then Maddie, who had been there all along, spoke up, "Martin, I think we not only need to keep it quiet here, but I also don't think we should let Ted listen in. He seems to be eavesdropping. This case is none of his business now."

Martin moved quickly away from Noletta. "Detective Zobel, you'll need to give us some space. We have some things going on here, and they're confidential."

Noletta shivered as she heard the voice that had mocked her only minutes before. It was Martin's former partner. "You're wasting a lot of the city's money," Ted snarled. "You may have Lieutenant Merrill fooled, but it won't last. You're as big a waste of a cop as I've ever seen."

Another officer, one whose voice she hadn't heard before, spoke up. "That's more than enough, Ted. Martin's right. Go on home before you get yourself fired."

Ted made a parting shot using language that made Noletta cringe, but she assumed that he'd left when she no longer heard him. "Thanks for getting rid of him, Sammy," Martin said. "Would you help us keep it quiet in here now? We'll be on an extremely important call in a minute."

"No problem," Sammy said. Then almost under his breath, but loud enough that Noletta still heard it, he said, "I don't know why they don't just fire Ted."

For the next several minutes, they discussed what Noletta needed to say and what they hoped they could accomplish with this call. Martin was proud of her. Despite her fear and all that she'd been through, she was willing to do whatever was needed.

"Okay, let me get this tape recorder running, and then you can call Creed back," Martin said to Maddie when he thought Noletta was as ready as she'd ever be. "I know this isn't the best way to handle things, and it isn't the best equipment. But under the circumstances, this will have to do, Maddie." Then he added, "Noletta, I'm putting a miniature tape recorder on the desk. You'll need to lean down as much as possible and try to tip the phone away from your ear so that my recorder can pick up his voice. I'd like to record as much of his conversation as I can."

She nodded, trying to ignore her trembling hands and legs.

* * *

Martin was angry that Ted Zobel was still trying to harass him. It was hard to believe that his former partner couldn't just move on and leave him alone. He'd ruined his own chances for promotion, and his whole career was dissipating fast. Yet now it appeared that Ted was bent on vengeance. As if Martin didn't already have enough to worry about.

Detective Pollard from Summit County joined them as Noletta began to make the call to Creed. Martin said to him, "She's calling Creed back."

"Is it being recorded?" Jerry asked.

"Just with that," Martin said, pointing toward his small recorder. "He called her on her cellular. She faked her phone battery going dead, but he told her to plug it in and call right back. And I don't have the equipment handy to do anything else right now."

"Okay," Jerry said, and he moved in close so that he, along with the others, could hear as much of the conversation as possible.

Noletta tipped the phone away from her ear as Creed answered. "It took you a while," he said.

"I know. I'm sorry. I wasn't sure if you said to call you or if you were going to call me back. So I waited, and when you didn't call for what seemed like an eternity, I decided you must have meant for me to call you. So here I am," she said, and Martin was proud of the way she improvised. She could do this.

"That's okay, sweetheart," he said, and Martin couldn't help but notice the way Noletta cringed. For that matter, he did too. "I'm really afraid for you," Creed went on. "First, you need to know that Walton isn't to be trusted. Stay away from him. He has his own agenda, and it has nothing to do with keeping you safe or loving you or anything else."

"Why do you say that, Creed?" Noletta asked. "I thought you liked Walton." Her hand was shaking, but she was doing remarkably well at keeping her voice steady and strong.

"I know him well," Creed said, even as Martin was vigorously shaking his head in anger and frustration. "And don't trust that cop, Atkinson, either. He's not only incompetent, he's crooked. And I'm not just saying that. I know it for a fact."

"Really?" Noletta asked.

"Yes, really. I have it from a credible source right there in his own department. I've got to get you out of there. Atkinson is leading you on, trying to make himself look good," Creed said. "And I love you too much to let him get away with it."

That sounded like something Ted Zobel would say—had said—to him. Surely he hadn't talked with Creed, Martin thought bitterly.

"When can you come get me?" Noletta asked, launching quickly into the plan the officers had arranged. "I'm ready to leave here. I should have gone before. There are so many police around my house now that I know there's something they're not telling me. I'm so frightened, Creed. You're the only one I can trust."

"Yes, you can trust me. But I think it would be best if you came to me," he said.

"But I don't know exactly where you are," she protested. Martin touched her shoulder for encouragement. She was doing very well, and he wanted her to know it.

"My house is kind of hard to find, to be honest with you. I live in a tangle of streets, a very confusing area," he said evasively. "I have a better idea."

"It's okay," she said. "I'll get help. I'll come down there, and I'll find your home."

"No, don't let anyone else know your plans. It's too dangerous. And I think it would be better if we met somewhere else. Then I would worry less. I'll make the arrangements. You can come by bus."

"Creed, I'd be afraid on a bus, especially without Taffy," she said. "I'd rather fly or have someone drive me down."

"No, that won't do. Believe me, sweetheart, you can't trust anyone else. Come by bus. You're not a coward, my love," he said. "You can do it. But I'll tell you what. We'll meet partway. That way I won't have to miss too much work, and we can travel much of the way together."

"Partway?" she asked. "Well, where do you mean?"

"Las Vegas. You could ride a bus there, and I could meet you at the bus depot. Then we'll come back to Los Angeles together," he said.

She heard Martin whisper softly in her other ear, "St. George. Insist on St. George."

"Oh, I don't know. Maybe St. George," she said. "If I can ride the bus as far as St. George, couldn't you get me from there? I really am terrified to ride on a bus, with all the people after me like they are, and especially without Taffy."

Creed didn't respond for a minute, but he finally agreed. "You're right. We've got to keep you safe. Okay, I'll arrange for a ticket," he said. "I'll let you know what to do. You can get to the bus station without Martin knowing, can't you? Or anyone else for that matter, even your parents or Terri, and especially not Walton. I mean, you could take a taxi or something without anyone knowing, couldn't you?"

"That's a good idea," she agreed. "I'll call a taxi. I'll make some excuse to my mother."

"Good girl," he said. "That's the only way I'm sure you'll be safe. To catch a plane would be too complicated without help, and you mustn't have help. No, do it this way, and I know you'll be safe. I'll be in touch," he said. "It will probably be tomorrow morning. And until I tell you to, don't leave your parents' house. It's too dangerous for you to go out until you're ready to leave. You've got that, sweetheart?"

"Yes, I've got that," she said.

"I love you, Noletta. And I promise I'll take good care of you, and I won't let anyone hurt you. And I'll get you a new dog. That's a promise, too."

"I'd like that, although what I really would like is to get Taffy back."

"I'm sure that's not possible," he said. "But I'll find you one just as good."

"My mother's calling me. She has dinner ready. I need to go," Noletta said. "Call me soon."

"I will, my love. You won't ever regret this. I love you." Then the call ended.

Noletta was shaking so badly she could hardly close her phone and return it to her purse. After the second try, she had it in place. She folded her arms tightly against her chest and sat silently.

"Noletta, you were really quite amazing," Martin said with affection and admiration.

"Yeah, that was great," Detective Pollard added.

"Still working? I don't know who you think you're going to impress."

Martin spun around when he heard Ted's snide voice. "I thought you'd gone for the day," he said angrily, wondering how much Ted had overheard.

"I have real work to do, unlike some of the rest of you," Ted said.

Sammy was on his feet and moving toward Ted. "Zobel, just leave. So help me, if you don't get out of Martin's hair, I'll file a complaint against you with the chief himself."

"As if he'd listen to you," Ted said.

"Zobel! Get in here this minute," the thundering voice of Lieutenant Merrill ordered. "I'd have thought two days off would give you a message."

Ted spun around, his face red with rage. "You'll get yours," he said to Martin. Then he stomped off in the direction of the lieutenant's office.

"Wow," Maddie said. "How could anyone possibly work with him?"

"Well, it wasn't my idea of fun," Martin said. "Boy, I'm glad he didn't come in while Noletta was still talking to Creed."

"So am I," Noletta said. She could no longer control the tremors she had been trying to ignore, and Martin put a comforting arm around her. "He frightens me."

"He's all talk," Martin said. "Don't worry about him. Now, Noletta, Walton will be here in a minute or two. I asked him to come down and tell us all he can about Creed. Are you okay with that?" Martin asked.

"I am," she said. "He's a good friend, and I trust him, despite what Creed says."

Walton arrived shortly. "It worked," he said, "thanks to you." He kissed Noletta's cheek. "It's only because of you that I was able to do the sketch. I know it's a shock with Creed and all. Believe me, I'm as surprised as you. I thought I knew him well, but I guess not."

"This is terrible, Walton," she said. "I hope they catch him soon."

"So do I," Walton agreed. "And when they do, I hope they fry him."

"Okay, Walton, let's get started," Martin said.

* * *

As Walton answered the officers' questions and talked about his cousin Creed, Noletta received surprise after surprise. Creed wasn't an active member of the Church. "I've encouraged him," Walton said, "but he always laughed it off. He always said he'd get going sometime, but to my knowledge he never has. I can't believe he told you he was and that he made it believable. But then, Creed always was a good liar. That's how he's been able to get you to like him. He's always been a charming guy."

Noletta shuddered. "He has charm, all right," she said. "He had me fooled."

After Walton had finished, he excused himself and started across the room. "I'll see you later, Noletta," he said. "You be careful."

"I will," she promised as she trailed him partway across the room. "Thank you for helping us."

"I'm glad I could help," he said.

* * *

Martin watched as Noletta followed Walton away from the cluster of desks. Walton had been a big help, but he still didn't care for him. At least now he was cooperating with the case. He was suddenly paged and told that he had a call waiting on his phone. He picked it up, and on the other end, a voice said, "Detective Atkinson, is it?"

"Yes, I'm Detective Atkinson."

"Are you the officer who sent flyers out on a missing guide dog?"

He felt his pulse quicken. "I am," he said. "Do you have news for me?"

"My name's Sergeant Jon Powell of the Whittier Police Department in California. And, yes, I think I may have found your missing dog."

CHAPTER 23

"They've found Taffy?" Noletta cried when she rejoined Martin just as his call was ending. "Where is she? When can we get her?"

"Slow down," he said gently. "It isn't confirmed yet. Sergeant Powell will call back later, and then we'll see. It might not be until morning that we hear from him."

"Oh, Martin, I hope it's her. Where is she?"

"*If* it is her," Martin said cautiously. "The officer that called simply said he was from the Whittier Police Department. That's in Los Angeles County."

"Where Creed lives," Noletta said.

"In the same county, but actually quite a few miles from Creed's apartment." Martin looked at his watch. "It's getting late. We've had a long day already. I suppose we should be getting you home."

"Will I be safe?" Noletta asked.

"You'll be safe if I have to stay outside in my car all night," he said with sudden intensity.

"Martin, you need sleep as much as any of us," she said. "I'll be fine, I'm sure." But what she said didn't sound congruent with how she said it. She sounded worried and frightened.

"I should get back home," Detective Pollard told them as he too looked at his watch. "The warrants are out there on

Creed, Virgil, and Skip. I'm not sure there's much more we can do right now."

"Call me if anything changes during the night," Martin said. "I'll keep my cell phone on."

It wasn't until after Jerry had left that Martin said, "I'll increase the security even more than I did last night on your folks' house. We can't be too careful."

"I know this is silly," Noletta said. "But just because we know Creed is a killer and there's a warrant out for him, that doesn't mean he knows we know. I'm sure he thinks he's beaten you all the way."

"You may be right, but we can't count on it. I'm still nervous. We're better to be a lot more cautious until we get Creed and his buddies rounded up."

While Martin was arranging for the increased surveillance, Maddie left, and his former partner exited the lieutenant's office. He was seething. But he didn't say a word to Martin. He just headed for the door.

Martin finished arranging for the increased surveillance and then drove Noletta back to her folks' house. "Do you think Detective Zobel's in trouble again?" Noletta inquired. "He sure seems like a troublemaker."

"Lieutenant Merrill sounded angry when he called him in. So I suppose Ted hasn't helped his case any. I just hope he didn't overhear what we were talking about."

"I hope he didn't either," she said.

"I'm so glad I have a partner now that I can count on," Martin said.

"Yeah, and a pretty one, from what I hear," Noletta said.

"Not nearly as pretty as you," he said.

"Do you mean that, Martin?" she asked.

"I do."

She reached over and touched his face but didn't say another word. At the Fahrs' home, they filled Terri in on all the day's developments. "Noletta, I'm so sorry that Creed's the one. I know he has been so kind to you the past week."

"Too kind," Noletta said. "And I'm sorry for what he did to Lamar."

"Well, at least now, once he's in custody, I can sleep better, knowing that justice is finally being served. But I wonder why he killed Lamar. I can't imagine."

"Nor can we," Martin said.

Terri, like Noletta, was more nervous than ever now. "I suppose I shouldn't be nervous, because we should be safer now, knowing that their pictures are being sent out all over the area, and that when someone recognizes them, they'll be arrested."

"That's right," Martin said.

Terri smiled. "But it doesn't make me feel any better," she said. "And I'm sure it doesn't reassure you a lot either, does it, Noletta?"

"I'm afraid not," Noletta said with a catch in her voice.

"So do you think Creed will be calling you back soon?" Terri asked Noletta.

"I'm sure he will, either tonight or in the morning, but it's getting really hard to talk to him. I'm afraid I'll slip up and say something I shouldn't."

"You'll do fine," her friend said reassuringly.

"Creed was going to make arrangements for me to go by bus to St. George, where he says he'll meet me," Noletta said. "I expect to be hearing back from him soon on that."

"Now that's not a good idea," Terri said sternly. "Surely you won't go on a bus to St. George."

"I think I might have to, unless somehow he gets caught first."

"Oh, Martin, don't let her," Terri pleaded.

"That's a decision for another day, I'm afraid," Martin said. "Or at least until Noletta hears from him again. But if we do decide to try to catch him in St. George, believe me, we'll have plenty of cops around. Also, Terri, there's no way I'm letting Noletta ride on that bus alone. In fact, there's no reason even to put her on a bus before Cedar City. Hopefully, Creed will have no way of knowing."

"What if all this talk of Creed's meeting her is nothing but a setup?" Terri asked. "He could be anywhere. What if he's waiting for a chance to grab her right now? I wouldn't put that past him."

"And that's exactly why we've beefed up security tonight," he said. "I even plan to drive by your place a few times myself."

"But you need sleep," Noletta told him.

"I'll be fine. I just don't want to let anything happen to any of you," he said.

Martin was exhausted by the time he pulled up to his apartment, parked his car, and approached the front door. He pulled his apartment key from his pocket and stuck it in the lock. As he did so, a shiver ran up his spine. He looked around, remembering that Virgil, or someone who looked a lot like him, had been in the neighborhood the night before. And although they had not yet made a tangible connection between Creed and Virgil, Martin was sure the two of them—and Skip as well—were involved in this together. Martin took a deep breath and bent toward the door again to turn the key.

"Hey, Martin, there you are." It was his elderly neighbor, a widower in his late seventies. Martin looked up at him, and the man spoke again. "I've been worrying all day." That was no surprise to Martin. Ever since the death of his wife, Walter Jones had worried over even the smallest things. Martin had lost count of the hours he'd spent reassuring him, checking his car, his appliances, his yard, his checking and savings accounts, and even, on occasion, his mail.

"Brother Jones," Martin said, "it's good to see you. What are you worrying about tonight?"

"Well, I was just thinking that if you were having trouble with your natural gas, maybe there could be something wrong with mine, too. I shut my furnace down, turned off the water heater, and haven't used the stove. I was hoping you could tell me what kind of problems you were having," the old fellow said.

Martin slowly pulled the key from the slot, a wave of nausea hitting him. He hadn't mentioned any problems with the gas to anyone because there hadn't been any. "What makes you think I'm having problems with the natural gas?" he asked.

"Well, it seems to me that you wouldn't call for the gas company to go into your house while you weren't home if you weren't having problems," Brother Jones said logically.

"Someone went in my house? You saw them?" Instinctively, Martin pressed his arm tightly against his knotted stomach.

"Yeah, I just happened to be standing at the window. It was a couple of the guys from the gas company," he said. "You did call them, didn't you?"

"No, I didn't," Martin said. "What did they look like?"

"You know I'm not good at remembering faces. Anyway, I didn't see them that well. They were in gas company uniforms. One was maybe a little smaller than you. The other one, he was really big."

"Was his head bald, or at least shaved?" Martin asked.

"Yeah, how did you know that?"

"Just a guess. Let me show you a couple of pictures," Martin said. "These guys are a lot older now, but maybe they'll at least look familiar to you."

Brother Jones looked at the old yearbook pictures of Skip and Virgil as well as the one of Creed that Martin had shown to the sheriff in Summit County. After only a short hesitation, Brother Jones said, "Never seen this guy before," while tapping a bony finger on the picture of Creed. "But it could have been these two." He pointed at the pictures of both Skip and Virgil. "But if it was, the big guy's bald now, like you said," he added.

There was no way Martin was going inside his home. He debated for a minute about what to do. Finally, he opened his cellular phone and called his partner. "What do you think, Maddie?" he asked her after telling her what his neighbor had said. "What could they have been after in my place? Surely they don't think that I'd keep official records there."

"We need to call the bomb squad," Maddie said flatly. "These guys have tried to kill you before. You can't take any chances. I'll be over as quickly as I can get there."

"I'll call in," he said. "And, Maddie, thanks for your help."

"What are partners for?" she asked.

"I'm just now learning about that," he said.

"I'll see you in a few."

All homes surrounding Martin's were evacuated—Brother Jones on one side, and the Abram family on the other, as well as three families behind Martin's home. Dogs were brought in and indicated almost immediately at the front door of Martin's apartment that there were explosives present. It was a painstaking process, but the bomb, which had been left just inside the front door, was eventually disarmed by an officer who entered through a window. It was midnight before Martin's house was declared secure.

"Well, I guess I'll go in and see if I can sleep," Martin told Maddie.

"Don't even think about it," she said. "Why don't you get a hotel room for the night? You can't take any chances. Creed and his men are desperate to stop you from completing this investigation."

"I suppose you're right," he said. So he packed a bag, drove by the Fahr home, and found a room at a downtown hotel.

After sleeping fitfully for only a couple of hours, he got up and again drove to the Avenues. He talked to each of the officers on surveillance, telling them to be extra vigilant and explaining the close call he'd had that night.

* * *

"I thought you said Atkinson was going to be taken care of last night," a very angry boss said to Virgil and Skip.

"He must not have gone home," Virgil said. "He'll get it when he does."

"Nice theory, but not good enough," the boss said. "I've done some checking this morning. It seems the bomb squad was there last night."

"I told you he was a hard man to kill," Skip whined.

"Shut up and listen, both of you," the boss barked, his eyes flashing with anger. "I guess I'll have to deal with Atkinson myself. I have another job for the two of you. It will pay well if you do it right for a change. Of course, Skip, I'll have to hold back five hundred of your cut for your foul-up on the sale of the dog. This job will take you out of town, where I want you anyway. Until this whole thing blows over, you're not to set foot back in Utah again. And I don't want to hear that you can't get this next assignment done."

"What do you need us to do?" Virgil asked.

The boss told them. They looked at each other in amazement. "You don't like it?" he asked, staring at them with contempt.

"No, no problem. Just surprised," Virgil said. "This one will be easy. We'll call you when we're finished."

* * *

Creed's call came at eight that morning. "Are you at work?" Noletta asked.

"Been here since six," he said. "That would be seven your time. I got it all worked out, my love. Here's what you need to do. And remember, don't say a word to anyone. Call a cab once you get to campus. Have it take you to the bus depot. The tickets are waiting in your name. I'll meet you in St. George at six this evening."

"Creed, I can't take everything I'll need in Los Angeles to school with me, or even in a cab or on a bus."

"Bring one bag, one small enough to take up to campus with you," he said firmly. "Bring just the essentials. I'll see that you have whatever else you need. When this whole mess has died down, and you're no longer in danger, we can go back and get whatever else you want from your house."

"Are you sure I should be doing this?" she asked.

"Sweetheart, we're going to be so happy. But right now, your life is at risk. Believe me, you can't trust that cop or that jerk cousin of mine. We've got to get you out of Salt Lake now. I'll go crazy if we wait another day."

"All right. I'll see you tonight," she said.

"And when you do, I'll have a big surprise for you," he said, his voice suddenly full of cheer.

"What kind of surprise?" she asked.

"Sorry. You'll have to wait," he said, and he ended the call.

She sat for a moment, wondering what kind of surprise Creed could have planned. She was quite certain she didn't want to know. And since he would probably be arrested before she even saw him again, she most likely would never have to find out.

* * *

Although Sergeant Powell was a large, powerfully built man, he had a soft heart and gentle voice. He was easy to like, but as Fiona listened to him, she wished she'd never met him, or at least that he'd not come back this morning. It had been a blow the day before to learn that Scully was dead. Now she'd learned from the sergeant that he'd been running drugs, and the police wanted to know who his boss was.

"Mrs. Timmons, your husband died because of the man he was working for. And countless other lives are being destroyed. We believe that whoever sent Scully into Mexico is supplying drugs to hundreds—who knows, maybe even thousands—of people. He's got to be stopped," Sergeant Powell said.

"But I don't know who he worked for. I guess I didn't want to know," she said. "But he'd never have told me anyway. For the first time in our married life he was bringing home enough money for us to live on. He was even able to buy Ritchie a guide dog."

"Yes, about that dog. Do you know where he bought her?" Sergeant Powell asked.

"He said his boss got her for him. That's all I know. But it was the nicest thing Scully ever did for Ritchie," she said. "In fact, it was the only nice thing he ever did for our son. I wish I could help you, but I can't. I simply don't know who Scully was working for."

"Is the dog's name Taffy?" he asked.

"Yes, that's the name on her collar. And she answers really well to that name," she said.

"Do you mind if we look at her, Mrs. Timmons?"

"That would be fine," Fiona said. "She's in the backyard with Ritchie." She called Ritchie inside, then said, "These men want to see Taffy."

Sergeant Powell and his partner examined her more closely than normal, at least in Fiona's mind. Finally, Sergeant Powell said, "Mrs. Timmons, I'm so sorry to have to be the bearer of more bad news. But you need to know that this dog was stolen. We're going to have to take her, I'm afraid."

"But you can't!" Fiona cried. "There must be some mistake."

"I don't think so, but we'll let the dog's owner decide that for sure."

"Ritchie is her owner," Fiona insisted stubbornly.

"Actually, a dog by the name of Taffy was stolen from a young blind woman in Salt Lake City, Utah." He opened the folder that he had on his lap. "A flyer was sent out. Here, look at it," he said. "It not only has a picture of the dog that was stolen, but it has some identifying features listed here. That's what we just examined."

He held out the flyer, and she took it reluctantly, trying to read through her tears. Her world was in tatters, and now Ritchie's was about to come crashing down on him. She knew, even though she tried to deny it, that Scully had brought his son a stolen dog.

"I need to make a phone call," Sergeant Powell said. "Look that over for me. If you have any questions, my partner here can help you."

Then he stepped outside, opening a cell phone as he went. Fiona could scarcely breathe. Losing Scully had been a shock, but after the terrible things he'd done to her and Ritchie, she knew it was a loss she could live with. But this! If they lost the only good thing Scully had ever done for Ritchie—the one thing that had brought him happiness—she doubted she could pick up the pieces of her shattered life and go on. She dried her eyes and tried to concentrate. It was all there in black and white, she admitted to herself. The officers were right. Taffy belonged to someone else. Fiona reached out and cradled her son in her arms as if to ward off the world's cruelties.

* * *

For security, Martin drove a different car that morning. And he drove it alone to the bus depot. He wore a hat, something he seldom did, and dark glasses. He had no idea whether Creed or one of his men might be watching the depot, but from past experience he knew anything was possible. Maddie, also using a different car, followed Noletta's cab to the downtown depot.

Once Noletta was safely inside, she drove off, parked the car where it would be picked up later by another officer, and waited a few blocks away for Martin and Noletta.

Noletta picked up the ticket and got on the bus exactly as she and Martin had discussed earlier. Then, just a few blocks from the depot, she pretended to be ill and demanded that the bus driver stop and let her out. The driver was hesitant but finally complied when it appeared that he might have to clean and disinfect his bus if he didn't.

Martin, who had followed the bus, stopped, and Maddie ushered Noletta into the car. They had only to drive to Cedar City now, and they had plenty of time, although they knew they had to arrive before the bus so they could purchase Noletta a new ticket. The plan was that Maddie would follow the bus in the car from Cedar City while Martin and Noletta rode together to the bus depot in St. George. There, officers would be standing by to help them arrest Creed, once Martin spotted him.

About a block from where he'd picked up Maddie and Noletta, Martin's phone rang. "Detective Atkinson," he said into the phone when he noted the number that was calling.

"Detective, Sergeant Powell here. I've pretty well confirmed that the dog we stumbled onto yesterday is the one you're missing up there. I just had a close look, and she matches every detail, including the name."

"That's great news," Martin said brightly as he glanced in the rearview mirror at Noletta, sitting in the backseat.

"Before I'm one hundred percent on this, your victim ought to come down and give us a personal identification. I know that's quite a distance out of her way and yours, but I think we need to be sure."

"Absolutely," Martin agreed. "And as far as coming down, I'm sure that can be arranged. Taffy's owner and my partner and I are on our way to St. George right now. If all goes well, we'll have the man we believe arranged for Taffy's theft in custody by around six this evening. We'll put him in jail in St. George and then come on down."

"That would be great. When you get your man, we're going to want to talk to him. If he arranged for the sale of the dog, then he can probably help us find who he sold it to, if he'll cooperate. The man who sold it on this end seems to be a big-time drug distributor, but we don't have a clue who he is. For obvious reasons, we'd like to find him. But we can worry about that later. Right now, I guess we could pick the dog up and then hold her in an animal shelter until you get here."

In the backseat Noletta could hardly contain her joy. She was softly laughing with delight. The heaviness that had been over Martin began to lift. "I guess that would be okay," Martin told the sergeant.

"There'll be one heartbroken little boy down here, but it can't be helped," Sergeant Powell said. "I just feel bad seeing him hurt again."

"What do you mean?" Martin asked in a much subdued tone.

The celebration behind him stopped.

"Let me explain," the sergeant said. "The family that has Taffy consisted of a father and a mother and a little blind boy named Ritchie. The father was found dead on the Mexican border near San Diego over the weekend. Turns out he was running drugs and must have made a mistake along the way. We've been unable to identify the man he was working for, but when we do, we'll also have the man who bought the dog from your suspect."

"The boy's father's dead?" Martin asked.

"I'm afraid so. And his mother—she seems like a really nice woman—is having a struggle with this. From what she's told us, the guide dog is the only kind thing the father ever did for his blind son. Ritchie, that's the little boy, and the dog are inseparable, even though they've only been together for a few days."

"Sergeant, is there any chance that anything would happen to Taffy if you left her with them until we can get there sometime tomorrow?" Martin asked.

"I'm sure she'd be fine," the sergeant said. "Mrs. Timmons is a good woman."

"Let me talk this over with Taffy's owner, and I'll call you back in just a minute," Martin said.

"It's really Taffy?" Noletta asked after Martin's call ended. But her voice lacked the excitement of only moments ago.

"It looks like it, but the final identification will have to be yours. Is it okay with you ladies if we go to Los Angeles after Creed's securely behind bars in St. George?" he asked.

Maddie and Noletta both agreed. Then Noletta asked, "I gather that someone else has Taffy now? Is it someone who's also blind? A child?"

"Yes," he said. "I'll fill you in on it, but first, I need to know if it's okay with you if she stays with the family she's with now until we get there. The other choice is to have her picked up and held at an animal shelter."

"Did the sergeant tell you that she'd be safe at that home until we could get there?" Noletta asked.

"Yes, he assured me that Taffy would be well taken care of by the boy and his mother."

"Then tell him it's okay," Noletta said.

Martin made the call. When he was through, he began to explain where Taffy was and how she got there. Noletta listened, stunned at the story.

* * *

"Taffy's owner will probably be here sometime tomorrow to make a positive identification of the dog," Sergeant Powell said.

"Until then, she says it's okay if you keep Taffy here. But take good care of her."

"We will," Fiona promised. Then her face grew hard. "I just can't believe that Scully would do this to his son. It seemed so good, giving the boy a dog, but a stolen one?" She couldn't continue, her voice choked with emotion.

Ritchie was kneeling beside Taffy, his little face buried in her neck. Sergeant Powell swallowed the sudden lump in his throat. "Listen. I have an idea, Ritchie," he said. "I'll bet that my fellow officers and I could get you another guide dog."

"Would you really do that?" Fiona hardly dared ask. Could this fleeting glimpse of goodness actually happen?

Sergeant Powell smiled. "We can do whatever we set our minds to. It might take a little time, but you have my word. We'll get the boy a dog."

* * *

Virgil answered the phone and was surprised to hear the boss calling. He didn't think they'd hear from him until they had completed their current assignment. "What do you need?" he asked.

"There's a slight change in plans," the boss said, and he went on to explain. "So you know what to do?"

"Not a problem," Virgil said. "We'll take care of it."

"Then get it done and stay out of sight until I need you again. But don't leave the Los Angeles area until I tell you to. I'll see that you have enough money, and then some, if you do the job right this time."

CHAPTER 24

Maddie was parked across the street from the bus stop, and Martin and Noletta were waiting to board the bus in Cedar City when the officer he'd coordinated with in St. George called him. The message was fairly short and to the point. He couldn't believe what he was hearing. "Are you sure?" he asked the officer.

"We're positive. I went out personally to the scene. The description is right, the vehicle is right, and he even has ID on him."

"This is good news, I think," Martin said. "I'm stunned. How did it happen?"

"We're not sure. No one saw anything until the truck left the freeway and rolled over."

Listening to a one-sided conversation, Noletta had tried to fill in the blanks to ascertain what was going on. Her efforts left her frustrated. So, when Martin finally concluded his phone conversation a couple of minutes later, she demanded, "What was that about?"

"You won't believe this," he said. "But Creed won't be meeting us at the bus depot in St. George."

Noletta exhaled as if she were letting loose all the worrisome demons that had besieged her for so long. But she recovered quickly. "Why not?"

"He's dying," Martin said flatly. "He was shot by a passing motorist while he was driving on the freeway. His truck rolled after that. They say he's conscious but has lost a lot of blood. They're doing everything they can for him, but they don't think he'll make it."

"Oh, no!" Noletta moaned. "That's awful. Where did it happen?"

"Just outside of St. George. And get this, Noletta—he was coming from the west. He actually may have been in California. Although it's anybody's guess what he was doing."

"But who would do that to him and why?" she asked, stunned at the news.

"That's a good question. Come on, let's go find Maddie and head for St. George. I'd like to get there and see if we can talk to Creed."

Martin took Noletta's hand as they ran toward Maddie and the waiting car. Martin told his partner what had happened as he started the car and rushed away. They were back on the freeway, speeding south, when Martin said, "Oh, get this, Noletta. The officer that called me said there was a dog with Creed. It's a nice-looking dog, seems to be well behaved and trained, and it doesn't seem to be hurt. He thinks it's an Irish setter. They have it in St. George."

"He said he had a surprise for me," Noletta said numbly. "He said it was something he'd promised. And he'd promised he'd buy me a new guide dog. Maybe that's what he's been doing—finding a dog. And he was actually bringing it to me. I guess there was still some good in him."

* * *

Martin drove straight to the hospital. Two officers met them there and rushed them inside. "Are you Noletta?" one of them asked.

"Yes," she said.

"Mr. Esplin is asking for you. He says he's got to talk to you, that there's something he needs to tell you. He won't be able to see you because his eyes are bandaged. In fact, his entire head is bandaged. But he should be able to hear you."

Her mind was in a turmoil. One part of her had no desire at all to talk to Creed after what he'd done. But another part of her wanted to speak with him, wanted to ask him why.

Martin said, "Did you grab that little tape recorder, Maddie?"

"Yes," his partner responded.

"Whatever he tells you, Noletta, will be caught on tape," Martin said. "So, if you can, ask him some questions. I'll whisper in your ear if I need to. Only when he's told you everything he can will I let him know I'm with you."

Inside the hospital, the officers directed them to the ICU.

A nurse spoke then. "Is one of you ladies Noletta Fahr?"

"I'm Noletta."

"He's asking for you. Come with me," the nurse said. "He's conscious, but he's in awful shape. I think the only reason he's lived this long is because he wants so badly to talk to you."

"We're coming too," Martin informed the nurse, half expecting her to object.

"Certainly," she said, and led the way into the sterile confines of the ICU.

"But don't tell him we're here. We'll be very quiet unless I feel that I need to step in and ask something."

"That'll be fine," she said.

Martin led Noletta by the arm and silently followed the nurse. A moment later they stopped. "Mr. Esplin's right here, Miss Fahr." Then the nurse said, "Miss Fahr made it here, Mr. Esplin."

All Noletta could hear for a moment was the purr of the machines that were keeping Creed alive. The familiar smells that filled the room brought back memories she'd sooner forget. But, by trying to concentrate on Creed, she finally managed to speak. "I'm sorry, Creed. I was coming to meet you."

"I knew you would," Creed said. "Thank you. I had so much planned for us."

"That's okay," Noletta said helplessly.

"I can't see you," he said. "Touch my hand."

She complied, and he said, "I love you, Noletta,"

"I know you do," she said, as strange as that seemed, even to her.

"I brought you a new dog, just like I said I would. The cops told me she wasn't hurt. They promised that they'd see that you got her."

"Thanks, Creed," she said, reaching for his hand.

She felt him squeeze, but it was without strength. "Noletta," he began again, his voice more weak. "Your painting, it's in—"

Creed's hand jumped even as his speech was cut off. She could tell that he was literally shaking the bed. Then his hand jerked free from hers. A rumbling groan escaped his lips. The nurse shoved her way past Noletta, simultaneously calling for help. A doctor rushed in, followed by another nurse. "You folks must leave the ICU—now."

Noletta felt Martin take her by the arm, and together they moved toward the door. Once back in the corridor, Noletta asked, "What happened?"

"Some kind of seizure," Martin said.

"He was going to tell me where my painting is," Noletta said.

"The self-portrait that was stolen from your home?" Maddie asked.

"Yes, that has to be what he was talking about," Noletta said, her voice breaking with emotion. "I think he was going to tell me what he'd done with it."

"It's probably in his home," Martin said. "That will be easy enough to check out."

The doctor came out of the room. "Are you the folks who were just visiting Mr. Esplin?" he asked.

"Yes," Noletta said. "I've got to speak to him again."

"I'm sorry, miss. That won't be possible. Mr. Esplin is dead," the doctor said. "I wish there was more we could have done for him, but there simply wasn't."

"I wish there was too," she said as tears washed down her face. *Will the madness never end?* she wondered.

* * *

The decision to give Jewel, the guide dog Creed had bought, to the blind boy, Ritchie, had been an easy decision for Noletta. As sensitive as she was, Noletta knew how hard it would be for the little boy to give up Taffy, even if he'd had her only a very short time. She also knew it would lessen the blow if she could make the trade.

Despite all the terrifying things Creed had done, she nonetheless felt grateful to him for finding and buying another guide dog. And Martin, with the help of the police in Los Angeles, had already confirmed that Jewel's purchase was legitimate. Creed hadn't stolen her like he'd ordered Virgil to do with Taffy.

Another decision was also made that evening. Feeling that the danger was past with Creed's death, Martin suggested that he go alone with Noletta to get Taffy the next morning and that Maddie then drive their vehicle back to Salt Lake. A flight from St. George to Las Vegas and a connecting flight from there to Los Angeles were soon arranged for Martin, Noletta, and the dog, Jewel.

A return flight directly from Los Angeles to Salt Lake was also arranged for the two of them and Taffy. They checked into a couple of hotel rooms for the night, and Noletta anxiously awaited the next day's reunion with Taffy.

As they ate dinner in St. George that evening, Martin and the two women talked about what had happened to Creed. "Could it have been an enraged driver that shot Creed?" Maddie asked. "You know, maybe someone he cut off earlier while passing, who then went after him to make him pay. That happens a lot these days."

"I suppose that's possible," Martin said. "But under the circumstances, I'm more inclined to believe that someone just decided to bump him off for reasons of their own."

"Could it have been Virgil and Skip that shot him?" Noletta asked. "Maybe they had a disagreement of some kind with him. You know what they say about there being no honor among thieves."

"That's another distinct possibility," Martin agreed. "But unless we find that pair, we'll never know for sure."

* * *

The little house that Sergeant Powell stopped in front of shortly after eight the next morning was small and rundown. It needed paint and shingles—and the lawn, what little there was of it, was more weeds than grass. "This is where Fiona and Ritchie live," Sergeant Powell said to his passengers. "Like I told you earlier, we brought Taffy over here last night. And just to make sure nothing happened to her again, we kept surveillance on the place all night. I just felt like I needed to let Ritchie have a few hours to say good-bye to her."

"Thank you," Noletta said. "You're a kind man."

"Would you like me to take Jewel," he said, "so you'll be free to greet your own dog?"

"That would be nice," she said as she handed Jewel's leash to the officer.

Martin stood back and watched while Noletta followed Sergeant Powell and Jewel to the door. The door to the little house opened. Tears of relief and joy stung his eyes as he watched Taffy bound through the door and leap toward Noletta, and as Noletta knelt and buried her face in her dog's neck.

Then he saw little Ritchie step into the open doorway, his pitiful blind eyes streaming with tears. Martin himself could see only a blur through the tears in his own eyes as the sergeant tried to hand Jewel's leash to Ritchie. But Noletta couldn't do it. She realized after talking with Ritchie how much he had become attached to Taffy, how much he'd already come to rely on her in such a short time. Fighting back the tears, she walked Taffy back to the little boy and watched as Ritchie embraced his companion and protector. Ritchie needed Taffy now.

CHAPTER 25

When he realized it would take longer than expected at the Timmons's home, Martin had arranged for a later flight. It had been a hassle to make the change, and at times like this he was inclined to curse the airlines for all their regulations.

Even with the later flight, most of the passengers were already onboard by the time Martin directed Noletta and Jewel to the boarding gate. He led them quickly onto the plane and found their seats in the economy section not far behind first class. It had taken some persuasion by Martin to convince the airline to allow him to buy an extra seat and take Jewel on with them. Noletta's very real tears seemed to be the clincher in the dispute.

Soon after they had settled into their seats, the plane took off. Both Noletta and Martin were emotionally drained, and for the first hour of their flight, fatigue took over, and Noletta slept soundly. Martin tenderly watched her from his seat beside her, wondering what the future might hold for them, hoping their lives would be intertwined. After her nap, Noletta felt more refreshed and emotionally upbeat than she had in days. During the remainder of the flight, they talked freely, sharing stories from their pasts and talking about their families.

* * *

From an aisle seat much farther back on the plane, another passenger had watched with interest as Noletta boarded the plane. Occasionally, he checked to make sure she was still where he had seen her sit. And each time he did, he would see the back of Martin's head, and that made him bristle. He loathed the man.

* * *

During a lull in their conversation, Noletta leaned over to Martin and asked, "What time did you say we'd be landing?"

"Near eight," he said. "That's about twenty minutes. Maddie will be waiting for us at the luggage area. Even though you didn't check any bags, we thought it would be a pretty easy place to meet. It won't be long now. I imagine they'll be telling us to fasten our seat belts soon."

"I'm sorry I made us have to catch such a late flight," she said. "But I just couldn't leave that little boy before we had settled things."

Martin smiled. "It was worth it. You were great with Ritchie. I'm convinced his life will be better because of you. He learned some important things from you today, things I doubt he will even realize for several years. And I think you two bonded in a very special way."

"I hope so," Noletta said. "How could anyone help but love the little guy. Hey, did you say they'll be telling us to fasten our seat belts soon?"

"Yeah, why?" Martin asked.

"I need to freshen up," she said with a grin that was aimed in his direction. "If you'll tell us where the restroom is, we can make our way back here to our seats afterward without any trouble," she said.

Noletta grabbed her purse, but after a moment's hesitation she took a few items from it and placed them in her pocket. She handed her purse to Martin, indicating that he could place it overhead. Knowing the size of airplane restrooms, she didn't want to have to search for a surface on which to place her purse in such tight quarters.

Martin led her to the restroom in the center of the plane and left her there with Jewel. It was with mixed emotions that he walked away, but he knew she was anxious to reclaim her independence. Slowly he made his way forward and took his seat.

* * *

From his seat near the back, the other man looked up just as Noletta entered the restroom. He smiled to himself. Had others seen his face, however, they might have been more inclined to attribute his expression to malevolence rather than happiness. As soon as the detective had returned to his seat, the man impulsively rose from his own and made his way forward.

* * *

When Noletta opened the restroom door and stepped out, she noted the odor of a familiar brand of aftershave. She tensed just as a hand clamped around her wrist. Then she gasped.

* * *

Although he was almost certain that the death of Creed had ended the danger to Noletta, Martin felt a nagging worry eating away at his peace of mind. His unease was punctuated by the absence of his service pistol. Despite his strenuous protests, airport security had refused to let him take his weapon on the plane. Instead, he'd been forced to check it with the captain, who promised to return it once they were on the ground and ready to deplane in Salt Lake City.

Martin wondered what was taking Noletta so long. She and Jewel should have been back by now. He wondered if somehow she had become disoriented, although with her dog at her side, it seemed unlikely.

He looked at his watch, counting the ticks as the second hand made another complete sweep. Then he decided it had been long enough. He needed to check on her before the captain issued the seat belt warning. But as Martin rose to his feet, the huge plane suddenly pitched and rolled violently. The fasten-seat-belt signs came on instantly. Over the intercom the captain said, "We have encountered some turbulence. Please fasten your seat belts and stay in your seats until we are on the ground. This storm we're in will continue. If you are not in your seat, please take an empty one near you."

By now the plane was bucking quite violently. Despite that, Martin rose to his feet, determined to make sure Noletta was safe. But before he'd been able to move into the aisle, a flight attendant stopped him. "Please, sir. Take your seat."

"But my friend, she's blind. And she didn't come back from the restroom. I've got to help her."

"A girl with long brown hair and a dog?" the flight attendant asked.

"Yes, she's the one. I need to find her," he said urgently.

"Stay right here," she said in her no-nonsense voice. "I'm sure she's found another seat, but I'll check on her as soon as I can, just to be certain. When I locate her, I'll let her know you're concerned about her. Now please, sir, sit down."

The plane lurched violently again, and the flight attendant was thrown into Martin, knocking him off balance. He grabbed for the back of a seat and, with some effort, managed to stumble into his seat.

"Now fasten your seat belt and stay here, sir." The flight attendant spat out the words angrily, and she began to make her way toward the back of the plane.

Martin was restless. He felt that Noletta needed him. As the pilot continued to deal with the turbulence, Martin thought constantly of Noletta. And in the ten minutes that elapsed before the flight became relatively smooth and the captain landed the airplane, he knew that his feelings for Noletta were deep. He wanted to share them with her. He wanted to find just the right moment and then tell her that he loved her. He now knew that he did.

Although the fasten-seat-belt sign stayed on even after the flight had touched down, Martin rose to find the woman he loved. Once again he was interrupted by the pilot's voice over the intercom. "Please remain seated with your seat belts on," he said. "We'll be pulling up to the gate shortly. I'm sorry about the rough flight of the past few minutes. The storm we flew into was much rougher than expected. And it's raging on the ground here in Salt Lake City."

Martin tried to reassure himself that Noletta was fine, but doubts kept plaguing him. The normally slow progress toward the gate seemed closer to nonexistent. No sooner were the passengers given permission to begin retrieving their overhead luggage and exiting the plane than Martin began moving down the aisle toward the back. He searched from his side of the plane, through the center section, and into the far aisle, but he didn't see Noletta.

It was slow going since others were standing in the aisles, and they were not eager to let Martin crowd his way through. As more passengers began unloading their carry-on items, Martin realized he could no longer force his way through the impatient, determined human wall that filled both aisles. Defeated, he momentarily slumped into the nearest seat to wait.

Later, when he finally reached the center section, he tried the restroom door where he'd left Noletta. It was locked. That compounded his worries. *Could she still be in there?* he wondered. *Could something have happened to cause her to black out?* If she had been in there when the plane hit the turbulence, he supposed she could have fallen and hurt herself. But if that had happened, surely Jewel wouldn't have abandoned her post.

Martin moved on to the rear section of the plane, pushing through the few remaining passengers. Having seen no sign of Noletta or Jewel by the time he reached the back, he began to feel the early symptoms of panic, something he'd been trained to overcome. He kept watching for the flight attendant who had promised to look for her, but she wasn't around.

Martin grabbed his cell phone from his pocket and turned it on as he impatiently turned around and made his way forward, intent on checking the restroom again. If it was still locked, he decided, he'd either find help to get in or he'd yank the door off its hinges.

As soon as his phone had picked up a signal, he dialed Maddie's cell phone. She answered instantly.

"Where are you?" he barked.

"I'm at the luggage carousels," she said. "Is something wrong?"

Martin explained quickly, and Maddie said, "I'll contact security here and see if they'll let me come to your gate. If you see her, call me, and I'll do the same."

"Thanks," Martin said and clicked his phone shut. In a couple of minutes he'd managed to make his way back to the divider where the restroom was located. When he reached the restroom, he grabbed the handle, expecting to find it locked. But it swung open.

It was empty!

He dialed Maddie and told her. She asked, "Could she have gotten off the plane ahead of you?"

"It seems unlikely, but I suppose she could have passed me on the far side when I was in that dividing section," he said doubtfully.

"She's probably waiting for you, wondering where you are," Maddie suggested.

"Maybe," Martin admitted. "I'll get out of here as quickly as I can. Are they going to let you past security?"

"I don't know yet. They say they're working on it."

Martin was near the front of the plane when he met the flight attendant he'd been looking for. "I still haven't found my friend," he said urgently.

"You mean the blind girl? The one with the dog?"

"Yes. Did you see her?"

"She left the plane some time ago. She seemed fine to me. Some man had hold of her arm and seemed to be helping her."

"Did you talk to her?" he demanded.

"No, but she looked just fine. I'm sure she's waiting for you."

"What did the man look like?"

"I don't know," the flight attendant said, obviously annoyed. "She was standing between me and him. All I can tell you for sure is that he was wearing a baseball cap. Sorry, there are more than two hundred passengers on this flight. I wouldn't have noticed the girl had I not been watching for her at your request. But I'm sure she's okay. He was holding her arm, like I told you, helping her, it looked like. And the dog was right there with them. That's all I know. Now, if you'll excuse me—"

"Thanks," Martin said. Then he dialed Maddie again. As soon as she answered, he said, "She's with some man wearing a baseball cap and has already gotten off the plane. Are you past security yet?"

"Just barely," Maddie said. "But I can't see her anywhere."

"I'm hurrying," Martin said. "Start looking around out there."

By the time Martin had pushed his way through the last of the passengers and out the gate, he still couldn't see Noletta. His phone rang, and he snapped it open.

"Martin, I can't see her. I'm checking the restroom over here," Maddie said.

"That's good," he responded as he spotted Maddie's short, blonde hair moving through the crowd toward him.

He closed his phone and then snapped it open again. Swiftly he dialed Noletta's number. It went to voice mail. Then he remembered putting her bag in the overhead bin, and he wondered if her phone was in it.

"Detective Atkinson."

He turned. It was one of the flight attendants. "The captain said you left something."

His pistol. And their bags were still in the overhead bins. He ran back onto the plane, collected the gun from the captain, and quickly concealed it in the holster beneath his jacket.

"Are these yours?" another flight attendant asked.

She held out two bags. "Yes," he said as he reached for them and took off running.

"Hey, Martin, what are you doing?" Maddie asked as he nearly raced past her.

He stopped. "I'm hurrying," he said.

"Looks like you went back for your bags."

"Yes, and my pistol. Have you seen Noletta?"

"No. Martin, I'm worried."

"So am I," he said. "So am I."

Chapter 26

Noletta couldn't believe how quickly she'd been ushered from the airport. She had clearly misjudged the depth of Walton's feelings for her. He told her he'd headed for California once he realized that she was going there to be with Creed. Having been instrumental in helping her identify Creed as the man who'd shot her, Walton said that his blood had run cold when he heard that she was going there. He'd gone, he explained, to save her from his depraved cousin.

She wondered how he knew where she was going. She thought she, along with Martin and his partner, had been very discreet. But clearly he'd found out somehow. Perhaps Creed had called him and boasted. With their bickering over the past week, it wouldn't seem inconsistent.

She would ask him, she decided, but not just yet. It was gallant of him, she admitted, and it did show that he cared. In fact, it was clear that Walton had romantic intentions. *But he's too late now,* she kept telling herself. She knew now that her heart was with Martin. She couldn't help it. It had happened despite herself.

"Walton, we have to let Martin know where I am," she said. "He'll be worried. And I'll need to get my carry-on bag."

"Martin will get it for you. You and I need to talk. I can't believe I nearly let you slip away from me. I love you, Noletta. And I know you have feelings for me," he said.

"I'm confused, Walton. You haven't said anything like this before. I'll admit I had hoped you might feel something deeper. We've been good friends, but it seemed like that's as far as you wanted our relationship to go."

"I was afraid to tell you how I felt, and I was a fool," he said. "But I'm through being a fool. I need you. And you need me."

"I'm not sure this is a good idea," she said. "Maybe we should—"

"You're safe now, Noletta," he said, cutting her off. "You told me yourself that my killer cousin is dead. And I can't say I'm sorry after what I've learned he did to you and Lamar Kayser. And as for Martin Atkinson, he's just a cop. A better cop than I gave him credit for, but a cop, nonetheless. And he has no right trying to steal you away from me."

"Who said he was—" Noletta began.

"I'm not blind, Noletta. I can see what he's up to. Oh, sorry, I didn't mean that as an insult. Anyway, I know he thinks he has the inside track now. But please, please, don't let him come between us. We have so much going for us."

"Okay, I'm willing to talk," she said. "But at least let me tell Detective Atkinson that I'm with you. He can take my suitcase to my parents' house. I'll probably not be moving home for a day or two anyway."

"And when you do, I'll help you," Walton said as he pulled his cell phone from his pocket and turned it on. "You'll have to talk fast, sweetheart, because I forgot to bring my charger when I decided to fly to Los Angeles. It's probably almost dead."

He was right. There was only one bar. She punched in the number, and her heart fluttered at the very sound of Martin's deep voice a moment later. "Hi, Martin, it's Noletta," she began.

"Where are you?" he asked almost angrily. "We've been looking all over the airport for you."

"I'm fine," she said. "I'm with Walton, and I'm using his phone, and it's about to go dead."

"What are you doing with him?" Martin demanded. Noletta struggled to hear him as the wind roared outside the car and rain pelted it.

"He wants to talk. And we do need to. I'll call you later. Will you take my luggage to—" There was a beep, and the phone went dead.

"Did it die?" Walton asked.

"Yes, and I wasn't through talking to him," Noletta said.

"It's okay. He won't worry now that he knows you're with me. Actually, that may not be quite true. I suppose he'll know that I'm trying to win you back. And I can't lie; that's exactly what I'm trying to do."

Noletta was agitated by her friend. She'd wanted for more than a year to hear him say that he cared deeply for her. But he'd waited so long—too long. She didn't know how she was going to tell him that she was not in love with him, but she knew she had to do it. What worried her most, though, was hurting him. And in a way, what he said was right. She needed him. It was he who did so much in helping her make it through law school. She wasn't sure she could do it without him. Oh, she could use her readers more, but that was expensive, and they didn't give her the same personal attention that Walton did.

A particularly violent burst of wind rocked Walton's car, and a terrible crash of thunder accompanied it. The windshield wipers couldn't keep up with the rain. "This storm is unbelievable," Walton said loudly. "We're lucky the plane landed without problems."

"Where are we going?" Noletta asked. It was hard to carry on a conversation as the noise from the storm increased dramatically by the minute.

"I don't care. Just someplace private and quiet where we can have a serious talk. Probably my place. It's closest, and I can't wait to get in out of this storm. It's hard just to drive," he shouted.

Noletta supposed that was fine. She was familiar with his apartment, having studied there with him several times. Unless he'd moved his furniture around, she could maneuver easily in his living room and kitchen. She hoped it wouldn't take too long. She wanted desperately to be with Martin.

They rode without speaking for several minutes. It was too hard to make themselves heard above the noise of the storm. Suddenly Walton slammed on the brakes, throwing Noletta hard against the seat belt. "Sorry," he shouted. "The traffic light just went out, and so did the streetlights. Power must be out. Hope it's still on at my place. I hate the dark."

That was her world, the darkness. It wasn't so bad once she got used to it. She was surprised at first that Walton would say something so insensitive, but she quickly forgave him. It would be impossible for a seeing person to be attuned to every feeling that a blind person had. And anyway, he was usually quite sensitive to her disability. She knew driving in the storm was requiring all of his concentration. And she supposed he really was upset about the prospect of losing her to Martin.

Because the power was out over much of the city, the rest of the drive home took longer than usual. To Walton's disgust, his apartment was black also.

By the time they reached the apartment door, they were drenched. "You go on in," she told Walton, "while I see if she'll shake the water out of her coat out here. I don't want her to ruin your carpet."

"Don't worry about it," he said, but she did, and so he went inside, and she stayed out on the porch. Jewel shook her coat until she was reasonably dry, and then Noletta opened the door, and the two of them entered.

She could hear Walton moving about in the direction she knew to be his main bedroom. He called out to her as she began inspecting the layout of the living room to determine if it was the same as she remembered from her last visit.

"Make yourself at home, Noletta. I found my flashlight, but I haven't used it for so long that the batteries are dead. I'm going to run out to the car. I may have one in the glove box or the trunk. Man, now I know how it is for you all the time."

"It's not really all that bad, Walton," she called back as she made her way across the living room.

"Well, I've only stumbled twice, stubbed my toes three times, and crashed into the wall once," he said with a tense laugh.

"Are you all right?" she asked.

"I'm fine. At least, nothing's broken. I threw a towel on the kitchen table so you can dry yourself. If you can find my fridge, there's some pop in there. The Sprite is on the left on the top rack if I remember correctly. Help yourself if you'd like."

"Thanks, Walton," she called to him, and she heard the door slam shut.

She resumed checking out the room. Other than one chair, she found everything to be as she remembered it. That chair, a small wooden one, was next to the outside door. He'd never had a chair there before, and she wondered about it momentarily, not that it mattered.

She moved into his kitchen, where she had to be more careful. Things were not quite the same in there. Remembering how she'd tripped over the chair in her own house right after Taffy had been taken, a kitchen chair that Martin had moved—and how angry Walton had been at Martin for not putting the chair exactly where she usually kept it—she was careful not to trip in Walton's kitchen.

Soon she knew exactly where everything was. She found the towel on the table and wiped her wet hair and clothing. Then she opened the refrigerator, found a can of Sprite where Walton had said it would be, and opened it. She sat at his table and sipped for a few minutes. Then, restless, she left it unfinished and found her way back to the living room. Jewel stayed at her side, but Noletta moved on her own, as she usually did when indoors and in familiar places.

Noletta wondered what could be taking Walton so long. He should be joining her soon. She felt the tension return, dreading the discussion that lay ahead. He would want to talk as soon as he returned. He was still a good friend, and she cared for him a lot, but she didn't love him and was quite certain she never would, no matter what he said to her. Still, her gentle, sensitive nature didn't want to hurt him.

The wind outside had died down, and she listened for the hum of the refrigerator, knowing that it would signal her when the power came back on. She could hear the familiar ticking of a clock she'd given Walton for Christmas just a few short months ago. It was one that required weekly winding, and the ticking was soft but distinct. She hadn't noticed it when she first came in because the storm had been so loud, but she could hear it quite distinctly now. And she wondered, as she listened, why Walton had moved it.

He'd told her on Christmas day when she gave it to him that he would keep it on the wall that faced the doorway so that each time he came into his apartment he would see it and think of her. It was now on the wall to the left of the doorway. She walked over there, reached up, and touched it. In its current location, she didn't think it would be easily noticed.

So what did he hang where it used to be? she asked herself. And turning, she crossed to the wall opposite the door and reached up. Her hand touched an oil painting. *That's strange,* she thought. *He's never mentioned having a new painting.* She wondered if it was one he'd painted himself, although he mostly sketched.

Noletta fingered the painting. There was something eerily familiar about it, and the hairs on her neck and arms bristled.

She lifted the painting from the wall, her heart pounding fiercely, and fingered the back of the frame. She nearly dropped it when her fingers found a number etched there.

It was painting number twenty-three!

Noletta's self-portrait, stolen from her house, was hanging in the very spot in Walton's living room where he would be most likely to see it each time he entered his apartment. For a moment, she was puzzled. Then like a thunderbolt, it struck her. *Walton had either stolen it or had it stolen!*

The feeling of danger suddenly became palpable. If he'd stolen the painting, or had someone else steal it, then he was also behind the theft of Taffy. And if he was involved with that, then what else had he done?

The conclusion she came to in a matter of seconds was almost too terrifying to contemplate. Virgil had been at her door. He must have taken Taffy and the painting. If so, he must have done it at Walton's request. And if Virgil worked for Walton, so did Skip and Evan. Which could only mean that Walton had hired them to kill Martin. And that conclusion lead to another one. She had conveyed to Walton only a rough, very basic description of the man who shot her. And he had sketched a man he clearly detested, his own cousin Creed. That conclusion led to the worst discovery of all. A terrible one.

Creed was innocent.

Walton was a killer.

Walton had murdered Terri's husband, and he had stolen Noletta's sight. Then she remembered Creed trying to tell her something about where the painting was. And she knew that he'd been planning to warn her about Walton just before he died. Noletta came to the only conclusion that made any sense now. Creed had been murdered either by Walton or by one of his men. He'd been trying to warn her. And he had died before he could.

Now she was alone in this house with a cold-blooded killer, a man without a conscience, a man who had once tried to kill her, who discovered that her blindness was as effective for him as her death, and who then decided to take her for his own. And she had willingly gone down that path, *almost to the end.*

But now she faced the possibility of a different kind of end—if he discovered that she knew he had the painting. Although he loved her in some sick, enigmatic way, he would undoubtedly kill her to save himself. Of that she was certain.

Noletta knew she had to get away from him. She listened for a moment. The refrigerator made no sound; the power had not yet come back on. So it was still dark. Now was the time to make her escape, while she possessed the advantage in the inky blackness of the apartment. But no sooner had that thought come to her than she heard Walton's footsteps coming toward the apartment door.

"Noletta," he called. "Where are you? It's so dark in here that I can't see a thing. And I couldn't find another flashlight."

For a moment she was silent as she considered her options. The painting was still in her hands. If the power came on and Walton saw it, he would know. *Can I rehang it without letting him hear?* she wondered.

She turned toward the wall, and as she lifted the painting back into position, she tried to conceal with her own voice the sound of the frame scraping on the wall. "I'm here," she said as loudly as she dared, the noise outside no longer justifying a shout. "Thanks for the towel. It helped, although I'm still very wet. I could use another one." She knew she was rambling. "And I found the Sprite. It was right where you said." She felt the wire on the back of the painting catch the nail it had been hung on. She continued to talk as she lowered it into place as silently as she could.

"Noletta!" He shouted her name, his voice sharper than she'd ever heard before. "What are you doing?"

"Just walking around," she said. "I'm nervous knowing that you are in the dark and that you're not as used to it as I am. I've been afraid you'd get hurt."

"I'm fine," he said, his voice lower now. "But I think you're lying to me. Your voice sounds like you've seen a ghost. But you can't see. So you must have felt a ghost. You must have touched something on the wall that you shouldn't have."

"Why would I do that, Walton?" she asked, her mouth dry, her words indistinct.

"You would lie because you found something you shouldn't have found. I know exactly where you're standing. You're next to my painting, the one hanging where the clock used to be. And I heard it scraping the wall just now. You've been snooping. You have no right to snoop, Noletta. This is my home." Walton's voice had never sounded like this before, full of anger and hatred.

"I was just leaning against the wall," she protested faintly. The terrible rage in his voice struck chords of terror through her.

"You filthy little liar!" he shouted. "I thought we were friends. I've tried to make up for everything I had to do to you. I fell in love with you, Noletta. I was so relieved that day to find that you hadn't died. I was willing to share my whole life with you, to make your life easier. But now you've compromised all of that. I even had Creed killed to free you from him. And that detective friend of yours, I'd have gotten him too. And we could have been so happy, you and me. But now you leave me no choice, Noletta. This time you will have to die."

It was only through sheer willpower that Noletta kept from fainting. Her life now depended on her strength, her cunning, and her resolve. She wanted to live. She couldn't let him win. She knew she had the advantage because the darkness was not a handicap to her as it was to Walton. She prayed that the electricity would not come back on. She reached up and again removed the painting from the wall. It was the only weapon

she could think of, although she hoped she could make it to his
door and get away without having to use any type of force.

* * *

Martin and his partner were still struggling to get to the police
department from the airport. Intersections were clogged with
impatient drivers and numerous traffic accidents. He too was
impatient, and he was upset that Noletta had gone with
Walton. It didn't make sense. Something was very wrong with
the whole scenario. He just couldn't put his finger on it. It was
so wrong, though, that he'd already called Lieutenant Merrill.
He'd made a request of him, hoping he was wrong, but having
to know.

There was no way Walton could have known that Noletta
had gone to California, or that she would be on that flight.
And yet he had. Yes, he'd known something he shouldn't have,
something he couldn't have. But he had, and that meant there
were things that he and Maddie and Detective Pollard had
somehow overlooked in their investigation. He and Maddie
had talked it over, both agreeing that there was something else
they needed to know.

"Martin, could he have been watching us or having us
watched?" Maddie asked. "Maybe that's how he knew we were
heading south."

"That's what I've been wondering," Martin agreed. "Or
perhaps Ted somehow figured it out. He would have let Walton
know if he thought it would botch my investigation. And then
there's Creed's death. That really bothers me, Maddie. That
wasn't a random shooting. In an investigation like this, there
are no coincidences."

Martin's cell phone rang.

"Detective Atkinson, this is Lieutenant Merrill. I'm afraid
you were right. I located a report, just like you suspected.

Creed Esplin's gun was stolen just a couple of days before the murder of Lamar Kayser. It was taken from his truck and never recovered."

"Oh no," Martin groaned.

"Martin, didn't you say Noletta was with Walton Pease now?" the lieutenant asked.

"Yes."

"Martin, how Walton Pease was able to make that sketch from such a flimsy description as you say Noletta gave him has bothered me," Lieutenant Merrill said.

"It bothers me too," Martin agreed. "I think it's a fraud. Walton drew it, not from Noletta's description, but to frame Creed!" He slammed on his brakes and made a U-turn. "Walton has Noletta. We've got to find them."

"Where should we begin to look?" Lieutenant Merrill asked.

"Send some officers to Noletta's house and some to her parents' place. And send some to back up Maddie and me. We're headed for Walton's apartment."

"Martin, could it be?" Maddie asked in a stricken voice.

"Yes! Walton's the killer!" he said. "Stick that red light on the dash. There's no time to lose!" As he spoke, he turned on the siren and jammed his foot to the floor.

* * *

Noletta gripped the painting firmly. She didn't care if she ruined it. She had to stop Walton if he was somehow able to reach her in the dark. She could hear his tentative steps moving toward her. The darkness was a definite handicap to him. She decided to try to stall him again. "How did you know I was in California?" she asked.

Walton laughed—it was an unbelievably ugly sound. "It was easy, really. Ted Zobel's been a big help. After Virgil and

Skip took care of Creed for me, I came down to St. George. I just missed the flight you and your cop friend was on. But I knew where you were going. So I followed. It was just that easy. I wish what I have to do now was half as easy. I really do love you, Noletta, but you know that I can't let you live."

Noletta began backing toward the front door as Walton talked. She sensed how fruitless further conversation would be. What she needed to do was move quietly and quickly and get out of there. Jewel was so close that Noletta could feel her brushing against her leg as she kept pace with her mistress.

"It could have been so good," Walton said. "Why did you have to snoop?"

He was coming too fast. And he was veering in the direction she was moving. She had to hurry. Noletta reached the door, found the handle, and tried to turn it. But just then, Walton lunged at her. She spun to the side, knocking over the wooden chair that had seemed so out of place by the door. She managed to keep her balance as Walton crashed into the door, uttering words she'd never before heard from him. She swung the picture with all her strength and felt the frame break as it struck him. She had hoped to hit his head, but she knew it must have connected with his back. It wasn't an effective hit, and he lunged at her again. This time he grabbed her jacket, but as she tried to twist away, he stumbled on the chair she'd just knocked over.

Noletta managed to shrug out of the jacket. As she did so, her hand brushed against the front pocket of her pants. Instantly, she identified the two items she'd taken earlier from her purse. While Walton was trying to stand up, she scuttled across the room, attempting to remember exactly where everything was so she wouldn't fall. She passed the point where she judged Walton's coffee table to be, then silently crept around it.

She hadn't fooled him. Walton, once he regained his footing, came charging toward her. But when his shins struck the coffee table, he screamed and crashed to the floor a second time. Noletta grabbed the slender cylinder from her pocket and again sprinted for the front door, hoping she could keep herself oriented while moving so quickly. But she miscounted her steps and collided with the door a half-step quicker than she'd judged.

The impact sent her reeling backward and disoriented her slightly. It also disclosed her position. Once more Walton lunged. He connected with her this time, knocking her to the floor and landing on her legs. Noletta felt his hands begin working their way up her body, and soon she felt his breath near her midsection.

With courage she didn't know she possessed, she raised the hand holding the cylinder, aimed it directly at Walton's face, and depressed the nozzle—once, twice, three times. Walton screamed as the spray filled his eyes, nose, and mouth. He pulled himself off her, rubbing his eyes and coughing. As soon as Walton released her, Noletta again reached into her pocket. Grasping the other item firmly with both hands, she rose to her knees. Then, with all her strength she flung herself, arms outstretched, at Walton. She hoped she had aimed for his face, but she knew that any fleshy tissue would do. She connected— she wasn't certain where. But the expletives that suddenly filled the room convinced her that she had injured the man she thought was her friend—the man she had once hoped might eventually be her husband.

Once Noletta began her offensive moves, Jewel quickly joined her. With a low growl, she raced from her owner's side and attacked the assailant. Noletta shuddered as Walton began to scream in pain.

He tried to kick at the dog and roll away, but he was powerless against the enraged dog's brute strength.

A siren sounded a short distance away. Noletta cringed at Walton's panicked cries. "Call off your dog, Noletta. I swear I won't hurt you. Please, do it—now!"

Determined not to be deceived again, she stood carefully. Then, with a steady voice, Noletta spoke to Jewel. "Good girl, good girl. That's right. Stay, Jewel."

The shrill siren was now just outside the building, and a second one joined it within moments. As the sirens fell silent, Noletta heard the refrigerator begin to hum. The sounds calmed Noletta and helped restore her breathing to normal. She stared with contempt in the direction of the pathetic figure whimpering across from her. With determination, she backed toward the door, grabbed the knob, and yanked it open as she heard Martin's shouts. "Police! We're coming in!"

Martin said one more word as he bolted toward the newly opened door. "Noletta!"

Tears filled Noletta's eyes, and great sobs wracked her bruised body. She collapsed into Martin's arms.

"Are you okay?" he cried.

"Yes, I'm okay," she sobbed. "Walton's still inside. I think between the two of us—Jewel and me—we may have injured him pretty badly."

"Come on, Martin! I hate to interrupt this little reunion," Maddie shouted, "but Walton's not going to wait for us forever. He's trying to get up right now. Thank goodness for that dog."

"I love you," Martin whispered to Noletta as he tore himself away from her. It wasn't the way he'd planned to tell her, but he meant it nonetheless.

"I love you, too," Noletta whispered as he left her.

Officers from the second police car reached out and gently helped Noletta walk away from the building and toward the safety of their vehicle. She heard raised voices and a loud scuffle inside the apartment before Martin finally shouted, "We've got him, Noletta."

CHAPTER 27

Autumn of that same year

The cool evening breeze felt good after the heat of the Indian summer day. Dinner had been fantastic—that was Harmony's description. Elliot and Francine Fahr had hosted a family gathering and, to Noletta's delight, had invited a sprinkling of good friends, both old and new.

It came as no surprise to anyone that evening when Martin and Noletta announced their engagement and forthcoming marriage. Now, after the delicious food and long-anticipated announcement, the hosts and their guests were relaxing on the front porch of the Fahrs' home. Noletta's brother, Dirk, and his family had moved back to Utah a month earlier, happy to be with their extended family again and grateful that Noletta was still with them.

As dusk settled over the valley, the conversation turned, as it did so often, to last spring's "excitement"—that had become the family code word for the incredible events surrounding Noletta, Martin, Walton, and Creed. Because Dirk and his family had heard only bits and pieces and several abbreviated versions, they requested the full, unabridged story. Fiona and Ritchie were also eager to learn all of the details that had brought about their friendship with the Fahrs and their ultimate move to Utah.

Taking turns relating the details, the family and their friends pieced together the events that had culminated in tonight's announcement. When they reached the point in the narration where Walton had fallen on Noletta during the encounter in his dark living room, Harmony cried, "Wait! Let me tell it."

She walked to the front steps, turned back toward the waiting audience, and stood quietly, making sure she had their complete attention. Finally, she tossed her head and said, "Then Noletta reached into her pocket and pulled out the spray can—her hair spray—and sprayed it in Walton's face three times. Boy, he wasn't expecting that, and he started coughing and rubbing his eyes and maybe even forgot about Noletta for a minute. That gave Noletta time to pull out the other thing in her pocket and she stabbed him with it. Betcha can't guess what that was."

Ritchie, wanting to be part of the action, raised his hand. "Was it a knife?"

Dirk's oldest daughter said, "I know. It was a pencil."

"No," Harmony said. "It was a comb, a rat-tail comb."

"A what?" the children asked in unison.

"A rat-tail comb. It's half comb and half tail. And the tail is long and sort of pointed." Harmony's animated hands drew a picture in the air. "The handle looks like a rat's tail."

Noletta's father turned, sighed, and looked quizzically at his daughter. "Noletta, one thing I haven't really understood before is why you didn't use your pepper spray. I know you always carry it with you."

"Well, Dad, remember, I went back to the restroom just before we flew into the storm. With Creed gone, I felt safe and I certainly thought I had no need for it. Anyway, after I had been leaning against the seat and sleeping for an hour, my hair was full of static. I could feel it standing straight out. So I took the miniature can of hair spray, which I very rarely use, and my comb with me, but not my purse, which, by the way, I never did get back. Mom, you remember that rat-tail comb you gave me when I was thirteen, right after I broke my leg? I used it for scratching inside my cast when I started itching so much. That's the one I had in my purse and then put in my pocket when I headed for the restroom. Who would have thought it would save my life?"

Harmony was anxious to take her place in the spotlight again. However, because the last part of the story was Ritchie's favorite, he jumped in ahead of her the minute Noletta paused.

"Then Jewel decided she really was Noletta's dog. You see, Noletta let me keep Taffy—and that's why I love Noletta so much. Anyway, Jewel started biting Walton. She has the sharpest teeth in the world, and Walton couldn't get away from her. That's when the police got there," Ritchie said, sighing in contentment.

"Luckily, Martin and Madison were able to track down Virgil and Skip once Walton broke down and confessed where they were hiding," Noletta interjected.

"The thing I still can't get past is how long Walton was stalking me, pretending to be my friend. And his illegal drug business. *That* was the big shocker for me," Noletta said, as everyone in the group listened intently.

* * *

It always felt good to have the story behind them. It wasn't something they wanted to dwell on. Their guests had left, Noletta's parents had gone inside, and Martin and Noletta were standing on the porch.

"Fiona and Ritchie seem to be doing well now," Noletta said quietly. Because of the relationship they had developed with Noletta, Fiona and her son had decided to move to Utah. Ritchie was now attending the Utah School for the Deaf and

Blind, and Fiona was working nearby.

"I still can't believe that you just gave Taffy to Ritchie that day," Martin said as he put his hands around Noletta's waist.

"What else could I do?" she asked. "He was brokenhearted. He couldn't even acknowledge Jewel. That little guy had given his heart to Taffy."

"And Jewel," Martin said. "That's what she is and always will be to me. The way she came to your rescue after knowing you for only one day was incredible. Maybe she discovered the same thing about you that I did."

"And what would that be?" Noletta asked.

"That you are incomparable—that you are a precious jewel."

Martin kissed his fiancée lightly on the top of her head and abruptly changed the subject. "Did I tell you about my new morning mantra?" he asked, his laughter only slightly suppressed as he spoke.

"No. I didn't know you had one."

"Well, I do now, a very appropriate one. Here's a clue," he said as he gently nibbled her ear.

"So, what's the clue?"

"You mean you didn't figure that out yet? Here, let me give you the clue again." Martin moved his lips to her other ear.

"You're not making any sense," Noletta complained.

"All right, all right. You may thank your grandfather each day in your mantra. But I thank *Rattus norvegicus,* the unnamed rat, the little granivorous rodent that, along with his tail, gave his name to your favorite comb—which saved you for me."

"Always the romantic, aren't you," Noletta laughed, as they leaned against each other and listened to the crickets voice their goodnights.

ABOUT THE AUTHOR

Clair M. Poulson was born and raised in Duchesne, Utah; he spent many years patrolling the highways and enforcing the law in Duchesne County as a highway patrolman and deputy sheriff, followed by two years of service in the U.S. Army Military Police Corps. He completed his twenty-year law enforcement career with eight years as Duchesne County Sheriff. For the past fifteen years, Clair has served as a justice court judge in Duchesne County.

Clair also does a little farming. His main interest is horses, although he has raised a variety of other livestock, including cattle, pigs, and sheep. Both Clair and his wife currently help their oldest son run Al's Foodtown, the grocery store in Duchesne.

He met his wife, Ruth, while they were both attending Snow College. They are the parents of five married children and grandparents of twelve. Ruth has been a great support to Clair in all of his endeavors and now assists him with his writing by proofreading and making suggestions.

Clair has always been an avid reader, but his interest in creating fiction found its beginning many years ago when he told bedtime stories to his small children. They would beg for just one more story before going to sleep. He still practices that hobby with his grandchildren. He uses his life's experiences in law enforcement and the judicial arena to help him develop plots for his novels. With the publication of *Blind Side,* Clair has thirteen published novels.